◊ *GP* ◊

The Germania Press

Also by William Russell Sheridan

The Adamantine Heart

The Return of Wahkahchai

WILLIAM RUSSELL SHERIDAN

THE GERMANIA PRESS
Bavaria, Germany and California, USA

The Germania Press
Bavaria, Germany and California, USA

First Germania Press edition August 2018

Jacket design by Laura LaRoche

Manufactured in the United States of America

Library of Congress Cataloging-in-Publication Data
Sheridan, William Russell.
The return of Wahkahchai: a novel/William Russell Sheridan

ISBN: 978-0-9909682-3-8

ACKNOWLEDGMENTS

My dearest and most persistent readers deserve my gratitude.

In the United States and in Germany: my parents Bill and Helga, avid and critical readers.

In California: Janet Immel, who keeps me writing.
All my handball buddies who can read. Jim Pfouts for his erudition and excellent feedback.
Carl Grilli, a perceptive critic and fine storyteller in his own right.

In the Mid-west: Steve Doty and Marlene Ciorba, best friends and fishing buddies for life; Steve and Judy Schultz for unflagging support.
In the Pacific Northwest: Daniel Lippincott for perseverance through it all; JC for commentary, insights, and advice.

In Bavaria, Germany: *Erster Hauptkommissar* Roland Rüssel, who continues to regale and amaze me with his stories and insight into the human condition in all its perverse and beautiful manifestations. Special thanks to Martina Rüssel for broadening my readership among her German friends.

Unqualified appreciation for Marlies Reuther-Rüssel for her openness, honesty, and critical care.

Again, gratitude to Ernst Baur for his friendship and opening his home to me at Villa Ernesto in the Italian Alps high above Cannobio on the Lago Maggiore, where considerable portions of this book were written.

And, of course, whether at home in Bavaria or California, Nancy Clark, who never doubted me.

"*The hero of my tale...whom I have tried to portray in all his beauty, who has been, is, and will be beautiful—is Truth.*"

Leo Tolstoy-*Sevastopol in May (1855)*

CONTENTS

CHAPTER ONE

Eks Bay

The curved blade of time's carving knife had pared one or two inches from the bone and gristle that once made Farley Nilsson a six-foot-tall man and this perplexed him to some degree. Farley believed that once a genetically predetermined height had been achieved, it seemed only fair and fitting that a man's stature should remain constant the rest of his life-long days. As he stepped into his faded jeans, now too long for his white, skinny legs, Farley knew the peak had been crested and the slide down the back side had begun. Unfortunately for him, too much sun, wind, and snow had conspired to harden and compact his frame, had taken the moisture from his skin, and left him desiccated and smaller than in his prime. He was like a bar of soap after a long wash in the old galvanized zinc tub his mother used to bathe him before he outgrew its slippery fit and her slippery hands.

His lifetime exposure to the elements, first as a woodsman jacking lumber in Minnesota's great North Woods, and now as a fisherman, made his head seem unnaturally large on shoulders rounded by years of hunching against the wind or bending at his carpenter's bench to shave wood into an entirely new form. His hands—weathered by the sun and snow—were no longer graceful or particularly adept, which also aggravated him to no small degree. Arthritis now and then blew up in his joints and warped his fingers into a grotesque caricature of a human hand. It did not help matters that he had smoked since he was twelve years old and nicotine from the unfiltered cigarettes had leeched into the tips of his long, yellow-stained fingers. At least he had enough strength and dexterity left in his hands to pull the gray wool socks over his pink, boney feet. His toenails were too long and he thought about clipping them, but decided against it. Maybe if he waited long enough they would shorten on their own.

Farley had always maintained that he worked to live and unlike others he knew, did not live to work. He lived to fish and he lived to work with wood; not just saw it or chop it and drag it through the forest onto a dug road until the work killed him. As a young man still strong and straight and tall and impervious to the blade of time, he knew his job working as a faller in the timberland forests among the birch, pine, and fir was not conducive to living a long and healthy life. Knowing his was one of the most dangerous jobs in the world did put a bit of swagger into his step. His pay wielding an axe or a chainsaw was better than equipment operators or log truck drivers because the work was more dangerous.

On the day he watched a fit, seasoned logger in the prime of his life die at the top of a fir that twisted and kicked back with such force that it almost decapitated the sawyer, after Farley climbed up through the blood slickening the bole of the tree and belayed the dead weight of the man's body back to ground, Farley Nilsson made a life-changing decision. He unlaced his logging boots still smelling of boot oil, pitch, and the black blood of a friend. After wiping them down one last time, he put the high-standing uncut leather boots with steel in the toe and heel into the deepest, darkest corner of his pine closet. The day after he walked out of the woods for the last time, the day after he topped the last widowmaker, set the last choke chain, and breathed his last lungful of sweet sawdust, Farley took to the trades and became a master carpenter, a move that more than likely saved his life.

Despite the changes time and hard work and a northern climate had carved into the soft pine of his bones, his love for fishing remained undiminished. Ever the master carpenter, Farley had long ago made the requisite adaptations, treating his advancing years as nothing more than a knot that gave character to an otherwise fine piece of planking. He knew and accepted his limitations and worked around them. Each and every day the morning light tapped his eyes open and his white and purple-veined feet hit the wooden floor of his cabin by the lake, was another day he could spend on the water doing what he loved even more than turning a piece of maple into something useful and beautiful. And when it came to catching walleye, smallmouth bass, or even northern pike, no one, including any of the other professional guides who worked the lake, knew more about fishing the wide, deep waters of Lake Kabetogama than Farley Nilsson.

In one of those curious twists of fate he did not understand or even care to think about, Mother Nature had left Farley's eyesight clear as a window freshly washed with vinegar. He had a touch of presbyopia but could still see farther than most men half his age. When the distance to a deer pulling grass in the tree line on the bank across the lake was too great for unassisted clarity, he picked up his binoculars. At closer range he could still thread four-pound test fishing line through the eyehole of a one-sixteenth ounce crappie jig, even though it took him twice as long now to tie the knot.

On cold mornings, and most early-summer mornings in the North Woods of Minnesota were cold in his cabin until he restoked the wood stove into a warming, soft orange glow, the damned arthritis and rheumatism occasionally left his hands clumsier than an apprentice carpenter. The heat radiating from the stove's potbelly or the rising sun gave him back some of his diminished dexterity. However, unless he planned to fish the sunrise he had the time to wait for the swelling to subside and for the stiffness to abate, so even this did not bother him to any great degree.

He was meticulous about his fishing knots but not his hair, which had been white as the soap in his mother's tub since the time of his first bath, and he stole back some satisfaction in knowing he still had plenty to hide under a baseball cap. Unlike most anglers, he re-tied often. He rarely, if ever, lost a fish because a knot slipped or broke or the line parted just above the tie. Farley Nilsson took pride in doing things properly, in doing things that had to be done, and he considered this merely the price you paid for keeping fish on the hook. Many years of biting off the excess line had worn a ridge into both his upper front teeth, not that he cared, but his dentist had finally convinced him to use the toenail clippers that depended from the shoestring he now looped around his leathery neck. But if the truth be told, it was really the new abrasion-resistant lines, so tough that even a beaver could not bite through them, that had caused him to switch tools.

Farley Nilsson was going fishing and that made it a good day. The night before, he had lined up his reel with thirty-pound test monofilament thick enough so that the Palomar knot snugged down tightly to the ring on the bait with very little fuss and very little spit. A gentle morning breeze rising in the south and west pushed the water up against the sides of the boat and that helped things considerably as he readied his fishing gear. There was nothing worse than trying to rig lines or tie on lures in a twenty-knot wind. Cooler aboard and raingear stowed, he loosed the lines from his dock, powered up the motor for the big red Lund, backed her out into the shallow draft of Deer Creek and burbled into Slatinsky's Bay before heading downlake. Once past the unmarked rocks that crunched the lower units of the outboards of many a tourist running in a camp boat, Farley trimmed the big motor until the red Lund skipped neatly across the emerald water of the lake agitated by the wind into a feathery chop.

Farley Nilsson intended to run all the way out to Eks Bay for big northern this morning and he was not messing around. He was after a big one and he would not be satisfied with anything under forty inches or twenty pounds. Farley knew where and when to catch five pounders—the best eating fish save the walleye bar none—and his freezer back at the cabin was a testament to his hunting and fishing skills. He had enough bear, venison, and fish fillets to last into the long, cold shank of the Minnesota winter before it bended back into the coming of spring.

One of the things that made Farley a local legend on the water was the fact that he always fished with a plan in mind. He spent the early part of the week fishing for his supper: crappies or perch for the pan, perhaps a walleye or two for the wok. He gave the middle part of the week over to fishing for a living. Most of the daily fish specials featured on the menus of local restaurants within a twenty mile radius of the lake owed their natural organic gluten free piscatorial offerings to the fishing and catching prowess of Farley Nilsson. At least one day a week, if he had filled his personal and professional quotas, Farley Nilsson went after the big ones. More than anyone else on the lake, he knew where the trophies lived. Fish the size worthy of Farley's attention tended to be very smart fish or they would not have achieved either the size or the longevity that interested him. He could catch uneducated fish all day if the weather conditions were right; it was the educated fishes that presented him the greatest challenge.

At the mouth of Eks, he throttled back, checked the depth finder, and found the edge of the submerged weed bed where baitfish ran to hide from the big, predatory pike cruising the lake. He went to his tackle box and pulled out a deep-diving plug dressed in the fire tiger colors mimicking a large perch. He shook it to make certain the three large treble hooks swung freely beneath the red belly of the hand-painted, orange and black lure, one he had carved from a heavier plug of balsam fir. Farley disdained the use of the steel leaders recommended by most guides when fishing for such toothy creatures as northern pike or muskies, and he occasionally lost a fish as a result; but he more than made up for it by allowing the big baits to travel through the water in the natural motion conducive to catching more fish.

Satisfied with the geometry and the lay of the knot, he flipped the bait into the water and watched it swim as he reeled it back to the boat. It wobbled and wanted to dive just like a wounded perch. There was nothing special about his tackle. He used a medium-heavy action, six-and-a-half feet graphite rod that carried a dependable Abu Garcia 5000 reel that he maintained himself. Other guides and many weekend fishermen used five hundred dollar reels and four hundred dollar rods and fished all week without catching anything but weeds. The equipment did not catch the fish—knowledge and experience did, he was fond of saying. A man needed just enough tackle to meet the needs of the fish, not the man. Farley Nilsson was just about ready to put his knowledge and philosophies to work.

He had the bay to himself, which was a good thing. He did not need other people bothering him when he fished with a purpose. He donated enough of his time to helping out the greenhorns and the hopeless, especially if they had a kid or two along. But not today since he was fishing big, so it was good that he was alone on the water with no one to interfere or mess up his strategies. If they could find it, most tourists took a while and a long run to reach the easternmost water on the great lake, even with 200 horses screaming behind their sparkling fiberglass bass boats, not that Farley could afford the price of that much power hanging off the butt of his boat.

He had started from home after the false dawn leaked a little color into the receding night sky. Now in the protection of the back end of the bay, wisps of fog slid just above the surface of the water, snaking back toward the cool shadows thrown on the water by the pines and birches lining the sloping bank. With the sun still behind the trees, he sat in his old dented and scarred Lund, studying the water. One more look around, another quick check of his tackle, and it was time to fish.

Farley Nilsson pulled the 50 horse Johnson back to work and flipped the gear lever forward. He had a fine Minnkota electric trolling motor up front, but today he wanted speed. The propeller bit and he throttled up looking for the edge of the weed line just under the water. Once he had the depth and water temperature, he did not bother with the fish locater. He trusted the one in his head. Besides, he knew the bay like most people know their sock drawer. He knew the depths, he knew the structure, and he knew the weeds. He was not casting today; he was trolling, and he intended to go deep. One thing Farley knew for a fact was the bigger *Esox lucius* grew, (the *Esox* was also the name of his boat), the more they loved deep, cold water. This time of year, at the edges between spring and summer, most water in the lake was still cold except in the shallow back bays and colder, deep water meant forty to sixty feet under the boat.

He fired the heavy bait into an arc behind the Lund, his thumb acting as a brake on the line as it spooled out. Just before it hit the water, he stopped the line and the foot-long perch imitator gently slapped the surface like a big-bellied pelican coming in for a landing. He turned the handle of the reel and listened for the satisfying click as the gears engaged. He was about ten yards out from the weed line and he ran the boat parallel to the edge in about fifteen feet of water. The motor chugged along and the bait dove and wobbled under the surface. Before he could get halfway across the bay, he felt the vicious strike. To be certain he set the hook, backed off the throttle and put the motor into neutral. The rod bent as if divining some supernatural force under the water. He had one on! There was nothing supernatural or mysterious about it for Farley Nilsson. The creature, now aware that it was once and properly stuck, took off with a vengeance, stripping line from Farley's big reel. This concerned him not in the least. He had checked and reset the drag on each of his four rods before he left the cabin. This was only standard and proper procedure. Let the fish run.

He kept the rod tip up and used just enough pressure from his callused thumb to help retard the smooth strip of line from the reel. When it stopped, with controlled patience he carefully cranked against the weight in the water, letting the big girl know he was on the other end. A second run against the drag took the northern toward the weeds. This was something Farley could not allow and he had expected as much. If the fish got into the leafy maze of all that coontail and cabbage, Farley would be defeated. He needed to turn the brute and to do so he needed to trust the strength of his knot and his line, an excellent German product worth the extra cost. He stood in the boat to bring the graphite strength of the rod's backbone into play. He had yet to see his adversary—only the movement of the tight line through the water gave him any indication that he had a big one on.

Suddenly the line slackened and Farley reeled in for all he was worth. He knew what was coming next. The fish geysered up out of the water like a missile shot from a submarine. At the apex of its jump, the green monster tried to shake the lure from its mouth—once, twice, three times—before its extraordinary length concussed the water. Having anticipated the jump, Farley was able to catch up with the slack and kept just enough tension on the fish to hold the barbs in place. The next run was into deep water and this time Farley screwed the star drag down, putting even more pressure on the fish. Every run and each jump burned that much more energy out of the fish and now was the time to impose his will on the finny creature. He wanted the fish to think it was dragging the Lund. At the end of the run Farley methodically cranked the big Abu Garcia and this brought the exhausted fish to the surface.

The fight seemed over as she lolled a bit, showing Farley her white belly before she tried to throw the bait once more with a vicious headshake. To the untrained eye, it seemed Farley Nilsson had won his battle and was now leading the fish to the boat like a well-trained dog heeling to the leash. But Farley knew better. With an explosion of water from the broad fan of its tail, the big northern made one more line-popping, rod-snapping, heart breaking run just before it reached the boat. Not so easily conned, Farley had already triggered the reel, his thumb acting as a brake as the line spooled out. Its last desperate run to freedom defeated, Nilsson brought the northern to the boat respectfully, aware that its last tactic would have defeated most other anglers not quite so wise to the ways of the wily northern pike. Its energy now exhausted, Farley knew this was a critical time for a fish that big, so he got to work.

He wet his left hand, right hand holding the rod up to keep enough tension on the fish so that its nose pointed parallel with the boat. The fingers of his left hand found the gill plate and the thick vee of cartilage just under the jaw. He got all four fingers into the grip and lifted the fish out of the water and into the boat, careful not to get his fingers caught by treble hooks sharpened by lasers. Tired as she was, he felt the strength of the creature as it thrashed against the steel lock of his grip. "Easy big girl," he said, "I just want to get this pretty bait back and then I'll send you on your way."

The northern had struck the bait from the side, a slashing attack typical of the lake's apex predator, and two hooks of the back treble had seated into the tough, armored mouth of the fish. He used his pliers to unhook the pike, minding the razor sharp teeth that could slice through his hand faster than a bandsaw. Now free of the bait, the big girl gave another sensuous wiggle or two as Farley grabbed her under the belly with his right hand to give her further support. He gauged her length against the tape measure glued to the inside of the boat. Forty-three inches from stem to stern. Not bad. A twenty pounder to his eye. Tail first, he dunked the fish into the water like a tea bag, but maintained his grip under the jaw. He did not move the fish forward or back; he merely held her horizontal in the water as he watched her lateral fins gentle pulse, stabilizing herself in the dock of his grip. He waited two minutes, then three. The tail began to wave softly. Another minute and he felt the charge of energy as the fish revitalized. At precisely this moment, he released his grip. The northern hung suspended in the water for two seconds before it swam into the deep with a slow but steady dignity befitting her size and her age.

Farley washed his hands over the side and dried them on his towel. He checked his bait. The brand new yellow and black paint scheme was now scarred by the rake of the pike's stiletto fangs. Time to check the line. Three or four times, he slid his thumb and forefinger up and down about twelve inches above the knot. Satisfied that there were no nicks or abrasions in the line, he got a beer from the red and white plastic cooler; he allowed himself exactly two a day and it did not matter what time of day. He drank down a third of the cool golden liquid, and then wiped the suds from his lips with a swipe of his tanned forearm. He re-seated his Twins baseball cap; he had recently gotten his wilding hair cut—a nuisance at his age when most of his cohorts could comb their hair with a washrag. Curiously enough, Farley had lost more teeth over the years than hair.

He looked into the bay where the broad thatch of vegetation dimpled the surface. As a young man, he could remember powering into the mass of green with his outboard at full throttle using the propeller blade to chop and slice and pull the vegetation up from the bottom by the roots. Smaller and medium-sized northern used the weeds like a hotel, lying up among all the greenery, and the commotion from the churning drove them out and made them easier to catch. Those were the good old days but those days were gone. The Department of Natural Resources had put an end to that tomfoolery. He did not mind all that much. He supported conservation as much or more than the next guy did. Hell, he put more fish back into the water in a week than most guys caught all season. It's just that the fishing had been so good then, he remembered. Now you had to know what you were doing or risk getting skunked.

He finished his celebratory beer and his reminiscences at the same time and threw the empty green bottle back into the cooler. He would eat the ham sandwich and drink the second beer around noon up on the shore of some island somewhere and might even take himself a little nap on a Forest Service green picnic table until two, when he knew the fishing would get good again. He reached into his tackle box and selected a couple of gray dots that he placed on the deep-diving crankbait. These were weights that could be glued on the sides, top, or underbelly of a lure once you peeled off the backing. Neatest thing in the world, Farley thought. Fishing junk was getting better all the time, although it was also getting so goddammed expensive that a retired gentleman such as himself could hardly afford to pay the prices anymore. Fifteen bucks for a lousy titanium spinner bait, for Christ's sake. Next they would be making them out of depleted uranium that glowed underwater so you could watch the lure as you dragged it back to the boat. That is why Farley made most of his own baits, tuning them to his specifications.

"Not a bad start," he said to himself as he trolled out into deeper water. "Now let's go get a big one."

CHAPTER TWO

The Catch

Finished with his adjustments, he sent the heavy lure singing into the distance and again let it thump the water like a beaver's tail as it splashed down behind the boat. Sometimes that concussion alone was enough to rouse the big ones off the bottom, curious about all the commotion. He popped the motor back into gear and began a fast troll. He wanted the bait to run deep because Farley knew what most guys did not: speed triggers northern and muskies to bite. He knew for a fact that you could not retrieve a lure faster than a northern could strike, even at this speed. He backed off the throttle a little, just to check and make sure the bait was running right. He patterned the mouth of the bay, taking wide, gradual turns, covering the water carefully and efficiently. In the middle of the bay, with the depth finder reading 45 feet, Farley felt the line go taut and he set the hook just to be sure before he threw the motor into neutral. And for the first time this season, Farley Nilsson felt a surge of excitement that tingled in his toes and fingers.

It was big; he could tell that much. His rod bent almost double, so he eased off the drag. He had seen big muskies and northern snap rods like brittle bones. But something was wrong. He had stuck big ones before and it was not unusual for such monsters of the deep just to lie there, their dead weight suspended in the water. Being at the head of the food chain, what did they care? Eventually, though, they made a run and that is what bothered Farley now. No run. No line stripping off the reel. Could not be a northern then, or a musky; had to be something else. He had put the treble hook in the bent up snout of a prehistoric looking sturgeon once, and it had pulled his boat around the bay for almost an hour before he finally cut the line, he had to pee so bad. Even at his age, one beer was not enough to require taking a leak over the side, and he was damned certain that he was not going to cut the line this time and lose a perfectly good lure. Then he felt a give, but it was not moving like a sturgeon either, or a big fat lake trout, which would have been fine too.

"Damn it all," he muttered to himself, beginning to sweat. Maybe he had hooked into a small log; he had probably snagged a branch sticking up out of the log and now he had to haul its dead weight up to the surface if he wanted to recover his lure. He knew logs were down there. During the early part of the 1870s, some of the forests surrounding the lake had been logged. There were still huge iron rings hammered into the granitic stone outcrops of selected islands where the massive timber rafts were tied before they were towed up the Ash River. He stood now for additional leverage, working the rod, letting the graphite modulus blank do its work. He lifted against the weight on the other end and reeled in the slack as he dropped the tip of the pole toward the lake. He was making progress, he noted with satisfaction. Should not be too much longer now. He was going to get his lure back.

What Farley Nilsson saw when he finally got it to break the surface shocked him so much that he almost stumbled backward out of the boat. Only the high sides of the Lund saved him from going over and in. He managed to sit down before he lost his balance completely, but he never let go of the rod. In fact, he still had the rod in his right hand held high above his head as if he had indeed fallen into the water and wanted to keep it dry. Farley had seen a lot in fifty years on Kabetogama: fish kills from lack of oxygen, bears swimming from island to island and mauling campers, even an entire family of raccoons in a tree when the naturalists said there were none around anymore. He had seen northern rise from the deep and eat unsuspecting ducks paddling amiably along; once he saw an eagle drop down and take a northern that had just swallowed a walleye. He thought he had seen it all, but this was worth a second look. As soon as he recovered his balance and got his hat back on straight, he was ready for another look to confirm what he thought he had seen the first time.

It was the color that threw him—the lack of color to be honest. He had never seen a human being with patches of skin so white that it looked like all the color had been leeched from the naked body, as if the lake water had been turned to bleach. In places the body was mottled black and gray; in others, white. The front of snow geese were that white, or the crown feathers of a mature eagle maybe, or the first fall of snow, or his feet. Break apart the fried fillet of a walleye and see the same color inside, a white untouched by sun or pigment. And he had certainly never seen a human being, dead or alive, with both eyes eaten away. The gruesome hollow sockets stared at him as he stared back into the hideously blind face.

The lower jaw wobbled before the body gently rolled over, face down in the water. Farley could not turn away now, grimacing against his need to look, and for the brief instant of half a second he felt a visceral panic as an arm waved toward him, seemingly of its own volition. He feared the water-bleached corpse might yet be alive. Then he realized it was simply the water pulling on the limbs to play a joke on old Farley Nilsson, who thought he had seen it all, until today. He managed to convince himself that he had nothing to fear from the grotesque object in the lake now slapping gently up against the side of his boat. Farley had a quick look around; he sure would not mind somebody else running up to the boat just about now. This was one catch nobody would believe.

Farley was faced with a more immediate problem: he wanted his bait back and he was damn sure for certain he was not giving it up after what he had just been through, no sir! He thought about the problem for a minute, not given to rash action when a situation called for a certain amount of pondering. He had a mesh fillet glove he called Ol' Stinky. No matter how much he washed it, the meshed material protecting the fingers from a fillet knife, or raking gills, or razoring teeth, refused to surrender all the rotting fish smells accumulated over the years. He put the glove on and reeled the drifting corpse closer to the boat. The glove smelled infinitely worse than the body. At one time, the body had been trussed, he observed. This was not just some poor slob from Minneapolis up for the weekend who had gotten drunk and fallen in. A bright chartreuse-green length of nylon rope trailed the body's midsection like an umbilicus cut free from the mother. Evidently this had been used to secure the body to some kind of weight that had served as an anchor, he surmised. The knot must have slipped and his constant pulling had tugged the line free.

He could not get the lure out of the man's calf muscle; two treble hooks, like a cobra's fangs, had bitten deeply into the flesh. There was no blood. It was a dry bite. He knew what he had to do. He considered cutting the lure from the body with his fillet knife, but decided against it. He had seen a national park boat restoring a campsite near Lost Bay, a short run to the west. He grabbed the nylon rope, moving like a snake in the gentle roll of the water, and tied it off to the side of the boat. The body thumped the Lund as if signaling its readiness, startling Farley at the sound. Grimacing, he cut the fishing line at the lure, stowed his gear, and readied the boat for the short, slow run to Lost Bay. Then, not unlike the old man in Hemingway's story, Farley made way to bring his catch to shore.

When Ranger McManus looked up to answer Farley's hail, he saw the familiar Lund and the grizzled old fisherman, famous on the lake for his skill and his uncanny ability to catch fish when no one else could get them to bite. He always looked forward to exchanging information and chewing the fat with Nilsson. The old Scandinavian was an encyclopedic fount of fishing knowledge acquired from years of working the Boundary Waters system of lakes that included Kab, Namakan, and Rainy to the north. The dull grind of prepping a campground proved tedious work, and when he heard the dented Lund putter up, smoke burbling and rising from the motor's exhaust, it was a relief to see his old friend. As Farley putt-putted in and backed off the throttle to dock the boat, McManus did not immediately see what old Farley had in tow this fine bright bluebird morning. When he finally did see the floater on the other side of the red and white Lund, Ranger McManus gave his rather substantial breakfast to the fishes, which Farley thought was disgusting. He had considered McManus a better man than that.

"Well, give me a hand on deck," Farley said, shaking his head at the weakness of some people. "That is, if you're done chumming for the fishes."

McManus sheepishly washed his mouth with lake water from the other side of the dock and said, "Sure don't see that coming ashore every day." In fact, Ranger James McManus had never seen anything like it in his twelve years on the water. There had been a bear attack last year where a camper was mauled and a goodly portion of his haunch torn out and eaten, but that was an understandable act. A hungry bear will eat a man, and that is to be expected. A mother bear had been out showing her two cubs the true delicacy of wild blueberries, and the camper had startled the three, their attention focused on gorging themselves with the luscious fruit. It had been a poor year for berries because of the drought, and the bears were ravenous. Thinking her cubs were in danger, she attacked. One of her fangs punctured the helpless man's carotid artery. Already unconscious from the ferocity of her mauling, he quietly and painlessly bled to death under a pine tree just off the trail leading back to the blueberry patch. The mother bear, not one to look a gift horse in the mouth, made a meal of him. When the unfortunate man's girlfriend noticed him missing from the campsite, she flagged down McManus, who was checking fishing licenses that day from under the canvas canopy of his national park boat. It did not take him long to pick up the trail and find the body. That had been a bloody mess, but not unexpected, given his understanding of bears and campers.

When the cry had gone out about a man-eating bear preying on hapless tourists, McManus had to get in high gear and persuade the press and all the resort owners that this was really nothing more than an unfortunate accident of nature. Killing the mother bear, he finally convinced everyone, would serve no purpose but to orphan the cubs. She was just protecting her babies, he said to the reporter from International Falls, and that seemed to make all the difference. Cries for the bear's destruction died down as watchers of the nightly local news moved on to other more important items such as whether or not the local paper mill was hiring, or the University of Minnesota's football team might win more than three games this season. McManus and his team located the bears, trapped them, and relocated them within the eastern end of the vast national park.

But not this. He sure as hell did not expect to see Farley pulling in a corpse like a walrus lashed alongside an Eskimo's umiak, he told Farley in no uncertain terms, as he helped wrestle the inert dead weight of the waterlogged body into his boat. A white and gray waxy looking substance coating parts of the body rendered it even more slippery, and both men resorted to handling the body with gloves.

McManus, who considered himself a fairly observant guy, given all the time he spent outdoors, was puzzled by Farley's catch. Farley was tracking a thought in his mind, and his expression showed that he was on the trail of an interesting idea, but he was not letting on just yet. McManus had learned to trust the old laker's intuition, given his experience and time on the water. "Whaddya think, Farley? An accident or a suicide?"

"This was no accident of nature," Farley pointed out in his laconic style.

"Whaddya mean?" McManus asked.

"Well," Farley drawled, as was his habit when he had to teach the young pup a thing or two about the way the world worked. "I don't think he ran all the way out to Eks Bay just to dunk his willy in the water."

Farley had made a good point, but he still seemed troubled. With the toe of an old blue and white tennis shoe, Farley gently pushed the corpse's head to the side so the black holes where the dead man's eyes should have been, stared away from him.

McManus, on the other hand, with all respect for his good friend, believed they were looking at the result of an unfortunate accident. The poor fool probably got liquored up, stumbled and fell out of the boat. The ranger had seen it before.

Farley Nilsson, not given to summary judgment before he had all the facts, found himself in a position of uncertainty. Farley shrugged. At this point, he explained, he was only venturing a guess, for the sake of discussion. It might be an accident made to look like a suicide. He scratched the grizzle of his jaw. Nope. That did not make much sense unless you believed the man had stripped himself bare-butt naked, tied a concrete block or some such anchorage between his legs, and then jumped over the side of his boat into the drink. Nope. Farley was pretty much convinced that it had to be a suicide made to look like an accident, but that was only his unofficial opinion as an amateur. He was more than willing in this case to append his conclusion to the official report of the ranger who, after all, had received some professional training in the handling of suicides.

They agreed to leave Farley's Lund behind, and now that they had the body settled in a gray pool of water on the bottom of the national park boat, there was nothing to do but transport it to the ranger station near the Ash River and let the county sheriff and coroner come and have a look for themselves. On the short run out of the bay and into the main waterway to the ranger station, they debated motives and convinced each other that a proper investigation would no doubt reveal some sort of insurance scam.

The riddle of the man's death solved, McManus pushed the twin outboards to full throttle and got the boat on plane. Farley reversed his baseball cap just in time to keep it from flying off his head above the windscreen of the high-powered marine-gray boat. At the station, Farley jumped out and took her by the nose before the big Lund nudged the white bumpers depending from the pier, and tied off the bowline and the stern. Holding hands behind his back, he waited with the body as if he were attending a wake while McManus got on the radio to the sheriff. Farley was not too crazy about his vigil with the corpse, mottled gray and white, eyes eaten from the head. He noticed that the male had a rather substantial willy, even for a dead man, floating in the moss of his black pubic hair. Farley decided that would not do. He pulled out an emergency tarp stowed under the front seat of the boat, and delicately covered the body. There were kids and ladies coming in and out of the ranger station. It would not be proper for them to sight the corpse, which would be shock enough, and then be exposed to the man's privates lying there for all the world and God himself to see under these clear blue skies. Nope. It just did not seem right. After Farley tucked the dead man in properly, and with his sense of decorum restored, he resumed his position and stood watch, doing his duty out of respect for the unfortunate dead man.

CHAPTER THREE

In Custody

Law enforcement in Voyageurs National Park is a shared and cooperative governance, a testimony to the competent men and women who serve the federal government, the state of Minnesota, and Saint Louis County. VNP, established by the federal government in 1975, falls under the jurisdiction of the National Park Service. The linked chain of lakes that constitute the Boundary Waters Canoe Area Wilderness to the east is handled by the National Forest Service. Rangers within the National Park Service are responsible for law enforcement, search and rescue, firefighting and emergency medical assistance. Rangers receive their law enforcement training at the Federal Law Enforcement Training Center in Glyncoe, Georgia. Before they return to their current duty station proudly wearing a hand-sewn Department of Interior law enforcement badge on the shoulder of their gray and green uniforms, they are assigned to a Field Training Park. The lake waters under Minnesota jurisdiction are also served by the Minnesota Department of Natural Resources Conservation Officers. These men and women receive law enforcement training during a fifteen week course at Hennepin Technical College in the Twin Cities.

Because national park rangers and DNR conservation officers, or game wardens, wear relatively similar green coats and pants, tourists often confuse the two, unable to differentiate between the two services. But a discerning eye notes that a DNR game warden sports stripes down the side of the pant leg, with shoulder epaulets and flaps above each breast pocket that match the color of the olive pants. In contrast, the pocket flaps of the gray shirts of the NPS rangers are of a uniform color. They also wear a distinctive campaign hat with its wide flat brim—envision the iconic Smokey Bear—a throwback to a time when the United States Army Calvary once was in charge of the National Parks.

Law enforcement duties on the water can also overlap. For example, a warden might ask to see your fishing license, but if you have walleyes in the boat, a ranger might check to see if you are adhering to federal slot limits. Adding to the confusion, the St. Louis County Sheriff sees to it that all boat and water safety regulations are followed.

NPS Ranger McManus called the sheriff's office because it handles both missing persons and unsolved homicides, and McManus reasoned they might have one or both on their hands. McManus told Farley that since the body did not seem to be violating any federal law like selling methamphetamine, and since he obviously was not fishing without a license, and thus under the purview of the DNR, it had to be the sheriff. Farley nodded his agreement. He had worked with members of all three departments and to his mind all three seemed to be mostly a good group of hardworking men and women who cared about the land, the water, and the citizenry who enjoyed it.

The sheriff arrived in less than fifteen minutes, taking the opportunity to run hot, lights flashing and siren on, and he was duly impressed with the catch. He let Farley give him the particulars and used McManus to fill in the details as Farley tended to be circumspect and concise to a fault. Every word wasted in conversation took time away from his fishing, so Farley was known around the lake as a short talker. The discovery of the mottled and swollen body alone came as a considerable surprise to the sheriff, but the gruesome sight of a head without eyes was an even bigger shock. Sheriff Clayton, an army veteran of Desert Storm, managed to hold on to his lunch unlike his friend, the younger, more inexperienced ranger. He told the boys not to mention any details about the suicide if, in fact, that is what it was, although the introduction of this element of doubt did not play well at all with Farley or McManus, their opinions already considered and formed.

The sheriff asked them to keep their knowledge of the details an official secret, as a professional courtesy, which swelled Farley up a bit; such facts would no doubt be central to the investigation once they identified the body. The local press, if anyone in fact showed up nosing around for a story, would be asked to report the discovery of the body as an accidental death due to misadventure, and hold off calling it a potential suicide until the investigation had proceeded far enough to close the case, one way or another. This made imminent good sense to the principals and they were more than happy to give their allegiance to the story, particularly if it would help further the investigation.

Immediately after Sheriff Stan Clayton took official possession of the body, to help document chain of custody, he went to the SUV and got his digital camera. At first Farley thought he was going to get his picture taken as some kind of reward and was preparing his "I'd rather not have my picture taken" excuses, when he saw, instead, that the sheriff was going to shoot the corpse. He felt a bit silly then and took off his cap to scratch his head as he watched. Sheriff Clayton took shots fore and aft, top to bottom, upside and down. He explained that the more pictures they had, the better it would be for the medical examiner. Finished with the photography, they hauled the heavy, cumbersome body rewrapped in the tarpaulin for modesty, to the sheriff's Ford SUV, and with the combined effort of all three men working together, loaded it in the back. Clayton promised McManus the return of the tarp, but was told not to bother. He thanked the men again for doing their civic duty, which puzzled Farley to some degree. Was he supposed to leave the body floating in Eks Bay for the tourists to admire and poke at with a stick? They all had a good laugh at Farley's unintentionally funny morbid humor, then set up a day and a time to fish together in the coming week and discuss what had come of the investigation.

Nilsson and McManus watched Clayton drive off into the green curve of the woods, relieved that their duty was done, at the same time a bit sad now that they had developed a kinship, so to speak, with the dead man. It was a tragedy, they agreed, as Ranger McManus ran Farley back to his boat. More than anything, it had disrupted the harmony of the lake, disrupted their routine, and more importantly, disrupted their notions of the national park as a safe place with little or no crime, absent the drunken boaters, poachers, dope smokers, meth labs and an occasional theft of opportunity from unlocked cabins. It was not the man's death per se that bothered them; and it was evident in the way they talked that the event clearly had disturbed both men. It was the circumstances of the death. Hell, people died of mishap, stupidity, and natural causes all the time. Voyageurs National Park certainly was not exempt from the Reaper collecting his grim bounty of watery souls. The facts were that the man had killed himself: that is what sent the chill up their spines as they both shivered and shook their shoulders. For whatever desperate purpose, the man had decided to dump himself in their lake like so much human jetsam. The waste of a life like that just was not right, they both agreed.

Clayton transported the body to the hospital at International Falls and signed it over at the admissions desk. In his report, he noted that the case, although it had the appearance of an accident, upon further investigation would most likely go down as a suicide, and wrote it up accordingly. At the autopsy the next day, the medical examiner did in fact substantiate that conclusion in her official findings report.

STAN CLAYTON WORKED the case with no success, given the staffing and budgetary limitations of his office, but it was not for lack of trying. The local paper ran the story of the mysterious unidentified dead man and reported it as an accident at the sheriff's request, pending notification of next of kin and all that. Farley Nilsson became a celebrity of the moment and drank free for the next couple of weeks until the notoriety of his story wore off and he was well into reruns. To be honest, he was good and damned tired of telling the same story over and over, but he did manage to suppress his need to tell someone the full details of the case. The discovery of a suicide victim would have counted for much more notoriety than a mere horrific accident, here in these parts where a fair population of Catholics was sprinkled in and among the great North Woods. Nevertheless, Farley kept it under his hat as he had been asked and let the sheriff get on with his work.

Clayton ran the latent prints from the swollen fingers of the body but they came back with no matches. He sent them to the Integrated Automated Fingerprint Identification Service maintained by the FBI, but thirty minutes later IAFIS sent back a "no hits" message. There was simply not enough detail left in the water swollen, washed out skin of the corpse. He scoured the Missing Persons bulletins and sent out his own. No hits there either—no one reported back. He made the rounds of the resort owners, asking quiet and discrete questions, knowing how important it was not to disrupt the tourist trade that would peak toward the end of summer, high season for the men and women who made their living catering to the campers, hikers, and anglers coming up to spend time in the North Woods and on the lake.

Convinced that he had made every professional effort to bring closure to the case, given the limitations of his office, he closed the file in good conscience. Besides, in the spirit of inter-agency cooperation, he was working on a new case with his friend Ranger McManus, and this one was personal for both men.

THE BRENNAN BROTHERS, notorious scofflaws known to law enforcement in Saint Louis, Koochiching, and Lake of the Woods counties, were at it again. The three brothers were not apart three years in age. Before methamphetamines had wrecked and rewired his brain, old man Brennan could throw down in the bedroom with the best of them, that is, until he caught a felony conviction for grand theft auto with a firearm and the judge dropped a twenty on him. He now looked out at the world from behind iron bars in Faribault.

Like rust chipping and flaking off the old cast-iron engine block decomposing in the backyard, the brothers were hell bent on following the fine example set for them by their derelict dad. Following in their daddy's footsteps from the time they were old enough to break into and steal a car, they were determined to make a name for themselves. They were undeterred by the state's relocation of their Pap, which, truth be told, freed up a lot of refrigerator space for beer in the familial trailer parked just outside Ray. The twenty year stretch imposed by the judge seemed somewhat harsh, but in light of the old man's philosophy, oft echoed in his claim that "If you can't do the time, don't do the crime," the sentence made a certain amount of fatalistic sense.

For Sheriff Clayton, the brothers were nothing but a nuisance, and he knew the day would come soon enough when he would be able to reunite the clan once and for all, given the state's current reticence for offering parole to career criminals. He hoped only that he could catch them before they escalated their criminal pursuits and shot someone. At present, they seemed content with stealing the odd SUV from a drunken Ojibwe stumbling out of the casino and fumbling with his keys, rolling him for winnings if he was lucky, and selling the vehicle to the chop shops in the Twin Cities. Otherwise, they occupied themselves with poaching, infuriating Ranger Jim McManus when they decided to expand their culinary tastes to sample the more exotic or even endangered species resident in Voyageurs National Park.

They were a poaching ring unto themselves, those three, killing bear out of season for the paws and gall bladders, and shooting deer over bait on the islands of Kabetogama. McManus had finally gotten a break when he captured the youngest of the three idiots on a duck hunt. At the bottom of the miscreant's crudely hand-painted camouflaged duck boat, McManus found a dead loon—a protected species—in among the pelicans, cormorants, and mallards. Making conversation with the teenager after reading him his rights, his face still pockmarked with juvenile acne and his teeth stained with tobacco juice, McManus asked, just between the two of them, what did loon taste like. Willing to give the question proper consideration, the young felon-to-be scratched his head under his green woolen watch cap and thought on it for a second or two. To show that there were no hard feelings, he said, now on equal terms, one woodsman and hunter to another, "To tell you the truth, Jim, it tastes a lot like eagle."

This was the last straw for the park ranger, and with the blessing of the Minnesota Department of Natural Resources, who had spent too much time and money tracking the wilding crew all too willing to scoff at county, state, and federal laws, he quickly and quietly formed a confederation with the sheriff, this union of law enforcement resources more likely to bring in the other two outlaws. But the two still-at-large Brennan brothers were not so easy to apprehend, knowing the backwoods and the water as they did, and proved harder to catch than a northern timber wolf. In desperation, Clayton and

McManus turned to the Professor, a relatively new fishing buddy. Aware of his international reputation and his work as a special consultant for the FBI, they came to the door, each in his appropriate uniform, hats in hand, and apologized for the intrusion, but the Brennan boys, despite being their daddy's pride and joy, were an embarrassment to the entire community.

For Dr. William Russell Sheridan, an interesting case and a timely interruption, he said, as he needed a break from his writing. Moreover, he said he would consider it an honor to help the two men, and so the three formed an allegiance based on their friendship. He seated the men on the tan leather couch in his living room overlooking the lake and after offering diet sodas to drink, which the two men accepted, asked them to recount their investigations to date. The two shared turns describing the various crimes and misdemeanors committed by the Brennan brothers. Will Sheridan could sense the men's frustration as they told him of their near misses and failed apprehensions. "To sum it up," Sheriff Clayton said, "we've chased those two incorrigibles up one side of the map and down the other."

Will nodded. "That seems part of the problem."

"What do you mean, Professor?" McManus asked.

"Now don't take this the wrong way, but all the signs point to the fact that you two are educating the Brennan boys. The chase is not working."

The two officers looked at each other, surprised by the self-evident conclusion and had to agree: they either showed up too late to catch them in the act, or would lose the trail. Usually they could not bring enough evidence to bear even if they did manage to track one or both of the pair. Frustrating. McManus allowed that the apprehension of the youngest Brennan had been more a matter of serendipity than applied policecraft. A tourist had called in a report that some idiot was shotgunning anything that flew and McManus, helping the DNR check fishing licenses and boating safety violations on the lake that day, happened to be in the vicinity. That was indeed the problem, they admitted; on water and on land the two older boys could not be caught.

"This is an important realization," Will suggested, "and highly significant. It suggests the need for an entirely new strategy. What we do," said Will, taking a sip of his iced tea, "is use their strength against them." Will's newly formed crime-fighting team looked puzzled as they drank their diet sodas, still on duty. "And what exactly is their strength?" Will asked, vocalizing the question written on both men's faces. "They are extremely efficient and competent poachers; fine hunters and excellent shots, the pair." Damnation if that wasn't the truth, to the continual embarrassment of both men who could hardly sit down peaceably to a cup of coffee and a donut in any café in International Falls without some local yokel razzing them about the elusive Brennan brothers. "Here's what we do...," Will said, reaching for a sheet of notepaper on which he outlined his plan.

THE BRENNAN BOYS had been drinking tequila since breakfast, washing down the pungent liquor with their favorite beer—shoplifted—and drank merrily through the lunch hour, trying to figure out what to do with themselves the rest of the day. They decided they were just drunk enough to hunt. They were in a fine humor when they loaded the rifles into the rack of the old Dodge Power Ram pickup truck, painted an unnatural orange that had rusted through in enough places to make the truck seem as if it were infected with some malignant form of automotive chicken pox. They made a quick run into town to buy some .400 magnum rounds for the Weatherbys and picked up another bottle of breakfast tequila for the next day. They passed one of their happy hunting grounds just in time to spot the deer moving out of the trees and into the edge of a field where he could browse the clover among the native grasses. An elbow into the rib cage of the oldest brother driving alerted him to the fact that his sibling, scouting through the collapsed passenger window, had made a spot. He slammed on the brakes, shifted into reverse and idled back for a look. A fine buck stood at the periphery of a clearing; they were close enough to see his head swivel as he watched the curiously colored truck in the distance.

They knew the drill. Driver Brennan eased open his door and slipped from the seat, taking the loaded rifle his brother passed across to him. The big stag looked up from his grazing, but seeing no movement from the passenger, lowered his head to pull at the grass again with a flick of his white tail. "Ten points easy," the younger brother whispered as he slid across the bench seat and out of the cab to join his brother, both thumbing the safeties of their bolt action rifles. The younger Brennan sidled up to the front end of the truck. The older brother duck-walked along the bed of the pickup truck shielding him from the big buck's view. At the tail end of the Dodge, he sat and scooted under the rusted chrome of the step-bumper. He carefully propped up the rifle atop the wad of his camo hunting jacket and dialed in the scope.

He knew the deer was likely to spook at any time, and he hurried to locate the spot just behind and below the front shoulder of the animal. He took a deep breath and squeezed the trigger. He saw the animal jerk as the high powered round slammed into the deer and its head came up. "Damn," he thought to himself, "must have shot too low." In that split instant his brother fired before the buck could bolt. Another shot struck within a half-inch of the first, and this time the deer dropped its head, but it was still standing. He heard the report of his brother's rifle. "That's got to be one tough motherfucker," he thought, shaking his head, still not believing what his eyes told him. He felt the cold press of a gun barrel against the warmth of his exposed neck.

"Pretty good shootin' from this distance, but it's still out of season, you're shooting from the road and across a state highway, and I doubt if you have a hunting license," the sheriff informed him as he took the rifle and helped Brennan to his feet with a pull at the scruff of his collar. He cuffed the man and watched McManus do the same with the younger brother. At this point, the professor stepped out of the woods, the remote control transmitter in his hands, antennae still up.

"Watch this, boys," he yelled, and Thumper lifted his head and turned to them, then twitched his tail.

"That deer should be stone cold dead," the older Brennan complained, refusing to believe they had been trapped.

"Oh, he is," Will assured them both.

"Damned if that don't beat all," said the younger Brennan, who as a courtesy to law enforcement, turned his head to spit as he waited his turn to acknowledge his rights. "Ain't this some form of entrapment or the like?" he asked, the one brother who had excelled in school all the way up through the third grade before he pursued alternative forms of personal home schooling. Given their outstanding warrants, their extensive rap sheet of priors, and the evidence at hand with all the action videotaped from the sheriff's vantage point, Clayton knew the district judge would happily reunite the Brennan brothers with their good old Pap. Sheriff Stanley Clayton and Ranger James McManus, having perfectly executed the plan designed by Professor Sheridan, were pleased that they would once again be able to take their coffee and donuts in relative peace.

As the three men shook hands on a job well done, Professor Sheridan asked Clayton and McManus if anyone had been able to identify the John Doe dragged up from the cold depths of Lake Kabetogama. McManus looked to Clayton. The sheriff shook his head. "I have tried every technique available to law enforcement in the state of Minnesota. Finger prints, face recognition software, the national crime database, interagency missing persons reports, everything. No hits. Nobody knows this guy. Everyone told me just close the case, log it as a suicide, and move on. And that's what I had to do. I feel sorry that we will never know who the poor bastard is or how he came to such an unfortunate end, but it's time to move on. I don't have the resources or the manpower to continue," he said, with a note of resignation in his voice.

"We certainly don't," Ranger McManus echoed. With this last round of budget cuts, it's a wonder we can keep the park open at all."

Sheridan nodded his understanding.

"Are you interested in the case, Will?" Clayton asked.

The professor thought a minute before he replied. "I'll have to take a pass on this one. I'm finishing up another book for the general reader on how I have applied semiotic theory and analysis as a method for solving capital crimes. I have to meet a deadline by contract or I'll piss the publisher off." Both men nodded, although neither had a clue as to just what in the hell semiotic theory might be, but then he was a professor and they were not.

"And my uncle, a chief of detectives from the German state of Bavaria, is flying into the Twin Cities tomorrow for an extended vacation, his first visit to the United States. So thanks again, Stan, for asking me. As interesting as this one is, I better let it pass."

They shook hands all around and both men invited Will and his uncle, once he was sufficiently recovered from jet lag, to join them for introductions and a beer or two after work. Will accepted the invitation and all three men went their separate ways, looking forward to the story they now had to tell about the capture of the infamous Brennan brothers, no longer at large scoffing at the law and the law enforcement officers who had apprehended them.

Chapter Four

Sylvie

He woke to the alarm for the first time since he had left the routine of teaching at the university. The radio was set to the weather channel and he lay in bed just long enough to hear the weather forecast for the northern and central part of the state. It would be a good day to travel: overcast with possible thunderstorms developing by mid-day; humidity near one hundred per cent with a rapidly falling barometer. That part did not bode well for the return trip to the cabin. He threw off the blankets and let the early morning chill that had snuck into the house during sleep push the warmth out of his bed. The cool of the morning roused him into full consciousness. He had not slept well, unable to calm the flurry of mental activity caused by the expectation of seeing his uncle again. So much had happened since he was last in Germany assisting his uncle with solving the case now published as *The Adamantine Heart*. It amazed him that time could pass so quickly. They would have new stories to tell and he was excited by the prospect of being with his uncle again and bringing their lives up to date. Neither men were diligent with an old fashioned pen or modern email, confident that the time to meet again would come soon enough and they would be able to speak face-to-face, as it should be between close relatives.

In the kitchen he poured a glass of iced tea to help chase away the last foggy wisps of sleep. Glass in hand, he padded on bare feet into the greatroom that looked out onto the lake. He watched where the cool fingers of the morning trailed wisps of fog across the surface of the still water, a ghost-like movement of vapor as it crossed the placid surface of the lake, resting flat and calm as if asleep. From the north a loon's piercing cry penetrated the smoky mist. He recognized the eerie note as a locating call and soon after it died on the surface of the lake, he heard the answering cry. A mated pair, drifted apart in the night, had found each other again as the first rays of light slipped under and lifted the dark off the water. The wild cry of the loons settled him; exotic but familiar, its presence reassured him. There was something right and correct about the fact that the two birds had found each other. It was a good sign. More than anything else in his life, he had come to rely on and trust the signs of nature. He had taken pains to learn and understand them and now he relied on their presence. Unlike people, who often manipulated signs intentionally for the purpose of deceiving each other, most of nature's signs and signals, although they could be ambiguous at times—he admitted to himself—were usually not designed for deception.

The sun poured itself into the cold cauldron of the lake, filling it with green, amethyst, and emerald, the colors shifting as the angle of the sun changed. Will was almost finished with his oversized glass of tea. He remembered that he had once found a clear and unambiguous example of lying in nature. Reviewing Jane Goodall's work for a paper he was writing on the origins of lying behavior in human beings, he discovered the example of an enterprising chimpanzee in the Gombe forest of Tanzania that had stumbled upon a tree laden with heavy, ripe fruit. The young chimp, excited into near hysteria by the bounty of his discovery, jumped into the tree and began to gorge himself on the lush, sweet fruit.

At that point he heard the rest of his group wending their way down the trail heading directly toward his treasure trove. In an inspired act of near-genius he did what any selfish young chimp would do: he lied his little hairless butt off. Before the file of chimpanzees searching for breakfast fruit entered the clearing where his tree stood, he produced the cry that signaled the presence of a predator. In response to the warning the troupe of chimpanzees ran for their lives screaming, and scattered back up the trail and into the trees for protection. The opportunistic liar, his bounty preserved, scuttled off into the bush, both arms full and overflowing, carrying all he could eat and more, unwilling to share his good fortune with his mates. By sending a false signal the young rascal had intentionally lied.

A clear indication of intentional lying in a non-human species, he remembered telling his graduate students in the zoosemiotics class. Now there was a word his students loved to bandy about, once they learned what it meant. He grinned to himself. Zoosemiotics was the study and interpretation of the signs and signals produced by animals in nature. He went into the bathroom and brushed his teeth still thinking about nature and deception. He decided that his initial premise was false. Chameleons changed their skin color to fool the eyes of their predators. Opossum feigned death in order to escape attack. The coloration of the nonpoisonous king snake had evolved to closely mimic that of the deadly coral snake. No, he was wrong. There were many examples of natural signs that were used for the purpose of deception. Some were intentional; some were not, and that made a world of difference. It made him feel a little sad as he brushed his teeth, rinsed his mouth, and spit into the sink. He dried his hands and looked at his reflection in the mirror. He wanted to believe in some sort of inherent goodness in nature but he knew he was imposing a human value system on a non-human system and therein lurks the fallacy. He could not generalize across systems. Loons were neither true, good, nor beautiful, in spite of what Plato might have us believe; they were simply loons.

As he applied the shaving lather to his face, he became more obstinate in his thinking. To Hell with philosophy. If he wanted to see the loon as true, good, and beautiful, then by god, that was his prerogative. The loons would not care one way or the other, and he derived a sort of guilty satisfaction from the idea that he was violating a philosophical truism. He smiled through the wreath of white foam as he lathered his face to shave. That was it: he was no prisoner to philosophy or dogma or pedagogy. Not anymore. Free from the strictures of university and academic thinking, he now had the freedom to believe as he wished, even if he knew his beliefs were dead perfect wrong. Loons were beautiful and that was a good thing and he accepted the essential truth of his belief. His cheeks gleamed from the close cut of the triple-bladed razor and he gave himself a smug smile as he applied the aftershave. The beauty of philosophy is that once you understand it, you can use it against itself.

He pulled on a yellow polo and a pair of tan khakis. He slipped his feet into his sneakers, not bothering to unlace them. A quick run of the brush through his black hair and he was ready for the door. Five minutes later he was out the garage and headed south for the Minneapolis airport about six hours away. He fed the player a CD of Beethoven's *Pastoral Symphony*, set the cruise control and let the Subaru Forester do most of the driving. The truth of the matter was that he looked forward with great excitement to the prospect of seeing his uncle again, the redoubtable *Erster Kriminalhauptkommissar* Roland Rieger of the Bavarian State Criminal Police. That was certainly a mouthful. He regretted the fact that he had been less than diligent in practicing and maintaining his native tongue. Chief of Detectives seemed so much easier to say now.

He reached forward and took the edge off Beethoven—after all, the man was completely deaf by the time he wrote his *Ninth Symphony*. Syphilis will do that to a fellow, he reminded himself. Let that be a lesson. He thought about his uncle as he turned onto the highway and headed for Cloquet. Not much traffic this fine Sunday morning, as expected. Saturday was the bad travel day and all the locals knew enough to stay off the roads and highways up to the North Woods during changeover Saturdays. On those days throughout the summer months tourists up for the week headed home, and campers coming to take their place clogged north and southbound motorways from Albert Lea all the way up to Ely. A cultural phenomenon of northern Minnesota, once a week the transient population of the resorts and campgrounds changed over until Labor Day, the end of the summer for most, when life on the waters of Voyageurs National Park reverted back to a more natural rhythm.

HIS MOTHER'S OLDER brother, uncle Roland lived in Kaufbeuren, Germany, in the foothills of the Bavarian Alps. Rieger investigated serious crimes such as murder, rape, and serial killings, and had made his reputation in Europe by cracking cases that were deemed unsolvable. About two years ago—could it really be two years?—Roland had called Will and asked him to work as a consultant to the Bavarian State Criminal Police to help solve a case involving a serial killer. That had been a tough one. Sheridan laughed out loud. The levels of deception in that particular case had been damn near three layers deep. Applying his method of semiotic analysis to the case, he had been able to peel away each layer of deception, not unlike skinning an onion, and they had ultimately solved the case. Roland's work on the Adamas File, as the Bavarian criminal police or *Kripo* called it, had resulted in his promotion to *Erster*

Kriminalhauptkommissar, the highest rank for criminal detectives in the state police.

Will's work on the case resulted in the publication of *The Adamantine Heart* and solidified his growing international reputation as a criminologist working so-called cold cases, the small percentage of frustrating crimes that remained unsolved but open for investigation. As his reputation grew, Will was able to resign his position as professor of semiotic theory at the Iowa Polytechnic State University and work full-time as a consultant to Interpol and the FBI Special Investigative Unit. He had also authored a textbook on the application of semiotic theory to solving cases that could not be cleared by more traditional methods of criminal investigation, and the residuals from that book were enough to pay the mortgage on his cabin. Given the fact that things were going so well, he was not taking on any additional consulting work at the time. He had received a rather generous advance from a major publisher for his next book. He had been given a year to write the book, which had not posed much of a problem, given his extensive collection of field and case notes, and the manuscript was now with his editor.

In all, it could not have been a better time to invite his uncle to Minnesota's famous North Woods for a fishing vacation on Lake Kabetogama. Only a year or two from retirement, although still in his mid-fifties, Chief of Detectives Roland Rieger planned to use his seven weeks paid vacation to spend time with his nephew in the United States, which he had never visited. It was going to be great fun, Will thought to himself, turning up the Beethoven again to hear the crescendo of horns thunder through the excellent speakers of the Subaru, and he had laid in a selected provision of wine, beer, and booze large enough to hold a regiment in camp contentedly for the better part of a month. As the symphony ended and the player gave the CD back, he thought wistfully of Sylvie.

As a professor at university, the demands of teaching and research had taken most of his time, and he had never married, unwilling to spend time on the mundane courting rituals required for dating. Besides, he valued his independence too much. As much as he loved women and being with women in his own good time, he also needed time for himself, time to be alone. It was an act of selfishness, he admitted, but it had allowed him the freedom to discover new theories, to travel, and to meet other interesting women. In turn, he had given up the security and constancy of the marital bed, which he thought highly over-rated. Even when he was in a longer-term relationship he preferred to sleep alone; he insisted on it.

He could not stand cloying, clinging women who begged to be slept with as if they were children afraid to be left alone in the dark. So great was the insecurity of such women that they often traded sex for the comfort of a man lying next to them as a shield against the night. How utterly sad, he thought to himself, but he understood the need. He accepted the fact that his needs were different from most men, German or American. He did miss the companionship a steady relationship afforded. And to be honest, he had been happy as a graduate studies professor. He liked having an audience in the graduate classroom and enjoyed sharing what he knew; he missed teaching for that reason, but not for the endless hours reading hastily cobbled together papers, or dealing with uninterested or unmotivated undergraduate students when he had to teach a general education class. Now that he thought about it, when he first met Sylvie, she was just about the age of a graduate student starting a Master's degree.

He saw the freeway sign for Hinckley and decided it was time for a hamburger and a pee and a chance to stretch his long legs. He sat and as he ate his hamburger and french fries, read the Minneapolis paper starting with the business section, checked the sports page, saving the headlines for last. The metro section did not interest him. Finished with the paper and waiting for the bathroom to clear, he watched the day-to-day routine of the young women working behind the counter. Like Sylvie they were invariably blonde, by nature or by bottle, and invariably wore glasses. Tow-headed myopic females and he was not stereotyping. This was nothing less than a documented anthropological fact. Two of the three teenagers taking orders showed the bloom of pregnancy beneath their untucked corporate shirts. Not all behavior was genetic, he reminded himself; environment was also an important factor. This far north of the Cities there was not much for a small town teenager to do but get drunk and screw, as the country song blasting through the speakers exhorted customers willing to listen between bites of their triple-sized bacon cheeseburgers with extra-large fries.

The sad part of these kids doing what comes naturally was that their religion forbade them the use of birth control or an abortion at a time when their hormones would not let them say no. So they got pregnant and dropped out of school and were forced to work for minimum wage or, tethered to a child, go on welfare while they watched others lead TV lives of the sort they aspired to but could never have. Every now and then a rare beauty with enough brains to keep her legs closed long enough to escape the persistent young Romeos quarterbacking the local high school football teams, driven by their own set of biological imperatives, gained acceptance into one of the many competent state universities in Minnesota, got the hell out of town, and never looked back. In instances more rare, a willowy blonde too tall for her polyester uniform pants, found the right agent in Hollywood or New York and was able to move from behind the fast food counter and into the magazines her envious girlfriends back home bought from the stands fronting the check-out aisles in the local supermarket. He finished his drink and his cultural analysis and had a long stand at the urinal, mildly surprised that his urine was not the color of diet cola, and felt much better for all of it.

Back on the road and southbound once more, he made good time until, about an hour out of the Cities, a blinking electronic arrow on wheels pointed traffic to a single lane. In Minnesota the joke was that roads were either under repair or it was winter. For his peace of mind there was too much truth to the joke and he fell in behind a long line of cars, trucks, campers, trucks, boat trailers, trucks, pickups, and more semis. As the traffic slowed he thought again of Sylvie: she was certainly pretty enough for Hollywood—and he meant the movies, not television and the post-pubescent cuteness that passed for good looks among the teenage reality show crowd. No. He meant beauty in the classic style of Catherine Deneuve, not in the big assed, big-mouthed, rubber lipped, artificially whitened horse teeth style of American women that seemed all the rage these days. She was certainly tall enough to be a model, but she had natural breasts unenhanced or augmented by science and silicone. No doubt about it: hers was a natural beauty far more appealing than the sallow complected, hollow cheeked mannequins walking their knobby knees, bony asses, pointy elbows, and skeletal shoulders behind their blown up tits as they clomped down the runway.

Sylvie had one of those faces that stood out among the crowd, not for any sense of the exotic or the bizarre; rather, for its rare mixture of harmony and symmetry. It was simply a beautiful and beguiling face, and the more deeply and the longer you looked into it the more beautiful it became. Perhaps Plato had a point after all, he conceded to himself. She had the odd pimple now and then and he used to kid her about that because he knew she was sensitive about her appearance, not out of any belief that "I am gorgeous but temporarily imperfect," but because she did not yet believe or trust her own emergent beauty. He shook his head. The day when that momentous realization came would no doubt send a shock wave throughout the ranks of European men. They already stared—young and old—and this had always disturbed her—why were they staring at me, she had asked him, and he smiled to himself at the memory. Those were not stares; those were slack-jawed, gaping leers that said "I am not worthy in the presence of such overwhelming, paralyzing, perfect beauty." She would wonder aloud whether she had perhaps dropped a dollop of her favorite sweet mustard down the front of her white blouse while she ate her veal sausages for lunch. It seemed no matter how carefully she ate, invariably a drop of spaghetti sauce, or sandwich condiment, usually mustard but ketchup also, or egg yolk even, was bound to find its way down the front of her shirt, embarrassing her in the process. He realized then how much he missed her. He missed her easy laughter and her whole-hearted companionship. He missed the enthusiastic but occasionally clumsy sex when she tried too hard to please; he missed her unencumbered and natural beauty; but most of all he missed her surprisingly real and surpassingly fine intellect.

Roland, to give credit where credit was due, had noticed it first, veiled behind her elemental and dominant physicality, protected and hidden from others in her youthful clumsy vulnerability, and for that reason had taken her on and accepted her as his partner even after learning she had been assigned to him as a punishment, a rookie policewoman fresh from her studies at university. A quick and easy study, Roland had shaped and nurtured her keen intelligence until the two officers had become a team famous throughout Interpol for solving notoriously difficult cases.

Will met *Kommissar Sylvie Schumann* for the first time when Roland invited him to work on the Adamas File and he spent the remainder of the summer with her after the case was solved and before he had to return to the United States and complete his teaching assignments at the university. Behind kisses, they had promised each other to stay in touch, but distance, work, and the proximity of others had done them in. He simply did not have the heart for it and one day, as expected, the Skype calls became more and more infrequent, the letters and email simply stopped coming, replaced by a line or two appended to his uncle's letter when he wrote concerning some case or criminal proceeding. It was his fault, he admitted to himself. He also knew that she understood his silence. She was smart enough to figure it out. Men are really the sensitive ones, he had told her once. They suffer most when relationships fail and she could not help but agree based on the fiascoes of her personal experience with previous relationships. He shook his head again, wondering how a woman with such an unusual combination of brains and looks could have such difficulty in her relationships and then, of course, he found his answer in the question. The traffic just above the Cities pulled him from his reminiscences and he was glad now to give her up once more.

Instead of relying on his memory, and given the proliferation of lane closures and increasing traffic, it was time to let the satellite navigation take over. Once he found the proper exit for the airport, he indulged himself again. The sad fact of the matter was that she was in Bavaria, Germany and he was here and that was not going to change anytime soon. Dwelling on her much more would eventually become a painful indulgence, not a pleasurable one, and he wanted to remember her for the happiness and joy she had given him during their time together. Enough. He reprimanded himself and gave his attention over to the difficulty of managing the traffic pouring into the airport. In half an hour he would have Roland in the car and they would be happily on their way back to the cabin and the undisturbed freedom of a Boundary Waters fishing vacation.

He left the Subaru in short-term parking. His notes on his uncle's email directed him to Terminal 2 Humphrey at the glass exit doors at the south end of the Baggage

Claim Level near Baggage Claim 2 and Door 6. Once there he checked the monitors displaying flight information and noted with satisfaction that the Lufthansa/United flight from Munich was on time and on schedule, due to arrive around 5:30 pm. He expected as much from the Germans. He double-checked the flight number because the plane had landed first in Chicago and he knew Lufthansa and United often shared flight numbers. He arrived at the waiting area just as the massive Airbus A340 rolled up to the extended walkway and waited for it to accordion out and engulf the exit door with a welcoming kiss. Shortly thereafter, the flight crew disengaged the lock on the exits and international travelers emerged from the artificial tunnel, searching the signs and monitors for directions to other flights, other gates, customs and border protection for some, and for others directions to baggage or transportation.

Business travelers and first-class passengers deplaned first, most in overcoats and carrying briefcases, most talking on their cell phones or hurrying immediately to the kiosks where the charging stations were located. He knew his uncle would not be among them so he relaxed as the crowd streamed by. He could afford to fly first-class on the salary of an *Erster Kriminalhauptkommissar*, a Chief of Detectives, but he was frugal to a fault—a trait Will respected—and would not allow himself such an unseemly indulgence. No. He would rather take a seat toward the back of the plane where he could observe, ever the inspector and always a cop, where he would no doubt spend time chatting up the flight attendants once they had finished their duties. He wagered that by the time his uncle came down the ramp into the airport he would have the number of at least one new uniformed female friend, eager and willing to spend some of her layover with the handsome and charming police detective from the Bavarian Alps.

The flow of passengers ebbed or streamed, depending on the amount of luggage or children or both that had to be dragged along. Still his uncle did not show; but this was no cause for worry: it merely reinforced his initial thought that his uncle had booked a seat well back in the capacious plane and was allowing the impatient crush of travelers to flee the confines of aluminum and Plexiglas as they rushed to the nearest toilet or to meet connecting flights. So he waited patiently, holding the purple and gold box containing the Crown Royal whisky behind his back—a ritual gift for his uncle: a giving started by his father, Roland's best friend, more than twenty years ago. Now the number of bleary-eyed, jet-lagged flyers was slowing considerably from what must have been a full flight, and now he saw mostly itinerant students hunched under formidable backpacks like sherpas—one, in fact, wore a leather and wool sherpa cap pulled down over his ears. Then came the occasional serviceman travelling in desert uniform, or a couple too much in love to hurry. Just to be certain, he checked the itinerary one more time and once again satisfied as to the correct place and time, he looked up into a pair of the most beautiful, enchantingly blue Bavarian eyes, looking for him and only him.

"Sylvie," was all he could say, waiting for the flood of emotion to crest and his breathing to resume, forcing her name through the uncontrollable smile her presence engendered. She raised her eyebrows so that her own smile became beatific.

"Surprised?" she asked superfluously, the question posed in German and within the context of her own genuine happiness at seeing Will again. "And not too disappointed that Roland couldn't come?" He could smell the delicate perfume of her hand as she reached up and gently closed his mouth. "It's unbecoming for a professor of your academic rank and scholarly stature to stand and gape," she reminded him when he did not speak. Then she closed his eyes with a kiss that left him even more breathless. Finally, he had to step back and breathe again, hardly believing she was there, standing in front of him, and he could not resist kissing her again full on the lips, and then on both cheeks in European greeting as he slowly recovered his composure.

"What have you done with my uncle?" he asked her, looking over her shoulder, unable to stop smiling.

"Roland was delayed," she explained, taking his hand in hers. She walked him over to the rows of chairs, out of the way of the last few passengers arriving at the baggage carousel, wondering what language the two were speaking. She had forgotten just how tall he really was and how large and strong his hands were. Safely out of the flow of traffic she continued, "He's tying up a case for Interpol and will arrive next week. He thought it might be a nice surprise if I took his place. I hope you're not too disappointed," she said for the second time, and he knew she was asking if he was happy to see her again. Instead of speaking he took her into his arms and this time it was she who had to pull away from the passionate kiss, breathless. "Well, you certainly know how to greet a girl, I have to admit," and she accepted the gift of whisky intended for Roland. "I will drink this bottle by myself," she promised.

He laughed, but he had also seen her drink. "Come on, my gorgeous alcoholic," he said, and took her hand again by right of rediscovered familiarity. "Let's get your luggage and then get the hell out of here. You can tell me the whole story on the drive home."

Chapter Five

Black Miniskirt

Sylvie had cleared customs in Chicago, her flight's first stop before proceeding on to the Twin Cities. They waited for the horn and flashing light above the quiescent baggage carousel before it began to disgorge her bags. She held his hand more tightly than she needed and took the time to surreptitiously watch him as he waited for the carousel to lurch into movement. Now that the initial nervous excitement of meeting him had passed, she allowed herself to relax into his confident lead. He always seemed to know where he was going and even when he did not, it never seemed to bother him very much, and this calmed her, now swept up in the maelstrom of new people, new places, and new ways of doing things. Even though she had forgotten how tall he was, she did remember his handsome good looks, although he wore his hair cut much shorter now.

She blushed to think that she had asked Roland for a picture of his nephew, a picture she kept for herself, out of her boyfriend's sight, a picture she allowed herself to look at from time to time. The haircut suited him by accentuating the planes and angles of his face, making him seem both handsome and masculine; he was not a pretty boy at all. She blushed again to think of it; her current boyfriend Freddi was exactly that: a pretty boy. She grimaced. He fussed before the mirror like a woman.

He claimed he was merely expressing his sensitive side. She had also forgotten how good Dr. Will Sheridan smelled. She allowed herself to breathe him in deeply. He mistook the breath for a sigh and asked if she were tired from the long flight. She just smiled and shook her head. Excitement had replaced her fatigue.

As the first bags emerged and travelers crowded closer to identify and locate their luggage, he held his ground, letting others move around him. He was one of very few men she had to look up to. She liked that about him; it made her feel good about herself: it drew attention from her height to his. A bit of gray showed through his black hair at the temples; a new shock but she remembered too that he was almost ten years older than she, although you certainly could not tell by looking at him. As usual, he seemed fit and in excellent condition. To be expected, she thought.

He was an avid outdoorsman who hunted and fished and still played tournament handball. He had explained the game to her once after she had confused it with the perverted European mélange of hockey, soccer, and basketball called team handball. He had explained handball to her as being similar to racquetball, but without all the technology. He had even threatened to make her play once. She played some tennis, but she was primarily a runner, taking part in many of the six kilometer *Volkslauf* held almost every weekend in every village in Germany for walkers and runners of all ages and abilities. She had recently joined a martial arts club, she told him, knowing his interest in the sport, and had brought her running shoes and her karate gi.

As the conveyer belt revolved, bags of all sizes, colors, and shapes were offered on display like mismatched chocolates rejected by quality control. They approached the back of the throng watching the luggage ride by until every now and then one or two passengers pushed forward and wrestled a heavy bag off the jointed metal belt. Others who could not capture their bags in time were forced to wait out another revolution before rescuing their movable possessions from the trail of yet another circuit. Will walked Sylvie toward the end of the orbit where the bags disappeared again into the building and where fewer people stood waiting and watching, talking only until they spotted their bags. He asked if she saw anything belonging to her.

"That one coming toward us." She pointed out a large Gucci Tian piece done in Chinese jade and wrapped with yellow Customs tape. He timed his grab and easily lifted the bag by the handle off the carrier and onto the floor.

"Geez, Sylvie. What do you have in there—a piece of the old Berlin Wall?"

She just giggled and this pleased him immensely: in all her worldly sophistication and exposure to the dark underside of life, she had not forgotten her girlish giggle. Another bag of the same marque and configuration slid into view and she said, "That one too, please." This time he groaned dramatically as he lifted the heavy, full weight of the bag and set it next to its fashionable mate. "Just one more," she said, rubbing the small of his back in sympathy. "Can you do it?" He seemed doubtful so she pushed him aside and pulled off a smaller version of the first two.

"Planning to stay awhile?" he teased.

"I can always buy whatever I need."

He looked one more time to the carousel but she assured him that was all. He seemed dubious so she asked what he was waiting for. "A sink or a toilet," he told her and she said, "Grab the bags, big boy, and take me somewhere I haven't been before. And on the way, make sure you buy me something to eat. I'm famished."

Sylvie hungry was not to be taken lightly. Sylvie famished required immediate and careful attention. She said she could wait just long enough to forgo the pleasures of airport food and he promised her relief not too far up the road. They walked the wheeled bags to the car park. He loaded the bags into the back of the SUV and waited while she removed the dark blue coat of her expensive, tailored pantsuit; once in the passenger's seat, she pushed off her black open-toed pumps, toes to heels, and placed all behind the driver's seat. She folded down the sun visor above her seat, pleased to find a mirror behind it and dug a brush from her oversized carry-on garment bag laid out on the seats behind them.

He started the engine to run the air conditioner and waited patiently while she made repairs and brushed her light blonde hair into place. She dropped the brush, and then rummaged for a lipstick. Before she applied the color, she leaned over and he took the offer of a kiss from her lips. He broke it quickly, to be polite, since there was still cosmetic work to be done. He knew it would be improper to interrupt a lady in the process of reconstructing her makeup, but she surprised him by pulling him in for more, now within the privacy of the vehicle within the protection of the parking garage. This time she was serious about it and only after reclaiming her breath did she return to the mirror and apply the red from the stick to her freshly kissed lips. Only when she finished did he meander the vehicle down the sloping turns of the garage back out into the light of day.

"I excite you, don't I, Sylvie?" he said playfully, asking the obvious.

She looked across the seat to him, deadpan in her expression. "Don't make the mistake of confusing jet lag and hunger with sexual attraction, my good doctor."

"I never have," he said, grinning.

Commuter traffic exiting the Cities for the suburbs drew his attention from her and she was content to look at everything new as they drove north. Traffic on the freeway seemed just as heavy as on the *Autobahnen* surrounding Munich. Once in the steady flow of interstate traffic he told her, "I'm really glad to see you again, Sylvie Schumann. I have missed you."

She thought for a moment before she replied, crossed her arms and gave him a hard look. "Well, I'm still mad at you, whether you missed me or not. Why did you stop writing?"

It was a fair question and he understood what she was asking. When he spoke, it came out more harshly than he intended. "We're adults, Sylvie, not love-struck teenagers trying to keep a summer romance alive through the school year." If anything, she glared at him with even greater intensity, and he frowned. He had made a dreadful mess of what he wanted to say to her. She noticed his discomfort as he squirmed and repositioned himself within his seat.

"A call now and then or at least an email on my birthday would have been nice." She was not letting him off so easily.

He sighed and looked over at her. "My feelings for you haven't changed in the least, you know that."

He knew exactly what to say, the bastard, and she could not help but smile. She pulled the seatbelt off her shoulder, leaned in and kissed him on the cheek. She was finished scolding him and told him as much as she wiped away the red curve of her lips impressed on his cheek. Done with the repair of her makeup, she decided it was time to rebuild and strengthen the relationship.

"This really is a wonderful surprise and I want to take advantage of every minute we have together and show you everything: the cabin, the lake, the woods, how to fish, my books, everything." He was gushing like a teenager now, summer love or not and in spite of himself, and she was caught up in his unabashed enthusiasm. She remembered this was one of the things she found so attractive about the man; he was not at all embarrassed to show her his unadulterated boyish joy for the things he enjoyed. She was pleased at the honest surprise her unexpected arrival had caused him, and all her nervousness about how he would react when he saw her was now gone. She knew again how he felt about her, but one small matter required her attention.

"Well, what about your girlfriend?" she asked carefully.

"Girlfriends," he corrected her, and this earned him a pretty good shot to the shoulder.

"You been lifting weights?" he asked, and then continued. "Don't worry. I throw everybody out of the house while I'm working on my latest book."

She was not certain if she liked that answer and while she mulled it over, pushed her lower lip into a gentle glistening pout which, if anything, made her look all the more beautiful.

Unlike many of the women he knew personally and professionally, some of whom were considered fairly attractive by any standard, Sylvie surpassed them all with the simple addition of unconscious grace. There it was again, evident even in the casual way she recrossed her legs toward him, or the delicate way she held her head when she walked. Had she not been a natural beauty, she would still be graceful, making her all the more attractive. "I can't believe how much you love me," he said out of the blue, shocking her to the core in that effortless, damnably self-assured manner of his.

She stared at him for two solid uncensored minutes, wondering how he could know, how he could possibly see so deeply into her most private thoughts and desires when they had been together again only for such a brief time. She knew he was a master of language, fully able to manipulate every nuance of meaning and ambiguity as he constructed his messages. He had no way of knowing how much she really loved him, how much she had missed him, and how desperate she had been to see him again. He could not have known then or now, no matter how smart he was, how many degrees he had, or how competent a detective he was. She had told no one: not Roland, not her mother; she had barely admitted the truth of her feelings to herself. He could not know and she was absolutely certain of it because it was her greatest secret in life and she was certainly not ready now to divulge it to him or to anyone else for that matter.

She decided to use his strategy against him. His statement was clearly designed to get her to admit that she did indeed love him. He was fishing, despite his smugness and confidence. She decided to hide behind the same ambiguity he was using to test her feelings for him. Let's see: I can't believe how much you love me, he had said.

"You'll just have to force yourself," she replied, giving nothing away, intimating that he might have been right, suggesting merely the possibility that she did love him. She was nearly breathless after she said it.

He laughed out loud at the elegance of the design of her reply. "Sylvie," he said with honest admiration, "you're becoming quite the semiotician."

"Thank you," she said, politely accepting the compliment, and remembering that before she met him, she had not the faintest idea of what a semiotician was. She offered her cheek like a lady and he kissed her, and then she held his hand in both hers as they drove ever north.

Will had not forgotten about Sylvie's need to eat, although she had, at least temporarily. He knew a place below Hinckley where you could get a decent sirloin steak and baked potato served on a heavy, white cafeteria plate. Soon, he promised her, and they pulled into the parking lot of the restaurant five minutes later. Sylvie was eager to try all things American and she let Will order for her while she went to pee, taking her shoulder bag along. She came back to the table in walking shorts and a blue top that matched her eyes. She had switched her pumps for Birkenstock sandals, but she wore socks in the German fashion. He did not comment. She seemed cooler and more comfortable for the change, not being used to the stifling humidity that had settled into the air. She ate her steak, every bite of her baked potato, and even stole one or two crinkle cut fries from Will before he slapped her hand. Because he could tell she was still hungry, he ordered her a piece of chocolate cream pie with dark chocolate shavings sprinkled atop the shoe-sized wedge. She wanted to devour it all, giving in to the sheer enjoyment of eating for pleasure, but thought better of stuffing herself into discomfort.

She left the last three or so bites for him, but not without regret. "You sure?" he asked, fork ready. She remembered her mother's warning about making an unattractive pig of herself and sighed wistfully. She decided discretion was the better part of gastric distress and assured him that he should finish the pie for her. He made short work of it, amazed that a woman of her weight could eat so much; afraid that she might ask for it back. The last of the crumbs in the tines of his fork, he gave the plate to the waitress, who asked Sylvie—for whom she now had a legitimate and begrudging respect—if she required anything further. Sylvie asked only for a refill of her iced tea, brought immediately to the table.

"So where the hell is my uncle?" he asked with such dramatic intensity that it forced her to laugh.

"I still can't believe I'm here," she said, starting her explanation. "Everything happened so fast. Roland was excited about coming to spend time with you and seeing the States for the first time—more excited than I've seen him for some time." Will smiled. "And then, about a week before he was to leave, he told me he couldn't go. We were working on a case for Interpol—we helped catch a serial killer moving from country to country—and Roland had to go to Brussels to prepare their officers for testimony.

"Let me guess," Will said. "An international truck driver."

"How could you possibly know that?" she asked in disbelief.

He chuckled. "We have plenty of that sort cruising our freeways as we speak."

She nodded in affirmation and continued her explanation. "At the last minute they decided to use him as an expert witness with the promise to put him on a flight right after the trial." She took a sip of her tea, ignoring the straw.

"And that left his original ticket available," Will said.

"Right. And it was one of those non-refundable sorts, so he offered it to me. I simply couldn't pass up the opportunity..."

"To see me?"

"To see the United States, but when I went in to see my boss—you remember that prick, Steinmetz?" He nodded. "Well, he said no. He used the excuse that with Roland leaving too he wouldn't be able to manage the case load."

"Seems he still has it in for Roland," Will observed.

"He's worse, if that's possible, now that Roland and I are solving cases together." She paused for a little laugh. "And that crazy uncle of yours did screw his teenaged daughter at one time. She still calls him now and then." Will was not surprised. There was no doubt that Sylvie relished the idea of what Roland had done to the *Kapitän*, even though it was before Steinmetz had assigned her, fresh from university and academy training, to Roland as punishment. "When I called Roland in Belgium to tell him that Steinmetz wouldn't let me go, he was furious. He told me to wait and that he would call my *Handi* back in an hour. But he didn't." She looked at Will, listening expectantly.

"*Direktor Bruno Hauptmann* called your cellphone and arranged for your official visit to the States, on behalf of the Bavarian State Criminal Police, or the *Kripo*, as you say," Will told her. He remembered Hauptmann, Roland's dear friend through his father, with fondness and admiration. He had been impressed with the man—head of the *Kripo*—from the very beginning of the work they did on the Adamas File.

"How did you know that?" Sylvie demanded, once again caught by surprise, shaking her head in disbelief. Then she answered her own question. "Semiotic analysis, right?" She looked forward to hearing his chain of reasoning and he was happy to oblige.

"You are here; therefore, I have to reconstruct the most likely chain of events resulting in your arrival, given the circumstances you described."

She nodded and sipped from her tea. She loved to watch the transformation in his face as he concentrated, recounting for her the cascade of logical reasoning from which he would derive his conclusion.

"You tell me if my premises are correct." She agreed. "You cannot put in for vacation leave with less than a week's notice."

"Correct."

"You did not tell Steinmetz to go to Hell and then resigned, looking to start a new life with an old flame in the States."

"That's right too," she giggled, "especially the part about the old flame." He ignored her, deep in thought.

"The only person with the authority to countermand your captain's orders is *Direktor Hauptmann*."

"Yes."

"But Hauptmann is also an expert at playing the political games he needs to survive within the state police bureaucracy and would most likely have disguised his motives in overruling Steinmetz by inventing a plausible deception." He watched her carefully while he spoke. He knew that when people listen intently they often lose awareness of their nonverbal behaviors. Without knowing it, she was telling him that he was on the right track. "He would thus invent a sanction whereby you could travel to the U.S. on short notice." She nodded unconsciously. Now fully confident in the accuracy of his analysis, he pushed on to the conclusion. "Given that we worked together successfully in the past and have co-authored with Roland, a manual on the application of semiotic analysis for solving intractably difficult crimes, Hauptmann, no doubt, 'asked' you to liaise with me in order to edit and revise the manual. Given my subsequent work with the FBI Special Investigative Unit, you are here in an 'official' capacity, charged with working hand-in-hand with me on the revision and no doubt were ordered, I repeat, officially ordered to use every personal resource at your disposal to get the job done—even if it involves offering sexual favors in return for my vast and considerable knowledge." He grinned.

"I don't know what intractable means but if you pay for my dinner, you might get lucky, even though I am on an expense account. But dammit again Will, how could you possibly know exactly what happened and in such detail? Have you become psychic or something?"

"I knew you were going to say that." He laughed at her pained expression. "The suit gave it away, Sylvie, if you must know, and the fact that you had a change of comfortable clothes ready in your shoulder bag."

"What do you mean the suit gave it away?" she asked.

"Although you didn't travel in your dress uniform, you were wearing clothes suitable for official business. No doubt Hauptmann called you to let you know of his plan, faxed the orders to Steinmetz, and on the day you were to travel, you had to go in, sign the requisite vouchers, forms, and other paperwork that bogs down good police work in every country. You felt it necessary to wear the pretty suit you had on when you deplaned, thereby playing your part in Hauptmann's political game with Steinmetz. A tourist on vacation would have dressed much more informally and comfortably for a transatlantic flight with a stop in Chicago. What could that official business possibly be, given your destination? Liaise with me. Steinmetz remembers our work together in Germany."

She looked at him with the admiration of a student for the professor. "So the suit gave it away?"

He nodded and looked at the addition on the check. "Within the context of your sudden and unexpected arrival in place of Roland, wearing the suit was highly significant. A trained semiotician, I interpreted the selection of the suit to be meaningful beyond simply dressing for travel. It just didn't fit, pardon the pun, based on what I know about you, Roland, Hauptmann, and your boss. Given the premises and the scenario I created, a plausible explanation for wearing such a formal suit, which flatters you wonderfully, I might add, requires the inference of official business. I then reasoned through what official business might entail, given the short notice of your switch with Roland." He put down a nice tip for the waitress.

"One more thing," she said after she readied her bag for her shoulder, "Even though you were correct and alarmingly accurate with your analysis, how did you know that I didn't wear the suit merely to impress you?"

"Excellent question, Sylvie." He paused dramatically.

"Well...?" she prompted.

"To impress me you would have worn your black leather miniskirt."

She brushed her cheek against his, letting him smell her perfume and whispered, "Bastard. I packed that, too."

He smiled in gentle surprise and admitted, "That, I did not know."

Chapter Six

Tornado

As they stepped out of the air-conditioned coolness of the steak palace into the late summer heat, the thick heavy air enveloped them like a sodden sheet taken too soon from the dryer. Sylvie gasped a little, unused to the hot moist air that soaked her clothes from the inside and outside at the same time. By the time they managed the short walk to the car, she was glistening. Will drove the Subaru across the parking lot and pulled into a nearby gas station. He was suddenly quiet.

"What's the matter?" Sylvie asked, delicately patting her forehead with a silk handkerchief embroidered with Belgian lace.

Will pointed up to an eerie sky, a sky unlike any she had ever seen, not even high in the Alps of Bavaria.

"See that lens shaped cloud that seems to be flattened and elongated?" He indicated the direction for her through the broad windshield.

"Not a good sign?" she asked, sensing his concern.

"Not a good sign at all, Sylvie. Meteorologists call that a lenticular cloud and it is almost always a sign of bad weather to come. Along with this extraordinary humidity, high heat, and the direction of the winds, I'd say we're in for a classic northern window-rattling, eye-blinding thunderstorm."

"Should we try to get a room and wait it out? I wouldn't mind if we have to do that."

He smiled at the kind offer and he was tempted. "Let's do it this way. We'll gas up here and then hit the road, keeping an eye on the weather as we travel. Once we get above Hinckley the traffic thins out rather nicely and we might very well drive right out of this." She agreed to the plan and he took care of fueling the vehicle. In the convenience store he bought her four liter bottles of Evian. "You'll need to up your fluids in all this heat. It will take you a couple of days to get properly acclimated."

"Thanks," she said, already taking a drink from one of the bottles. It was exactly what she needed, even after the big dinner.

He drove them back to the interstate and they headed north again on 35. Fifteen miles up the road she smiled beatifically and announced, "I have to pee." When she saw the reaction pulling at his face she laughed. "Just joking. You looked exactly like your uncle when I said that."

"I owe you one. You got me good. I was ready to pull over for you."

"So tell me, big boy. Where are you taking me?"

"Excuse me just a minute," he said, listening closely to the weather station on the radio before he switched it off. "I'm stealing you away to my lake cabin in the North Woods, my Bavarian beauty."

She liked the sound of that. "Do you really think I'm beautiful?"

He took a quick look to see if she was joking. She seemed genuinely uncertain. She had never thought of herself in those terms. She knew men considered her attractive, but beautiful was a term she reserved for movie stars.

"Without a doubt, Sylvie Schumann, you are one of the most beautiful women I have ever known, and I've known quite a few in my day. In all the years I taught in the Midwest and before that in the Pacific Northwest, I've seen maybe ten women I would classify as legitimately heart-stopping drop-dead gorgeous. And I don't mean the big-mouthed, swollen-lipped, post-pubescent pouting skeletons that the American media present to us as their exemplar of beauty. I mean classically beautiful women with the right hair cut to flatter the shape of their head, women with a harmony of features in the face, a geometry of form and shape that coalesces to make a woman beautiful. The race doesn't matter, the skin color doesn't matter, but the complexion does. The hair color is red, black, brown, white, blonde—long, curly, short; bald I have to think about. It's the confluence of form that matters. That's you, Sylvie. It's what Verdi called 'recondite armonia di belleze diverse,' a recondite harmony of diverse beauty. You asked and that's what I think."

She considered what he had told her, sat up a little bit straighter in her seat, and smiled a beautiful and harmonious smile. After a minute or so of sublime, peaceful radiance, like sunlight filtered through a pure white cloud, she said, "Will. In light of what you said, I have to consider the possibility that I'm much too good for you."

He could not help but chuckle. She was probably right. She had a strength and confidence about her now that he had seen only as a glimmer of possibility when they had worked together for the first time. "That is very likely true; but just remember one thing."

"What's that?"

"We haven't talked about your personality yet. You are, after all, your mother's daughter," he teased, tickling the vulnerability below the strength.

"I can change," she promised, the smile now a frown.

He looked doubtful. "It's hard to overcome both one's biology and so many years of social conditioning."

"Will you help me?" she pleaded, exaggerating the plea with her eyes.

"I'm here for you kid, because that's the kind of guy I am. We'll work together to rebuild your personality so that you can be more than just a shallow beauty of little or no substance."

She smiled vacantly. "A beauty with substance—I can't wait to begin the transformation. And Mother always told me that it was the woman who tries to change the man."

"Don't change a thing," he told her in all seriousness.

"But you don't think I've become too fat?"

"Oh god. Here we go again," he said in mock exasperation as the first fat drops of rain spattered across the windshield, hinting at what was to come, interrupting their verbal play. He was forced to pay attention to his driving in earnest now as they ran through the sunshine under the burgundy colored clouds until the rain eventually washed away the last of the sunlight. He came off the cruise control and backed his speed down as the force of the rain increased. Thunder rumbled in the distance and wind bent the straining tops of the firs. The torrent of rain lashed against the windshield, defeating the furious pace of the wipers unable to keep up with the slew of water pushed at them by the rising wind. Given the poor visibility, he dropped his speed another ten miles per hour. The water sluicing across the road made it seem as if they were driving through a shallow stream and he worried now about hydroplaning the tires.

"Time to give in," he said to Sylvie, as if he had just made up his mind. He indicated a Minnesota map in the side pocket of the passenger door. "Open that up for me and find Minneapolis."

"Why don't you just use your on-board navigation?" she asked, puzzled.

"I will once we do a quick location on the map. I can't afford to make a mistake based on the weather signs I'm seeing."

She unfolded the map and laid it in her lap. "Got it."

"You'll need to turn it around." He waited while she reoriented the map and smoothed it out again across her knees. "See 35 running north above the city?"

She traced it with her finger and nodded.

"Good. Find Hinckley and look north about 30 kilometers or so, and let me know the number of the first exit or road coming off the interstate."

She studied the confusing jumble of lines and colors and numbers and then called one out.

"Nope. Already passed it. Try a little farther north."

She called out the next highway and he said, "Perfect; should be coming up in less than a mile."

Despite the windshield looking like a dirty aquarium, they found the exit, left the interstate, traveled another half mile or so before he turned onto the hard-pack dirt and gravel of a two-lane logging road that wound back into the wind-whipped forest. He pulled over to the side as far as he could and parked. "Just in time," he said with satisfaction.

Sylvie thought she detected a hint of relief in his voice but did not say anything. The wind, blocked by the trees sequestering them, howled as if enraged and grew even more ferocious. Whipped by the wind, rain lashed the vehicle, rocking the SUV on its suspension. Gusts of wind pushed beneath the four-wheel drive vehicle, threatening to lift the Subaru off its chassis. In the distance they heard the terrifying sustained crack of a lodgepole pine unable to bear the full weight of the wind any longer. The force of the gale breaking its back, the tree splintered and crashed to the earth, the horrendous fall pushing the bole through the cushion of its branches. Sylvie started at the noise, unable to keep the panic from her eyes. She reached for his hand.

"What an ungodly sound," she said with a dry shiver through the shoulders. "It seemed to go on forever."

"Green snap, it's called," he explained, holding her hand tightly. "Nature's own way of pruning out the weak and the diseased." The information did not comfort her in the least. "Aren't you afraid that one might fall on us?"

"No," he assured her. "I parked so that we have the best protection possible given the circumstances." He left it at that but she wanted to know.

"What circumstances?"

"I think we're in the middle of a legitimate full-blown tornado." He tried to look through the rain-smeared window. "Wind is definitely coming from the south-west and is moving north and east, the typical direction of a tornado around here. Listen."

She heard a sound like a massive locomotive powering up its enormous diesel engines, but it was only the roar of the wind. "It sounds like we're parked at a railroad crossing and a locomotive pulling a freight train just passed in front of us," she observed. Sylvie felt a pressure change and worked her jaw, trying to clear her inner ear. She swallowed with force and asked, "Are we in danger?"

He nodded. "The danger is there but I tried to minimize our exposure to it. I think the tornado is moving on a line just north of us. It's going to be close but I built in a margin of error. There's nothing to do now but hunker down and hold on."

She did not know what hunker down meant but she was all for holding on. He checked to see that she still wore her seat belt. There was nothing more they could do but wait and let nature run her course and hope that course took the danger north and ahead of them. Wind and rain slammed the vehicle, rocking it from side to side, trying to push it off the road and then, seemingly frustrated by the immovable weight of the vehicle, gradually gave up and moved off into the distance. The high-power roar of the tornadic winds was suddenly gone. The downpour was steadier now, and as the wind abandoned it, the rain maintained a constant saturation and a constant force. Then the pressure abated as if someone had throttled back the big engine of the powerful storm. Five minutes later Will was able to use the wipers and they could see brief glimpses of brightening in the gloom.

Will keyed the ignition, selected D2 on the automatic transmission, and let the four-wheel drive slowly pull them back onto the graveled surface of the service road. The rain had reduced to drizzle now and he backed the wiper speed down to its lowest intermittent setting. He rolled down the window on her side. "Smell that fresh air."

She put her head out the window and drank in a great draught of air. She detected a tinge of coolness and the hot sticky wet humidity was gone, as if the winds had completely purged the atmosphere of all its moisture. Will switched off the air conditioner. Once back on the rain blackened asphalt of the interstate and heading for Cloquet, he found a station broadcasting an update on the weather. The tornado had passed within half a mile of their location and was pushing on toward Duluth. "Are we okay now?" Sylvie wondered, studying the map again.

"Yes. We'll be moving north but more westerly and at a tangent to the storm. We have survived the worst of it." He pointed through the windshield and she could see the back edge of the massive storm system, blue skies pushing it out of their area. "Looks like we'll see the sun again today, Sylvie, and maybe even a pretty good sunset."

She took a good long pull from her water bottle and then offered it to Will. "That, without a doubt, is one of the scariest things I have ever experienced. What about you?" she asked ready to make conversation again.

He shook his head. "The scariest would have to be the first time I saw your mother in the morning without makeup."

That admission cost him a punch to the shoulder and it smarted, Sylvie having been trained to exert a certain level of violence as a police officer.

Every stream, every creek, every ditch that held water was gorged with run-off from the storm. Along the highway and into the clearings of the forest she saw evidence of the storm's ferocity. Traffic moved at a much slower pace than normal, drivers and passengers alike chastened by the awe-inspiring fury of the storm.

"We'll take a rest at Cloquet," he promised her and as an afterthought added, "If it's still there." She could not tell if he was serious or not.

At that instant, he hit his turn signal and moved to the right lane, then slowed and edged over onto the shoulder of the road.

"What in the world now?" she wondered out loud and followed his eyes to the rear-view mirror. She saw the lights of the emergency vehicles before she heard the sirens. The Minnesota State Patrol cruiser clipped by them at a high rate of speed, blue lights flashing and siren pulsing. An ambulance followed a few seconds later, chasing the officer. A few minutes up the road they came upon the tail end of traffic slowing and moved left into a single lane. They saw the carnage among the emergency vehicles and the confusion of flashing lights.

One vehicle lay on its top, exposing its belly to the sky, one wheel still turning slowly. A semi pulling a trailer had jackknifed into the grass of the roadside ditch. A small lake was growing where the trailer damned the water in the ditch. They saw the nose of a boat pointing straight up a large oak as if it were sniffing up the tree. Farther on they saw the remains of the recreational vehicle that had been pulling the boat. An exploding bomb could not have done more damage. Pieces of the vehicle were strewn everywhere, littering the highway and the ditch where the chassis lay on its side; there were even pieces of metal and glass among the trees. The boat trailer was bent and twisted but still attached to the rear end of the vehicle by its emergency chains. Two more cars ahead of the RV were piled up in the ditch, long deep furrows marking the slide to the wreckage. Sylvie, ever the good investigator, put the pieces together as Will negotiated his way through the debris field.

"The two cars piled into the ditch first. For whatever reason the big long vehicle, I think you call it an RV, hit its brakes and skidded, lost control and probably rolled, throwing the boat up that tree. The tractor-trailer rig following behind also hit his brakes, jackknifed, and went off the road. That's the way I see it. Those Minnesota guys have their work cut out for them," she said referring to the state patrol.

Will knew what had happened. The unfortunate drivers had tried to beat the winds and the rain but they could not outrun the tornado. Unwilling to heed the signs, and in their foolishness and unwillingness to give in to the unrelenting forces of nature, they had paid the price. Traffic speed gradually picked up again as they drove beyond the catastrophe and Will shook his head at the grim scene they had just witnessed. In that instant, the realization came to Sylvie, the sudden understanding of the meaning of the actions that had probably saved their lives. He had read the signs, and instead of ignoring them, he had acted, saving them both. She took his hand again, silently reaffirming that she knew what he had done for her, for them both. Had they continued on the interstate during the storm, they could very well have been part of the carnage and destruction they just passed. She sighed with relief and smiled at the man she had not seen for more than two years.

In Eveleth, they stopped to stretch their legs and get a soft drink and a candy bar. The jet lag and the storm had conspired to drain the last vestiges of energy from her and he could see the fog of fatigue settle into her face, gathering below the lashes of her eyes. The caffeine from the soda and the sugar from the chocolate revived her enough to survive the last leg of the trip while still conscious. She was not interested in seeing the Hockey Hall of Fame, and she had to laugh when she realized he was not being serious, but did agree to a short stop at the Leonnidas Outlook, which provided a panoramic view of the Minntac Mine, an iron ore producer.

After the respite and the look around and once again on the road north, he explained that it was the mining industry in Minnesota that had given rise to the logging industry and not vice versa, as many people believed. Gold had been discovered just north of Eveleth at Vermilion Lake and a road was built from there to Duluth around 1895. The road led to a miniature gold rush that soon went bust but did lead to the discovery of iron ore in the Mesabi mountain range, through which they now drove.

Compared to the Alps, it was not much of a mountain range, she noticed—she would have called them hills— and what did iron mining have to do with the onset of a logging industry, she wondered. She enjoyed her Snickers bar and the historical commentary relating to the different vistas she was seeing, grateful for both in helping her stay awake.

"Mines needed timber for shoring up," he said. "Tunnels needed support and ore carts rode atop rails anchored to wooden ties. Unfortunately, as is too often the case when it comes to human beings and the exploitation of natural resources, most of the forests in the area were logged off by the early nineteen twenties."

"That explains all the skinny trees," she observed.

"That's right, he continued. "But not those. The logging done currently is for paper and pulp, and the forests you see now are second and third generation stands. In fact, there is still an enormous paper mill in International Falls, about half an hour or so from Voyageurs National Park where we happen to be headed."

"Tell me more about these Voyageurs," she directed, fighting back the fuzziness of impending sleep. She settled back into the comfortable seat, sandals off. "And try to keep it interesting, will you? You're putting me to sleep. Why the French name? I thought Minnesota was settled mostly by Scandinavians. You're making all this up."

"Just be good and pay attention and understand that everything I'm telling you is certified as correct and true by the Minnesota Bureau of Tourism."

She doubted that but he continued anyway.

"The first indigenous people in the area were probably the Dakota. They were driven out by the Chippewa, now known as the Ojibwe, whose descendants still live here and in Canada, just across the border."

She perked up at hearing this. Like many Germans, from her school days she had carried forward an abiding fascination with the history and culture of the American West and American Indians. "Tell me more," she said.

"The first whites arrived in the early 1600s looking for furs and a Northwest Passage to the Pacific. Early French explorers such as Du Luth and others came to trap beaver. Beaver pelts were hammered and compressed to make felt hats for European gentry. For this reason, the beaver was very nearly trapped out of existence. But to be honest about it, the Indians did most of the actual trapping and sold the pelts to the Voyageurs."

"Who were these damned Voyageurs?" she demanded, slapping her knee in mock anger.

"I can see I still have your attention—that's good. The Voyageurs were French traders—for the most part—who would canoe the Boundary Waters between Canada and Minnesota to the farthest outposts west. There they collected the pelts and furs, mink, otter, rabbit, fox, raccoon, and so on, loaded them in their birch bark canoes, which the natives showed them how to make, and paddled their load back to the major depots in the east. A round-trip journey could last a year or two, depending on the length and severity of the winter. Get it? Journey, voyage, *voyageurs*? And that's why there are names like Voyageurs, Sault Sainte Marie, Grands Marais, or Lac Qui Parle."

"I get it," she acknowledged. "The lake-that-talks; I like that. It's quite poetic," she said.

He nodded. "Probably a translation into French of the original Indian name. That happened quite a bit. Now don't interrupt. I'm not finished yet."

She groaned dramatically and looked out the window at another line of trees, hiding her enjoyment of the narrative.

"By the 1870s trapping was mostly finished, but with the discovery of iron ore, mining flourished and brought the loggers to Minnesota: Swedes and Finns settled in the northeast, Poles in the central region, Germans and Bohemians in the south and southwest parts of the state. There's even a New Ulm in the south-central area."

Sylvie lived about one hundred kilometers south of Neu Ulm in Bavaria. He ended his exposition and turned off highway 53 at the sign of the huge walleye, a fiberglass imitation designed for tourists. The jumping walleye had a saddle on it for children to sit while their parents took their pictures.

"I want my picture taken on that fish," she demanded as they drove by without stopping. "*Ist das ein Zander?*" Sylvie asked in German without thinking.

He ignored the pout and told her "Later. Another ten minutes and we're home. And yes it is *ein Zander*. Here it's called a walleye. Lake Kabetogama is a famous walleye fishery."

Placated by the promise, she watched the sun disappear into the tops of the fir trees as the evening softened.

"*Warum walleye?*" she asked, pronouncing both w's as v's.

"Because of the way the eyes of the fish are oriented on its head. The Americans say the eyes are looking at the wall."

The explanation satisfied her and she giggled when they passed the sign outside a restaurant built of logs that read, "Eat here and get worms," surprised at the honesty of the owners.

"Not quite," he explained. "It's a combination restaurant and bait shop. I'll take you there some evening for pizza and ice cream, if you're good."

She clapped her hands and promised.

He turned left on a graveled road, drove another mile or so, and then turned into a paved drive that wound through the trees and ended in a broad spread before the double garage of a magnificent log cabin. He let her out to stretch and admire the two story structure as they waited for the garage door to rise.

"It's absolutely gorgeous," she said after he parked the Forester and came to stand with her, pointing out the features. The log house was built entirely atop a granite escarpment that trailed down to the lake, which she could not yet see, her view blocked by the enormity of the two-story building. He walked her around to the deck at the back and she could see Lake Kabetogama and islands in the distance, and a boat or two running for home atop the choppy waves of the water as the sun disappeared below the horizon. Along the southern shore to the east of the cabin, she saw the flickering lights of the resort cabins coming on against the lowering of the night.

"Let's get you settled and show you your room," he suggested, waiting patiently while she took in the wonderful view. In the distance a loon cried, seeking its mate. The unusual song and the cool air off the lake gave her the chills.

"What a beautiful and mournful sound, she said, leaning into the warmth and comfort of his side. "It sounds almost like a wolf."

"He's welcoming you to his lake," Will explained. "Actually, males make that call when mating or calling to a mate when separated. He wants to join up before it becomes completely dark."

"What a romantic and sensible creature," she said, and let him lead her inside. He brought her bags in from the foyer and then took her in his arms. "Just between the two of us, I made the same call every night for two years, and now here you are."

It was a silly romantic thing to say, but she loved it nevertheless. She looked up into the gray of his eyes and kissed him properly now in the privacy and protection of his inner sanctum. The intensity and passion in the kiss surprised him. When they broke the kiss, both stepped back a pace, breathless, and recovered enough to laugh at each other.

"You are a loon," she said, "and a romantic nut," her smile as intense and passionate as the kiss. "But the most important thing is that I'm here with you now."

"Yes," he agreed. "The most important thing is that we're together again."

Chapter Seven

Canoe Ride

She could hardly bring herself to leave him even for the overpowering physical necessity of sleep. But the travel across time zones, the long car trip north, and the excitement of the tornado passing by so closely, had all conspired to pour lead into her bones and her eyelids. Not even the cold water on her face as she washed for bed enlivened her. She stretched into the luxury of the fresh flannel sheets and pulled the comforter up to her chin. The last thing she remembered was the taste of his lips.

The smell of bacon awakened her. She was ravenous. She pulled down the covers and her feet found the thick shag of the area rug covering the polished oak floorboards. Her unpacked suitcase sat at the end of the bed on a varnished cedar trunk topped with a velvet seat. She found some of her clothes neatly hung in the closet, the rest carefully folded in the massive chest of drawers that stood five feet high. She stepped into a pair of blue bikini briefs and pulled on an oversized T-shirt that stretched to mid-thigh if she tugged with both hands. She grabbed her makeup kit and padded into the en-suite bathroom beyond the walk-in closet. A quick look in the mirror confirmed that she had some sleep damage to repair. The shower rejuvenated her and she lingered in the relaxing spray until she felt guilty about using too much hot water. Properly restored—a moisturizer and a touch of the lipstick was enough to do the trick—she combed her hair into place, still moist after toweling. She decided against perfume after thinking about it seriously; it would clash with the wonderful smell of bacon drifting in from the kitchen. She stepped into her walking shorts, tucked in the T-shirt, slipped on her sandals, no socks this time, and like a good detective followed her nose to the kitchen.

He was barefoot in front of the stove holding a spatula and singing *Nessun Dorma*, one of her favorite arias. Her giggle turned him from the iron skillet and she knew he was singing "no one sleeps" just for her. He greeted her with the smile that never failed to send a tremble of anticipation deep into the space behind her stomach.

"I see the *Principessa* has awakened from her beauty sleep," he said in greeting. She regally presented her cheek, which he kissed.

"Uhmm," she said appreciatively, "You smell good."

"I think that's just your tummy talking," he said. "You're just in time for breakfast."

At the curve of the great dining table she settled into a comfortably padded oaken chair with a high curving back, and crossed her legs, all the while extending her arms, hands clasped, high above her head. Her back arched into a perfect, feline morning stretch. "What?" she asked, catching him in a full, unabashed stare.

"Oh nothing; just remembering."

"Remembering what?" she teased, but he ignored her, making busy with breakfast preparations.

"How many eggs and how would you like them? Be advised you'll also have blueberry pancakes with maple syrup on the side."

She wanted three of each, but she asked for two cooked in the American style, turned over once, and two hotcakes. The toaster popped the bread and he buttered it while still hot. He plated the eggs with panache, sliding them directly from the skillet to the plate, added rashers of bacon, cut the toast on the diagonal and presented the meal to her. As she unfolded the linen napkin in her lap, he returned with another plate warming in the oven, piled high with the pancakes, blueberries showing through the sides. He poured freshly squeezed orange juice and set it next to a larger glass of milk cold from the refrigerator.

She waited until he sat and told him, "This is simply wonderful. I can't remember the last time I had such a sumptuous breakfast."

"For your information *Kommissar Schumann*, it's now two o'clock in the afternoon."

She covered her surprise behind her hand. "I had no idea that it was so late," she stammered. Her mother would have killed her for getting up so late in the day.

"Eat," he said. "You needed the sleep and I had shopping to do. Remember—I expected Roland, not you."

"Disappointed?" she asked, looking at the plate of bacon in the middle of the table. He pushed it across to her and she smiled her thanks.

"Roland is a helluva guy and we do go back a long way," he said, hedging his answer.

This time she ignored him, enjoying the luxury of the bacon, thick and chewy, smelling of hickory smoke. She was lost in the glorious taste of fresh blueberries buried in the buttermilk pancakes, smothered in the mélange of melting butter and rich, warm maple syrup. He shut up and let her eat. To her dismay, she finally had to stop. She could not manage another bite; yet there were still rashers of bacon uneaten and two more pancakes still warm on the plate brought directly from the oven. Before she could resolve the struggle between need and want, he cleared the table of the dishes and that was that.

They sat together for the longest time, catching up on friends in common and work, getting comfortable with each other again. They talked away an hour, then another half, then he asked her if she wanted to take a run. She decided she needed the exercise, remembering ruefully what and how much she had eaten. They got ready together, helping each other stretch on the rug in the living room with the enormous windows looking out onto the lake. After a quick trip to her bathroom, she was ready for the run.

He drove to a nearby trailhead where they studied the metal sign laying out the track and the distances. They agreed that four miles should be enough. She let him lead because he knew the trail. He took her through the pine and birch forest at a slow jog at first, giving her muscles time to warm up, then he increased the pace until he could hear her breathing behind him. He kept the run leisurely, allowing her to enjoy the beauty of the run on the trail through the woods, thick and heavy with green on either side.

This was a young and unruly forest untouched by a power saw or an axe blade, making it quite unlike the sedate, heavily managed forests of Bavaria. To show off a little bit, she passed him and took the lead, giving him an altogether different perspective. Well into the second mile she heard him slow, and when she looked back, found that he had stopped. She wondered if it was to give them a rest. Sweat dripped along the curve of her chin. She noticed he too was sweating heavily from the exertion and his shirt was almost soaked through. The heat had come up again after yesterday's thunderstorm but the humidity was not nearly as oppressive as the day before, although she could still feel its effects.

He walked ten meters or so off the trail and motioned her over. He bent down and picked among clusters of red and green berries, pushing the leaves aside. He took her hand and turned it up and small thimble-shaped red berries spilled from the cup of his hand to her palm. He took one and she automatically opened her mouth and he placed it on her tongue. The taste was a perfect mix of sweet and tart.

"Wild raspberries," he said, and she wanted more after she finished the delicious treat in her hand. He let her have the pleasure of picking them from the scattered bushes along the trail. Then she noticed something unusual. He was watching the trail intently.

"What are you looking for?" she asked, her lips and tongue red from the juice of the berries.

"Black bears," he said as if it were the most natural thing in the world.

"You can't be serious."

"Bears love raspberries almost as much as you. They were here earlier today. I've seen the signs."

She did not believe him. She knew when she was being teased for excitement. Then he pulled her to his side, shielding her slightly behind him. Twenty meters ahead and just off the trail in another patch of berries, a black furry head with ears standing at attention, popped up and looked at them with curiosity. Instinctively she clung to Will.

"Hold still," he whispered, "and watch." They were standing downwind of the bear and for that reason he had been taken by surprise. He rose to his hind legs for a better look and a better sniff of the air, moving his head from side to side, trying to pick up their scent. His front paws were held slack in front of his body like an airline attendant moving down the aisle of the aircraft. Satisfied with what he saw and smelled, he dropped down again with a grunt and cautiously ambled toward them.

"What do we do now?" she whispered, genuinely frightened. "I'm not carrying my gun."

"Don't worry," he assured her, "he's not breaking any laws. He thinks the berries are sweeter where we are and he wants a taste, but I'm not interested in sharing at the moment." With the bear less than ten meters away, Will suddenly yelled "Hey!!" and violently clapped his hands together. The concussion sounded like a rifle shot cannonading through the trees and startled the bear to such a degree that he tumbled over backwards in his haste to stop, reverse direction, and get the hell out of there. Without missing a beat, he rolled over onto all fours and after showing them his hairy black behind, made a mad dash for a large white pine. In less than three seconds he had shinnied up the bole of the tree. Sylvie held her hand in front of her mouth, covering little gasps of surprise. She did not know if she should speak, or whisper, or what.

"Come on," Will said, taking her by the hand and pulling. "Follow me."

They walked out of the bushes and back onto the trail as they watched the bear in the tree. To Sylvie's horror, Will stopped under the tree branches where the bear hung on like some enormous and improbable Christmas ornament, and started talking to the animal. Sylvie was petrified. She had never been so close to such a creature in the wild. The only bears she had seen were pathetic creatures behind the bars of the Munich zoo. Now Will stood, making soothing sounds to the poor creature, as if they were long lost friends who had just found each other again after all the years. Suddenly the bear lost his precarious purchase and slid down the trunk three meters or so before he managed to arrest the slide. He scrabbled back up to his original position and looked down over his shoulder with some consternation evident in the warm, luminous ursine eyes. The sound his long, curved claws had made on the thick rough bark of the pine was unlike anything she had ever heard.

Will laughed at the young bear's plight as he looked down over his other shoulder. He seemed forlorn, and then to her utter amazement, he whimpered. "Seen enough?" Will asked. She thought he was talking to his friend in the tree before she recovered and nodded, yes. "He's scared to death," Will explained. "He's a two-year old and probably just separated from his mother this season. It's still a bewildering world out there for a lonely young bear without his momma. Let's leave him the berries. I think we scared him enough so that he will think twice before he tries to get friendly again with the strange creatures that walk on two legs all the time." He walked her another two hundred meters up the trail and stopped, letting her have a look back. Once the coast was clear, the young black bear got his courage up enough to slide down the trunk of the pine and waddle off into the protection of the forest.

"Care to lead?" he asked.

"Oh no," she said without hesitation. "You go right ahead."

RUNNING THE TRAIL became part of their daily routine; the breakfast did not. Will wrote late into the evenings and usually stumbled out of his bedroom between ten and ten-thirty in the morning. Sylvie preferred to rise at eight and make herself a cup of tea. She read away the waiting hours on the deck when the day was pleasant and the lake behaved itself. Book in one hand, teacup in the other, she relaxed on the heavily padded chaise longue in the shade thrown by the immense log home. At other times, somewhat embarrassed by the sheer whiteness of her legs, she pulled her chair out into morning sun before it became too intense for her skin. She enjoying the peace and solitude and admitted to herself how much she needed the same.

When she heard him fumbling about in the kitchen, she marked her place in the novel or one of the many reference books on nature Will kept in his extensive library. He had moved all his professional books from his university office to the cabin and she found the breadth and depth of the works stunning. There were titles on semiotics, hermeneutics, phenomenology, pragmatics, forensic pathology and psychiatry, forensic anthropology, and hundreds of other titles related to his professional work. One shelf was reserved for the chapters, articles, monographs, and books he had authored during his tenure as a professor at the university and his later work as a special investigator and consultant to various agencies, including the FBI, Interpol, and her own state criminal police force in Bavaria, Germany. It was a daunting collection, but she was more impressed by the collection of classic works lining the opposite wall of the study. There he kept the major works of world literature arranged not by author but by nationality. She was reading Milan Kundera presently and had just finished a work by Gabriel Fielding, an English author previously unknown to her, but evidently a personal friend of Will's. The book had been hand-signed with a personal note from the author. There were also representative works from the great American, Spanish, French, Russian, and Italian authors. He even kept works by Chinese and Japanese writers. There was poetry too, not merely fiction.

Like his uncle Roland, also a voracious reader, he had a fine collection of international erotica, and after the Kundera, she was looking forward to reading Anais Nin. She had teased him about his "porn collection" and he justified the works two ways: some were indeed literature by any aesthetic measure; some of the works gave insight into the further darker reaches of human sexuality. Besides, he told her, she had not seen his porn collection yet. She remembered that when she was a student at university in Munich, a professor made the class read de Sade and she had been both fascinated and disgusted by the depravity of which he wrote. She could not bring herself to believe that human beings were capable of such bizarre sexual practices and dismissed the work as the product of a deranged mind. Her disbelief had gradually suffered the corrective of her direct experience as a criminal investigator working rape and other sex crimes. She had come to realize that when it came to the full range of perverse human sexual experience, fictionalized, invented or real, in many instances de Sade had gotten it just right. Now she understood exactly what Will meant.

He came out through the sliding glass door, barefoot and bare chested in khaki shorts, an enormous glass of iced tea in one hand. He stood at the railing of the redwood deck, treated to be weather resistant, and looked into the sun reflecting off the lake at an angle that turned the water to burnished, hammered copper. Sylvie watched him silently as he stretched, taking pleasure in observing him during an unguarded and unprotected moment, her right hand shielding her eyes from the sun in the east. Her smile must have alerted him.

"There you are," he said, finding her off to the side, taking equal pleasure in finding her, and in their first kisses of the day. He noticed the book she was reading, Kundera's *Unbearable Lightness of Being*, and gave her his lost little boy look. "I'm sorry that I don't adequately satisfy all your sexual needs and force you to read such sexy books as a supplement. And you don't need to salute me."

She quickly dropped her hand from her forehead now that his body was keeping the sun from her eyes. She had to laugh at his little inanity. "Maybe I'm reading it to get new ideas," she teased him, for making her feel silly about shielding the sun from her eyes. He raised his eyebrows with theatrical exaggeration and came down toward her but she thwarted him with her foot against his well-muscled chest. "Not so fast, big boy. I want a canoe ride."

"Hmmm," he said, considering the request as he stroked his unshaven chin. "Using sex as a weapon now?"

"Not a weapon," she corrected, "an inducement."

He nodded his head in agreement. "I like the sound of that: an inducement. Fortunately I am immune to any and all forms of sexual inducement, seduction, coercion, or hypnosis—whatever the case may be, and whatever you want to call it. A thousand coeds have tried and a thousand failed."

She disagreed vehemently. "Perhaps in the case of your American..." she searched for the word, "floozies, I think you call them, you might very well be immune. However, I know you to be entirely susceptible to my Germanic charms." She dropped her foot and he fell to her, catching himself at the last instant before his weight crushed her, his lips just above hers, and looked deeply into the infinite Bavarian blue cabochon of her eyes.

"A canoe ride and a picnic," he promised her. "But just remember that a canoe signifies the phallus," and he kissed the protest from her lips.

She pulled him fully atop her length like a blanket, placed both arms around his neck and allowed him to nuzzle her neck just below the ear. His gentle bites and kisses made her tingle the entire length of her body and she did not resist when he reached for the silver button of her shorts. She did not care if the boaters fishing for walleye in the distance could see them or not. Let them look.

SHE HAD NOT been in a canoe before, not even as a child growing up around Lake Forggen near Füssen. And she looked forward to the prospect. She considered a canoe an essential element in the romantic adventures she had dreamed of as a young girl, and she told him so. An hour of paddling into a stiff wind coming out of the north and west would disabuse her of any romantic notions, he thought but he kept his silence, unwilling to diminish her enthusiasm with anything so base or intrusive as reality.

It was a long steep walk down the timbered stairs of the granitic scarp that sloped into and under the lake. He had built a dock on pontoons from segments, like an army engineer's bridge, which allowed him to disassemble it and load the sections into the big Lund fishing boat tied up on the other side to keep it safe when the lake iced over. During the long hard Minnesota winters, Will harbored the boat and the canoe in the garage on the lake shore, winched up and out of the water for safekeeping and maintenance.

He made her wait before getting into the aluminum canoe. He lifted in the picnic basket and blanket and threw a seat cushion forward. "Can you swim?" he asked. She nodded. "You don't have to wear your life vest then, but keep it near you." She nodded again. He took a paddle, left hand above the blade, right hand atop the pommeled handle. "Dip into the water ahead of you, pull toward you and as the blade of the paddle passes, push back and sweep out and away from the canoe. That's called a J-stroke. You can do it on either side as you get tired of one or the other. I steer the canoe from the back, so don't worry about the direction."

She feigned a pout. "I want to steer the canoe."

He shook his head. "Not until you're older and have mastered the basics. Besides, you have the better view up front. Step into the center of the canoe, keeping your center of gravity low and forward." He handed her in carefully as the canoe began to rock. "That's it; use the side to hold on and now move forward but stay low." She gingerly stepped over the middle bench, rocking the canoe even more and quickly sat, turned, and looked back for reassurance. "Not bad," he told her. "You're still dry. Now hold steady while I board." He untied the forward and rear lines and stepped in, pushing the canoe away from the mooring with his trailing leg.

His powerful strokes sent them out into the big water toward Ram Island and past Camp Wooden Frog. After a few clumsy attempts she got the hang of the J-stroke and was quite proud of her contribution to the canoe's forward momentum, at least until she soaked her lap with her first attempt at a crossover stroke. She learned quickly to let the paddle drop its water before changing sides. She was working hard now, enjoying the rhythm of the stroke through the water, feeling the exertion of the pull against her arms, shoulder, back, and even her stomach muscles. After ten or fifteen minutes she decided this was hard work and she rested, paddle across the gunnels of the canoe and turned around to talk to Will. He was stretched out full-length, feet crossed at the ankles, his Aussie-style outback hat pulled down low across his forehead, eyes closed under the shade thrown by the brim of the cloth hat. "Hey!" she yelled at him as if he were a lazy, recalcitrant bear. "No fair making me do all the work." Using the paddle's blade, she sprayed him with a whack of water.

"All right, all right," he said. "I was just letting you refine your stroke."

She cinched up the string under the broad brim of her straw sun hat and got back to work now that she had taken care of the dead weight of the slacker in the rear. "Just like a man," she said loud enough for his ears, shaking her head.

"How so?" he asked, changing the direction of the canoe by angling his paddle like a rudder.

"Slowing me down and trying to hold me back," she said defiantly.

"Amen, sister, amen."

Chapter Eight

Dream Work

For half an hour they paddled without talking, and in that time synchronized their strokes, their combined and syncopated energies propelling the canoe at a respectable pace through the brilliant blue-green water. He guided them through a white and black flotilla of sea gulls and cormorants. All lifted ahead of the approaching canoe, squawking their displeasure at the disruption. The simultaneous beat of wings and the slap of webbed feet pedaling atop the water thrilled Sylvie. She was sweating now but did not mind at all. She had removed her shirt and slipped off her shorts, stripped down to her red bikini. He admired the definition and flow of the muscles in her back as she worked the paddle. They glided among the islands in the lake and he pointed out a beaver hut within the cut of a small bay. "Look left!" he shouted. "There he is!"

At first glance she did not recognize the glistening object swimming so smoothly and steadily away from them. It was the size of the animal that confounded her. Will quickly angled the canoe to follow the wake of the swimmer and she hurriedly unzipped her day bag to find her *Handi*. The beaver looked almost as big as a black Great Dane paddling through the placid water of the protected bay, its efforts sending ripples across the calm water to lap against the shore and the oncoming canoe.

Suddenly the beaver smacked the water with the broad plank of its tail, rose up and dived quickly—black wet fur shining in the sun—and disappeared under the protection of the water. At the spectacle she laughed out loud in delight, the mechanism of the camera in her phone clicking, ready for the next shot.

Will explained that it was relatively rare to see such a big boy during the light of day. Although not originally nocturnal, the unrelenting pressure of hunting and trapping had forced beavers under cover of the night for protection. This was a good sign, he acknowledged, highly significant, in fact. It meant that the animal felt safe from predators. The wolves could not get at him on the islands during the summer, and hunting and trapping were prohibited in the national park. She looked back at him as she zipped the phone back into its watertight case, concern on her face. He had sparked a primal ethnic fear.

"Wolves?" she asked.

He nodded seriously as he turned the canoe back out into the open water. "I'll tell you a true story about a wolf attack." She turned around to face him so she could hear better, eyes wide with excitement and expectation. "A couple of years ago, before I met you in Germany, a friend and I were hiking up around Locator Lake. On the trail ahead of us we spotted an enormous timber wolf, probably the alpha male of the pack, and I tell you Sylvie, for whatever reason, he looked angry and he looked hungry."

"Ohmigod," she interjected. She had no choice but to believe him, now especially after the run-in with the young bear on the trail. She could hardly imagine such a thing: an encounter with a wolf in the wild. She heard the faint and distant echo of the archetypal wolf whose howl still resonated through her country's fables, legends, and myths when wolves roamed the forests and ruled the night. "What in the world did you do?"

"There was only one thing we could do: we ran for our lives."

She shook her head in disbelief. "How could anyone expect to survive an attack by such a creature?"

"We took off the instant we saw him and when we finally risked a look back—sure enough—he was rapidly gaining on us, although we were still about eight hundred meters ahead of him. We were both carrying packs and so I stopped, tore off my hiking boots and pulled on my running shoes. 'That's not going to help,' my buddy Mike said. 'No human can possibly outrun a wolf.' That's right, I said. But I don't have to outrun him—I only have to outrun you."

He waited for her laughter to subside and she wiped a tear from her cheek, mouth open, shaking her head.

"Just a little joke," he assured her, "although I have had encounters with wolves in the wild."

She looked at him through narrowed skeptical eyes, her distrust fostered by his previous story. "No worries," he said. "To my knowledge there has never been a recorded instance of a wolf attacking a human being in the entire history of the Boundary Waters." He watched her let go a little sigh of relief. "Now bears—that's another matter altogether." Before she could swat him with the long paddle he pointed and said, "We're here, bosun. Prepare to ship oars and land the boat."

They had rounded into another protected bay about four hundred meters in width and she could see the sandy shore fast approaching. They paddled vigorously for two strokes in unison and he yelled "paddles up" just before the canoe grounded its nose in the sand. "All ashore," he commanded. She leaped nimbly over the curve of the stern onto the beach without getting her sandals wet and held the canoe steady for him as he moved forward. Together they beached the craft and unloaded. They placed the food on the picnic table of the campsite maintained by the rangers of the Forest Service. She looked around and saw a fire pit and a metallic square box near the table. A trail led back into the woods of the island.

"What's that?" she asked, pointing to the strange green box.

"That's called a bear locker."

She looked incredulous.

"No silly, it's not where we keep bears locked up. It's used to store food overnight so the bears can't get at it if you camp on the island."

She did not like the sound of that explanation either. But she had something else in mind. "Oh, Will. Can we please make a fire?"

He considered the request. The big white pines and tall spreading cedars cast the plateau of the campground in cool shadow, so why not? "Okay," he told her, "but you have to collect the firewood while I unpack the food basket. And I want to put the wine in the water to cool."

Off she went, singing happily and loudly, just in case. She returned shortly, arms loaded with deadfall. He had already prepared the fire pit. In the center he had laid a neatly constructed nest of tinder: dried pine needles and birch bark shaved into curls. Atop this he had constructed a lean-to of similar-sized twigs. Using selections from the wood Sylvie had brought, he built a foursquare structure of small sticks. He pulled a match from his survival pack, showed it to her, and grinned. She looked down at the example of his woodsmanship in the fire pit and said, "If you can get that mess started with that little wood match, I promise you an outdoor dessert you won't soon forget."

Without further ado he struck the match. It fired into flame behind the protective bay of his palm. He placed it at the bottom of his tinder pile and let the sere material catch the flame. The needles glowed and burned orange and went out, white ash edging the burned black as the little fire danced from needle to shaving trying to catch enough wind to burn. She was certain that he had failed and suddenly felt sad, disappointed for them both, but he blew gently into the center and a gout of flame erupted, consuming the small sticks piled above it.

Strengthened by each puff of breath, the flame pulled the sticks above down into itself. Now the fire licked at the belly of the larger sticks making up the roof of the square and he rocked back on his heels, waving the smoke away from his face with his hat. Another minute and the sticks the size of his fingers ignited and sparked into flame. He leaned in again and made a few adjustments with a poke here and there to reposition burning brands that had fallen away from the center. Standing at his shoulder watching, she could now feel the heat of the fire as it rose higher and consumed the larger branches he was steadily feeding it. There was something primal about the man concentrating with such focus on the fire, and as she smelled the wood smoke, she could hear the fire roar and snap at the wind as it gained strength. She undid the tie of her bikini top, handed it to him for his consideration, and then stepped out of her bottoms.

"Going for a swim?" he teased.

"Afterwards," she said, pulling him atop the blanket spread on the picnic table, no longer willing or able to wait for dessert. Not a single boat passed by to disturb them; not a single bear, nor a wolf, at least none that she noticed in her preoccupation with paying off her debt.

Stretched out across the length of the table top, a lifejacket under his behind and a seat cushion supporting his head, the sound of the wind slipping through the pine branches awakened him from his short nap in the shade. He rolled over on his left side and propped his head onto the support of his hand, arm angled at the elbow: he was just in time to watch her rise from the water, finished with her swim. She pulled the moisture from her hair with both hands, her eyes closed, and he watched the water run over the shoulders of her sleek white body. It occurred to him that he had seen a similar scene once before. Then he had it: Botticelli's *The Birth of Venus*. The similarities were astounding. There was the water bordered by the trees, Sylvie emerging from the lake, Venus from the sea. In the painting, a breath of wind from the mouths of angels floated the giant white half shell on which Venus stood toward the shore. The gentle breeze that had awakened Will now caused Sylvie to shiver, pushing at her back, forcing her out of the water. Sylvie's hair was much shorter than the golden tresses of Botticelli's model, but Sylvie Schumann was equally graceful, equally tender and delicate, but even more beautiful in the nearly perfect esthetic of her symmetrical form. She slipped into her sandals to protect her feet from the stones on the rocky shore beyond the sand. He threw her a towel as she approached, she happy to see him awake and waiting for her. She stopped and rubbed herself dry with the oversized and gaudily colored beach towel, her eyes locked with his, neither blinking. She placed the towel down on the bench and sat, naked but dry, taking the breeze on her shoulders. She kissed his stomach and shocked him on purpose as she pressed her still moist and cold hair against the warmth of his belly. She watched the towel draped across his lap for modesty seem to rise of its own accord, tenting in the center.

"Leave me alone, Sylvie," he begged in mock desperation as she slowly and steadily pulled the towel away, inch by excruciating inch, until finally he was exposed in all his glory like a pine to the sky.

"I'm not talking to you," she said, "I'm talking to my best friend and he's listening like a good friend should." She pushed him back down as he tried to sit up and make his escape. "Don't worry—I'll do all the work," she promised, and before he could protest further, he felt the cold press of her lips followed by the exquisitely warm heat of the inside of her mouth. He flopped his head back down on the cushion and let her have her way. What else could he do? Botticelli no doubt had to deal with similar problems.

Afterwards she left her head lying in the flat pillow of his stomach, facing him, riding the gentle swell and fall of his abdomen, waiting for his breathing to return to normal.

"Sylvie," he said, with high drama, "I am impressed," and he stroked her hair, now almost completely wind-dry.

"Can I tell you a secret?" she asked.

"You can tell me anything you want."

"I've had more sex with you in four days than I've had with Manfred in the last four months."

He assumed Manfred was her boyfriend back in Kaufbeuren where she lived and worked. He could tell that she had more to say—she had paused merely to judge the effect of her statement. To his consternation, and despite the fact that he already knew as much, the realization that she in fact did have a boyfriend back home caused him a twinge in his stomach, an unexpected soft ache of jealously that he quickly controlled. She grinned as he pulled a face.

"Freddi is a good man," she explained. "He really is, and he cares for me deeply, make no mistake about that."

He shook his head. There would be no mistaking Freddi's feelings for her.

"In his own way, I think he loves me very much. And I do enjoy sex with him; it's just that we're both so busy from time to time with work." She waited for him to nod his understanding and to show that he accepted what she was telling him.

"Tell me more about Freddi," he said.

She sighed in relief. She had been afraid of how he might react to the confession of her relationship with another man. She could tell he was not the least bit concerned she was with someone else. She felt she could tell him anything now. "We've been together about a year."

"Is he a cop?"

"My dear god, no!" she said emphatically. "I could never see myself in a relationship with a cop. I know what the Job does to couples: never with a cop. He's a lawyer." She said it with such sincerity that he laughed.

"What's the matter?" she asked, a little put off by his laugh at something so serious and so important.

"I guess a lawyer is somehow better than a cop, in terms of relationships, I mean."

"He's a corporate lawyer," she huffed, defending her Freddi. "Anyway, I just don't know what it is, Will, but it's completely different when I'm with you. I seem to lose all control of my rational self and that scares me. I'm just not used to that happening. I feel voracious when I'm with you—something comes over me and I feel possessed and I give in." She shook her head. "Don't get me wrong: I'm not complaining. I'm just trying to make sense of what has been happening to me. It's as if the real and the true me has been unleashed and set free and finally I can be the woman I have kept locked up and protected for so long." With his index finger he gently collected a tear from the swell of her cheek. Both eyes were brimming now. "Why can't I feel that way with Manfred? I know he loves me, you smug bastard. I hate you for what you've done to me. I can't figure it out. What's missing between Freddi and me? Why can't I bring myself to love him as he loves me?

He sat up now and pushed the sun-streaked hair behind the comb of her ears. "Do you want the truth?" he asked. She nodded, ready for it.

"Passion."

She looked into his blue-gray eyes, searching for the truth and knew he was correct.

"Promise me one thing, Sylvie.

"Anything."

"Don't ever be afraid of your passion for me."

She promised. "God, I'm hungry," she said out of the blue.

"Well duh," he mocked, "So let's eat. I'll get the wine."

After lunch they sat atop the green metal table at the campsite, shoulder to shoulder, taking in the splendid vista afforded them through the frame of the lodgepole pines and birches on either side of the campground. They could see the Grass Islands in the distance. "Good fishing for smaller northern there," Will assured her, using the German word *Hecht* for the fish, as he pointed out the lazy swoop of a white egret in the sky, hopping from island to island. They could hear the motor of a distant boat moving to a better fishing location.

Sylvie, turned to Will and asked, "Want to hear a dream I had before I left Germany? Maybe you can help me interpret it."

"Sure," he said, always glad to do a little semiotic interpretation of dream symbols. It had been part of his training in semiotic theory. He heard her take a deep breath before she began.

"Now don't laugh, but in my dream I saw a beautiful woman alone in a canoe. I remember she was wearing a deerskin dress, you know, with tasseled fringes and moccasins. She had a beaded band around her head. She was paddling the canoe by herself, but she seemed certain she had to leave, but she was also afraid because she didn't know where she was going. I do know that she was paddling farther and farther away from the shore and there were men standing there watching her leave. I think they might have been Native Americans, but I'm not sure. One of them seemed to be white and didn't want her to go. One of the Natives, and I'm certain of this, seemed very old, as if he might have been her grandfather, but I'm not certain about that. I think he and the others on the shore wanted to follow her but didn't have a canoe. The last thing I remember is that she looked back at them and they motioned to her. Then I woke up. That's it. What do you think? I can't figure it out."

Will thought for a couple of minutes before he began his analysis. "What a beautiful dream. Freud showed us that there are two parts to a dream. The first is the manifest content, in other words, what you just described to me. The latent content is the symbolic meaning contained in the manifest content. There are three or four significant symbols in your dream: the woman in the canoe, movement across the water, the water, and the men on the shore. For example, the water suggests change and a canoe trip most likely is a wish to change your current situation in life."

She nodded. That seemed to make sense, given what she was facing back home.

"Jung would say that the person in the canoe is an archetypal symbol, a Native American princess perhaps."

"Why would I dream of a princess?"

He laughed. "The question should be why did you dream of yourself as a Native American princess."

She shook her head. "How can that be me?"

"Think about it," he said. "Most likely you had been mulling over the possibility of seeing me here in Minnesota for quite some time and if I know you, you probably read up on our state and its Native American cultures. And don't all little girls at one time or another fancy themselves as a princess?"

She leaned away to make room for a punch to his shoulder. "I did not," she lied, grinning.

"Yes, you did. And it seems you have been thinking quite a bit about your relationship with Manfred back home. Thinking of leaving him?" he asked.

She covered her open mouth with her hand. She knew there was no need to affirm his analysis. "All right, smart guy, what about the two other men on the shore that I wanted to follow me?"

He thought it through. "Don't know," he finally admitted, pursing his lips. "Freud says dreams are either about wish fulfillment or anxiety. Your dream seems to contain elements of both. However, some cultures see dreams as portents of the future. All I know is that you are here sitting next to me and that makes me very happy."

She grabbed his arm and snuggled in. Perhaps she had made the right decision.

The paddle home was more leisurely, the wind at their backs helping instead of hindering. She docked the canoe rather expertly now, and he told her so, and she took pride in the accomplishment. They unloaded and carried their gear up the long incline of steps to the deck of the cabin. Suddenly she stopped short, dropped the life vests and seat cushions, and froze next to him as if she had just run into another bear.

"There's someone inside," she whispered.

"It's okay, Sylvie," he assured her. "Friends often come by for a visit and help themselves to whatever is in the fridge. Let's go see who it is." He pushed the sliding glass door open and the person in the big chair held up his shot glass in greeting and said, "Hope you don't mind, but I took the liberty of helping myself to the Crown Royal."

"Roland!" Will hollered in joyful surprise as he went to greet his uncle, first shaking his hand man to man, then hugging him. Sylvie came next and kissed him on both cheeks, evidently not altogether surprised by his sudden appearance.

"You look like you could use a drink," he said to his nephew, as he unscrewed the cap to the whiskey. "And Sylvie—well, Sylvie is positively glowing. Must be something about this North Woods climate and wilderness that agrees with her." He nodded to himself for being correct as she blushed into her eyes, down the length of her graceful throat and across the top of her chest. "I can see now that I did the right thing by sending you here ahead of me, even without Will's permission."

Chapter Nine

The Job

They spent their first night together catching up on the lives of relatives and friends in common, telling new stories as they changed from wine to whisky before tiring of both. They laughed and joked as only relatives who are also close friends can and after a third bottle of an excellent German Riesling from the Mosel river was added to the line of empties, they sang a little concert to each other. Sylvie was impressed with the power of both men's voices, despite their infidelity to the songs they sang: Roland's light baritone supporting Will's dark tenor. But what the hell did they care about hitting the right notes? They were together again, recementing the familial bond that kept them united across the distance of time and space. The more familiar Sylvie had become with each man, the more convinced she was that the two had evolved a shared philosophy and outlook on life, a curious symmetry given their disparate generations and circumstances. It showed in the way they talked about life and people and in the way they tried to make sense out of the chaos they caused.

Roland had progressed from service in what was then West Germany's elite federal border police to the *Schutzpolizei*, the everyday police force charged with patrolling the streets and highways, to the *Kripo*, or *Kriminalpolizei*, the criminal police responsible for such crimes as murder, kidnapping, rape, and other high crimes. Roland had come up the old way and the hard way through the ranks of the *Schupo*, making his reputation on the autobahns in and around Munich, until he was tapped for the advanced training required for criminal investigation. Sylvie, by contrast, had come into the ranks of the criminal police directly from university, part of the new social plan to introduce more women into the force. She had persevered, excelling despite the resentment and hard-liner attitudes of the old guard. They considered policing a paramilitary endeavor right down to the polished jack boots, one unsuited for females with the exception of clerical work, of course, parking enforcement, or police outreach in the local schools. It was a testament to her intelligence and personality that she had survived. She was the first to admit that she could not have done it without Roland's careful tutelage and abiding friendship.

Their pairing was an unexpected and unwanted match. Still in her first year of duty as a criminal investigator, she was suddenly assigned without request or warning to then *Hauptkommissar Roland Rieger*, whom she knew only by departmental reputation and gossip. Her commander informed her in no uncertain terms that her assignment to Rieger was intended as a punishment for him. Known as the iconoclast of Group I-Violent Crimes Division, his methods were unorthodox, and to the chagrin of his commander, highly effective. Rieger consistently had the highest rate of success among his cohorts, solving cases other investigators in the Bavarian State Criminal Police avoided or gave up. Rieger worked in KK11 and 12 within Group I handling the toughest cases, almost all having to do with murder or sex crimes and often both. In fact, her first case with Roland had been the Adamas File, detailed in Will's memoir *The Adamantine Heart*, wherein he recounted a series of murders and sexual mutilations that had required the services of Will's semiotic analysis to solve the case.

Roland, familiar with his nephew's contributions as a consultant to the FBI's Special Investigative Unit, had convinced the Director of the Criminal Police to hire Will as a consultant on the case. That is when Sylvie first met Professor Sheridan. Together, using his semiotic methods, the three had solved a case deemed unsolvable by the so-called experts working with them and exposed a highly sophisticated scheme for smuggling stolen diamonds from Sierra Leone, Africa to East Berlin. Now the three were together again.

Sylvie was the first to succumb, readily admitting that she was no longer in top drinking shape. She kissed both men good night and headed for the comfort of her bed as the dawn tried to climb through the golden oak window slats and into bed with her. The men were sad to see her go. Sylvie was one of the few women, Roland admitted, with whom he genuinely enjoyed sharing a glass. Will knew this was high praise from his uncle, whose daily routine back home included taking a glass or two at the *Stammtisch* of the local *Gasthaus*. The *Stammtisch*, literally the tribe table, was reserved for a select few regulars who came and sat and solved local and world problems as they depleted the reserves of the fine local beer and the neighboring region's wine.

Will laughed when he remembered how the owner of the same *Gasthaus*, St. Peter's, had tried to gently lead him from the table to other accommodations, despite Will's insistence that the particular table at which he sat would do just fine, thank you. The poor man was distraught to the point of tying his bar towel into knots, unable to convince the handsome young giant that he needed to move. He almost fainted with relief when Roland came in and introduced the owner to his immovable nephew, the *Professor Doktor* from America. He revealed to the owner that as a practical joke he had put Will up to camping at the *Stammtisch* just to gauge the man's reaction. The owner was so pleased and proud to be victim of Roland's practical joke that he immediately called for a bottle of iced Stoli, an original Stolichnaya vodka predating the collapse of the Soviet Union with "Made in the USSR" still on the label. That had been a good night, they both agreed, toasting the memory.

"Getting along with Sylvie?" Roland asked, "Not that it's any of my business," he allowed.

"At first she was a bit mad at me for not writing, but once she got that out of her system she has warmed up to me again rather nicely, if you know what I mean."

Roland nodded sagely. He knew his partner. She was not the type of woman who suffered a slight gladly. She protected herself and one of the ways she protected herself was by remaining cool and aloof in her interactions with others, not impolitely or rudely, he explained. She was simply unwilling to give of herself to others until she trusted them implicitly. Roland stood and went to the liquor bar for the Crown Royal bottle. It was time for serious drinking. He returned with two shot glasses full to the brim with the amber liquid. Will noticed his uncle's hands were absolutely steady and he did not spill a drop on the trip back to the lounger where he reclined, pillows propping up his head, feet in black socks crossed at the ankle.

"Go ahead and help yourself to my booze," he told his uncle, who rightly ignored him. Roland knew full well his house privileges as uncle. They touched glasses, smelled the sweetness of the whisky appreciatively, and drank down the shot. This time Will hopped up from the massive leather couch, set in a horseshoe before the fireplace, now cool and dark, and returned with the bottle. They savored the second drink and Roland remarked that if Sylvie had indeed warmed up to Will it was a sign that he was forgiven. Roland asked if he could build a fire, and Will told him to suit himself. It was indeed a bit chilly in the large open room with the high cathedral ceilings and exposed beams soaking up most of the heat. He had not thought to turn the brass bladed fans on. They sipped their drinks, transfixed by the flames as the chimney began to draw properly and the tamarack pine logs caught and sputtered, sparking into a shower of yellow as the superheated moisture in the logs expanded and exploded up into the brick wall throat of the fireplace. Once the fireworks subsided into a steady burn, Roland smoothed down the sides of his mustache and said, "Don't tell her I told you this but I'm worried about Sylvie."

This surprised Will and he pushed himself up into a sitting position. He prided himself on his ability to read people. There was nothing about Sylvie's behavior or general demeanor that indicated to him anything amiss. In his involvement with her perhaps he had missed the signs, a possibility which troubled him greatly. He waited for Roland to continue.

"One more year on the Job and I'm taking early retirement." This too came as a surprise. Roland was still in his mid-fifties, far too young to retire. He explained: "I'm presently an *Erster Kriminalhauptkommissar.*" Will nodded. His uncle, a chief of detectives, wore four silver stars on the epaulets of his dress uniform—the highest rank possible among the investigators in the criminal police. The next step up was an administrative promotion to captain and the one gold star that went with it. "With the marks against me on my record, they'll never put me in management. Not that I have any great love for the move to administration. I am an investigator and I need to be in the field solving crimes, not pushing paper and screwing up the lives of good detectives. Anyway, even if I work another ten years or so, it won't increase my pension one euro when I retire. I've invested well and next year I'm going to buy a house in the Allgäu and manage my stock portfolio. Sylvie is the only other person I've told—so she can plan her career moves accordingly." He got up from the chair, took the poker from its stand, and resettled the logs. "That puts out a pretty good heat," he remarked and settled back into his chair, pleased with the results of the redistribution.

Will fully understood and appreciated his uncle's decision. The man had given his adult life to law enforcement and despite black marks on his record—most of them placed there as retribution—he had served the Bavarian state and its people with honor and distinction. And Sylvie would need the early warning to make her own decisions. The current captain of their division, a man of Roland's age named Steinmetz, would be nothing but an impediment to her advancement because she was female and had not come up through the ranks. Moreover, she was Roland's partner, and what galled her captain most was the fact that she had thrived as a result, much to his growing frustration and embitterment, as he was responsible for assigning her to Roland in the first place, a delicious irony, Will noted.

Roland continued. "Sylvie is disaffected. You won't see it because it only becomes apparent at work. She has seen too much of the underbelly of society at too young an age. She's not yet thirty and we've already worked twenty major homicides and sex crimes. For example, take the case we just finished for Interpol in Belgium," he reminded Will. "When we finally caught the bastard he had the vagina of his last victim still in his coat pocket, carrying it around in a plastic bag as if it were the most normal thing in the world. When we asked him what he was going to do with it he said in all honesty that he was taking it home and was going to cook it and eat it for his supper." Roland finished his drink and debated whether or not to have another. He pushed the glass away from the bottle. "It's starting to get to her—seeing the depravity that human beings are capable of. And things are only getting worse."

Will nodded his agreement. "Not only is it getting worse, in the U.S. we're seeing killers getting younger every day. And out here in the Wild West or the North Woods any kid can get his hand on a gun at home and take it to school. We're also seeing the rise of an entire generation of amoral children. Both parents work, the kids are dropped off at day care from the day they're old enough to keep a diaper on and they grow up without a moral code. I've seen ten year olds in the larger cities who would kill you stone cold dead if you cheated them on a dope deal."

In the face of such stark depravity, Roland changed his mind and poured one more half glass for them both. "In Europe, we're also seeing more women commit capital crimes." He shrugged his shoulders. "I don't know—it's probably time for me to get out, but if Sylvie quits, she gives up her pension and any hope of financial security from the Job. That's what has me the most worried."

"You think she'll leave the force?"

"Count on it—once I'm gone she'll last six months. Steinmetz will see to that.

Will did not doubt his uncle's insight. What he had just heard troubled him. "What about her personal life? Isn't she involved with a corporate lawyer or something to that effect?

Roland had to laugh. "It never ceases to amaze me, the choices some women make when they refuse to listen to their heart. Don't get me wrong Will—Manfred is a nice enough guy and he's crazy about her. I have no doubt that he can give her the security and the lifestyle she needs to be comfortable, but that leaves only one problem, if I am to trust my highly trained criminal mind, I mean legal mind," he quickly corrected himself.

Will laughed and asked, "What's that?"

"He doesn't get her wet," he said, lapsing into the familiar vulgarity of two men who understand each other.

"There's more to a relationship than mere animal passion," Will said, playing the devil's advocate.

Roland looked him squarely in the eye, defying him. "Tell me you don't get hard just looking at that woman."

Will laughed to hide his momentary embarrassment at having been so easily read, his attraction for her so easily uncovered, but the blush gave him away.

Roland grinned, pleased with himself in the exact center of his euphoric inebriation, where only the pure and undiluted truth would do between two men who respected one another and expected nothing less. "I don't want her to leave the Job for the wrong reasons. She has to go because she hates the people, the regimentation, and malfeasance, not because she thinks she's in love with some limp-dicked lawyer." He shook his head for emphasis. "You leave the Job because you have a disability or you're burned out from chasing the bad guys and the terrorists. I can't let her use him as an excuse to get out. It will be a mistake twice compounded and she'll live in regret."

Now, for the first time, Will fully understood why Roland had sent Sylvie to him. And make no mistake about it: his uncle was a mastermind extraordinarily skilled at manipulating events to suit his sense of what should be and how it should be. All the signs were there—the coincidences, the confluence of events, the good luck, karma, fate, whatever you wanted to call it, Roland's fingerprints were everywhere. He saw the wisdom of Roland's plan. It was essential for Sylvie to leave the force on her own terms. It was even more essential that she not enter into a relationship as a matter of having settled. Either could destroy her, if he knew Sylvie near as well as his uncle did, and the combination of the two factors would most assuredly guarantee her destruction. Roland had certainly not lost his touch; Will was in fact glad to see that the master strategist still knew how to play a hand, at least where others were concerned. Will's father, Roland's life-long friend, had told him as much some years ago.

They had had enough of talk and drink and decided to find their respective beds even as the fire smoked and popped for the last time. Outside the great heavy logs of the cabin, birds were in full song, welcoming the bright light of day.

SYLVIE SPENT THE next day nursing her two bad boys back to health, despite their protests. She knew better than to lecture: besides, she had walked both sides of that fence. On the rare occasion when she did come home drunk, having stayed too long with Roland or two or three other investigators from other departments, Manfred cared for her, but not without his usual prattling lectures on the perils of alcohol poisoning or cirrhosis of the liver, his attempts at affection. That was the last thing she needed to hear when her stomach felt as if it had been turned inside out and her head ached with such a metronomic regularity that it made her dizzy; or was that caused by Freddi's medical harangues? When she could stomach it no longer—even the sound of his voice would begin to increase her nausea—she would leave the apartment and go for a walk.

The last time it had happened she fled and escaped to the peace and serenity of a walk through the woods on the trail that ran along the banks of the Wertach where she experienced an epiphany of sudden and shocking realization: he was exactly like her doting mother. This manifest knowledge filled her with such dread that she was forced to pollute the river with the tea and toast Freddi had given her in an attempt to settle her stomach. At Roland's apartment, where she had run to seek sanctuary, she recovered on his couch and blamed the violent physical reaction on too much alcohol. Roland knew better. At the very least she understood the misery of the two men now under her care and, laughable as it was since it had been entirely self-inflicted, she offered empathy more than sympathy administered in carefully measured doses.

By two in the afternoon the groaning had largely subsided and there was movement afoot in the cabin after the earlier desperate forays to the bathrooms. She had let the sun bake out the last of the alcohol in her system, replacing it with water and a little lemon juice. She watched the two from the chaise longue on the deck.

They had managed to dress and shave and sat at the smaller white breakfast table under a red and white striped umbrella for shade, one across from the other, sharing sugar and cream for their tea, butter and apricot jam for their wheat toast, passing sections of the daily newspaper back and forth. She had made everything ready for them, and then left them alone. She knew they would sit like this for an hour or so quite contentedly, rarely speaking unless one or more of the daily events reported in the paper warranted a brief cutting comment. Then the other looked up from his section to listen, nod politely, and return to his place with a snap of the folded newsprint. So it went and it gave her a little giggle, watching the two, and she happily returned to the pages of her book until they needed her.

Chapter Ten

Invitation

When the call to come in sounded, it was to thank her. After a proper kiss from both men, which she knew was in gratitude for her gentle nursing and her considerate silence, Will announced that Roland wanted a trip to Canada. They would make the drive across the border at International Falls and she was invited if she was so inclined. She was pleased to be included and accepted gladly, asking if passports were required. Will said usually not in the days before terrorists commandeered the world stage, but now bring them. He cautioned both against carrying firearms. Although legal for law enforcement officers, a weapon even properly declared would slow them up considerably and they decided to do without. Will also promised them dinner out on the return so she put on a touch of lipstick and dab of perfume at the neck. Will assured her that khaki walking shorts, a cool top, and sandals were sufficient— he said not for you Sylvie, for Roland, who said he still had the legs for short shorts. Dressed and ready, Sylvie gave up her position in the front seat of the Forester to Roland.

Will drove them to the oversized replica of the Kabetogama Walleye; Roland insisted on having his picture taken astride the monstrous leaping fiberglass fish and they took photos with Sylvie's cell phone. Sylvie wanted one of herself to send back to Manfred and Will suggested that she send just the picture of the big jumping green and gold fish. The photo op concluded, they drove to the border at International Falls, a city reported to be the coldest winter spot in the contiguous United States. Mt. Washington in New Hampshire was actually on record as being colder, Will informed them, doing his duty to disseminate the truth. After a question or two about their intent on the Canadian side and inquiries about the transport of firearms, they were waved through by the border guard who showed the proper respect for the starburst Interpol shield Will had placed on the dash, and crossed the International Bridge over the beautiful Rainy River into Fort Frances, Ontario, Canada, but not before Will groused about paying the toll. Sylvie laughed. He was just like his uncle.

In Fort Frances, a town that still owed much of its existence to logging and paper production, Will took them to a replica of the original fort that had given the town its name, the earliest known outpost in that neck of the woods, and let them out to walk around. Will was only too glad to indulge Roland's interest in all things northern and Native American, but he grumbled as he reached for his wallet to pay the entrance fee for three. Their curiosity satisfied and duly impressed, Will took them to the duty-free shop before they left Canada and let them nose around for souvenirs, T-shirts, and memorabilia. Sylvie found the perfume and leaded crystal and Roland found the Canadian whisky.

Roland's low whistle of appreciation brought Will running. Roland refused to believe the prices for the Crown Royal and damned the German government for taxing such an essential human necessity and looked around for a shopping cart. Sylvie strolled by just in time to divert his attention, modeling for them the most gorgeous sweater depicting a timber wolf under a moonlit night, perfect for the cool of the evening. They assured her she looked wonderful in it. Then the man that groused about paying the toll and grumbled about the entrance fee to the museum at the fort, would not listen to their protests as he bought the booze for Roland and the sweater for Sylvie, putting everything on his platinum, frequent-flyer charge card. The transaction finished and everyone happy with their purchases and foray into northwestern Ontario, they drove to a customs zone just before the border crossing and waited for a van from the store to deliver their goods. They declared their customs to the U.S. Customs officer at the border checkpoint and he waved them through with a big smile for Sylvie.

"A bit cheeky of him, I thought," Will declared, "coming on to Roland like that."

"My beauty is renowned world-wide and crosses international borders and gender boundaries," Roland said with regal satisfaction, the hint of a lilt in his voice.

"You two are both international idiots," Sylvie grumped until Will handed back a Swiss chocolate bar, which she refused to share.

An hour later they pulled into the gravel parking lot of the Bite'n Bait, which had rolled out the portable billboard announcing the Friday walleye feed: All you can eat for less than ten dollars. Will told Roland that was still a pretty good deal, especially when you figured in how much Sylvie could eat and she nodded from the back, confirming the truth of that statement. They were relatively early and all the tables had not yet filled. Will led them to the back of the dining room despite the posted sign asking them to wait to be seated. They walked past the glass counter behind which tubs of home-made ice cream were kept refrigerated, and Sylvie lingered, already planning her dessert selection—the blueberry cheesecake ice cream seemed a divine mixture—and Will waved at the blonde waitress, a senior in high school, punching keys on the cash register. He seated his crew at the round of a highly polished heavy oak table placed under the mounted trophy of a giant northern pike. He must have weighed at least twenty pounds in his prime, he told Roland, who was admiring the terrifying fish, its mouth open to show razor sharp teeth to best effect.

As he pulled out a matching oak chair for Sylvie, Will noticed an old friend and waved a hello to Farley Nilsson sitting three tables over with the proprietress of the establishment, Liliana Popelka. In response, Farley and Mrs. Popelka picked up their beer glasses and came over to the table. Roland stood as Will made the introductions all around and Lili took the open chair next to Roland as they were invited to sit and visit. Roland was already casually acquainted with Lili Popelka and seemed quite pleased to see her again. She was the person who had given him a ride to Will's cabin from the commuter airport outside International Falls. Farley was always happy to see Will—they were friends and serious fishing partners—and he blushed like a teenager when Will said the pike above their heads guarding the table was Farley's catch. Will was always welcome in Nilsson's boat he told Sylvie, because he was an avid student and because he knew when to shut up and fish. Will called for another pitcher of draft beer and once the glasses were filled, he turned to Farley.

"Something's got you troubled today, old friend."

Farley stammered a bit, choked down a drink from his beer to wet his whistle and said with averted eyes, "I just don't believe I've ever seen such a pretty young woman," then blushed again into his baseball cap all the way up to his sunburned ears. "Beggin' Miss Popelka's pardon, who ain't no slouch in the good looks department either."

"You're quite right Farley," Lili said magnanimously, "She's quite beautiful indeed."

Farley relaxed with an audible sigh and repositioned his Minnesota Twins baseball cap, grateful for the end of that line of talk.

Will helped him out of his difficulty. "How's the fishing?"

Lili Popelka immediately interjected. "Have Farley tell you about his most unusual catch. He's famous now and even got his picture in the paper."

Anyone expecting the old man to spin a tale or tell a story full of adventure and excitement would have been disappointed. He sat, as if formulating his narrative, but Will knew he was essentially a shy man not at all fond of speaking in front of other people. Farley knew all the details; he just had trouble figuring out how to string them together. In fact, sometimes the details actually got in the way of Farley's stories because he had particular difficulty deciding what should go where and when to say what. So he sat in silence, pondering the order, trying different combinations in his head, remembering the sequence of events while his companions at the table waited bemused, as Farley's internal struggle played itself out on the old man's face. Will knew his friend simply needed a little help getting started. "What did you catch, Farley?"

"Caught me a corpse."

Nobody laughed, uncertain whether he was kidding or not.

"Where?"

"Pulled him up out of the mouth of Eks Bay."

Roland had already caught on, having interviewed thousands of people during the course of his investigations. "Can you describe it for us?"

Farley looked uncomfortable again and took his hat off completely before replacing it. "Can, but I shouldn't."

"Why not?" Will asked, knowing that Farley appreciated the direct approach above all others.

He stammered again. "Because of the ladies."

"I understand," Will said, putting him back at ease. He knew Farley did not wish to seem impolite so he must have been motivated by some higher purpose. Will knew that if anything, Farley was a gentleman of the highest Norwegian order and this implied that he must always treat a lady as a lady should be treated and never offend.

Will knew that he must try to disarm Farley's sense of impropriety.

"Lili, as you know, was a nurse and worked in the operating room of the International Falls Hospital. Miss Schumann is actually a specially trained detective in the Bavarian state criminal police force in Germany and has investigated many murders and sex crimes. Roland is her boss and partner."

Farley had known about Lili's work as an emergency room nurse, but Miss Schumann's work surprised him and he thought about how much the world had changed in just the last twenty years or so. But Farley was a relatively flexible man when it came to social change—his own philosophy was live and let live and stay off my land and my boat and we'll get along just fine. As he considered the information he decided he was impressed. Given the credentials of both women, he decided an objective description was not only warranted but also well within the limits of acceptable behavior between fellow professionals. And Farley considered himself nothing less than a professional fisherman.

"He was nekkid as a baby jaybird." This factor alone explained Farley's reluctance to describe the corpse. "Not even a sock or a watch on him," Farley explained, adding technical detail for the professionals. "Fish had eaten out his eyes," he added, lowering his voice, certain now that he would not cause offense or shock the delicate sensibilities of the ladies present at the table.

"Not to be rude," Roland said, "but how do you know it was fish?"

Farley did not take offense. He considered it a damn good question at that. "You would make a good fisherman," he said to Roland and Will knew this was high praise indeed. Roland thanked him for the compliment. Farley's success on the water was due in very large part to his ability to observe and detect emerging patterns. He saw things on the lake most people overlooked or had no appreciation for even if they did notice something out of the ordinary. "I could still see parts of the eyeball in back of the sockets where the fish couldn't get to," he explained, careful not to make the description too graphic or gruesome, thus his reliance on anatomical vocabulary.

"That's a very important detail, along with the fact that he was nude," Sylvie acknowledged.

Farley was not quite sure why that was, so he asked.

"It tells us something about his relationship with the killer or killers," Roland said.

This statement surprised Lili more so than Farley. "Very interesting to hear you say that, *Erster*." As an example of one of those it's-a-small-world coincidences, Lili Popelka had been born in Oberammergau, not too far from where Roland and Sylvie lived in Kaufbeuren. She had come to the States twenty-five years ago after having married Robert Popelka, then a sergeant in the American army stationed just outside Munich. A cook, he retired after his last duty rotation in Germany was up and took his new bride home to Minnesota where he opened the Bite'n Bait. He had died five years ago from a stroke and Lili, tired of the stress of working as a nurse in the operating room, quit to manage the restaurant full-time.

She continued. "Most of the folks who know about the body think it was a suicide. You imply that it was not."

Roland nodded in the affirmative. "I don't know the particulars of the case but generally people don't commit suicide in the nude unless they're at home."

Farley nodded in agreement. He considered this imminently reasonable, as no self-respecting male that he knew would commit suicide in the all-together, leaving a body for just about anyone to see. No, he had too much respect for the sensibilities of others to let them find him in such dire straits. You just could not be certain as to who might find the body or, heaven forbid, pictures might be taken and show up in the local newspaper. He shuddered. That is not how he wanted to be remembered.

At this point the young woman who had greeted them from behind the cash register brought to the table a basket of freshly caught, lightly breaded deep-fried walleye fillets, served with peppered coleslaw, mashed potatoes, and sweet corn on the cob. Farley beamed when Lili credited him with the catch of the day and its impeccable freshness. Farley could fillet a fish with the precision and speed of a surgeon. As the food was being plated, Will invited Lili and Farley to stay, but they had already eaten and Lili was needed in the kitchen as the dinner hour approached and more tourists—unable to catch the famous fish of the lake—came in for supper. As the three detectives ate, wisps of steam rising from the walleye fillets broken open to expose the firm white flesh, Lili asked Will what he thought about Farley's catch.

"Delicious," he mumbled through an enormous bite.

Lili gently elbowed him in the triceps. "No, silly. I mean the poor dead man he brought to shore. Do you think it was a suicide, a murder, or what?"

Will accelerated his chewing and swallowed, giving himself time to prepare an answer. "On the face of it, it sure looks like a suicide, but I have to agree with Roland and Farley. Something doesn't add up here and I have my suspicions. Unfortunately, I do not have all the facts of the case, dear Lili, so anything up to this point is conjecture." Everyone at the table nodded in agreement.

The conversation shifted to the qualities of the meal, its preparation, and a little discourse on the walleye itself, which Farley, now comfortably in his element, was happy to deliver. Then Lili and Farley made their excuses politely and Farley made Will promise to an excursion on the water before too long and he even remembered to invite Sylvie and Roland, although he considered four in a boat two too many to fish comfortably. He figured Will would attend to Sylvie and he would gladly work with Roland, who already had impressed the old fisherman as a capable and competent individual. Will said he would call later in the week and they would make the arrangements. That suited Farley just fine and he shook hands all around for the second time.

After they had finished feasting on the delicious walleye, Lili brought an entire apple pie to the table and the young blonde waitress followed with a gallon of the homemade ice cream. Sylvie wondered how Lili had known to bring the blueberry cheesecake flavor and then remembered this was also Will's favorite. The oven heat still in the pie warmed the ball of ice cream sitting atop each serving and slid it toward the nose of each slice. After they had finished, Lili came to check on them once more, a bottle of authentic German *Schnapps* and four iced glasses in hand, as the waitress collected their dessert plates and forks. Speaking in German and using Bavarian dialect, Roland complimented her on the pie, ahead of raised glasses and a toast to everyone's health and well-being, and Lili smiled as she drank the shot. Will had not missed the fact that her forearm had touched Roland's as she reached for his empty plate, helping the young waitress clear the table for talk and another round. They sat and talked for a while, shared one more round as they watched the tourists interspersed with the locals come and go, some sitting for the walleye dinner, others coming for the ice cream alone, others looking around and shopping in the adjoining bait and tackle stop.

Will offered to show Roland and Sylvie around the place but Roland politely declined and said, "You needn't wait up for me."

Will took an extra house key off his ring and flipped it to his uncle, wishing him a good time. Sylvie raised her eyebrows, puzzled for a moment until she got it figured out. Then she kissed her boss on the cheek, wished him goodnight and whispered good luck in his ear.

Chapter Eleven

Walleye

All three were up much earlier than the day before and well into their individual routines. Will was at a logical stopping place on his next writing project, research for a new textbook for the FBI Special Investigative Unit, and was eager to unchain himself from the desk and get back on the water. Roland had come home from Lili Popelka whistling and was still in the bathroom, fixing his hair. Will shook his head and smiled: Roland spent more time with his hair than a teenager. He heard the muted drone of the hair dryer as his uncle continued the process of arranging his coiffure. Curious, Will thought to himself, the man never troubled to dye the gray but spent more than half an hour every single day in front of the mirror getting the curls in their proper position. Will wondered if Roland did not have some sort of personal styling map that he followed to avoid making any tonsorial mistakes. Will did not have the heart to tell him that once out on the water and exposed to the damaging rays of the sun, he would most assuredly sit his uncle under the protection of a wide-brimmed hat, no matter how much he protested. The man was used to exposing his face to the morning sun; in fact, the *Erster Kriminalhauptkommissar* enjoyed lying out on those rare and special days when the sun warmed the waters of the *Forggensee*, the lake below the famous castle *Neuschwannstein*, King Ludwig's monumental legacy to the Bavarian Alps. But here the noonday sun was far too brutal and after ten o'clock, as a rule of the boat, it was the hat for his uncle.

Sylvie was in the kitchen making sandwiches to take along on the fishing expedition. Will sat on the couch, preparing the rods and reels, checking the baits and drags, seeing to it that the equipment was ready for use. His position in the living room afforded him the luxury of watching her as she moved from counter to refrigerator and back. He looked up from his work and watched Sylvie go about hers. He decided he liked her with her hair cut shorter. It accentuated her cheekbones and brought out the line from the plum of her cheek down past her ears and into the graceful length of her neck. It was this very same line he enjoyed kissing so much. Longer hair got in the way and to be frank, Sylvie's ears were perfectly formed and highly kissable. He sighed as he put down one rod and picked up another, going through the same checks for drag, feeling for any cuts or nicks in the line above the knot securing the bait, and readjusting the magnets on the reels to minimize backlash, always a problem with the rookies in the boat. Sylvie turned to watch a blue jay fly outside the kitchen window. She was one of those rare women beautiful even in profile.

To his practiced and highly trained objective eye, the only flaw in her otherwise perfect beauty was also natural. When the last row of her back teeth came in, they crowded the others at the front, causing the canines to overlap the incisors. It was noticeable only if you looked closely or if it was something you studied from force of habit, like a dentist. Having conquered the horrors of an onset of teenage acne, however mild, and surviving this trauma, as her wisdom teeth came in her once proud and shining white smile was gradually being reduced to a source of personal shame. The orthodontist had offered her two choices: she could have the back molars removed, thus alleviating the problem; or she could wear adult braces for a year, guaranteed to be practically invisible. Right. Just what she needed on the Job, braces, as she was painfully pulling some modicum of respect from the males with whom she worked.

Sylvie had a difficult enough time during her first year working in an empire of men who perceived her as a princess intruding among the paramilitary elite; barely tolerated but never accepted. And so she did what any attractive, overtly intelligent young woman bent on survival would do under similar circumstances: she stopped smiling. Everyone wondered about the once happy and outgoing young professional who now seemed overly introspective and uncommonly sad and they all blamed it on the rigors of the Job, her mother in particular. Sylvie had reasoned that it would be far easier to curb her natural predilection to smile than it would to bear the merciless ribbing she knew she would have to endure if she wore the braces.

Although the male officers with whom she worked would kid her good-naturedly, she also knew it would be a test of how well she took the teasing and how well she fit in. One good thing she had learned from her mother was that to get along in a man's world, and the ranks of the criminal police were nothing less, a woman had to understand the behavior and culture of the men with whom she worked. Once she learned that their actions were often predicated on treating her as they treated their male cohorts, usually because they just did not know any other way, she began to understand. Over the course of the years, as she gave as good as she got and learned from Roland not to take what the idiots said personally, she gained acceptance from some of the men. Not to say that there were not the ever-present percentage of jerks that still did not get it and never would; for the most part, she was able to interact with her colleagues and go about her duties without unreasonable bother. As her percentage of solved cases rose, she earned a growing reserve of respect, however dearly won. Therefore she was entirely unwilling to sacrifice those hard won gains to practically invisible braces.

She had learned to smile less and it made her seem all the more serious because of it; probably not a bad result on the Job where she was perceived as taking the Job seriously which, for a woman, was seen as a good thing, if it was not overdone to the point where it made others look bad, mind you. This was one of those fine lines that she had learned to negotiate with a little help from Roland, mostly in those cases when he had crashed over the line himself and, by observing, she learned what not to do. Of importance was the lesson learned, Roland emphasized, not necessarily the process of teaching it.

She made the decision not to smile at work and the force and power of her naturally ebullient personality became muted like the orange light of the sun filtered through an eyelid. Her personality had not changed in the least, only her manner of presenting herself. She learned to smile without showing her teeth. She learned to smile by turning up the corners of her mouth and keeping her lips closed. It worked: she was no longer perceived as withdrawn or even melancholic. Through the force of natural circumstance—her work within the milieu of male testosterone and the dental crowding of her molars—-she developed a rather effective yet somewhat wistful alternative smile.

Will knew the emotional work Sylvie was forced to do; he had seen it first hand as they teamed with Roland to solve the Adamas File. He knew she could be radiant and unreserved, but that part of her was reserved only for those people about whom she cared a great deal. If anything, it was a sure and certain sign of her affection: a full, unrestrained smile that said here I am, hair uncombed, underwear unchanged, crowded teeth unbrushed; take me as I am. Roland was the recipient of her unabashed and uncensored joy. Will had seen as much in Germany when they rode together to investigate a crime scene or shared dinner afterwards, or worked through the troublesome logic of the case on Roland's couch in his apartment in Kaufbeuren. Will wondered if Freddi had seen the real and authentic smile. Somehow he doubted it. At least not in the bedroom. The thought gave him a secret sense of satisfaction.

Roland had earned his access to her happiness. Roland's force of personality and his legend in the criminal police protected her. Over the years the *Erster* had established a reputation for competence and efficiency—his percentage of solved cases was unmatched. His methods and habits were unorthodox: for instance, he rarely, if ever, reported to his office, explaining that he had yet to see a crime committed there and this served to infuriate his boss, which Roland considered nothing more than an unexpected benefit. The longer she worked with him the more Sylvie came to appreciate what others saw as idiosyncrasy was actually the result of refined method and long experience working in the field. She saw that Roland was a successful investigator because he could separate conventional wisdom from the reality of what worked and what did not.

She had also discovered, to her surprise, what an observant student of human nature the man really was. His study transcended the empirical and the observational; in other words, the day-to-day casework necessary in the field: interviews, ringing doorbells, talking with informants and people who knew the street. What made Roland great was the fact that he constantly read and kept abreast of the latest findings in the study of criminal behavior and forensics. In a sense he was as much a scholar of the criminal mind as Will was of semiotics. Sylvie had come to realize that this was a familial trait. This was a family of readers and scholars, formal and informal. From the stories they had told her she gathered that they were all informed and well-read and their natural intelligence, fueled by the information gleaned from their bookwork, pushed them to the edges of the circle. She saw that in both men. It served both to make them successful and, to a similar degree, distance them from others. No doubt this was why she felt so comfortable in their company, a kindred spirit secure with her own kind.

She finished wrapping a sandwich in cellophane and smiled at Will, showing all her teeth, crooked and straight, happy in the reverie and the understanding it had brought her. She was pleased to catch him watching and it was only the instant of her smile that drew him to her and out of his own thoughts. When he saw no hint of sadness or reserve whatsoever in the dazzling radiant smile that exposed the imperfection in the line of her teeth, he gave as good as he got. Placed within the context of the woman's overwhelming natural allure, her golden white hair, her blue eyes, her perfectly shaped mouth, and the exotic contours of her face, the smile seemed almost supernatural. He understood at once the profound implications of her willingness to share it with him. He made a mental note to tell her she was exaggerating the crookedness of her teeth. She had convinced herself over time that the perceived effect was much greater than the reality of the phenomenon. The mirror in which she examined herself was distorted. In reality the imperfections of her teeth were hardly noticeable. It was similar to noticing someone's shoes— you knew they were wearing them but who took the time for anything other than a cursory glance?

"What are you looking at?" he asked with mock aggression.

"A gorilla," she said with all the carefree ease of an observer safe behind the security of the iron bars at the zoo.

"Don't forget to pack a banana for me in the picnic basket, pretty-please."

She held up a fine representative of the thick, curved yellow fruit and showed it to him. "You be a good boy and maybe later I'll peel it for you and then you won't be so grumpy."

He showed her his gorilla fangs and she tittered just as Roland came into the living room, finally satisfied with the result on top of his head. Looking his finest, he presented a shining and freshly shaved cheek for a morning kiss, which Sylvie gave gladly. He always smelled good, making it even more of a pleasure to kiss him, and before he could go she restrained him with a hug. Although Roland had never been much of a public hugger, he closed the distance and clinched like a prizefighter, sharing her unexpected enthusiasm. To add even more intrigue to the surprise, she kissed him quickly on the lips, a favor usually reserved for birthdays, holidays, or highly significant thank-yous.

"All this public police love is making me nauseous," Will said behind a grimace as he checked the action of a bail spring on a spinning reel.

"Don't be jealous," Roland chided. "I consider it unbecoming conduct in such an overeducated man."

"Can you blame a guy?" Will asked, working his lower lip into a shiny wet pout. "You spend all night gallivanting around with that good-looker, Lili Popelka, then you come waltzing in here and start stealing kisses from my girl while I'm busy doing all the work so you can catch a damned fish."

Roland came over to the couch and picked up a rod, testing its balance in his hand. "For your information, my dear *Professor Doktor*," he said using the German inflection, "I do not gallivant, I consort. And Sylvie's affection for me is duly earned, not stolen, and someday you will learn the difference when you can no longer trade on your looks and your money." To help underscore the point, Sylvie came over and sat defiantly on Roland's lap, arms around his uncle's neck.

"Very well," Will acknowledged, bowing in the face of overwhelming peer pressure. "I apologize: you consort, not gallivant, and I have been properly put in my place.

Never let it be said that I would ever interfere with or in any way try to disrupt your mutual admiration society."

"See that you don't," Sylvie admonished with a wag of her elegant finger as she rose from Roland's lap just as he started to groan. "Roland and I have a bond forged in duty, a love developed and nourished in respect and confidence, the product of protecting and caring for each other every day we put our lives on the line. It's a love that far transcends the simple, base, and purely primal attraction I have for you," she said with a certain amount of smugness and a toss of her head to elevate her nose.

"I'm certainly sorry to hear that," Roland said, rubbing his thighs with greater effort than needed to get the blood flowing back into them.

"Not I," Will said, affecting grammatical correctness, cool as the inside door of a refrigerator, and she could not resist his sang-froid another second and hoped to warm him up with a promise whispered into his ear as she crashed his lap. Little did she know that it would have exactly the opposite effect: the touch of her warm breath against his ear and the innocent press of her breast against his bare arm sent a chill deep into core of his spine. "We have to go fishing now," he said, unable to hide the desperation in his voice. Roland joined his laughter with Sylvie's, both enjoying his discomfort and his willingness to join in their play. "Grab some gear you two, and let's get on the water," he said, retreating into the business at hand. "Against the three musketeers, those poor walleye don't stand a chance."

Because she asked, insisted really, he let Sylvie operate the electrical winch that lowered the big red Lund Pro V into the water under the shelter of the boathouse. When she drew enough water, he climbed in, and trimmed back the powerful motor. It coughed into life as he pushed the button for the electronic ignition. The motor sputtered, smoked, and died. He adjusted the throttle and thumbed the ignition again. This time the motor caught and he poured in the fuel as it thundered into high revolutions. He backed off the throttle quickly until the motor burbled in the water, a signal that she would sit at idle and not die again. He checked the trim once more, fuel indicators, wattage for the batteries, saw to it that the radio was tuned to the weather channel, then backed her out smoothly and pulled in alongside the dock where Sylvie and Roland waited, hands full of gear. He took Roland aboard first with the wet weather gear, and Sylvie handed in the tackle, rods, bait boxes, Styrofoam rounds of live leeches topped with plastic lids to keep the wigglers from floating out and lastly, an ice chest full of provisions for their afternoon meal.

He stowed the gear bags up front, the rods and reels in their long lockers on either side of the boat, the tackle boxes behind the seats with the ice chest. He took a minute to carefully place the leeches in the chest to keep them fresh and lively. Sylvie ran forward, holding the boat until she reached the prow and at Will's signal, pushed the nose out and away from the dock. Will slowly throttled forward and Sylvie nimbly jumped in to Roland's steadying hand. She plopped down on the seat next to Will as he swung the windshield into place, bridging the middle gap between the right and left windscreens and access forward, locked it into place and idled out and away from the dock. He checked his depth finder, turned to make sure his crew had settled in, and after he stuck his hat between his legs he hollered "Hang on!" and let the big 200 horsepower Honda outboard bring the nose up as he shot them out of the hole.

As he increased the throttle and trimmed the planes, the nose dropped smartly and they were running at speed. Sylvie gasped at the sudden acceleration and the sharp turn up-lake that rolled them over onto the side of the boat until he accelerated them back into a flat and even running position. She had just managed to save her hat and looked back to check on Roland hunkered down into his shoulders, trying to find protection beneath the rush of wind, already too late to save his elegant coiffure.

"This is wonderful," Sylvie shouted over to Will but he answered only with a smile, his attention fixed on his piloting as they sped east and north, looking for the buoys that marked the ever-present danger of rocks below the surface, rocks large enough to rip a titanic hole in the hull.

The Lund clipped along at fifty, a speed which kept them flying across the backs of the green waves showing their white beards, called a walleye chop by the locals and a sign of good fishing. On their right they passed the marinas and cabins of the resorts dotting the shoreline; on their left the islands that stippled Kabetogama. Out on a Wednesday, they had the lake practically to themselves, wide open for a long and fast run. He eased the throttle forward and the needle touched sixty. He listened carefully to the tune of the motor, concentrating to hear the false note that might signal a problem. He satisfied himself with the steady roar and the rooster tail thrown by the motor in a high arc behind them. On a calmer day he could peg the needle at seventy, but enough was enough—there was always the danger of driftwood in the water and unmarked boulders hidden all too easily by the light chop on the water.

For good measure he backed off and ran at fifty as he passed a small flotilla of local boats marking a school of walleyes lying deep. Those who knew the big red Lund, or the BRL, as Will called it, waved in recognition over their rods and his crew waved back, Sylvie ever mindful of her hat flopping in the wind. Will was up on one knee now, needing a better look forward. He pointed to an island ahead in the distance, now little more than a dark green mole on the face of the water. "Pine Island," he shouted. "That's where we'll start fishing today." He let the speedometer touch sixty again for a second or two then slowly throttled her down to thirty as they closed on the island.

Chapter Twelve

Catching the Case

Will did not head directly for the big island but swung around to the windward side. Ahead of them a pile of rocks broke the surface of the lake and to her delight Sylvie saw that this was a rookery for pelicans, seagulls, cormorants, and even a roost for one or two old men of the lake, blue-gray herons. Will idled into position between the rocks and a marker buoy, and the presence of the boat sent the birds into flight with the most awful screeching and squawking, as if the call of one incited the other into even greater noisy cries. They lifted in waves, rising in cacophony, circling their barren retreat, returning inexplicably, but not without giving further strident voice to their displeasure at having been disturbed.

"A godawful noise," Roland remarked at the avian hullabaloo as he pulled up a seat cushion in his search for a hat stowed there, still hanging on to a forlorn hope of saving the remnants of his morning's tonsorial labor. The wind of the fast ride had blown his hair stiff and he looked not unlike a frozen woodpecker. Once he found the hat it took him more than a minute to stuff the mess under the protection of the baseball cap, and only then did he feel ready again to face his public, clamoring for his attention on the sanctuary.

"I told you to wear a hat," Will reminded him.

"Never wear them," Roland said, nonplussed. "Let's catch one of these walleye and see if they are appropriately named. Had a girlfriend once who had a walleye," he explained to Sylvie, who was not the least bit surprised, having been privy to quite a few stories about Roland's old girlfriends, some of them even true. But before he could get into the meat of his narrative, Will filled his hands with a fishing pole and explained the Lindy rig to him.

"I know you're familiar with spinning gear because I've seen you catch trout in Bavaria. This is called a Lindy rig and it's excellent for catching walleye in these conditions. The lead sinker here," he said holding it, "is designed to bounce along the bottom with the drift of the boat. The spinner attracts the fish to the leech on the hook. Hand me one of those containers, will you Sylvie?" he said, pointing to the ice chest. She took one out dutifully and popped off the plastic lid. The black shapes wiggled in the water of the Styrofoam, swimming wildly in their confined space, twisting and turning in and among each other.

"Ick," she said, looking down into the writhing, wet, brown and black mass. "I'm not touching one of those," she said with the absolute certainty of a girl who knew what she should and should not touch.

Will knew all she needed was a little schooling. "It's easy," he said, picking up a three-inch specimen and watching it contract along its length between his two fingers. "Take the broader end that has the biggest sucker—they have one on each end. The anterior end has the eyes and the tail is at the posterior end. Let the sucker attach to the fingernail of your thumb." Both Roland and Sylvie leaned in for a closer look and watched Will turn his thumb upside down, the leech firmly attached to the nail. He handed the leech to Sylvie.

"Oh, I can't do it," she said, grimacing and shaking her head.

Roland took the leech and let it attach to the table of his thumbnail. "I'll be damned," he said, trying to shake it loose to no avail. "The little suckers hang on pretty tight."

"Some of them have three rows of teeth with a hundred teeth per row. And believe it or not, that little guy has thirty-two brains."

"Can they hurt us?" Roland asked, more for Sylvie's sake than to satisfy his own curiosity.

"Not really," Will assured them. "Even if they do manage to penetrate your skin, they're easy to get off. They're also very clean. When they bite they inject an anticoagulant called hirudin, and this thins your blood, making it easier for them to suckle. When they're fully engorged, they just fall off. One thing to keep in mind though: once the anticoagulant is in your bloodstream, the wound site will bleed for up to ten hours."

"That's amazing," Roland said, studying his bait with renewed respect.

Will nodded as he showed Sylvie how to hook the leech. "That's why hospitals use them. And walleyes eat them like candy."

With the leech properly hooked about half an inch behind the sucker, he handed the rod back to Sylvie, now in control of her little girl's disgust of anything that wriggled or bit or boys played with.

"Open your bail, drop the rig over the side, and let it fall until you feel the thump of the sinker hitting the bottom, then close the bail." He watched her dunk the line as the sinker's weight carried the rig down until the line went slack. "Okay. You're on the bottom. Close the bail and reel up a turn or two so you can lift the sinker with the rod and feel it as it touches down again. Then open the bail and hold the line with your index finger." She did exactly as instructed; Roland did the same from the rear of the boat. "I can feel it thump the bottom," she reported.

"Me, too," Roland said.

"Good," Will acknowledged and dropped his line, satisfied to have all three in the water with minimal fuss.

He had the nose of the boat facing the rock island bird sanctuary, the aft end pointing toward Pine. The wind caught them broadside by design and pushed them into a natural drift across the sunken ledge where Will knew walleyes congregated as they came up out of the deeper waters to feed. Everyone was paying proper attention to his or her line. "Typically a walleye will pick up the bait from behind and engulf the leech. You'll feel the weight of him as he lifts the sinker and swims off a ways. He'll then stop and try to swallow the bait. When you feel the pick-up as it's called, your line will also begin to straighten as he moves off and at that point, release the line from your index finger; in other words, let him have the bait and swim away. He won't go far. Count two or three seconds, close the bail and set the hook by sweeping the rod upward."

He paused for an instant as his line began to move. He relaxed his index finger and dropped the rod tip ever so slightly in the direction of the moving line and closed the bail. He lifted the rod up and yelled, "Got one," watching to see if the line remained taut. It did and he began to reel in line. "Fish on," he said and the rod bent to reinforce his claim. "Bring your line in, Sylvie, and please hand me the net behind you."

She hurried to reel in and brought him the net, excited to see the emergence of the fish.

"You go ahead and net him," he told her and she made a stab at capturing him, but the fish darted away, pulling against the drag. "Not from behind, Sylvie, just the other way so he has to swim into it." Will backed off the drag a bit and reeled the fish back to the side of the boat, turning the walleye's nose toward the net. Sylvie leaned forward and down and smoothly combed the net through the water, scooping the fish up out of the lake, taking its thrashing weight in the net with both hands on the handle.

"Good job!" yelled Roland from his position where he had watched the proceedings with interest. He too had reeled in eager for his first look at the fabled Kabetogama walleye, which he knew in German as the *Zander*. "Yep," he said after a close observation of the fish, now out of the net and in Will's hand, "Looks just like my last girlfriend, only the fish has a smaller mouth."

With his audience close by, Will showed them how to properly handle the wet gleaming golden fish without getting hurt. "Never grab the big spiked dorsal fin," he warned, showing them the webbed fan of spines on the fish's back. "And don't try to lip him either." He carefully opened the mouth and showed them the needle thin teeth useful for catching minnows and leeches. "Not as bad as a northern or a musky, but they can do damage, so keep your fingers clear at all times." They both nodded, seeing the danger. Will demonstrated the proper hold, letting them both have a turn at sliding a finger up under the jaw, thumb on the gill plate. Fortified and confident with their new knowledge, they returned eagerly to their lines, hoping for a fish. Will measured the fish to make certain it fit the required length, then started the pump for the live well, set the aerator to blowing and dropped the fish in with a splash. "A good start," he said, watching his crew for mistakes or trouble as they dropped their rigs into the water.

Not five minutes later Sylvie giggled nervously and waved Will over. "I think I've got one," she whispered not wanting to frighten the fish or alert him to the fact that he was caught. She had already released the line and was watching it slowly wind off the reel. Then it stopped.

"Easy now," he said. "Close the bail, reel in so you can feel a bit of tension in the line, and then set the hook."

She swept the rod tip up as she had seen Will do and was rewarded with the heavy dull weight that signaled the undeniable presence of a fish on.

"Reel him gradually—not so fast," he cautioned, "and keep your rod tip up." He could tell she had a good one hooked and his suspicions were confirmed when the walleye breached for the first time.

"Fine fish," Roland yelled in encouragement.

"Get the net, Will. Get the net," she yelled at him in the panic of not wanting to lose the fine specimen now fighting against the drag. "And don't forget to take him from the front," she implored as Will leaned over the side. The net disappeared and she thought she had lost the fish as her line went slack just as Will swung the black net back on deck, heavy and dripping, wet and full of one four pound golden-green thrashing walleye.

"Get my camera, Sylvie," he said, "Just there under my seat." He unwrapped the nylon net where it had looped over the walleye's fins and nose, unhooked the fish in mid-flop, saving the leech in the process, and handed the fish to Sylvie. She held it as proudly as any mother holding her baby for show. Will caught the pair with Pine Island in the background, Sylvie happy and face full of glee at what she had accomplished. About the time he stowed the camera and loaded the fish into the live well, Roland was hooked up.

A little after one o'clock when the action settled down, a count showed they had eight keepers in the boat, two each for Roland and Sylvie, four from Will. Sylvie still had the biggest fish and although she had released a walleye too small to keep, she demanded that it be counted, thus placing her ahead of Roland. Roland contended that if it was not in the live-well, it should not be part of the total. Will let them work it out for themselves as he moved the boat toward Pine Island and shore lunch.

After the lunch of walleye fillets and wild rice, Roland stripped down to his bathing suit, found a fairly level piece of ground aboard a large sloping hunk of granite, and fluffed out his towel for a short tanning session. In the heat of the afternoon Sylvie took off her long-sleeved denim shirt, dropped her khaki shorts and showed her white firm belly below and above her black and red string bikini, her first time wearing it, her first time having the courage to wear it in public and not merely in front of a mirror.

"I need to get a little sun," she offered in explanation, checking Will's reaction. "Do you like my new bathing suit?" she asked, presenting herself to him for approval.

"I like nothing better," he said, but she did not get it, so he added, "It looks very good on you."

Will and Sylvie used the interlude for a walk into the interior of the island and he showed her an eagle's aerie on a neighboring island, a nest high up in the bows of a stately pine, a nest so large that it could easily accommodate a person. Some nests were revisited every year by their inhabitants and were added to and remodeled and expanded to the point where they eventually became so large and unwieldy and weighed so much that they crashed from the treetop to the ground. The current resident was not on the nest; they spotted her perched on the limbs of a snag on the edge of the waters where she could see down into the lake. The feathers on top of her head were piebald white, an indication of her maturity, and she was on the hunt.

She jumped into flight and cut a circle in the sky while gathering herself. She gauged her distances before she started her sky dive and plummeted to the lake surface. At the last instant she opened her massive wings to break her fall and raked her talons through the water. She pulled out a two foot long, twisting, curling northern pike. Her struggle now was not in the success or failure of the hunt; it was her desperate attempt to overcome the aerodynamic problem of lift, the problem of trying to keep her wings dry while gaining enough altitude to resume her flight, fish stowed below in the hangar of her talons. The angle of her descent had been just enough to maintain some forward momentum, an angle that allowed her to spear the pike but keep from plunging into the water. They watched the titanic struggle between the air and water—the northern pierced by the raking sharp claws still writhing in an effort to escape the hold and the flight into suffocating air; the female eagle beating her magnificent broad wings against the slide back down into the drowning waters. She rose and then fell, and for an instant they both thought she would go in, the weight of the fish simply too much to bear, unable to release the still fighting, writhing northern either by instinct or because of the too efficient lock of her talons.

The fish went back into the water and it appeared that all was lost for the eagle. The impact caused her to release one hold, one talon opened and freed, and her wing tips brushed the surface of the lake, as if she were trying to smooth the disturbance caused by the thrashing northern. With one more powerful thrust of both wings, she swept the air back behind her in a rush loud enough to be heard on their island and she was up. A second, massive concentrated thrust and she was gaining, the fish still hanging from one feathered leg. She rescued the fish, reestablishing her toehold and was once again firmly in control of the flight. But the ordeal had exhausted her and she did not fly to her nest on the neighboring island to secure her prize as she needed to land soon, secure the fish, and regain the energy for her wings and her flight to safety.

She was so depleted by the struggle that she was unable to gain the height of her protective aerie. She landed not 20 meters from where they stood, using the broad plane of a granitic promontory for her emergency landing. She folded her wings into her back and looked around, sunlight glinting from her golden eye, the fish flopping one last time beneath her as she repositioned her death grip. Once suitably recovered she attended to the task at hand, the curving, slicing beak first tearing, then gulping morsels of white flesh from the barred, green fish.

Will walked Sylvie back in silence, both in awe, both respecting the honor of what they had witnessed. Roland waved a greeting from his hot rock, the muscles of his upper body delineated by and glistening with sweat. He was sitting up now, arms around knees, letting the breeze off the water cool him. In the distance, they saw the twin plumes of a high-powered boat approaching at speed and they watched as it grew in size, nearing the island. "A park boat," Will informed them, hand shielding his eyes from the glare off the water, "and they're headed our way. Probably got a complaint about Roland lying around in the all-together, a crime against nature, I would think." Sylvie agreed.

The captain of the approaching boat cut the throttles and the spray of water behind the twin outboards died as Will and Roland—back in his swimming trunks—ran to receive the boat on the sandy beach. Ranger McManus threw them a line and Will secured it to a nearby cedar tree. Sheriff Clayton, in the passenger seat, waved a hello. Both men were in shorts and water sandals and did not mind getting their feet wet as they stepped from the boat to the beach. Will welcomed them ashore and made the introductions. The two men complimented the catch as reported and offered the appropriate comments on the heat of the day. But it was obvious that the two men had not come to give the weather report or check licenses, and they in fact apologized for the intrusion, considering Will a local by now and a professional comrade. They briefly explained their need to involve their business with the Doctor's pleasure.

Ranger McManus, the younger man, caught himself staring at Sylvie and tried to cover himself by wiping the sweat from his forehead with a green handkerchief as he reseated his green ranger's cap. Will and Roland let the two men finish paying their compliments and awaited their request as Sylvie discreetly pulled her long sleeved shirt on over her shoulders. The three had a collective hunch why the two men had come, but Clayton made it official. The county would consider it a professional and personal favor if the three investigators would have a look at Farley's Catch in International Falls. Recently, the county had received a special grant for interdepartmental law enforcement services in Voyageurs National Park and

Clayton could not think of a better opportunity to put the money to work.

Will looked to Sylvie and then to Roland—it was their vacation after all—and Clayton took advantage of the pause to assure them that all expenses, within reason of course, would be paid with the addition of a generous stipend given for their consultation. Roland and Sylvie agreed readily; they shook hands all around and a time was arranged to suit them. Declining the offer of beer or sodas, the men returned to the boat and Will and Roland shoved them off with a wave.

As they idled out into deeper water, Ranger McManus at the wheel and a reasonably married man still, said to Sheriff Clayton, a bachelor, "Bet you can't tell me the color of her eyes."

Stan Clayton swabbed his brow with a blue handkerchief now darkened with sweat and admitted as much. "I can sure as hell tell you the color of her bikini. Remind me to think about booking a vacation to Germany next year..."

The rest of his quip was lost in the full-throttle roar of the twin engines as they powered back to the ranger station at the mouth of the Ash River, both men still in awe of the unexpected natural beauty in the wilderness they had been privileged to observe.

Chapter Thirteen

Semiotic Analysis

Roland begged off: he had seen more than his fair share of stiffs on the table and—not that it was any of their business—Lili was on her way over to pick him up for a day in Duluth. He trusted Will and Sylvie to do the analysis of the post mortem examination and wanted to review their findings when they returned. He knew this was Sylvie's first experience with a floater. He warned them not to set their expectations too high: a body immersed in water for a length of time is very hard to read. Even in the cold-water depths where Farley Nilsson hooked the body, he explained to Sylvie, maceration takes place, whitening the body and softening the skin to the point where many times you cannot take prints off the fingers; the skin sloughs off to the touch.

They assured him they could handle it and looked at each other guiltily. They had been right about their guess: the nearly two hour stint in the bathroom had exceeded even Roland's extraordinary routine. When he did come out only after Will had threatened to send in rescue, his hair was perfect and his cheeks gleamed from a fresh razor. The long scar that ran on a diagonal from below his ear, across his jawline, and down to his throat—the souvenir of a high-speed pursuit and crash—pulsed carnation but did not bleed. The fleeing felons had suddenly stopped, turned their stolen Mercedes around and rammed his cruiser, effectively committing suicide by cop. Their actions forced Roland to shoot to kill in order to protect himself. And this was a mantra Roland relentlessly drilled into his partner and his nephew. Always protect yourself first. Sylvie said he smelled good enough to be kissed, so she did—careful not to muss— and she received the same in return. Will was left standing by expectantly.

Roland told him, "Don't look at me with those puppy eyes." He checked his watch as he heard the rumble of Lili Popelka's Ford pickup truck coming up the driveway. "Right on time. I appreciate punctuality in a woman," he said, looking at Sylvie, who shrugged.

"That's not all you appreciate in a woman," Will offered facetiously, showing his uncle to the door as he helped him shoulder into a black leather jacket. "Be home before midnight."

"What day?" Roland asked, allowing his collar to be turned down.

"Just have fun and be safe," said Sylvie.

Roland had had just about enough of this fawning attention and he grumped, "To allay your fears, I intend to wear not one, not two, but three condoms tonight in the very real probability that I will climax with enough force to burst through even a neoprene fishing glove. And I do so not to protect myself from any sort or insidious or nefarious sexually transmitted disease. I do so for the express purpose of protecting Mrs. Popelka's uterus from the explosive and potentially damaging force of my substantial ejaculation."

Sylvie rolled her eyes in mock surprise. "I had no idea, Roland, that you were such a bull."

"Yah, yah," Will said, having none of it. "Get out the door. Your friend is waiting."

Sylvie and Will stood arm-in-arm, hip-to-hip and waved to the couple away on their adventure. As they watched the truck disappear down the drive into the forest Will said, "Runs in the family, you know. It's a good thing we let him out of the chute and into the field."

"Poor woman," Sylvie said, thinking of her own womb. "I hope she survives her evening with him."

Will closed the heavy door with his foot and took her into his arms and told her she looked particularly ravishing today but she knew exactly what he wanted and only after a sufficient teasing delay did she give in. They did not bother with the decorum of bedrooms or beds or covers, choosing instead to make convenient use of the big couch in the living room. In order to protect her womb from any possible damage, Sylvie made him demonstrate distance and trajectory, although she was left to determine aim, and came away suitably impressed. It never failed to please her when she managed to find the truth in the fable.

"Ready for a little work" he asked once they were decent again and presentable to the public.

She stood composed and ready. "Let's go. I'll drive."

SHE POUTED ALL the way to Ray. "Why can't I drive? I let you drive the car when we were in Germany. Roland doesn't let me drive either. Did you notice he had absolutely no qualms about letting Lili drive? Let that be a lesson to you. That's why Roland is going to get lucky tonight and you are not. Men are such pigs."

During her rant, she had evidently forgotten that he had very recently gotten lucky, but he held his tongue and let her vent. He thought she was finished but she was just pausing to breathe. He was not the least bit disconcerted by her gentle rant, his right hand captured firmly in the grasp of her two hands. He showed her a buck and three does standing at the edge of a copse of trees, taking to the grass of the field for the last vestiges of vitamin C in the last of the fresh, green shoots of the season. The splendid vista restored her to good humor and good mood. To maintain it he promised her a late lunch out after the visit with the chief medical examiner at the hospital in International Falls.

On the road into town he showed her mountains of sawdust almost high enough to toboggan down, dumped from the local lumber mill that processed living trees into pulp and pulp into massive paper rolls weighing tons per unit. At the hospital they checked in at the nurse's station and were asked to wait in the reception area. They sat together on one of the uncomfortable ugly, green chairs two seats wide with aluminum arm rests that lived in doctor's, dentist's, optometrist's, and chiropractor's offices throughout the country. Among the coughers, hackers, nose blowers, children running unattended, and the aged with the look of desperation in their eyes, they waited in good health trying not to look guilty or self-satisfied.

It took CME Dr. Hansen ten minutes to answer her numerous pages before she made her way to the waiting room. She arrived in a hurry, wisps of hair escaping the heavy combs in her brown bun rising off the back of her head. She wore her glasses low on her nose, which must have been somewhat uncomfortable, given the size of both, but it did not seem to bother her. As she approached, she pulled her dirty, wrinkled white coat together across the top of her breasts, leaving it unbuttoned. She carried a clipboard in her left hand like a mother carrying a child on her left hip, and a frown of displeasure under her nose.

Sheriff Clayton had arranged the meeting and she had consented only out of professional courtesy to him; nevertheless she was none too pleased about the imposition. She was really much too busy for such shenanigans and to her mind it all seemed very irregular and unwarranted, a waste of her precious time. However, in order to maintain good relations with the sheriff's office, as a personal favor she had acceded to the request. Of all the law enforcement officials she worked with, Clayton was the least bothersome and the most charming. When the two strangers stood to greet her, her displeasure deepened and she made no effort whatsoever to hide it; to Hell with social niceties. She had never been one to give in to social conventions just to make nice and she had work to do; she checked the clipboard to make sure.

The blonde was altogether too pretty and much too tall and Dr. Hansen disliked her immediately, despite her pleasant closed-lips smile: it was affected surely. The big man's hand swallowed hers and caused her an instant of panic. He was easily 6 feet 5 inches tall, and the heels of his hiking boots accentuated his height. She had to tilt her head back to look him in the eyes and she did not like that in the least. She was used to looking down at men, usually men in a supine position on a metal-framed hospital bed. This one had life in his eyes and a hundred years ago would not have been out of place in a lumber camp bucking a two-man saw. She looked away quickly— the eyes more so than his imposing height and musculature bothered her. She went immediately on the offensive when she realized the utter certainty of the fact that the intelligence behind the intense gray-blue eyes of the man was superior to her own. She checked the chart again, and his academic credentials confirmed her suspicion as a fact.

"Follow me," she said peremptorily, showing them her back as she led them down the hall marked with yellow directional lines and arrows bending right and left—some running under closed doors—until they reached the elevator. They rode in silence to the basement as Dr. Hansen checked each light illuminating floor levels on the ride down and studied her clipboard in the interim. When the steel doors clanked open, she stepped out first and led them through the twisting corridors of the basement to the cold white rooms of tile and stainless steel or aluminum where autopsies were performed and cadavers were kept, some in shrouded repose, others undraped awaiting the scalpel, the toe tag, and the jar.

"What exactly is a Doctor of Semiotics?" she asked abruptly, filling the silence in which they stood looking at each other. Her tone of voice served to impugn his academic credentials and simultaneously demonstrated her ignorance. Will decided to be patient and polite; after all, she was merely a physician. But she continued in the same arrogant tone of voice. "I mean, what is it exactly that you do? I can't imagine that a Ph. D. would be useful for investigative work. Sheriff Clayton did say you work with the FBI in some capacity," she allowed, trying to moderate some of what she thought to be the sting of her incisive but honest appraisal. "I guess what I'm really asking," she said getting down to it and dispensing with any further social niceties, "is why exactly are you here?" The question implied that she was perfectly capable of handling a routine autopsy that even an idiot could see was a suicide and she resented the imposition of this obvious intrusion into her domain.

Sylvie took note of the color rising in Will's cheeks, despite the decidedly cold temperature in the room, but he was smiling yet.

"I read signs exactly, Dr. Hansen."

Margaret Hansen blew out her cheeks, a habit of exasperation carried over into adulthood from the very first time she had ever experienced that emotion as a young girl. That was no answer. She pushed through the double stainless steel doors, sending them swinging, expecting to be followed. Once through and into the room of four flat metal tables on rollers, each carrying a draped body, Will stopped and waited with Sylvie, forcing the chief medical examiner to stop, turn, and walk back to them, wondering why the hell they had not followed her to the office in the corner.

"Dr. Hansen, let me make one thing explicitly clear. I am not responsible for the fact that your boyfriend has abandoned you. I am not responsible for the fact that your long-awaited engagement has been called off, nor am I responsible for the fact that you have been stranded in a town you do not like and in a job that you obviously despise. In other words, I am not responsible for your current miserable situation in life, so please do not take it out on me or Detective Schumann."

Sylvie took a big breath in through her nose and compressed her lips to keep from grinning. Margaret Hansen looked as if her father had slapped her. Her mouth was open in shock and embarrassment.

"How could you possibly have known those things about me? No one knows that Jack left me on Sunday. I haven't even told my parents. That bastard must have told you himself," she said, her face now poisoned with suspicion.

"I can assure you, and Detective Schumann will vouch for the fact that I do not know anyone by the name of Jack."

She was not buying it. That son-of-a-bitch ex-boyfriend of hers was already spreading the news around this godforsaken refrigerator of a town. "Then how could you possibly know such intimate details of my private life? We've never met and I haven't told anyone."

"Semiotics, Doctor, is the study of signs and I am considered an expert in their interpretation," he said calmly and as a matter of fact. "I conclude from my reading of your signs that you have been in a rather lengthy engagement, judging from the band of exposed white skin on your ring finger. The absence of the ring and the color contrast indicate to me that you have worn it through at least a summer and a winter. You have transferred the ring to the opposite hand, indicating that the engagement has been broken. The fact that you continue to wear the ring not as a sign of engagement but as a piece of jewelry, suggests to me that you believe the ring is owed to you: ergo, payment for a long engagement unfulfilled by the promise of marriage. No wedding ring to add to the promise ring tells me that he has left you and terminated the relationship suddenly and without explanation."

He continued. "You most probably took this job, which you consider to be beneath your training and your talents, simply to be with him. Although you tolerated the job before, now you hate it because it serves as a constant reminder that you traded career possibilities for a relationship and the possibility of marriage. Against your better judgment, and bowing to the pressure of family—you are getting older, Dr. Hansen, and your relational prospects have never been exceptional—you settled, and that more than anything else about your situation eats at you like hydrochloric acid spilled on the skin."

"The white coat, which symbolically represents your job, is dirty, unwashed, and unpressed, indicating that you have given up any sense of loyalty to the position. Your demeanor and rude behavior toward Miss Schumann, who represents someone your Jack might very well have run off with, to your mind at least, is the result of your unhappiness with yourself. You have projected your discontent on to us because you typed us as a happy couple in spite of knowing nothing of our relationship, private or professional. The fact of the matter is that we symbolize to you something you and Jack were not, but something you have desperately wanted. In all, this has resulted in your inappropriate and unprofessional behavior, and surly and sour treatment of us. And that Dr. Hansen, although I could go on in even greater detail, is the power of inductive observation and semiotic interpretation."

Dr. Margaret Hansen took a step back for self-protection and looked to Sylvie for assistance, a desperate plea behind her panic to have someone help her as she faced the truth of what Will had shown her. In the instant when Hansen's face told her that Will had nailed it, the discomfort and chagrin served to verify the accuracy of Will's analysis. The woman was near tears as she took off her bifocals, carefully folded them and placed them in the breast pocket of her coat. She tried to push a wayward strand of hair back into place but it floated away. Her chest heaved as she tried to regain her composure.

"He does the same thing with me," Sylvie admitted. "It can be very uncomfortable. Sometimes it's as if he has some sort of unique vision that allows him to see into the private world of a person, the world we keep only for ourselves and hide from everyone else. He has an uncanny knack of walking around in that world as if he belongs there." Sylvie comforted the woman in her moment of distress with an arm around her shoulders and Will offered Dr. Hansen his handkerchief, which she accepted with a sniff of thanks before she forcefully blew her nose into it. He told her to keep it after she finished the wipe and carefully folded it for the return. Nevertheless, she pressed it on him, not wanting the obligation of keeping it. She took a sigh of breath so deeply into her lungs that it lifted her shoulders.

"I hate what that bastard did to me."

Will and Sylvie nodded compassionately, waiting.

"We were engaged almost three years. I had to threaten that I would leave him before he finally proposed and gave me the engagement ring." She held it up for them to see, wiggling her fingers so that the cold artificial fluorescent light from overhead sparkled through the diamond. "I took this dead-end job to be with him," she continued as they admired the stone. "I sacrificed my career for him. Now I'm stuck in International Falls, Minnesota, the coldest place in the continental United States." Sylvie nodded knowingly. She had seen the enormous digital thermometer that stood as a proud civic testament to the city's frigid reputation. "And do you know the worst of it?" Hansen asked Sylvie, who shook her head. "On top of everything else, the son of a bitch was lousy in bed. Sylvie moved closer to Will, unconsciously guarding and protecting her knowledge of his accomplishments in that regard. But it was something that women knew without saying and she breathed out the last of her resignation, wiping under each cheek with Will's blue bandana, handed over again for the purpose. Why were all the good men taken?

"I apologize for my behavior. I'm really not like this at all and I hate myself for what I've become. I'm just a mess," she said stating the obvious as she looked up and away to better sop up another tear. "I've just been a complete wreck these last few days."

"Apology accepted," Will said graciously, with Sylvie's affirmation. "And may I offer a bit of advice?"

Margaret Hansen, once more in control of herself, if not her flyaway hair, looked up into his kind eyes and saw through the handsomeness into the goodness of the man. Seeing him for the first time, she started as if someone had silently approached her from behind while she was concentrating on the resection of a cadaver's chest. She nodded, a little bit anxious at what she might hear.

"Today after work go and immediately sell that ring."

She laughed spontaneously, it was so unexpected, but she slipped the ring off with some difficulty—she was retaining water today on top of everything else in her miserable life—and grimaced as it scraped over the first knuckle. Once in the palm of her hand she examined it one last time before dropping it into the large side pocket of her clinic coat. She suddenly felt much better. "I don't know why but that seems like a very good idea all of a sudden," she confessed. "I wonder why that is?" she asked, thinking out loud. "Not ten minutes ago I was determined to keep it forever as a reminder to me about what a jerk that bastard was, pardon my French."

Will and Sylvie chuckled at the attempt to be light-hearted and Hansen smiled at her accomplishment. Will explained, "The ring is a significant symbol. Usually it signifies the happiness of the union between two people, but in your case it has taken on a new meaning. You keep it to remind you of his betrayal of your trust. It now signifies your failed relationship and, ultimately, your sense of failure. As long as you keep it he has that last vestige of emotional control over you. Sell it, a behavior which will signify that you are taking control back, and use the money to buy yourself an indulgence."

Dr. Hansen promised she would do exactly that and for the first time in five days felt a sense of relief, as if the weight of her failed relationship had been lifted from her shoulders. She put her glasses back on, signaling that she was ready to return to the task at hand. Sylvie smiled to herself as she watched the change in the woman. Will's advice had been excellent. In fact, she would have sold the damn ring a long time ago were she in similar circumstances. Then she blushed as she remembered that she had not called Manfred during their agreed upon time yesterday. He would have to wait until she returned to the cabin.

As Dr. Hansen took them to the nearest table and used her foot to trigger the switch for the overhead light just as Sheriff Stan Clayton entered the room, leaving the steel doors swinging behind him.

"Hey, Will," he said enthusiastically, shaking the professor's hand. He took Sylvie's hand with far too much energy and for far too long in an effort to prolong the time he could look at the gorgeous blonde without causing offense. He gulped and returned her the use of her hand, and she laughed politely at his awkward enthusiasm. He was a likeable fellow, despite his clumsiness, she decided. "Maggie," he said in greeting as he turned to the chief medical examiner. "Hey, you look different today. Are you losing weight?"

She blushed to her ears, dropped her eyes and tried to tame the stray wisps of hair all at once. When she returned his approving glance, along with the use of his hand, her interest in him was both new and evident. Will had certainly seen those signs before. He likened Hansen's reaction to his own pleasure in revisiting an aria he had heard many times before, discovering heretofore unexpected and delightful insights upon hearing it once more.

"We were just starting," Will told him. "You're just in time to hear Dr. Hansen's review of her work."

Chapter Fourteen

Autopsy

After providing her visitors with tear-away blue scrub suits, plastic booties, latex gloves, and surgical masks, Dr. Margaret Hansen suddenly felt as nervous as a first year intern on rounds reviewing case notes for the resident physician. She cleared her throat twice before she found her place and began her narrative overview of the autopsy. In preparation for the visiting detectives, the body had been retrieved from cold storage and placed on the examining table. For better access around the table, she pushed aside the scale and aluminum trays designed to receive resected organs. She lifted the evidence sheet draping the cadaver and pulled it efficiently over the head and down to the toes. It was important now for her to appear competent and professional. Stan Clayton came around the table and stood at her side, affording himself a better look, holding the mask over his nose and mouth with one hand. She became very much aware of his presence and, at the same time, aware of herself. She liked his cologne, not so evident anymore below the formaldehyde and bleach smells pervading the autopsy room, and remembered she had not worn perfume for the longest time. She knew exactly what she would buy with some of the money from the sale of the ring. Across the table, Will gently nudged Sylvie with an elbow and she stepped on the toes of his big booted foot in return.

The CME had conducted a classic autopsy, following all prescribed protocols and procedures. She had taken an X-ray of the body, given its time underwater. Her examination within the mandated characteristic Y-incision that opened the chest revealed early stages of cirrhosis of the liver, but in all other aspects, the internal organs of the corpse were entirely unnoteworthy. When resected, the lungs had been full of water, to be expected given the location where the body was found and recovered. There were no signs of blunt force trauma—she smiled at Will as she said it—and examination of the brain showed no evidence of contra-coup. The term was new to Sheriff Clayton, who was not at all embarrassed to admit it, and Will explained that a blow to the head could result in a blood bruise on the opposite side of the brain, the force of the blow slamming the spongey tissue of the brain against the inside of the boney cavity of the skull, a phenomenon also evident in the brains of professional boxers, soccer players, divers, and quarterbacks. Sylvie stepped on his toe again, this time with enough emphasis to make him grimace, and he apologized for jumping in when he should have kept quiet.

Dr. Hansen smiled at him, suitably impressed. "In fact, I did check for subdural hematoma, the bruise one would expect with contra-coup. There was none. I saw no signs of ocular petechiae, the shower of red bumps in and around the eyes that would indicate our John Doe had been strangled either by ligature, by hanging, or by manual force. All the structures of the throat including the larynx and pharynx were undamaged. The cricoid cartilage and the hyoid bone were examined and found to be intact and unremarkable," she said, pointing to the throat. "The autopsy revealed no wounds to indicate gunshots or stabbing, absent the punctures caused by the treble hooks that snagged the body. Given these findings and the absence of anything contradictory, I concluded that this man died of cardiac arrest brought on by drowning. Therefore, I intend to write it up as a death by suicide."

She folded down the last page of her notes and looked up expectantly, waiting to have her findings verified. Stan Clayton nodded in agreement, the findings verifying his own gut feelings about the matter.

"I respectfully disagree, Doctor Hansen," said Will.

Margaret Hansen, M.D., after the first wave of a flush rising in anger at having her conclusions contradicted, took a deep breath and treated the disagreement exactly as if it had come from a colleague with a difference of medical opinion. "On what grounds, Professor Sheridan; if you don't mind my asking?"

"Not at all. I would expect nothing less from a competent professional. If you will permit me a small digression? The essential conundrum of this case, whether it be death by suicide, death by misadventure, or a death by murder, is that we have no verifiable identity for the victim."

Sheriff Clayton happily interjected. "I can confirm that fact. We do not know who he is and his identity does not appear on any of the numerous state and federal databases I checked. Basically, all we know is that he is a he."

Will agreed. "But a semiotic analysis will permit us to construct and build some semblance of an identity for the man, who is presently and perhaps forever after, known as John Doe. We owe that much to our fellow human being, whoever he might be."

Everyone around the table nodded in agreement.

"What we know is this: the victim is a person of identity to those who knew him in a context before his demise. We see him now after his death. If we can ascertain the facts of that demise, in other words, the facts of the case post mortem, it will assist us in discovering his identity ante mortem.

Will turned to Maggie Hansen. "So you see, I do not disagree with your observation of the medical signs: that was excellent. Nor do I disagree with your interpretation of those signs. Your work in that regard is much appreciated. In ascertaining the medical details of the man, you have moved us forward in determining an identity for our unfortunate John Doe. I merely disagree with the conclusion derived therefrom that the poor man committed suicide."

"Now what makes you say that, Will?" Stan Clayton asked, more surprised than anyone there about the motive behind the death. He too had concluded that it was a suicide, a rather strange one, truth be told, but everything he had just heard Maggie Hansen say had confirmed his own conclusions.

"Almost all signs—with the exception of some natural signs—have the potential for multiple meaning; that is, many signs present us with the problem of ambiguity," Will explained.

"So we need to resolve the ambiguity," Sylvie suggested.

Dr. Hansen was interested but puzzled. All the medical signs had seemed pretty clear to her. "I'm not sure what the ambiguity is, to say nothing of resolving it," she admitted.

"An important realization, Maggie. To first understand the ambiguities and then resolve them can only be done by interpreting the entirety of the signs before us within the context of their initial expression."

"Lost me there, Doc," Stan Clayton said with a chuckle.

Will continued. "In other words, Dr. Hansen's conclusion is based on an excellent analysis of the signs presented to her at the autopsy table. But this is not the context in which the man died."

"I begin to see what you mean," Hansen said, the respect in her voice catching Sylvie's attention.

Clayton was still a step behind and had to scratch his head while thinking it through, to no avail. "All right. I give up. What are you eggheads getting at?" He smiled at

Maggie Hansen to let her know that the term was one of respect.

Will nodded. It was time to do a little professing. "Let's look at what we know, Stan. You were the first person to see the body after Farley Nilsson and Ranger McManus brought it to the Ash River Ranger Station."

Clayton agreed. That was an indisputable fact of the case.

"What was the first thing you noticed about the body?"

From head to toe and in between, Clayton took a good hard look at the corpse. "Other than the missing eyes, and the fact that he was buck naked?" he said in the form of a question. Will nodded. "The slit wrists," the sheriff said, "indicating a possible suicide."

Here Dr. Hansen interrupted, anxious to make a contribution. "But it's not at all unusual for suicide victims to strip, sit in the bathtub, and slit their wrists."

"A perfect example," Will allowed, and for demonstration, turned over the corpse's wrists. "Look at the lacerations you noted in your report; signs that might be interpreted, despite the degradation and swelling of the skin, as slash marks or slit wrists."

Everyone leaned in to take a closer look and agreed.

Then Will moved them to the ankles and the shins. "What do you see, Sylvie?"

Her eyes widened. "Similar marks."

"Slash marks that would indicate suicide?"

She gasped her surprise at the now obvious conclusion. "People rarely commit suicide by slashing their ankles."

Will stepped back and crossed his arms. "And yet, the marks above the ankles and the wrists appear to be similar. Does everyone agree?

All nodded that they agreed.

Very well. "Is there another possible interpretation of the signs we see on the ankles and wrists?"

Dr. Hansen immediately said, "Signs of the use of a ligature thin enough to cut the skin. Oh my god," she said, covering her exclamation within the cup of her hand. "It's possible someone tied his hands and feet!"

"Possible indeed," Will affirmed. "However, for the sake of argument let's assume this was a suicide and those were indeed slash marks on the wrists. Would this not result in a high degree of exsanguination before death?" he asked Dr. Hansen.

She nodded her agreement. "I see where you are going." She read from her notes. "There was more blood in the body than I expected, but I noticed very little livor mortis—what we call post-mortem stain." She explained. "This happens shortly after death when the blood in the body pools to areas where the body makes contact with the ground. Obviously, that could not have happened in this case. I also was unable to reach a conclusion regarding algor mortis—the cooling of the body—because of its immersion in cold water. I do know that in death from submersion, water enters the lungs and quickly dilutes the blood—medically we call this hemolysis—so that it cannot carry enough oxygen to the brain and other vital organs, and cerebral hypoxia begins. In most cases, after about three minutes, death by asphyxiation occurs." At this point, she paused to check her notes again. "I did find that the lungs were full of fresh water, unremarkable given that he was found in a lake and not in saltwater.

To further make his point Will said, "He was found completely naked in a cold-water mesotrophic lake, not in a warm bathtub, and according to Farley, brought up from a depth of about forty feet."

Clayton slapped his forehead with his palm. "Aha," he said with such dramatic overemphasis that they all laughed. "Context rears its ugly head."

Sheriff Clayton was sharp enough when he got started in the right direction. He reminded Will of some of his better graduate students.

"You got it," he told Clayton. "Let's assume for the sake of argument that the nudity was not volitional."

Now Sylvie jumped in. "That would suggest someone forced him to strip."

Will raised his eyebrows. Roland had done a good job training this one. "Now take the next step in your thinking. What does it indicate when a person is forced to strip naked?"

"Humiliation," Margaret Hansen blurted out, having experienced the same recently at the hands of her now absent fiancé. She pulled her coat together across the tops of her breasts.

"Yes," Will acknowledged, noting the embarrassment in Clayton's face once he understood the tenor of Hansen's meaning. "And what is the purpose of such humiliation?"

"Control," Maggie said calmly, without a second thought.

"Uhmm," Will grunted. "And what might we say is the ultimate form of control by one person over another?"

Dr. Hansen's eyes grew wide as she became aware of the conclusion. "Rape."

"A very close second only to murder," Will said. To be safe, he asked Dr. Hansen if she found evidence of sexual assault.

Maggie checked her notes for confirmation. "I found nothing to indicate sexual assault."

"Thank you, Dr. Hansen. This confirms my conclusion that he was not raped. My semiotic reasoning takes me to the inductive hypothesis that he was stripped for another more practical reason. It is a known fact that murderers will often strip their victims to give the appearance of a sex crime when they are actually trying to minimize the discovery of forensic evidence. However, that is not likely in this case as the victim was not expected to be found."

Sylvie and Stan Clayton nodded together in agreement. Sheriff Clayton took a minute as they considered the possibility and mulled it over. He checked his jawline to see if it was ready for a shave and then asked, "But isn't it also possible that the John Doe might have set up the situation to make it look like he was murdered, whatever his motivation to do so might have been? I mean, he could have stripped himself, tied his feet, then tied them to a concrete block or something similar, tied his hands, and then thrown the weight over the side and followed it down."

"It is a possibility, Stan, and as objective criminalists and criminologists, it is our duty to consider all possibilities, but in this case there are other significant behaviors that rule against your possibility as stated."

Clayton waited patiently, not sure what they might be.

Sylvie posed the question: "If a man committed suicide by tying himself to a concrete block and throwing it overboard, why would he want to make it look like a murder? It would seem that the act of using a concrete block or some other weight as an anchor at the bottom of forty feet of water would indicate that he didn't want to be found ever again. If this is true, how would anyone ever know he was murdered?"

Clayton was forced to admit, "That's a pretty convincing point. I see what you mean."

Will paused to think for a minute as he reexamined the corpse. "The fact that the corpse was submerged in the cold water below the thermocline of the lake is significant. We know that cold water retards putrefaction and decomposition, so forensic entomology—the science of how insects aid the decomposition of dead bodies on land—doesn't help us much here. We have no flies, no maggots, and little or no signs of bacterial decomposition. On land, we know that an exposed body can break down to bones in less than two weeks. I assume you found some traces of methane, carbon dioxide, and hydrogen sulfide in the body," he said, turning to Dr. Hansen in a collegial manner.

"Correct," she affirmed. Some was detected. Even in cold water the bioflora of the body will decompose, but at a much slower rate."

Will nodded, pleased to have his conclusion supported. "We note too that the skin on the body is wrinkled, mottled, and sloughing off in places, making the observation and interpretation of the marks on the wrists and ankles confusing and ambiguous. We will revisit our conclusion of forceful ligature of the wrist and ankles when we have more evidence for support."

"We observe that on some parts of the body the color is bleached white, on others a greenish black. These signs will help us with a chronosemiotic analysis and give us a relative guess as to the amount of time the body spent in the water."

The other three nodded as if they understood what a chronosemiotic analysis was. As he continued his observations, Will said, "An analysis of the uses of time."

He pointed to the dead man's cheeks, the sides of his breasts, his abdomen, and the sides of his buttocks. That waxy looking, whitish-gray substance is called adipocere."

Sylvie repeated the word, trying to get her tongue around it.

Dr. Hansen chimed in. It's also known as grave or corpse wax."

"Thank you, Maggie. It is a significant finding for our chronological analysis."

"How so?" Sheriff Clayton asked. He'd never encountered the phenomenon before.

Will explained. "Adipocere is the result of a chemical reaction when fatty or adipose tissue reacts with water and hydrogen in the presence of bacterial enzymes. The reaction breaks down the body's fat into fatty acids and soap, believe it or not. This process is called saponification," he said, turning to Sylvie, writing diligently in her case notebook. "Ironically, once formed, it is mostly resistant to bacteria and retards further decomposition, thus protecting the body. On land, adipocere has been found on some bodies more than one hundred years old. We do know adipocere forms in bodies submerged in water in the winter. The conditions of the lake where Farley recovered the body were suitable for enabling the body to saponify, which forensic science tells us most likely begins about a month after submersion. We also know, in contrast, bodies discovered in warmer waters are skeletalized within one to three months. Our John Doe remains relatively intact. So we can conclude definitively that the body was in the water for at least a month, more likely three. This gives us significant chronological information."

Clayton looked at Will with profound respect. "Now I know why you work for Interpol and the Feds."

Sylvie smiled as she finished her notes.

Dr. Hansen took a moment to re-drape the whitened, lifeless body of the man exposed on the metal table, drawing the white evidence sheet up to just below the chin. She invited her guests to finish their discussion in the warmth of her office, out of the cold aluminum and stainless steel of the autopsy room. After removing the latex gloves and the surgical masks, they followed Dr. Hansen to her corner office.

Once settled, Will took up the narrative. "There are two additional factors that would warrant the conclusion of murder disguised as suicide and not suicide or suicide disguised to resemble murder." He paused and looked at each of the three bright living faces watching him, and then spoke with the eyeless deceased man in mind. "There are easier ways to commit suicide. The pattern for males is usually to do something much more violent— eating a shotgun, for instance."

That was a fact, Sheriff Clayton agreed, at least in law enforcement where the cherished service revolver was most often the weapon of choice. Barrel in the mouth, pull the trigger, slump to the side.

Will continued. "To my mind there is one conclusive sign that speaks against the idea of suicide once and finally. Actually, it is the absence of a sign; in this case, perhaps even more persuasive for its absence."

Sylvie put her hand to her mouth to cover her surprise. Of course. "If he committed suicide in Eks Bay, how did he get there? They never found a boat!" she exclaimed for them all.

"I'll be damned," Sheriff Clayton said. "There was no boat where the body was found, nor have we had a report of an abandoned craft anywhere on the lake."

"It is also highly significant that no clothes were ever found," Will said. "We can conclude therefore that someone else was in the boat with him and returned with it and the naked victim's clothes. And we can conclude therefrom that murder was committed designed to resemble a suicide, even with the problem of the obvious oversight, which probably would not have occurred to the killer in the boat at the time."

"Amazing," said Dr. Hansen, suitably impressed.

"Damn, Will," said Sheriff Clayton, "you are every bit as good as the FBI boys said you were."

"Yes, he is," said Sylvie proudly, thinking back to the Adamas File.

Clayton took the exclamation to mean something entirely different than intended, but it served only to heighten his appreciation and ratchet up his admiration for the man by one more notch.

Now deep in thought, Will sat with his admiring public largely unaware of the adulation. Something else had just occurred to him and he was almost ashamed to admit he had overlooked it. He tapped his finger to his lips and thought it through before speaking. "There's one more thing that bothers me, and I have to thank you all for helping me discover it. Without our discussion today I don't know if it would have occurred to me. Dr. Hansen alluded to it earlier. There were no signs of a struggle. There was nothing at all to indicate force; humiliation without force. How is that possible?" he asked, inviting the others to think along with him. "Even at the point of a gun, I would think that a man facing death would make some sort of last minute attempt to resist. But we found no signs of resistance, no defensive wounds, no broken fingernails, nothing. This is highly significant," he said with finality.

There was nothing for them to say. It was an indisputable fact. There were no signs of struggle.

Dr. Hansen asked, "Was there anything else in my report that you wanted to see?"

"Yes. You said you did you find fluid in the lungs, but did you find any internal bruising there?"

What a strange question to ask, thought Sylvie. A drowning without fluid in the lungs? That did not seem possible, but the question about the lungs being bruised puzzled everyone. She waited for Dr. Hansen's reply, wondering what Will had in mind.

Dr. Hansen referred to her notes again. "A resection of the lungs did show that they were filled with water…" She hesitated before continuing. "And I did find that the stomach was full of water. The brain showed cerebral hypoxia and thus I concluded death by drowning as a result of cardiac arrest, that is, the lack of oxygen to the brain caused heart failure and death. And no, I did not notice internal bruising of the lungs." She had regained her composure, now certain that this conclusion was correct and sustainable.

Will sat with legs crossed at the knee and thought about Dr. Hansen's finding. Two minutes went by. Sheriff Clayton was forced to shift his weight from one buttock to the other and looked at Margaret Hansen. She smiled back and blushed and both looked at Sylvie. As they waited, they could all hear the white large-faced clock on the opposite wall as the thin black hand pointed away the seconds. Another minute in silence passed. Sylvie knew Will was working through what must have been a rather complex chain of reasoning. In silent thought, he had lost awareness of time and of the others, his thinking unaffected by their presence. Sylvie had learned it was best just to wait and let him work. But the time was fast approaching when she would have to pee.

He startled all three when suddenly he said, "One conclusion obtains." Dr. Hansen, have you done a toxicology scan?"

"I did one as a matter of protocol. The scan showed no drugs such as cocaine, methamphetamine, or marijuana in his system. There were trace amounts of alcohol, but some of that is accounted for naturally in the body. Are you looking for something specific?"

He smiled. "I am indeed. Would you indulge me?"

"Of course," she offered, one professional to another.

"Please resubmit your samples to the FBI forensic pathology lab in Minneapolis and ask that the assay be done at the highest level of sensitivity."

She made a note on her clipboard. "Very well. Anything in particular they should be screening for?

"Yes. I'll tell you later privately, but as a control I won't say anything now so we can keep the analysis purely objective. If you will allow...." He reached across her desk and tore a sheet from Dr. Hansen's memo pad. With his pen he wrote a few words, signed and dated it, folded it in quarters, and handed it to Sylvie for safe keeping and her promise not to read it until given permission

"You have my word," Sylvie said, and placed the folded note inside her casebook.

"I'll call you soon as we get the results back from the lab," Dr. Hansen promised, curious to learn what Will had written on the memo paper. But you've got me curious now. Are you looking for a poison, perhaps?"

Will shook his head, grinned and said, "Not a poison, but I can tell you that it has something to do with what is called the mammalian diving reflex. I won't go into detail now, but based on my semiotic analysis, I have reasoned that the assay will show one or two anomalies, and those should support the conclusion that I wrote on the memo."

Sylvie swiveled her chair next to his, directly facing him now. "Don't think for one minute, buster, that you are leaving this room without sharing that chain of reasoning with us."

"I agree," Clayton echoed. "Let's have it. Two more minutes won't kill anyone," he joked.

"Very well," he said with a laugh. I was just thinking about everyone's need to pee, so I'll be brief. Drowning is a violent act. As the body struggles to breath and the lungs fill with water, there should be some evidence of internal bruising among the lung tissues. This was not noted in the autopsy. This is an anomaly that raises the question of why there was water in the lungs, but no bruising. I need an answer to that question; an answer I believe will emerge in the analysis."

"While we're waiting for the mysterious drug analysis to come back, what do you suggest we do in the meantime? Sheriff Clayton asked. He was not quite sure what an anomaly was, but it sure sounded important.

"We need pictures and then we need to show them to every resort owner, hotel clerk, camp ground director, et cetera on Kabetogama, and Namakan too, for good measure. And if we have to, we'll canvas all the way up and down Rainy as well."

Sylvie led the team out of the office as they looked one last time at the eyeless corpse in repose in the autopsy room. "That's going to be one horrible, ugly picture," she said, shaking her head in sympathy for the poor man.

"That's nothing but a fact, ma'am," Stan Clayton said to Sylvie Schumann, who was as attractive as the corpse was repugnant.

"You two have a point," Will admitted. "Let's try this." He reached over for Sylvie's sunglasses and put them on the corpse. "I'll buy you a new pair," he promised as she groaned. He next added his Minnesota Twins baseball cap and stepped back to study the effect. "Much improved, I think."

As Dr. Hansen positioned the medical camera for the shot she said with unexpected candor, "Even I would go out with him now," and they all laughed at the morbid humor.

Sheriff Clayton said he would have copies of the photos printed on flyers and would bring them around on Monday, if that were convenient. He apologized for not walking out with them under the pretext of having another question or two for the CME. Will winked and Dr. Hansen blushed into her rather large, reddening ears. Sheriff Clayton, she noticed, was decidedly more handsome and certainly livelier than the poor fellow she was wheeling back to refrigeration with Clayton's willing assistance.

After they said goodbyes all around and thanked each other, Sylvie, without apology, pushed through the swinging stainless steel double doors of the autopsy room, and after a short run down the basement hall found a bathroom. Will heard sighs of relief emanating through the closed door. He stood by dutifully as he waited for the toilet to flush, the water in the sink to run, and the warm air blower to stop before he took his turn. They walked out of the hospital holding clammy hands.

Chapter Fifteen

John Doe

It was too early in the investigation to be frustrated and too early to be encouraged. No one had reported the John Doe missing. A search of the Missing Persons reports for Minnesota, Iowa, North and South Dakota, Wisconsin, and even Illinois came back without any hits. None of the photos or descriptions matched their floater. This was an anomaly to be taken seriously, Will told Sylvie after she handed him the last batch of downloads. They gathered the flyers containing the photos and descriptions and the numbers to call and made ready to make the rounds of the resorts. Sheriff Clayton had faxed the flyer to all requisite law enforcement agencies on the off chance that someone had taken an MP report and would be able to match it with the person in the flyer. They were still waiting for the toxicology report to come back.

Sylvie grabbed her purse and laid a sweater across her bare arm for later when the cool, early evening wind skipped off the lake. She had her hair pulled back, which Will did not particularly like, but she was pretty enough to pull it off under her favorite straw hat worn to protect her delicate complexion from the September sun. She smelled good and he told her so. She accepted the compliment with a smile. Roland had come home early in the morning and would probably sleep past noon so they left him to his rejuvenating slumbers. Besides, this was the sort of detective grunt work he detested and he was more than willing to leave it to them. He promised assistance later in the day and they sent him off to bed, his hair severely mussed.

As they drove toward Gappa Road, which gave them access to most of the fishing camps and resorts lining the south shore of Lake Kabetogama, Will mused out loud, "It's rare for someone to be so completely alone that they could disappear without someone at least raising a question or two, if not a full scale alarm. Like it or not in this land of the individual and independence, we're all members of some tribe," he said. "Everyone is born into a language, a culture, and a family. Families are part of clans and clans become tribes. Tribes become nations. We're all linked in one way or another to somebody else, literally and figuratively, from the belly to the umbilicus, to our mother, to the person who formally and officially pronounces you dead."

Sylvie nodded. "It is practically impossible to join a society and a culture at birth and leave it in death without another human being taking official or unofficial notice, at least in Germany."

"My point exactly," he agreed. "So where the hell is JD's tribe and why isn't somebody hollering their heads off about this guy?" He shook his head. "This is significant. Something is not right. It's almost as if there is some sort of conspiracy of silence surrounding JD."

"A conspiracy of silence?" Sylvie asked.

"As soon as you admit that you know someone, you have admitted something about yourself," he explained.

"Ahhh," said Sylvie, grabbing the stack of flyers. "So the question becomes: what is it that they don't want us to know? In this sense, if you'll allow me to steal a phrase, JD's death is significant. It takes on a meaning beyond the mere act of dying—meaningful enough in itself." She put on her straw hat and smiled at him.

They turned left off Gappa onto an access road that led to the first of the fishing camps set back in among the pines on the south shore of the lake. Will shifted the Forester into Park and looked at her in mock amazement. "Sylvie, I swear that you are turning into one fine doctoral level semiotician which, in my book, merits a quick kiss."

She kissed him back and repaid the compliment. "I have a fine teacher." She thought for a minute. "May I be so bold as to propose an alternative hypothesis?"

"Of course," he allowed.

"The silence might well be due to the possibility that no one knows him here."

Will nodded gravely. "That thought too had crossed my mind. Unfortunately, if that proves to be the case, then I am left with very little hope that we will be able to solve this case. At the very least, if this is so, we will have learned a significant fact."

"And what might that be?"

"He was deliberately brought here to be killed, a deliberate decision designed to assure silence."

She nodded her agreement. In that regard at least the possibility of suicide would be eliminated and, in so doing, open up the possibility of a murder investigation. Unfortunately, it also occurred to her now as she wrapped her head around the idea, that although they might be dealing with a premeditated murder they had not one scintilla of evidence as to a possible motive.

Before they walked to the main cabin with the sign "Office" written in neon above the front door of the Four Pines resort, Will returned to her line of reasoning. "If we can build an identify for this guy we might be able to figure out what killing him means and that, in turn, might lead us to the killer."

"Right. And then he won't have died in vain or anonymously, which is probably even sadder."

"I hope not," said Will, "but that might depend on how good we are, or how lucky." They were on their sixth interview of the day, six fishing resorts crossed off Sylvie's list.

Under the klingaling of a bell, he pushed through the screen door fronting the large log cabin at the Four Pines resort. They stepped into a carpeted waiting room with a bar counter and an antique cash register and admired the stuffed, glassy-eyed ten point stag mounted on the wall behind the brass cash register with its elegant high curve down to the cash drawer. Still chewing a bite of his lunch sandwich, the resort owner came through the curtains screening the entranceway to a back room. He knew Will and after introduction to Sylvie, they spent five minutes or so talking about the fishing conditions of the past week. After the social demands of civil conversation had been met and dispensed with, he looked closely at the photo on the flyer, eager to help.

He pulled at the whiskers of his beard and said, "Ya know, I'm sorry, Will. I can't help you with this one there. I just don't recognize him, don't ya know."

"Quite all right Dave, but thanks for trying. We'll head next door and let you get back to your sandwich. Someone is bound to recognize this guy. It just takes time."

Dave saw them to the door and the bell tinkled again as he opened it ahead of them.

At the twelfth resort, Whispering Pines, the dock boy, up from Bemidji to work the approaching Labor Day weekend before he had to return to St. Cloud State and the Fall semester, pointed to the photo and said "Yep. He was here like earlier in the summer. Like with two other guys, I think, to fish the walleye opener. They were booked into the lodge for the weekend and only took the boat out once, which was very strange, don't ya think?" Will thought it was very strange indeed but made no comment. He did not want to interfere with the young man's roll.

"No, I didn't see them go out; they were gone at first light before I opened the fish cleaning shack." He pointed to the photo again. "He wasn't with the two guys who came back when I landed and tied up the boat. I just assumed he stayed in his room while the other two putzed around. They weren't fishermen, don't ya know," he added, disdainfully. "No offense to those two. And if I recall, they were back like before ten. Very polite fellows, I might add, despite the fact that, ya know, they were green."

This observation interested Will so he asked, "What makes you say that?

He grinned. "Oh, just the fact that all their equipment, rods, reels, clothes, boots, everything on them or with them in the boat was new as a baby loon." Will complimented him on his astute observations.

"What made you remember our man in the flyer?" Sylvie asked the young man, who puffed up now like a tom turkey in front of a hen. Not too far past his twenty-first year, her beauty forced him into an embarrassed stammer. There were plenty of pretty girls at SCSU but none of them were in this woman's league. She was pretty enough to be a movie star.

He gulped and tried again after another false start. "It's just that we don't get many Indians, I mean Native Americans, staying at the resort," he explained, correcting himself as he remembered the lessons from his required university class on Diversity in the Americas. "They either live up here on the res or work at the casinos. We don't see them much at all like on vacation or staying at the resorts."

Will nodded. "Did you notice anything else about him?"

Darrel Sanderson shook his head after giving the question some serious thought. He played with the earring in his right ear. "Ya, you betchya. He spoke English better than me." He grinned and shuffled his tanned feet in his flip-flops.

"Thanks, Darrel. You've been a real help. And if I don't see you again before you head back for school, have a good senior year."

"Thanks, Professor. I sure will." He remembered to tip his baseball cap to the lady. From the fish cleaning shack he watched them walk all the way down the hill to the log building that served as the lodge and residence for the resort owners. He let go a low whistle as he turned and got back to the job of filleting and cleaning the three walleyes sliding and flopping in his sink. He hoped she had not minded the fish smells emanating from his hands.

"For a minute there I thought he was actually going to drool on himself," Will said to Sylvie as they walked the narrow paved path down the hill.

"I thought he was really quite handsome and certainly charming," Sylvie teased. "And he seemed very eager to please. I admire that quality in a man."

"It certainly is an admirable quality in a man and I'm certain that in another five years or so he might actually become one," Will said, and gallantly held the door for her as they entered the Whispering Pines lodge.

Jean Berghammer sat in one of the lodge's overstuffed brown leather chairs, using the lull in her day to catch up on her reading. She put the magazine down when she saw Will and with some difficulty through the knees, pulled herself up out of the chair to greet him. Close to retirement now from her high school teaching duties back in New Hampton, Iowa, she too would be leaving in a day or two and turn the resort over to her husband Don. After the introductions, and the questions about Don's back— he was almost recovered from his fall from the roof of Cabin #7—she waved them into the sitting room of the lodge and served them Diet Cokes before she left to get her records from the office in back.

Up on the hill above the lodge they could hear the distinctive purrr-purrr and idle of a chainsaw as Don cleared his camping spaces of underbrush and dead tree limbs. Jean returned with a cardboard box full of filed receipts, limping a bit from the exertion and the rheumatism in her bad leg, an old volleyball injury from her years as a varsity player in college. She sat down, put her glasses on, and with apologies rubbed the swollen knee below her shorts for a minute before she fingered through the tops of the receipts in the file. She found the one she was looking for, pulled it and examined it over the top of her glasses, and handed it to Will. "There you are. I think that's the one you need."

Will thanked her and Sylvie pulled her chair closer, reading over Will's shoulder. "An Illinois plate," he remarked. "And a rented car at that." As he read he spoke aloud all three names listed on the receipt. "Mike Black. David Campbell. Steve Johnson. Not very imaginative." He handed the list to Sylvie and showed Jean the photograph.

She reset her bifocals and studied it with the concentration of a teacher trying to decipher a handwritten assignment. She looked across the top of the photograph and said to Will and Sylvie, "That would be Mr. Johnson."

Will smiled and thought better of asking her if she were certain. "Did you notice anything unusual about him?"

"Other than the fact he was a Native American?"

Will nodded.

"I got the sense that he didn't want to be here."

Sylvie had no doubt that Jean Berghammer knew full well when a person did not want to be somewhere.

"That doesn't surprise me in the least," Will said.

"If you don't mind my asking, why would that be, Professor?"

"How many Native Americans do you know with the last name Johnson?"

With one hand Jean Berghammer covered a nervous giggle like a freshman in high school caught with a love note. "I didn't even think of that," she confessed, smiling at him with admiration. Will stood and thanked her for her time and the Diet Cokes and promised that he would call Don toward the end of the season after the tourists had all gone back to work and the two of them would do some serious walleye fishing. Sylvie asked politely to use the bathroom—the caffeine in the Diet Coke had gone right through her and Jean showed her the facilities. As he waited, Jean beamed.

"What?" he asked, feigning exasperation.

"That one's a keeper, Will. A smart man like you shouldn't let her get away, if you know what I mean?"

Will kissed her on the cheek, thanked her for caring and was saved as Sylvie came back into the room. On the way out of the lodge he said to Sylvie, "Just between you and me, Jean said I should keep you."

At the car she paused for a moment and said, "I don't know if I like the thought of being a kept woman."

They drove the road back to Will's cabin, taking their time, no traffic to slow them. "You're right. Probably wouldn't be such a good idea."

"And why is that?" she challenged.

"Oh, I don't think I could afford you for more than a month or two."

She grinned and asked, "Do you know where that dirt road goes?" She pointed ahead to an old logging track that wound back into the woods. He slowed and stopped. "Back to a little lake that only the locals know about."

"Got a blanket?" she asked.

"In back for emergencies," he said.

She opened the top button of her blouse. "This is an emergency!"

Chapter Sixteen

Catching a Break

The east wind shoved the once placid lake into rolling waves that rocked the few intrepid boats still out fishing, braving a wind that tugged and pulled their anchor lines taut. As the wind picked up it blew the tops off the waves like foam off the top of a German lager, Roland observed. The big red Lund handled the turmoil but the ride was wet and unpleasant. Water sprayed every time the nose of the boat slapped the water. Sylvie did not seem to mind the intermittent dousing so much as Roland, who had hunkered down behind the protection of the windshield in an effort to save what remained of his carefully coiffed and perfectly arranged curls, steadfastly and stubbornly refusing to wear a hat while underway. Will smiled at the futility, taking glee in his uncle's distress, but it was his own fault. Once again he had offered Roland a hat, which he once again declined out of vanity, and now was victim of the ravages of the wind blowing out his curls. "Not much farther now," Will shouted above the howl of the water and wind.

Once in the leeward protection of the island they were making for, he opened up the throttle a bit and scooted the Lund into the protected waters behind Sugarbush. The trees on the island sifted and blocked the wind, calming the waters in the natural bay. He found the location he was looking for and hit the kill switch for the outboard, trimmed the motor to keep the prop out of the weeds, and opened the compartment that ran along the gunnels where he stored his rods. Roland studied his reflection in the windshield, obviously disgusted with the mess on his head and after trying to comb his hair back into place with his fingers, sighed and gave up. Will handed him a hat and a baitcaster. "Familiar with one of these?"

Roland nodded. "Your father and I used to fish quite a bit in Germany but we used mostly spinning reels. I have used this type of set-up one or twice but I would appreciate it if you would talk me through it so I don't hurt myself."

Will appreciated this aspect of his uncle's character. For all the man's competencies in so many different areas, he was not afraid to admit what he did not know.

"This is the thumb bar," Will said, pushing the bar on the black Abu Garcia baitcaster. "It allows the line to spool out." He released his thumb from the line and sure enough, the spinnerbait hanging from the monofilament at the end of the rod dropped slowly to the deck. He turned the handle and the reel clicked as it engaged, winding the line back up onto the spool, stopping about four inches before the white spinnerbait hit the last ceramic guide on the graphite rod. "Try it once." He handed the rod over.

"Got it," Roland said.

As Roland worked with the reel, Will showed him the star drag. "Crank this forward to increase the drag. Now try to pull the line from the reel. If you have it properly adjusted, it should pull slowly off the reel under steady pressure. Perfect. That black knob on the right side of the reel sets the magnets that control the speed at which the line comes off the spool. Tighten it and hit the thumb bar." This time the bait did not drop at all. "Okay. Loosen it and try it again. Right. Now we have this rod adjusted for you and the weight of the oversized spinnerbait. After you click the thumb bar, transfer your thumb directly to the spool so it doesn't unwind until you cast forward. As the weight of the cast pulls the line off the reel, ease up on the pressure with your thumb, but don't take it off completely until after the bait hits the water. Watch."

Will took the rod, clicked the thumb bar and turned the rig sideways. He bent his arm at the elbow so that the rod pointed back over his shoulder, then snapped the rod forward in a smooth continuous motion. The reel sang as the oversized white spinnerbait flew the line out toward the water. Just before it hit the surface, Will feathered the pressure of his thumb on the line and stopped the spinning spool. The perfect cast flopped the big bait into the water with a flutter and hardly a splash. The instant it landed, Will switched the rod to his left hand, clicked the handle and smoothly retrieved the bait through the water. The big nickel-plated Colorado blade rotated and pulsed through the water. At the boat, Will brought it up, shook it to dislodge a piece of milfoil, and then handed the rod to Roland.

"You make it look so easy," Sylvie observed.

"Ten thousand casts," Will said, watching his uncle concentrate on the task at hand. Roland clicked the reel, turned it one quarter to the side as instructed, brought the rod up and launched the bait. It slammed into the water just three feet from the boat, sending a geyser of water into the air. Sylvie broke out into startled laughter, unable to contain herself, but Roland was entirely nonplussed, his concentration unwavering.

"Too much thumb pressure on the line," Will suggested.

Roland nodded. His next cast arced out over the water and landed with a measured splash. Roland smirked at Sylvie as he retrieved the lure. "What are we fishing for today?" he asked.

"We're fishing for smallmouth bass, or smallies, as the locals say, and northern, of course." Will explained. "Holler if you need anything. If you feel the strike, and believe me, you will, set the hook and don't be shy. Cross his eyes."

Roland was already preparing for his next cast. Will moved forward and set the foot-controlled trolling motor into the water, then coached Sylvie into a competent cast or two. After the third, she pushed him away.

"Go drive the boat. I can handle this."

He grinned and obeyed and picked up his own rig baited with a chartreuse rattle trap as he positioned the boat for optimum downwind casting. He kept an eye on Roland aft and Sylvie fore, letting them work through their mistakes as they got the feel of the rods and the reels.

Sylvie made a particularly good cast, setting the bait down just short of the submerged weed line and looked back to see if Roland had noticed. He ignored her with a purpose, watching the run of the white spinnerbait coursing just below the surface of the water, ticking through the tops of the weeds. Sylvie turned back to her line and just as she was about to lift the bait out of the water, a medium-sized northern, locked onto the cavitating pulse of the blade, shot up from the bottom of the lake like a torpedo and slashed at the bait. Sylvie saw the gaping maw open and the razor sharp teeth strike the bait with such speed and ferocity that she recoiled, falling backward. This effectively set the hook on the eight pound pike even as she collapsed with a little scream and landed flat on her butt. This time Will and Roland had to laugh out loud. But she scrambled to her feet, never once taking her eyes off the fish or releasing the rod. As he watched her rod bend and the fish strip line off against the pressure of the drag, Will quickly reeled in his own line, set the trolling motor to slow reverse, and moved next to Sylvie.

"That's a good fish you've got on. Keep the rod tip up and let him run. Soon as he stops, reel him in but don't reel against the drag. Let your equipment do the work."

After the fish stopped his run, Sylvie reeled hard as she could.

"Not so fast," Will cautioned. "You don't want to horse him and possibly break the line."

This slowed her down. In all the excitement she was breathing heavily, determined to boat her catch. Roland moved forward to get a better look. Suddenly the line went slack and thinking that the fish had broken the line, a look of complete and utter disappointment flooded her face like a flush. An instant later the big green pike launched itself out of the water and into the air, shaking its head and twisting its sinuous body. They could hear the rattle of the blade against the body of the spinnerbait as the northern tried to throw the lure. It slapped into the water and took off, stripping more line from the reel, bending the rod with such force that Sylvie needed both hands on the cork handle to hold on. Sylvie was fierce now, every muscle in her arms and back taut as she fought against the strength and pull of the diving fish.

Will reached over and loosed the drag a touch. "Let him run, but then crank him back in steadily. Let him know who's boss."

This time she got him to the boat and the fish rested there in all his magnificent green length, now swimming slowly against the pressure of the line.

Sylvie relaxed and at that instant the northern took off again, almost pulling her over the side, had it not been for Will grabbing the top of her shorts from behind so she could steady herself.

She cursed in German and said, "Now it's getting personal." She caught up with the fish and gradually brought him back alongside the boat.

"That should be his last run," Will told her. "Now what are you going to do?"

"Don't look at me," Roland said. "I saw the teeth on that thing. If you want, I'll shoot it between the eyes."

Will grinned. "I don't think that will be necessary. Keep your rod tip up, Sylvie, and I'll get him for you." He leaned over the side of the boat, wet his hand and studied the fish. With a quickness of hand that surprised both Roland and Sylvie, Will grabbed the northern behind the head, thumb on one gill plate, fingers on the other, and lifted the eight-pounder out of the water and into the center of the boat, water streaming from his jade colored flanks. "Don't ever try this at home," he said grinning with satisfaction, "unless you are a highly trained professional. Please hand me those pliers, Roland." Will took the tool and levered the point of the hook out of the fish's armored mouth, careful to avoid the slashing teeth.

Sylvie stared as Will handled the fish. "The head on this *Hecht* looks just like a dog."

Roland nodded his agreement. "*Wir sagen auch Wasserwolf,*" he said in German. "We also call him the water wolf, an apt description."

Will let Sylvie touch the fish's flank. "He's slimy," she said, surprised.

"It's part of his protective coating and gives him that distinctive smell. Let's get him into the live well. You just caught our dinner for tonight." Sylvie seemed none too sure about that prospect.

"How big do you think he is, Will?" Roland asked.

Will measured the fish. "Just a touch over thirty inches and that calculates to about seven or eight pounds. He definitely has some girth." He showed Sylvie how to safely hold the fish with her left hand around the tail, using her right hand to support the fish from underneath. He took her picture with her cell phone and showed her the shots for her approval. He took the pike from her before he angled the fish into the live well, tail fin first, and started the aerator. He washed his hands over the side and dried them on a towel and threw it Sylvie. "Nice catch, Sylvie, but you don't have to fall down to set the hook."

"He startled me," she explained, with just the hint of a pout as she wiped the water from the elegant fingers of her hands. "I've never seen anything like it—that fish came at me mouth open, teeth flashing—and the ferocity with which he hit that bait is what forced me back."

Will grinned and watched Roland move back to his spot in the rear of the boat, ready to resume casting. As Sylvie retook her position, he said to her, "Just wait until you catch a big one." Sylvie looked back to see if he was kidding. He was not.

They fished another hour and caught seven northern and four smallies. Sylvie and Roland caught two each and Will boated three; Sylvie and Roland each caught their first smallmouth bass off the rocks edging the bay at Sugarbush. All northern were released but one and they kept the two smallies measuring over 15 inches. After the action died down, Will nosed the boat next to the wooden dock below a cabin that had been built before the park service had taken control of the land and placed a moratorium on private ownership and any future development. The cabin, deeded to the national park by its former owners, was maintained for campers and could be had by reservation, but it too was slated to be torn down, dock and all, letting the spot revert to its natural state. The cabin sat on a slope east of the dock about one hundred yards back from the water. It was unoccupied. The summer season was quickly coming to a close with the Labor Day weekend signifying the unofficial transition from summer season into fall, which would afford most of the resort owners a welcome respite, already preparing to busy themselves with make, mend, and repair of cabins and rental boats, and maintenance of grounds.

Now that most of the summer vacationers were gone, the three detectives had the vacated lake largely to themselves. Will tied up, set the cooler on the dock, threw out cushions for seats, and they took a break from the fishing. Sylvie handed out sandwiches and Roland opened the beer bottles. In the distance across the sheltered bay, they spotted a pair of juvenile eagles not yet bald on top but nearing the second year of their maturity, judging from their size. As they admired and commented on his noble bearing and majestic posture high up in his pine tree, the one nearest to them regally leaned forward, lifted his tail feathers and ejected a gout of liquid past his perch through the branches and into the lake twenty meters below. They could hear the impact all the way across the bay.

"*Mein lieber Gott*! Did you see that?" Sylvie exclaimed, laughing behind her embarrassment.

"That has to be the most impressive shit I've ever seen a bird take," Roland observed, deadpan. "I wonder if he had sauerkraut for dinner."

Will choked on a swallow of beer and joined his laughter with Sylvie's. He pointed to an exceptionally large pine ten meters past the house. "That's where his parents used to have their aerie. Two years ago it finally collapsed under its own weight. The nests can weigh well over a ton and are used over and over until the wind drops them out of the tree or they fall of their own accord."

"Where is the new nest?" Sylvie asked. She had seen the nests of protected storks in Bavaria but nothing to rival the size of an old, long-used eagle's nest.

Will pointed with the neck of his beer bottle as Sylvie looked through the compact binoculars. "See the tree he's sitting in?"

She nodded, but this caused her to lose her line of sight. He waited a moment until she found the tree where the young eagle sat, unperturbed at being observed. "Now look over one tree to your right."

Sylvie shouted excitedly, "I see it! It's bigger than a Volkswagen—and there's another eaglet sitting in it. He's the one making all the noise."

Roland pulled at the cord dangling from the binoculars and Sylvie reluctantly passed them over.

"That's young Alfred. He's the twin of Eddie, but he's a smaller bird. He's squawking because wants mom to come feed him, but she wants him to be more independent like his bigger brother there," Will explained.

Eddie gracefully launched himself from his perch, beat his wings twice to gain altitude and prepared to settle on a large branch about two hundred meters from his little brother. He missed, gaining purchase with only one talon and fell over backward, wings flapping, holding on for dear life with one leg. For a minute or two, he tried to regain his composure, left wing extended for balance as he hung upside down like a bat, making it appear that he had had every intention of hanging there under his branch instead of missing his landing.

Sylvie wrested the binocs back from Roland. "I can't believe what I'm seeing. What in the world is he doing?"

Will chuckled. "If I were to guess, I'd say that like most teenagers, he's still a bit clumsy and he just screwed up his landing. He doesn't know what to do now, but he's likely to get it figured out soon enough."

Two minutes later, Eddie the junior eagle released his hold and fell to earth still upside down. Sylvie gasped just before Eddie opened his wings, caught the air, and in a graceful natural curve, glided above the water. Two more beats of his wings and he was back into flight and joined his brother in the nest, who chided him for his misadventure. Eddie folded his wings and ignored his shrieking brother

"I feel privileged," Sylvie said, taking a deep breath. Few people will ever see such a sight in the wild. I'll never forget this."

"That's exactly why I love it here so much," Will admitted. "The fishing is great but there's so much more to see if you just take the time to look." He sighed deeply.

"What's up?" Roland asked, suspecting that the sigh might have been triggered by something else.

"This damned case has got me stumped," Will admitted.

The admission startled Sylvie. She believed that no case could ever be too difficult for *Professor Doktor* William Russell Sheridan to solve. Roland seemed not the least bit surprised. He opened a pilsner and passed it to

Sylvie. He opened two more, one for Will and one for himself. "I agree. It's a tough one."

"But is it solvable?" Will asked his uncle.

"Not now," Roland said. "Solving a case means different things to different people. It all depends on what you know and how much you know."

"We actually have quite a bit of information now," Will said.

Roland smiled. "Who did it?"

"I don't know."

"What was the motive?" Roland pressed further.

"I don't know, dammit."

"Who was he?"

"I don't know that either."

"Well goddammit, *Herr Professor Doktor Sheridan*, FBI and Interpol consultant and master criminalist, what exactly do you know?"

Will thought for minute, enjoying the repartee with his uncle and seeing the wisdom and guidance in the questions. "I know that Sylvie is quite frankly one of the most beautiful women I've ever met."

She blushed to her ears.

"Although indisputably true," Roland acknowledged, "entirely irrelevant to the case."

Will shrugged his shoulders and took another pull from his beer. "But not to me or to Sylvie. Okay. I know what I don't know."

"Start there. Find out who he was or is. His identity will lead you to a motive. The motive will lead you to the killer or killers. Start with what you don't know and grow the knowledge. Establish a database. That's where Sylvie is invaluable. Combine your analytical skills with her organizational genius and you have a good chance to crack this case. And while I'm thinking about it, don't forget that she's a whiz on the computer—she can find stuff I never knew existed."

She smiled her gratitude at the compliment. "I'll help you in any way I can," she promised.

Will thanked her for the offer and turned to Roland.

"I'll need you to continue your critique of the investigation."

Roland nodded and pursed his lips. "*Das versteht sich von selbst*. That goes without saying. And Will, just so you don't misunderstand me: you've both done fine work on the case so far. I think you are on the right track. In fact, you've gotten further than anyone could have expected, given the circumstances of the case. Don't get discouraged now. Keep this in mind—a case like this usually depends on catching a break. But you have to be prepared to make sense of it, if and when it comes. And if my experience is any guide, it will come. Find out who this guy was and wait for serendipity to make a contribution; then you'll really start to roll. Now that I've had my royal Bavarian say, I need to catch another northern—a big one preferably—to take to the delightful Miss Popelka, who will no doubt be more than generous in expressing her gratitude and appreciation."

To show his, Will put Roland on the fish he needed and Sylvie relaxed and let the men fish as she thought about what Roland had said. What she had misinterpreted as friction between the two men, she now realized was nothing more than their unique and inimitable style of communicating. No pretense, no subterfuge, no disguised motives or intent, nothing but the pure unvarnished truth between them. She wondered if she could ever be so honest with another human being in her relationships.

Chapter Seventeen

Gray Wolf

Dinner the next evening was a combined international effort and, by any measure, simply excellent. Roland started them with a beef broth consommé with Bavarian potato dumplings bobbing in the homemade soup. Sylvie volunteered for salad duty and worked as sous chef while Will sautéed the breaded pork cutlets, hammered thin and served with lemon slices. He tapped into his precious stores of wild rice harvested on the shores of Leech Lake in Minnesota. He carefully measured in a portion and combined it with white rice to stretch it. For dessert, he gave them fresh blueberries and apricots over vanilla ice cream. They drank a slightly sweet sauvignon blanc from California's Central Coast and then another as they laughed and told stories at the table. The dinner and dessert stretched to almost two hours.

After dinner, Sylvie prepared the dishes for the dishwasher since the men had done the majority of the cooking. She was impressed with their culinary talents, although she had not said anything to either one. Will and Roland were at the liquor cabinet that stood in the living room and were indulging themselves in the luxury of deciding between Scotch and Canadian whiskies. They settled on an old favorite of Roland's, Crown Royal, a Canadian whisky he had often shared with Will's father.

When Sylvie joined them in the living room, they had one down already, hers waiting atop a coaster on the oversized glass coffee table edged with burnished nickel. They had just poured refills when the doorbell chimed. Will looked to Roland. In the German fashion they had eaten later in the evening and were not expecting anyone. Roland shook his head. Lili was in Moose Lake visiting a relative suddenly taken ill over the weekend. Sylvie sipped her drink and smiled as the door chimed again.

"One of you will have to answer the door if you want to find out who it is," she said, inviting one or the other to the door with her eyes.

"You're closer," Will pointed out and reached for a pillow. "Besides, I'm afraid to answer the door after eight o'clock up here in the North Woods."

She bumped him with a hip on her way past.

"That was deliberate. She didn't even say excuse me," Roland noted. "This is an excellent whisky." He savored another sip and watched Sylvie at the door as she smoothed the sides of her white shorts with her palms, buttoned one button of her black blouse up over the lace of her black bra, turned on the porch light and opened the massive oak door. She stood so that most of her body was shielded by the heavy beams of the opened door, a habit of safety approved by Roland.

The man standing in the circle of light looked her over carefully and took a deep breath. He did not speak but readjusted the tie of his white shirt under a black suit. Sylvie waited patiently until she realized the man in the night at the door did not speak because he was giving her time to look him over. She finished her visual assessment, noting the man's clean and well-pressed black suit, tailored to hide his ample belly. The calm in his brown eyes put her at ease. His black hair was combed back off his forehead and pulled into a pony tail longer than any she had ever seen on a man.

"Good evening," she said, and before he could speak opened the door to admit him. "Won't you come in?" she invited the man.

"Thank you very much, Miss. Very kind of you to welcome a stranger in from the night." He stood in the foyer and waited as she closed the door behind him. "My name is Henry Gray Wolf. I've come to see Professor Sheridan about this man," he said, pointing to the poster in his hand. It was their John Doe.

Sylvie nodded. "I'm sure he will be interested in speaking with you. Please come in and sit down." She escorted him to the living room where Will and Roland stood waiting.

Henry Gray Wolf carefully walked into the room and shook hands with both men, repeating his name as they said theirs. Will indicated a comfortable leather club chair for the man and they waited as he thanked them, unbuttoned his suit coat, and they smiled when he patted his belly and said he was getting much too fat to wear such a fine suit.

"May we offer you something to drink, Mr. Gray Wolf?" Sylvie asked.

Again, the man did not speak, as if he were contemplating a variety of suitable answers, calculating the effect of each, sorting through a myriad of possible replies before he finally settled on one.

"Please call me Henry. Everyone does. And if it wouldn't be too much trouble, I wouldn't mind a sip of that Crown Royal."

"Not at all," Will said, opening the glass door of the high-standing liquor cabinet and taking down a fresh shot glass. "Do you take ice or water, or perhaps a glass of soda on the side?"

Henry Gray Wolf pondered the question. He looked at Roland, who had taken the second leather chair, this one a recliner, his feet in white socks against the black upraised bolster. Will and Sylvie were both in bare feet.

"I'm sorry," he apologized. "Should I take off my shoes?"

"You should make yourself comfortable," Will suggested.

"I do hate these things," Henry Gray Wolf admitted, as he shifted forward over his belly with an inadvertent grunt, and pulled at the laces of his black wingtips. "Give me my moccasins any day." Now shoeless and in black socks, he sat back and said with a small smile, "I prefer it the same way you are having yours."

Will poured four more shots and offered the drinks with a toast. "To comfortable shoes."

This seemed to please Henry Gray Wolf immensely. He drank the jigger of whisky down all at once and looked on with approval as Will poured his empty glass full of the amber and gold liquid.

"Canadians do know how to make a decent whisky," he observed, relishing the smell of caramel in the glass. The heat of the alcohol made him sweat a bit and he searched his back pocket for a handkerchief to pat dry his forehead and upper lip.

"Why don't you let me have your coat?" Sylvie suggested, and he shouldered out of it immediately, handing it to her with relief.

"Much better," he said, this time taking a sip instead of a gulp. "I can't help but notice your accents," he said to Roland, and then Sylvie as she returned from the hall closet.

"Sylvie and my uncle are visiting from Germany. Both are investigators in the Bavarian State Criminal Police force."

Henry Gray Wolf considered that item of information. He did not speak or acknowledge the statement and it occurred to them that he already knew, so no acknowledgment was necessary.

"I am Ojibwe," he said as a simple matter of fact and watched for their reaction. He was beginning to relax in the company of the three detectives.

"I have had a long and abiding interest in indigenous American cultures," Roland said. "As a very young man learning to read and speak English, I was fascinated with stories of the American West. In fact, Will's father taught me quite a bit about native cultures. I find it fascinating that in my culture as well as yours, native tribes played such an important role in the development of both countries. Will and I are both descended from a Germanic tribe called the *Bavari*, which settled in south Germany more than 1500 years ago."

"And the pretty young woman?" Gray Wolf asked.

"She's from a tribe called the Blondes," Will interjected and everyone laughed politely, except Sylvie.

"To be correct," she informed them, "my ancestors are traced back to the north Saxons."

Henry Gray Wolf listened intently. "I had not known this. I would like to hear more about the Bavari and the Saxons, but I know that it is late and I have come to your home unannounced. I thank you for welcoming me and for the drink, but most of all for making me feel comfortable." The little speech had made him sweat again and he took the time to dab at the perspiration and take another short sip.

"Not at all, Chief Gray Wolf. You will always be welcome in my house," Will said.

Again Henry Gray Wolf said nothing, but he was pleased that Will had figured it out. A chief, after all, need not announce himself.

Roland looked puzzled. "I have to admit that I am not familiar with the Ojibwe. About all I can remember from my reading is that they belong to the Algonquian linguistic family. I was led to believe that this part of the country was at one time populated by the Chippewa."

The chief smiled into the rounds of his ochre cheeks. "The history of my people, unfortunately, is most often written by those who have conquered them."

Roland laughed out loud. "That certainly is the case if you watch most American movies about World War II.

One would think that the Germans never won a battle. In fact, if you look at today's modern fighting forces, you'll see that most modern tactics and equipment are based on the German model."

"As the son of a German mother and an American father, I find myself forced to take both sides," Will interjected.

The chief nodded. He knew what it was like to walk softly between two cultures. He cleared his throat. "What causes me the most aggravation is the false information perpetuated about our cultures. If you will permit me, Roland, to add to your knowledge of my people."

"By all means," Roland said, filling glasses all around.

"There are about two hundred thousand Ojibwe living in the U.S. and Canada. The name Ojibwe was corrupted by the whites into Chippewa and this is the name still used by tribal organizations recognized by the U.S. government."

"Aha," Roland said, "that explains why I have seen the name Chippewa in my reference books and not Ojibwe."

"Yes, said Chief Henry Gray Wolf. He pointed to his toes. The word *Ojibwe* is said to refer to the puckered toes of the moccasins we wear."

"I would love to have a pair of moccasins someday," Roland said as an aside.

"Next time we're in International Falls I'll pick you up a pair," Will promised. "Chief, you were telling us about the proper name of your people..."

Henry Gray Wolf finished his drink and said, "Just between the four of us, most Ojibwe today prefer to be known as the Anishinaabe, which translates roughly as the first or original people."

"That's interesting," Sylvie said, "because the British and Americans call us Germans, but in our native language we call ourselves *Deutsch*, although I have no idea why that is."

"Perfect example," said the chief, admiring the young woman. He thought how much more beautiful she would be with a little color on her skin. In his dream, she had been darker. She was the primary reason he had come.

Will took the opportunity to explain. "It's as the Chief noted: the conquerors impose their language and their terminology. The Romans called that part of Europe Germania—hence, Germany. The French use *Allemagne* which, by the way, is taken from the tribal name of the *Alemanni*. Our tribe, as Roland mentioned earlier, is the *Bavari*. They originally settled in the southern Alpine region of Germany now called Bavaria. In Old High German, the word *Deutsch* is derived from *diutisc*, which refers to the language of the people. It was used to describe the tribal language of the indigenous people there to differentiate it from the Latin spoken by the Romans."

"I did not know that," the chief said, and with genuine interest asked, "Were there other tribes that settled in the land of the *Deutsch*?"

Sylvie smiled. "We do call Germany *Deutschland*."

The Chief smiled back and loosened his tie. The whisky was making him hot again.

"The *Alemanni*, the *Bavari*, the *Franks*, the *Visigoths*, the *Ostrogoths*, the *Angles*, and the *Saxons* were the main tribes. The *Franks* migrated westerly and established what is known in German as *Frankreich*, the kingdom of the *Franks* in France. The *Ostrogoths* established themselves in a region called *Oesterreich*, the eastern kingdom and the German word for Austria. The *Angles* and the *Saxons* migrated north to Scandinavia and then on to England. In early English, the land of the *Angles* is called *Engla-land*. There is a region in England still called Anglia and to this day the French call England *Angleterre*, the land of the *Angles*."

"I didn't know that," Roland said. "You continue to impress."

"Language is a semiotic system and I had to study the origin and history of language as part of my semiotic studies," Will explained.

After the little lesson on Germany, they all paused to consider the similarities between their tribes, languages, and cultures, until Gray Wolf took the opportunity to revisit the reason for his arrival.

"I am the executive director of the White Bear casino in Ely. I believe this man worked for us as a dealer," he said, indicating the picture on the poster lying on the coffee table between them. The reason for Henry Gray Wolf's visit now apparent, Sylvie and the two men sat forward, their full attention focused on their visitor.

"Who is he?" Will asked.

Henry Gray Wolf patted his pockets, searched through them and looked at Sylvie with a silent apology.

"I'll get your coat," she offered. She returned with it and he thanked her, pulled an envelope from the inside breast pocket and gave the coat back. He waited for her to rehang it in the foyer closet and retake her seat. Only then did he open the envelope and remove a photo, which he passed, along with the poster, over to Will.

"His name is Randolph A. Baxter."

Will handed the photo and, for comparison, the brochure to Roland. He studied both and passed them on to Sylvie. Roland noted, "Not exactly a name one would expect."

Henry Gray Wolf, thinking about his own name, his father's name, his grandfather's name, and the name of Randolph A. Baxter, explained that Native Americans often had two names, one given at birth or a name they had earned, or as it seemed in this case, a name they adopted to make movement through the culture of the whites easier.

"He worked as a dealer in your casino..." Will reminded him.

Henry Gray Wolf acknowledged the reminder but did not speak.

Roland used the silence to ask a question. "Does he have any family among the Anishinaabe?

"Most likely he does not," the Chief replied.

"How do you know this?" Will asked directly.

"For employment purposes he listed his tribal affiliation as a Canadian Ojibwe. But I know this is a lie of convenience. He is not of my people."

"You believe he is not Native American," Sylvie said gently.

He smiled at her, appreciating the radiance of her natural fresh beauty. He reminded her of the dawn on a spring morning during the first warm days of the ice-out. Her skin was the color of the morning fog as the sun reflected off the top of the mist covering the lake. Seeing her again gave him peace of mind. "I believe he is not Anishinaabe."

"Given your knowledge of the Anishinaabe and Native American culture, what tribe do you think he belongs to?" Will asked and sat back, expecting Henry Gray Wolf to take his time as he worked his way up to an answer.

Gray Wolf liked the way this man asked questions so he smiled at Roland, certain that this was where he had learned how to pose his investigative questions.

The two men's eyes locked for a moment in mutual respect and understanding and Roland said, "He has always been a good student, but he has already surpassed me."

Henry Gray Wolf nodded, understanding the importance of teaching the old ways to new minds. "Meskwaki."

Roland pursed his lips, mulling over the name and saying it out loud, trying it on his tongue like a drink of new whisky. "I do not know the Meskwaki either," he admitted, with a touch of embarrassment.

Will said, "You might know them as the Sac and the Fox, an Iowa tribe just south of Minnesota, now near Tama, Iowa. They have the distinction of being one of the first tribes in the U.S. who bought back land from the government and established themselves as an independent people. If I remember correctly they also have a casino in Tama."

Henry Gray Wolf acknowledged that he was correct.

Sylvie returned from the kitchen with a plate of roast beef sandwiches, paper plates, and napkins. The chief accepted the offer of a sandwich and as they paused to eat, Will picked up the thread of the conversation.

"Chief Gray Wolf, if you don't mind my asking, do you have a personal interest in this case?" Will emphasized the word personal.

The chief brushed a crumb of bread from his tie depicting a wolf peering from behind the protection of a stand of birch trees.

"As the chief, of course I am interested in and am responsible for the welfare of all my people. But I have to tell you that although Randolph A. Baxter was a Native American and worked for us at the casino, remember that he was not Anishinaabe."

Will excused himself for a moment, went into his office and returned with his case notebook in which he wrote an entry. Will looked up from his notebook. "Weren't the Anishinaabe and the Meskwaki traditional enemies?"

Chief Gray Wolf looked at Roland. "Your nephew has learned a great deal. Two hundred years ago, perhaps; now we are competitors for gambling dollars and nothing more."

Will nodded. "There is another reason then for your interest."

The chief scooted forward in the club chair, placed his sandwich plate on the coffee table and folded his napkin. "Among my people," he explained, we have a medicine society concerned with the physical and spiritual well-being of our tribe. To become a practitioner requires years of dedicated study, like a Ph. D. After I graduated from St. Cloud State, I was accepted to medical school at the University of Minnesota. Although I graduated with an M.D., I did not accept an internship. Instead, I became an initiate into the medical society of the Anishinaabe. In the old days there were eight degrees of training, but these now have been combined into four levels of achievement. During my study, I had to master the herbal knowledge and spiritual insights of our tribal elders. Fasting and a vision quest are part of the preparation and training. Although I have mastered all four levels, I continue my study as I attempt to integrate the best parts of Western medicine with the teachings of my forefathers."

"The philosophy of our medicine society stresses the balance between our personal life and other forms. We respect life with the goal of achieving harmony within the social order. The disappearance of Randolph A. Baxter has disturbed that harmony. When I learned that his body had been found here at Kabetogama, I fasted and set out on a vision quest. In my dream walk, I encountered a white spirit guide, a goddess dressed entirely in white deer skins and white moccasins. When I tried to speak with her, I could not understand her language. She turned and motioned for me to follow her. That is why I am here," he said with the deep humility and conviction of a man who has studied long and hard, and believes completely in what he has learned. He turned to look at Sylvie, who sat mouth agape in complete and utter amazement. Chief Henry Gray Wolf sat back in his warm leather chair and smiled to himself with the satisfaction of knowing that she too had seen him in her dreams.

Will looked to Sylvie, then Chief Gray Wolf, and nodded his head. Sometimes the universe was not so easily understood and mysticism crowded up against science. There was still much work to be done. He picked up the photo again for emphasis. "For the sake of argument, let us accept that this man is Randolph A. Baxter, a Meskwaki tribal member working in an Anishinaabe casino. This is slightly unusual but not outside the realm of possibility. Why do you believe that Baxter and the man in this photo are one and the same?" Will asked Henry Gray Wolf.

"I sit on the Inter-Tribal Council. The Sac and Fox of the Mississippi, as the U.S. government calls the Meskwaki, also has a representative. Every now and then we send each other extra help if one tribe needs it and we can spare the manpower. It's usually done as a favor and it's usually on a temporary basis. We need to keep our trained people. The Meskwaki rep asked me one day if I could take a man."

Roland interjected. "This was unusual."

Gray Wolf nodded. "Their rep said he would consider it a favor to the Meskwaki nation. At the time, I didn't need extra help, but in light of the request, I accepted."

"Why did you say yes?" Will inquired, despite what Gray Wolf had just told them.

The question made Chief Henry Gray Wolf uncomfortable as he considered his response, but he was not offended. He understood the need for the question. He also knew that the professor had an excellent reputation among the Anishinaabe and was known among them as a fine hunter and fisherman. More importantly, he was known to respect the land, walking lightly as if in moccasins. Nevertheless, the question disturbed him. He was not used to disclosing his motivations, especially to people whom he did not know, and certainly not to whites. He looked again to Sylvie and knew that he must answer. "At the time I thought the young man had gotten himself into some kind of trouble with Federal authorities and that he was perhaps the son of an important Meskwaki tribal member. I said yes on that basis."

Sylvie asked, "Did you have any specific information that Mr. Baxter was in trouble?"

"No," Gray Wolf said, "it was merely a guess."

"It makes sense," Roland observed. "A young man gets in trouble with the law or something happens that causes problems within the tribe and the best thing for the young man is to relocate until the dust settles, I think you say. By sending him north to you they solve their problem and yet are able to keep an eye on him."

For the first time that evening Henry Gray Wolf allowed himself the rarity of sharing a smile.

Will, observing the interpersonal dynamics of the interaction, cleared his throat gently to speak. "I think I understand now why you are troubled. A favor becomes an obligation and you might have felt responsible to the Meskwaki people when Baxter suddenly and unexpectedly disappeared."

Henry Gray Wolf finished the last of his whisky and did not speak. The Professor had an uncanny ability to say what others feared but needed to hear. It would be an honor to sit on the Council with him, although he was certain that it would be distinctly uncomfortable from time to time. He was most assuredly a truth-talker.

Will turned his attention from the chief to his uncle. "There is a problem, dear Roland, if you will permit me."

The *Erster Hauptkommissar* indicated that Will should continue. "I will always yield in the face of greater knowledge."

"Since when?" Sylvie asked sardonically.

Chief Gray Wolf almost grinned at the effrontery. The white female had a razor sharp edge of intelligence that lay beneath the surface of her beauty. For her, beauty was the scabbard that covers and protects but does not hide the knife. He waited patiently for the professor to make his point, appreciating all the while the deference the younger man paid his uncle.

"And I will always yield to greater experience," Will said. "Now where was I...?" he asked, forgetting his train of thought.

Sylvie reoriented him. "You found a problem in Roland's thinking."

"Not in the reasoning: it makes logical sense but only under one condition." He waited for Sylvie's prompt.

"Which is...?"

"The initial premise of Roland's logical argument must be true for his conclusion to be true. Since we don't know if the initial premise is true, that is, why the young man came to the Anishinaabe, then we can't assume the conclusion is true or correct."

Roland nodded. "I see exactly what you mean."

Gray Wolf was again troubled. He had not considered the possibility that his own assumptions were incorrect. It had all made sense at the time. He again waited for his host to speak.

"With your permission, Chief Gray Wolf, what we must do is discover the reason Randolph A. Baxter came to your casino. If we can discover that first, it may very well help us solve this case." Will did not disclose that they considered the case a murder and not a suicide.

Henry Gray Wolf felt the burden of his obligation lighten somewhat and took a deep breath. "I will do whatever I can to help your investigation. In fact, the tribal council has authorized me to pay you and your team a consultant's fee, in addition to covering your expenses, of course."

"That's very generous of you, Henry, but before I accept your kind offer, I must ask you a personal and private question."

Chief Gray Wolf nodded. He expected the question.

"Do you believe that either the Anishinaabe or the Meskwaki were in any way responsible for his death?"

He shook his head. "I do not. I have asked myself the same question. And this was the reason I did not come to you sooner. I needed time to ask around and assure myself of this truth. I feared the answer. In my heart I am convinced now that he was not killed by a member of either tribe."

The break in the tension was palpable. "Thank you, Chief, for speaking what you know in your heart to be the truth. But I must caution you—our investigation will seek the objective truth even as you have looked into your heart for the answer."

Henry Gray Wolf understood the implications. "I ask of you only one condition. The Meskwaki are a sovereign nation, as are we. If your investigation implicates a tribal member, we will want to deal with it within the dictates of tribal law, even if we must eventually turn the case over to federal authorities."

"I accept your condition," Will said. "If our investigation points to a tribal member, I expect either the Anishinaabe or Meskwaki to handle the matter. In the meantime, I need Roland to research the Meskwaki while Sylvie and I spend a day or two with you at the casino as we start our investigation."

Chief Henry Gray Wolf stood and thanked his hosts, his relief evident in his face. "I'll meet you at the casino tomorrow and have a representative there for your convenience."

They shook hands in agreement, waited for him to slip back into his uncomfortable wingtips and retie the laces, and then walked him to the foyer. As they waited, Sylvie said how much she admired his tie. "It's a beautiful symbol," she remarked.

He thanked her for the compliment. "You're one of very few who has made the connection, as obvious as it seems." He allowed Sylvie to help him shoulder into his coat and hand him back into the night.

"Well, that was certainly an interesting and unusual experience," Sylvie said.

All agreed. She then went to pack an overnight bag as Will wanted an early start the next morning. Will and Roland spent an hour brainstorming strategy. Roland promised he would have a briefing on the Meskwaki ready for them upon their return from the casino.

"Good job tonight," Roland said to his nephew as they wished each other good sleeping.

"Thanks," Will acknowledged. "I simply remembered who taught me to always check the initial premises leading to a conclusion if they aren't grounded in empirical facts."

Chapter Eighteen

Drugged

Against the chill of the early morning, Sylvie wore a light blue, cashmere V-neck sweater the exact color of her eyes. In sand-washed cotton slacks and black pumps with just a hint of rise in the heel, she presented an understated sexiness that lay just below the surface of her professional demeanor as an investigator. She crossed her arms under her breasts and shivered while she waited for Will to back the Subaru out of the garage. She could have entered the garage through the kitchen and stayed warm, but she wanted the shock of the cool morning air to help her awaken. She had let herself fall into the seductive rhythm of the men—after working on the case, hiking, fishing, or sight-seeing in the early afternoon, fishing again until dark, late dinners, and evenings filled with ribald conversations and stories that talked away most of the darkness. She often found herself snuggling into the warmth below the down comforter of her bed just as the surprising gray light of dawn pushed against the curtains of her bedroom.

This morning Sylvie and Will were up early to the call of appointments. Roland had enlisted Lili Popelka to drive him to the community college in International Falls where they would scan the holdings for information about the Meskwaki in Iowa. As Will reached across the passenger side to open the door for her, she could not remember when she had been happier. Then, in an instant of panic, she realized she had not called Manfred in over a week.

"What's wrong?" Will asked, seeing the frustration in her face. "Forget something?"

She looked at him for a moment while she attacked the seat belt. Locked into place, she decided to tell him the truth. "I haven't called Freddi in over a week," she said, her guilt mixed with a tincture of desperation.

Will knew the fault was largely his. He handed her his cell phone. "Be my guest; call him now if you wish; there's no rush." He turned the engine off. She thanked him for his thoughtful kindness, but Will noticed she needed a minute to look up her boyfriend's number in her address book. "If you want privacy I can step out," he offered.

Sylvie punched in the country code and a long string of numbers, put the phone to her ear, and as the computer processed the numbers she told Will that would not be necessary. "It's ringing," she said for no other purpose than to let him know the call had gone through. Then her attention was suddenly diverted to the *Handi*, as the Germans called the cell phone. In German she said, "Freddi, it's Sylvie. I'm calling from America. Everything is fine but I've been very busy working on a new case. Roland and I have been hired as consultants on a very interesting crime and it looks like I won't be back as scheduled. I'll give you all the details in an email. I'll also try to call you on the weekend when you're home. Be good and I'll talk with you later. *Tschüs*." She turned the phone off and replaced it in its holder. "Thanks," she said. "I got his answering machine. He's at work." The relief on her face was palpable.

"I wasn't listening," Will lied.

She reached over and punched him on the shoulder for being too brazen with the truth. "Of course, you were." She crossed her long legs at the knee and her arms under her breasts except this time she was hot. "What am I going to do about Freddi?" she asked, wrinkling her nose.

"Easy," Will said. "Tell him thanks for everything but you just want to be friends."

Sylvie glared at Will. "Don't be simplistic."

"I'm sorry," Will offered in all honesty. "I know that you care about the guy and that you have a history together. He's a big boy—give him the benefit of the truth and he'll get on with his life and find another girl."

"I'm afraid of hurting him."

"He's a lawyer. He'll get over it or sue you for alienation of affection."

She stared at his ear, but he refused to look at her. "You know what? You're a bigger idiot than your uncle when it comes to handling relationships."

Will keyed the ignition, backed out and turned the radio on but Sylvie turned it off. "Goddammit Sylvie!" Will said, not hiding the intensity in his voice. "It is much too early in the morning for us to have an argument about your lover, for Christ's sake, so I'm going to tell you this and tell you this once only, so you better pay attention. For what it's worth, and this is the nearest I will ever come to a verbal affirmation of love: you are my sweetheart and I don't really care what you do with or about Freddi. For all I care you can invite him to come stay with us and I'll even teach him how to fish, if it will keep you happy. He doesn't sleep in my bed and he doesn't drive my boat. Otherwise, I don't care what the two of you do. Accept the inevitable fact that you are my girl. That's it."

He looked away from her and attended to the demands of the road as he wound the SUV through the forest. He was handsome enough literally to take her breath away. She studied him and smiled to herself. "Don't you have anything to say?" he demanded.

She shook her head no and smiled demurely. She had heard exactly what she wanted to hear. Her eyes misted and she dropped the shade down and studied her face in the lighted courtesy mirror. Everything right, she slipped out of her seatbelt and snuggled up against him.

"Sylvie," he said in mock astonishment. "I didn't know you cared enough to put your life at risk." He kissed the top of her blonde head. He let her soak up his smell, his warmth, and the comforting presence of his physicality. When he felt her take a deep and relaxing sigh, with his right elbow he gently nudged her back to the center of her seat and made her put the seatbelt back on. As she shouldered into the belt she read the green highway marker as they passed.

"We're heading for International Falls."

He nodded. "Dr. Hansen, the CME, called while you were in the bathroom. The toxicology results are back from the federal lab."

She could sense the excitement in his voice, as if an expectation were about to be fulfilled. She remembered that he had been working on a hypothesis and the lab results would no doubt confirm or disprove his conclusions.

"You just love anomalies, don't you?" she asked.

"That's why I get along so well with you." She took it as a compliment.

AT THE HOSPITAL'S reception desk, they waited. Within minutes of her page, they saw Dr. Hansen coming down the hall, waving to them, her face radiant with a smile. Maggie Hansen stopped in full stride and faced Will, hands on the hips of her knee-length clean, freshly pressed white lab coat. She seemed in a good mood and eager to share information. Will asked how Sheriff Clayton was and Sylvie thought the woman would crack her makeup with the smile she beamed at them.

"We just got back from a weekend trip into Canada. I hadn't realized how beautiful it is around here." She blushed at the admission.

"Thinking of staying then, are you?" Will asked conversationally."

"You are an amazing and very dangerous man," she said without artifice. She wore highlights in her soft brown hair and a new, shorter haircut framed her face. Her engagement ring was gone. "I'll never understand how you can read people's most intimate thoughts. Watch out for this one, Sylvie," she said in her girl-to-girl voice.

"Oh, don't worry Maggie. I'm quite immune to his meager powers," she lied, as Dr. Hansen raised a skeptical eyebrow.

As they walked down the lined corridors Will told Dr. Hansen they had discovered a tentative name for the John Doe. When she asked, "Why tentative?" Will told her they had so far received no corroboration that the man's name was indeed Randolph A. Baxter. But at least they had a name for him.

She powered up her computer, logged in, and brought up a file. "Anyway," said Dr. Hansen, "you might explain to me just how your vaunted powers allowed you to predict this." The file contained a chart showing different levels of chemicals. She pointed to a spike in the chart and explained. "This is alcohol. It's within normal limits as a naturally occurring byproduct of the body's metabolic processes." Then she pointed to a spike that looked like an icicle. "This isn't." Will leaned in to take a closer look at the graph. Dr. Hansen watched him as he carefully scanned the parameters of the findings. As he turned to her and nodded she said, "You predicted they would find an anomaly, and they did." She turned to Sylvie. "Did you remember to bring the piece of paper with Will's prediction?

"I certainly did. I wouldn't miss this for the world. Let's find out if this man is as good as he thinks he is, or merely a side-show, circus charlatan."

Will looked at her askance. "Really, Sylvie? Is this truly what you think of my methods?"

Immediately, she knew she had gone a step too far in her attempt at humor. She quickly took his hand in hers. "No darling. I was just trying to be funny and it didn't come out quite right in translation." On the cheek, she gave him a quick kiss of appeasement.

Mollified, he asked her to hand the folded paper containing his prediction to Dr. Hansen. She carefully unfolded the paper, hoping for the best, hoping for Sylvie's sake Will had at least come close to finding what the lab had reported. She gasped at what she read and handed the paper back to Sylvie. Eyes wide, she read what Will had written above his signature and the date: "Expect to find succinylcholine chloride."

All three leaned in again to take a confirming look at the graph on Hansen's computer. With a measure of satisfaction in his voice, Will read, "High levels of succinylcholine chloride detected."

"What in the world is that?" Sylvie asked, leaning in to study the graph, hands on her thighs. Despite highly competent German expertise in the area, the capabilities of American forensic science amazed her.

"Succinylcholine chloride," Will and Margaret said simultaneously and both laughed.

"By all means...," Will said, offering her the opportunity for the explanation.

Margaret began with an aside to Sylvie. "Of course, he knows what succinylcholine chloride is." Sylvie laughed and said she was not surprised in the least, and shrugged her shoulders. He smiled, always appreciative of an impressionable audience, satisfied that his conclusion had been verified. Dr. Hansen again pointed to the largest spike on the chart.

"We took a sample of John Doe's, excuse me, Randolph Baxter's brain tissue, liquefied it, and analyzed it using electrophoresis and chromatography. This separates out all the chemical constituents of the tissue. Since we know what to expect from a normal assay, we can overlook things like alcohol, acetylcholine, serotonin, and other similar chemicals; that is, stuff that should be there. This should not, at least at these levels. Actually, the spike indicates succinic acid, and should not be present at these levels."

She saved the file once more and printed it out for Will on the color printer next to the monitor. As they waited for the copy to emerge, Will expanded on Dr. Hansen's explanation.

"My analysis from last time led me to believe we would find the presence of something unusual. The drug succinylcholine chloride causes complete muscular paralysis, but does not produce immediate unconsciousness at lower dosage levels. It was considered virtually undetectable until a few years ago because it degraded to other naturally occurring chemicals in the body. A spike in the levels of succinic acid, which we have here," he said, indicating the graph, "is presently the only way to detect its use and thus its presence in the body."

"Right," Margaret Hansen agreed. "And that's why we had to send the sample to the federal lab in Minneapolis. They're the only ones with the equipment sophisticated enough to run this kind of chemical assay. They ran the sample through their high resolution mass spectrometer."

"Wow," said Sylvie, realizing the import of the findings. "This seems similar to a date-rape drug like Rohypnol."

Will sighed dramatically. "I'm afraid you have found me out."

Dr. Hansen could not help herself and snorted a short laugh. "So that's the real secret of his power over women."

"On the contrary," Sylvie corrected, "I put it in his iced tea at night."

Will nodded. "Our relationship is based entirely on the use of industrial grade pharmaceuticals. Before we leave, would you mind writing Sylvie another prescription? And double the dose while you're at it. I seem to be building up an immunity." This earned him a punch on the shoulder from Sylvie, relieved that her gaffe had been forgotten. Dr. Hansen said she would have the prescription ready for pick-up on their way out of the hospital.

Will pointed one more time to the graph. "If you would indulge me one more time, I would like to see the carbon dioxide levels."

"Of course," said Dr. Hansen, pleased to oblige. She swiveled her chair to face the computer on her desk, opened a new file, brought up a graph and printed a color copy for Will. He studied it for a minute and smiled at what he found.

"There is our second anomaly, perhaps the most important one of all as it supports the initial hypothesis that led me to suspect the drug."

Dr. Hansen pointed to the graph in Will's hand. "That's the measure of CO_2 we found. It's within normal limits," she added, then inadvertently gasped again and covered her mouth to hide her surprise. This time Will grinned, and Sylvie knew Will had the confirmation he needed.

He explained. "The anomaly is that the CO_2 reading is normal. When a person jumps into or is unexpectedly thrown into water, especially cold water, the mammalian diving reflex is triggered. This is an evolutionary survival adaptation that allows a person, or any other mammal, to survive longer without oxygen when immersed in water. My hypothesis is that the use of the succinylcholine chloride, based on my reading of the chart, to some degree at least, was sufficient to suppress the diving reflex. The level of the drug we found in his system would also explain why Randolph Baxter did not struggle against his captors or flail as one would expect while a person is drowning, thus elevating the levels of carbon dioxide in his system. In other words, he drowned all right, but he drowned much too fast. It's as if he filled up like a bucket dropped in a well, and that is not how persons ordinarily react when being drowned against their will."

The two women sat in silence, considering the import of what Will had said, until Sylvie spoke. "I need to think through the ramifications of these findings," Sylvie said, back in her role as an analytical detective.

"Good idea," Will agreed. "I'll take notes, if you don't mind. Always glad to hear someone else's thinking on the matter."

In that instant, Sylvie blushed, knowing that he had given her the same honor of position that he normally shared with Roland. She thought carefully before she spoke.

"Our assumption that this was a murder and not a suicide now becomes a sustainable conclusion based on the two anomalies discovered during the assay. The perpetrator, or perpetrators as the case may be, inject Baxter with a drug that causes muscular paralysis, but keeps him conscious. Why?"

Will looked up to her question and decided she was thinking out loud.

"This way he does not struggle as they get him into the boat. He remains manageable as they take him out on the lake and then set the scene to make the murder appear to be a suicide. But Will's semiotic analysis of the crime leads us to the conclusion that argues against suicide. The finding of high levels of succinic acid in the brain, coupled with the unexpectedly low levels of carbon dioxide, support Will's assertion that this is indeed a murder and not a suicide, which it seems to be on the face of it."

Sylvie finished her synopsis and smiled her pleasure, gratified to see both Will and Dr. Hansen smiling back. She watched him finish a note, fold the little red notebook and put it back into the inside pocket of his leather coat.

Dr. Hansen looked as if she had experienced an epiphany. She covered her mouth again out of courtesy and then spoke. "And that would explain the anomaly of finding so much water in the lungs and in the stomach."

"Right," Will said. "He filled up like a sponge."

Sylvie, caught up in their collective excitement, was a step behind on this one. "How was that possible?"

Will took the liberty of answering. "He was probably given more than one injection. The first was measured to keep him quiet and under control while they walked him down to the boat. He was tied up before the second dose was administered to prevent him from fighting in a panic when he realized what was going to happen. Most likely that second shot was also intended to paralyze the muscles used for breathing. Ordinarily, when someone drowns and water enters the throat, the victim usually experiences laryngospasm, a constriction of the larynx and vocal cords that blocks the inflow of water for a time. It's an evolved survival mechanism. Based on the water in his lungs and stomach, that most likely did not happen and he filled up like a water balloon. To make it look like a suicide by drowning, the cold-hearted bastard, or bastards as you suggested, Sylvie, stripped him, tied some kind of weight to him, and threw him overboard. Then they calmly sat there in the boat and watched him die as his lungs quickly and inexorably filled with water, the weight pulling him deeper and deeper into the cold blackness of the lake bottom. The poor guy was fully awake and aware of every agonizing second, knowing full well what was happening to him as he was forced to drown and die."

They sat together in a collective moment of silence, contemplating the horror of being unable to draw a breath, lungs screaming for air, knowing that unconsciousness would follow shortly, then death. They could sense the desperation, the panic that had no effect, and the inevitable, gruesome certainty that you were going to die and there was absolutely nothing you could do to prevent that from happening.

Will broke the temporary silence of individual reflection. "One last thing before we go Maggie; where in the world would someone get access to a drug like this?"

"That's a good question," she said, thinking back briefly to her course on pharmacology in medical school. "Anesthesiologists have access, of course, and vets."

Will quickly took out his notebook again and made an entry. "That's where we'll start. And one more thing, Maggie. I know you have to revise your report, but it would help our investigation if the results were not made public until we finish our fact-finding." She assured him that with all the paperwork ahead of her and her yearly vacation coming up soon, the new report would take some time to complete. Sadly enough, no one was expecting anything from her office regarding Randolph A. Baxter anyway.

As she walked them out to the parking lot, Will thanked her and told her where they were next headed. He said he would contact Sheriff Clayton after they returned, brief him and ask him to sit on the findings for a while. Will asked her to pass along the results of the assay, which she promised. Dr. Hansen hugged Sylvie goodbye, took Will's hand and then on her tiptoes, impulsively kissed him on the cheek. He smelled the lilac and heather scent of her new French perfume. Her engagement ring had been put to good use after all. The automatic doors whispered closed behind her after she smiled and waved them back onto the highway.

WILL DROVE SOUTH toward Hinckley and the White Bear Casino. In all, it had been an excellent start to the morning. After fifteen minutes of riding in silence and obviously bored by the unchanging landscape of pines, aspen, birches and bass boats, Sylvie turned to Will at the risk of intruding into his deepest thoughts. "I think Dr. Hansen has a crush on you." With a tissue pulled from her purse, she dabbed at the two commas of lipstick on his cheek. Of all the things she could have said, that bald statement was so unexpected that he had to laugh.

"Can you blame her?" he asked, playing along, sensing that Sylvie was in need.

"I don't think I have ever met anyone so full of themselves as you, with the exception perhaps of your uncle."

"How can you blame me for something so clearly and obviously genetic?"

"There's only one thing I find even tolerably attractive about you, if you care to know."

"What's that?" he asked, curious to see where this conversational tangent would lead them. He had the Subaru set on cruise control in the light southbound traffic moving steadily through the North Woods.

"The fact that you are so irresistibly attracted to me." She grinned to her ears.

"Having a fit of identity crisis, are we?" he prodded.

In perfect honesty she nodded yes, a smear of shame on her cheeks.

"What brought that on?" he asked, coaxing her to talk, which he knew she wanted to do seriously now, the prior talk nothing but a prelude: an opening to set the stage for the important issues that needed to play out. She wanted to be heard and he was happy to oblige.

"You practically had to force that woman to do a toxicology screen, when she was absolutely convinced that it was a complete waste of time and money. You were already working from a hypothesis that allowed you to predict the presence of a drug. Somehow you reasoned your way through to the discovery of the succinylcholine chloride so that when you actually saw the report you weren't even mildly surprised. I watched your face. I consider myself a reasonably observant and intelligent woman. I am extremely well trained, and I am a very competent detective. Your uncle has told me as much. Once. But he meant it."

"He's right and you are all those things." He turned to her to let her know he was being serious.

She continued. "It's because I'm your uncle's partner, a man I consider one of the best minds working in the Criminal Police—when he's sober. And even when he's into his third bottle of wine, he can still think rings around most of the deadwood walking around the department these days. And yet, in spite of my training and experience, you did something today in International Falls that I cannot conceive of doing even if I work another twenty years on the Job. I feel completely overwhelmed when I'm with you."

She said it without regret or tears or even a sense of resignation; it was nothing more than an observation based on her honest appraisal of self. She seemed more wistful than anything else. He drove for a moment or two in silence, mulling over what she had told him, considering the import and the intent.

"Listen to me, Sylvie. I have a doctorate in semiotic theory, which you well know by now is the study of the interpretation of signs. I have studied with some of the best minds in the history of semiotic theory. My particular contribution to criminology was to take a method of analysis used primarily to understand symbols and signs in language and literature and other similar semiotic systems, and apply it to the reading and interpretation of a specific semiotic system called a 'crime.' I've had the good fortune to be successful at what I do."

"The key is to treat every crime as meaningful. Every crime has significance. Every crime is committed by a human being—a symbol user—and almost every crime is intentional. Because most crimes are intentional and significant acts, they can be read, interpreted, and understood. In so doing, we can infer motive. Criminalists and criminologists all the way back to Sherlock Holmes and Edgar Allen Poe have used some form of this reasoning, whether they know it or not. My contribution is the synthesis I've performed in developing my method: bringing together inductive, deductive, and abductive logic, semiotic analysis, and the particular idea that crimes are significant, contexted actions. By that I mean they happen in a place, at a time, and for a reason. And these factors can stand as significant interpretable signs which, when read and understood, more often than not, can lead us to the perpetrator. When you add the contributions of medical forensics and pathology in helping us understand the physical and physiological signs, we have a powerful method available to us. My particular skill is really a function of unifying all these analytical elements into both a method and a process of detection and, ultimately, for solving high crimes." He blew out his cheeks. He had not intended to give a dissertation but she deserved the depth and intensity of the answer.

"I know that, my darling, and I'm doing my damndest to learn everything you can teach me. But that knowledge still doesn't quiet my sense of uneasiness, nor does it explain how you could possibly have known that somebody injected that man with a doping agent."

He patted her on the thigh, leaving his right hand atop the slope of the muscle there. "I haven't told anyone this, so keep it under your hat: I think Randolph Baxter was the victim of a contract killing; a professional hit, if you will."

She looked at him with surprise. She had not considered that possibility either, but then who had? "Thanks for making my point," she said, mischievously.

He let the comment slide. "The complexity of the case itself is a sign. It suggests to me that it has been carefully orchestrated. As you know, we solve most murders in this country within the first forty-eight hours, if not in the first week of their discovery, or we don't solve them at all. This one, however, and I tell you this in all honesty, we may never bring to a resolution, and this again suggests to me the work of hired, trained professional killers."

He paused a moment to pass a double-trailer big rig slowed by the gravity of its load as it hauled its heavy weight of short cut logs up the hill before the turn off to the Potlatch pulping mill. Once safely past the train of logs and back in the right hand lane, he reset the cruise control and finished his thought. "Look at it this way. If you knew you were going to be killed, wouldn't you—even if you knew it was hopeless—wouldn't you at least try to go down fighting?"

She thought about the importance of the question. "I would go out kicking, clawing, scratching at the eyes, biting, and screaming my last breath out of my lungs," she offered with conviction.

He nodded. "So would I. At the very least I would die with someone's skin under my fingernails. But we saw not the least bit of evidence of a life-and-death struggle, not a single solitary sign. No sign that he was smothered, no sign that he was punched and knocked out, no sign that he was choked into unconsciousness. The only sign we have in this regard is that there were no signs of a struggle. And that is significant. It leads to the possibility that our man was somehow incapacitated. How? Something simple and efficient and untraceable. Remember, these are professionals. This has been carefully planned and thought out. They decided to construct a scenario—a suicide—so there would be no extensive post mortem. Ergo, they had to administer some sort of drug that would allow them to keep him from struggling and under their control at the same time. Professionals control the scene. What drug best fits the bill? SCC. It had to be there. That's why I forced the issue of the toxicology screen. I would have been shocked if they had found nothing at all. Had that been the case, we would have all gone home and gone fishing."

He took his hand from her thigh and pointed to the sign advertising the casino. "We're almost there."

She leaned over and quickly kissed him on the cheek. "I don't care anymore how smart or good looking you are. I've decided to like you in spite of all your shortcomings," she declared.

"Thank you, Sylvie," he said, affecting humility. "It's nice to have someone accept you for who you really are."

At the next exit, he pulled the car over and pulled her close for a significant and meaningful kiss.

Chapter Nineteen

White Bear Casino

The White Bear Casino resembled Los Angeles International Airport in more ways than architecture. Acres of parking lots, new hotels, and fast food restaurants surrounded the round building topped with a rotating tribal *wickiup*. Diesel buses parked one next to another and from a distance resembled loaves of bread resting on the cooling pan.

"I like that," Will said of Sylvie's observation.

"Shouldn't they have a white bear on top instead of a *tipi*?" Sylvie asked.

"White Bear is the clan name," Will explained. "And more properly, that is a *wickiup* because it has a rounded dome, unlike a *tipi*. Looks like we'll be able to park close to the front door today. On the weekends you practically have to take a shuttle bus to get from your car to the entrance. Ever been to a casino?

"Once, in Baden Baden. It was lavish and beautiful, but I thought it was much too pretentious; for my taste, anyway. I don't particularly relish the idea of having to dress up to lose my hard-earned money to the House."

Will chuckled, took her hand in his and escorted her across the street that carved out a horseshoe in front of the casino's entrance where cabs and shuttle buses queued up, doors open, engines idling. Sylvie wrinkled her nose against the acrid smell of diesel exhaust.

"You should like it here then. In the true spirit of democracy everyone is welcome to lose their money: rich or poor, regardless of race, creed, color, or fashion sense."

The automatic door parted to admit them. They walked into the din of money falling into aluminum trays, the crank of handles being pulled, and the electronic buzz of artificially produced noise from the slots as the red cherries, black bars, or yellow lemons spun to a stop. Cocktail waitress in ludicrously short skirts, low cut bodices, and cheap fishnet pantyhose, floated their trays of drinks ahead of them on a palm facing up and pointing back to the way they came as they pushed through the aisles of gleaming silver machines. The women dispensed drinks to indifferent drinkers, the attention of the gamblers riveted to the whirl of the canisters, diverted only by some nearby unit that clanked change back into a lucky gambler's bin. Floor managers watched their sections like hawks on telephone poles studying a field for mice, their attention as focused and unwavering.

"Wow," said Sylvie. "You weren't kidding." She tried to wave a pouch of fresh air into the hanging, lazy blue smoke of a hundred cigarettes. "This is amazing. They all seem hypnotized."

"You have the same effect on me, *Hauptkommissar Schumann*," he said.

Before she could reply he caught the eye of the nearest floor manager, introduced himself, and said Chief Henry Gray Wolf was expecting them. The man nodded, his black hair glistening inside a tight ponytail, took the radio from his hip and made a call. He replaced the radio at his hip, tightened the Velcro strap closed and invited them to please follow. He led them past the blackjack section. Sylvie noticed all the two-dollar tables were full, the five-dollar tables and ten-dollar tables had vacant seats, but all the seats at the 100-dollar tables were taken. He showed them through a door marked Authorized Employees Only and walked them down the hall past a suite of internal offices. Two uniformed Ojibwe guards stood on either side of two full-length polished steel doors opened by a combination lock.

"The counting room," the floor manager informed them, and nodded to both guards. Further down the hall they came to a glass-walled room. Again, their guide nodded to the receptionist at the desk, who acknowledged the signal and keyed the intercom to Chief Henry Gray Wolf's office before she announced their presence.

The chief greeted them at the door to his office, genuinely glad to see them, and thanked the floor manager, who returned to his station. They were invited to sit on an immense, shiny black leather couch beneath a painting of horses running through the dust of a buffalo roundup, their riders painted and carrying their hunting lances held high, ready for a throw or thrust.

"What a remarkable painting," Sylvie remarked.

"Thank you, Ms. Schumann. That's me third from the left. The artist is Robert A. Hudson. He likes to be as authentic as possible. He painted that from a picture taken during a ceremonial roundup."

Will smiled. "I have a few early pieces by Hudson myself. Quite an operation you have here, Henry."

"Have you played here before, Professor?"

"Yes. In fact, you have most of the residuals from my last book," Will said, and Chief Gray Wolf laughed politely.

"If you'll excuse me for a moment..." He got up from a leather chair designed to match the couch and keyed the intercom. Sylvie noticed Gray Wolf was wearing the same color suit and socks he had on when he came to visit them at the cabin on Kabetogama. His secretary entered.

Jennifer White waited politely for the introductions. Will and Sylvie stood and came around the clear glass coffee table edged in silver standing in front of the couch, careful not to bump shins on the edge. After the introductions were finished, the chief asked if anyone would like something to drink. Sylvie, to Will's surprise, asked if she might have a Diet Mountain Dew. Will asked for a Diet Coke and Ms. White accepted a glass of mineral water. The chief did not order a drink, but when the efficient waitress came in with the drink tray, she placed a highball glass before her boss atop a paper napkin inscribed with the casino's logo.

"To a successful resolution of the case," Chief Gray Wolf proposed. He drank a good measure from his glass, replaced it carefully in the center of the square napkin and said, "I have taken Ms. White into our confidence and she knows the circumstances of the case. Jenny probably knew Randy Baxter better than anyone at the casino. Will and Sylvie turned to the woman, the leather of the couch squeaking beneath them.

She was professionally dressed in a black Donna Karan business suit over a cream-colored blouse. Of medium height, her thin figure, the tailored skirt, and her pointed heels made her seem taller. She nodded. "We had dinner together now and then," she said with a trace of embarrassment.

Will looked to Sylvie and she asked the first question without missing a beat. "Were you seeing each other?"

Ms. White nodded again and blushed red into her mahogany skin. Sylvie guessed her to be in her late twenties; perhaps even early thirties and the blush seemed unusual for a woman her age.

"Yes and no," Jennifer White said. Sylvie waited for her to elaborate but she did not. She sat quietly in her chair, leaning forward, legs together at the knee, hands folded in her lap.

"Were you interested in him?" Sylvie asked.

This time Ms. White nodded emphatically and moved the thick black braid of her hair from one shoulder to another. "Normally I don't have any trouble with guys, if you know what I mean..." she said to Sylvie, who knew exactly what she meant. Will smiled when Jennifer White looked to him and she returned the smile. He nodded a gentle affirmation. She was just attractive enough to turn heads and she accentuated her natural attributes with careful grooming and attention to detail. "But I couldn't figure Randy out. At times I was sure we had a chance to make something out of the relationship. At other times it was as if he hid behind this Plexiglas wall that he kept between us. I could see him and hear him, but I could never get any closer to him." She shrugged her shoulders as she remembered.

"It must have been very frustrating for you," Sylvie reflected back to the woman.

Ms. White agreed instantly. "He drove me crazy with his hot-and-cold act. Sometimes he acted more like a white guy than an Indian." She stopped suddenly as she realized what she had just said and to whom, but relaxed her shoulders when Will laughed at the honest expression of her frustration. The chief was unable to suppress a grin.

"The good Doctor has had quite a bit of experience with different cultures and Detective Schumann, as you know, is our guest from Germany."

"Who has also had the misfortune of dating some rather difficult men," Sylvie immediately added. Will studied another Hudson painting on the far wall, intrigued by the bold and vibrant use of primary colors. Ms. White giggled behind her hand at the interplay between Sylvie and Will and relaxed farther back into her seat, her hands now on the sides of the chair, legs crossed. Sylvie took the opportunity to return to the issue at hand. "Would you care to characterize his behavior for us?"

"He definitely was not one of the boys, so to speak."

"What made him different?" Sylvie quickly asked.

"He seemed somewhat more mature and worldly—if that's the word—than many of the dealers or croupiers working here. And I think he was very smart and educated but didn't want the rest of us to know it. That hurt; he wouldn't open himself up to me."

At this point Will asked a question and Ms. White was ready to take it from him. "Did he ever talk about his past?"

Her eyes grew wide in surprise. "How could you have known that?"

The chief took a drink from his glass. "The Professor is a world-renowned student of criminal behavior."

Will wished the chief had not said that and Jennifer White went stiff again and asked, "Do you really think Randy was involved in some sort of criminal activity?" The expression of disbelief on her face suggested that the idea could not have occurred to her.

Will shook his head emphatically to reassure her. "There is a very good chance that he was the victim—and I emphasize the word victim—of criminal activity. That's why we're here."

She nodded and sighed the tension from her chest. She took a minute to think. "In the six months he was here he never spoke about his past. Not once. Everything he ever talked about concerned work or something in the news or movies or things like that. But I couldn't tell you where he was from, or if he had brothers or sisters. Don't you think that's strange?" she asked

Will agreed. "Very unusual and highly significant."

She looked puzzled but reassured. Before Will could explain, Sylvie asked if Ms. White would be willing to show them Randolph Baxter's apartment. Ms. White looked immediately to her boss, anxiety now tightening her lips.

He stood and smoothed the tie that sloped above the belly of his shirt. "I expected that would be the next step. By all means. Take the rest of the day and do whatever you can to help the detectives with the case," he instructed her.

She went to get her purse from her desk. Will and Sylvie took the moment to thank the chief for his hospitality and promised to keep him abreast of any developments.

Chief Henry Gray Wolf invited them back to the casino after they finished their investigation at the apartment and promised them a generous allowance of the House's money if they wanted to gamble after dinner. As they turned to leave with Ms. White, Will snapped his fingers and asked if the chief would be willing to pull surveillance tapes of the day before Randolph Baxter's disappearance. They left with Gray Wolf's promise to do so immediately.

On the key ring next to her canister of mace and panic whistle, Jennifer White still had the key to Randolph Baxter's front door. She led them up the concrete stairs and the black wrought iron balusters to the second floor of the apartment complex built specifically for members of the Ojibwe tribe working at the casino. Like the standardized layouts of an inexpensive motel, one unit resembled the next and in the dark it took the light above each door for them to find their way. As she stepped forward to insert the key into the deadbolt lock, Will asked her to wait for a moment while he carefully studied the door. There were no scratches to indicate the lock had been picked, and a spider's web stretched from the surround to the doorknob. To his eye, it was obvious no one had entered the apartment recently.

"No maid service?" Will asked.

"Just me," Jenny White joked and Sylvie laughed in commiseration. She knew exactly what that was all about.

The apartment, having been shut up for a time, still smelled of new carpet. The front door opened into the living room. To the immediate left, a dining room with breakfast table and four chairs on casters for the linoleum floor. Just beyond, a kitchen done entirely in almond. Between the kitchen and the living room, a hall led to two bedrooms on either side of a large bath at the end of the hall. The bathroom was large enough for two sinks. The second bedroom was furnished as a den.

"Ms. White, if you don't mind, Sylvie and I need to carefully go through all the rooms and do a pretty thorough search. It will take us some time," Will explained.

She nodded, "I'll sit on the couch in the living room and watch TV."

"That's fine," Will said, and walked with Sylvie into the bedroom. He flipped the light switch and studied the sparsely furnished room. The double bed, still made, dominated the room. A chest-of-drawers in ubiquitous pine with a matching nightstand stood against the wall by the bed. On the nightstand a digital clock/radio kept time. As Sylvie pulled opened drawers one by one and pushed through clothes, Will pulled a magazine from the drawer of the small nightstand. "Now this is interesting," he said aloud as he flipped through the magazine.

Sylvie looked back over her shoulder, still rummaging through the middle drawer. "Porno?"

Will laughed. "Not exactly, but I like the way your mind works." Will checked the name and address on the subscription label. Both matched. Randolph Baxter was in the fourth month of his subscription. "This guy reads *Popular Science.*"

Sylvie pushed the third drawer shut. "It certainly seems to fit the clothing choices he makes. He's worse than you are in his selection of colors. Everything is white, black, or gray. At least there is no camo."

"You're just a fashion snob." Will pushed open the louvered doors to the closet. On the carpeted floor he saw white tennis shoes, black work shoes polished to a high sheen, and a pair of gray flip-flops. Black pants and white shirts hung in ordered precision at the right end of the closet. At the left, two pair of gray casual slacks. The only color in the closet came from the denim blue of his Levi's. Even the polo shirts were gray, black, or white. Will thought Baxter did not dress so badly.

"There's really not a lot of stuff here," he reported to Sylvie.

"Same here," she answered, pushing in the bottom drawer with the toe of her shoe. "Just the basics. He wasn't spending his paycheck on clothes."

"Good observation," he told her. "Why not?"

She grinned at him. "He's an existentialist and an anti-materialist trying to make a minimalist fashion statement."

"I'm impressed, Sylvie," he said sardonically. "You've been reading again. Now tell me what you really think."

She came over and kissed him on the cheek. "I think you're too good-looking and too smart for your own good. But I'm learning to deal with it, as you Americans say. As far as Mr. Baxter is concerned, I can't help but think he was a man waiting to move on. I get the sense that he saw the apartment as nothing more than an extended stay at a hotel. He had just enough stuff to work in, go out now and then, and do his wash while he wore his last pair of underwear."

Will agreed. "Let's check the bathroom, but I'm certain the things we find there will corroborate your objectic analysis and assessment."

"What in the world in an objectic analysis?"

"The human uses of objects—things, if you will—within their space. Almost all the objects we surround ourselves with are significant—we have a reason for choosing them—thus they become meaningful. What he doesn't have can also be significant. Where are the pictures of his family, the knickknacks we clutter our lives with, mementos, books, plants, souvenirs? Where is all the stuff that says this is my life and this is how I live it?"

Sylvie opened the mirrored cabinet above the almond shaped and colored wash basin, removed a tube of toothpaste, and handed it to Will. "What does this signify?" she asked facetiously.

"It means we're going steady. Every time you give me a little squeeze, more love comes out of me."

"You're an idiot," she informed him, putting the tube back. The bathroom was entirely nondescript. It had the look of a hotel lavatory. The den was even more sparse. A coffee table sat next to an easy chair designed in the same southwestern pastel color as the couch and chair in the living room. A freestanding torchier pushed light up to the ceiling. Sylvie shook her head in disdain. "I can't imagine anyone making a conscious choice to decorate like this."

"I was thinking of redoing your room in this motif," he teased her. "Now I'm not so sure. Anyway, I think you'll find that this is all rental stuff."

She sighed, as if the idea released her from the thought of anyone actually having bought the furniture in those horrid colors. "That does explain the smell of the cleaning chemicals," she said, putting a cute wrinkle into her nose. "Let's go talk to Ms. White."

As they entered the living room Jennifer White clicked off the TV with the remote and stood. "Did you find what you needed?"

Will said simply, "Thanks for letting us have a look around. By the way, did he ever give you anything of his—perhaps something personal?"

"No," she said, rearranging her braid again, checking the black plaits for split ends. Then she brightened. "But he did install a new car stereo for me on my birthday. That was just about a month before he disappeared," she added helpfully.

"That's highly significant," Sylvie assured her, mocking Will at the same time. He merely smiled, maintaining his good humor.

"Imitation is the sincerest form of flattery," he said to Ms. White, who nodded in agreement, despite her bewilderment. "Let's get you back to work."

Will held the door for Sylvie and Jennifer White when the phone on the lamp stand next to the couch rang. Sylvie looked to Will and Ms. White made as if to answer the call, but Will held her arm and put a finger to his lips.

The phone rang four times. After the fourth ring a taped message announced the phone number, asked the caller to leave a message and a number for a promised return call after the tone. At the tone, they heard a man's voice.

"Randolph, I'm calling to let you know you've missed your check-in for the third month in a row. This is a violation of your agreement with us. If you do not contact us within the next five days, we will begin proceedings to terminate you from the program." The voice paused. "And you know we both don't want that to happen." The speaker paused again and when he spoke, a personal note of concern replaced the former officiousness in his tone of voice. "If something is wrong, Randolph, call me and give us a chance to make it right. We don't want to lose you. We're waiting for your call. Goodbye." They heard the dial tone, and the tape stopped recording. Will immediately extracted the tape.

Sylvie smiled. "Serendipity?"

Will grinned wryly, "Serendipity. And you're not going to believe this. He has Caller ID." He copied down the number on the phone's LCD display. It was a Minneapolis number and a Minnesota area code. Will wrote the number into his notebook, and then punched the numbers on the phone's keypad.

On the second ring a female voice answered. United States Marshals Office. How may I direct your call?"

Will said into the receiver, "Sorry, wrong number. I was trying to reach ATF," and hung up. "This case is getting more interesting by the minute."

"Who did you reach?" Sylvie wanted to know.

"A switchboard operator in some government office." He did not tell her it was the United States Marshal's office. He was formulating an hypothesis and he needed Sylvie to provide independent support for his prediction when the time came and not before. He told her, "On my authority we'll get a subpoena for his phone records. When they arrive, I want you to look for this number. I predict it will show up at least once a month."

Sylvie nodded and made a mental note to herself. She knew Will was again hot on the trail and would depend on her to provide evidence to support whatever conclusion he was working toward. She wanted to ask questions and to help, but now understood that Will did not tell her—or Roland for that matter—certain things until he could substantiate his reasoning. She did not take it personally; rather, she admired him for his sense of professionalism and for his discipline. She was flattered that he would trust her for the independent verification he needed in order to proceed. Too many times she had seen investigators develop theories of a case and then try to force the facts to fit the theory. She had seen the mess this could cause and she and Roland were frequently called in on such cases to clean them up. She had come to understand fully Roland's admonition not to theorize prematurely. "Gather the evidence and the data first," she could hear him reminding her at the beginning of each new case. "Then and only then, construct the theory so that it adequately accounts for the evidence." Will would tell her his theory when she brought him the results from the phone company. Until then she would wait patiently and not bother him with questions she knew full well he would politely decline to answer.

The chief was still in his office when they returned and Will and Sylvie formally thanked Jennifer White for all her help and patience, although she was not certain she had really done anything.

"I do hope you solve the mystery of how Randy died. I really liked Randy and I think if we had had more time together, he would have opened up to me."

Chief Gray Wolf walked her out and gave her the next day off in an attempt to quell the tears pooling in her eyes. "Is there anything else I can help you with?" he asked, uncomfortable in the face of Jennifer White's emotion.

"Actually, there is," Will said. "If you have them ready now, I need to look at the surveillance tapes from Baxter's work station."

Chief Henry Gray Wolf nodded, made a quick call, and then said, "Come with me, please." He led them to a private elevator at the back of his office, took a special key from his pocket and inserted it into the control panel above the numbered buttons. The door opened and the elevator rose as he again keyed an inside lock. The numbers lit as they passed three floors on the way up. The third floor was the last button on the polished brass console, but the elevator continued to rise.

After the elevator lurched to a stop, the heavy metal doors pulled back and the three passengers were immediately greeted by two armed and uniformed tribal guards. Both nodded to the chief and stepped aside to make way into the hall. At the next locked door the chief removed a card from his wallet and swiped it through the lock box on the side of the door. A red light went out and a green light went on, and they heard heavy tumblers click into place before the chief opened the door. They stepped into a room filled with video monitors, video recorders, and one wall lined top to bottom with row after row of numbered and annotated videotapes and DVDs. At the center console a technician sat in front of a computer monitor and a microphone.

"Jed, will you pull the tapes for station 7? We'll need, let's say seven days up to April 28." He looked at Will, who confirmed that seven days would be more than sufficient.

The technician tapped into his database on the computer, entered the dates and station number, wrote down the information that appeared on the monitor, and said he would be right back after he pulled the tapes. He returned with seven. "These record the shifts worked by Mr. Baxter, as requested. If you need tapes from the other dealers working other shifts at the same table, I can pull those too."

"Shouldn't be necessary," Will assured him. "This is exactly what we need. Thank you very much."

The chief echoed his thanks and the tech resumed his position in front of the monitor and the bank of video receivers.

"What do you expect to find on the CCTV, if you don't mind my asking?" the chief said.

"There is a chance, however slight, that the killer or killers first contacted him here at work. As professionals they would know about the surveillance cameras, but they would reason that since Baxter did not know them or their motives at the time, they could safely observe him under the guise of gambling at his table. It's just a hunch, but we won't know unless we look. It could also be a monumental waste of time, but I'm willing to take the chance for the sake of Jennifer White."

"I appreciate that," Chief Gray Wolf said to Will and Sylvie, escorting them back to his office. "You're welcome to leave the tapes here in my safe if you wish to gamble. And, of course, please be our guests at the hotel," he said, picking up the phone. "I'll put you in a suite with a VCR."

"That is a wonderful offer," Will said, agreeing with Sylvie's look of expectation. "Do you feel lucky?" he asked her.

She raised her eyebrows provocatively. "Let's go find out."

Chapter Twenty

Relationships

Sylvie had brought along her black spaghetti-strap dress by Givenchy just in case they might have to do a night out. The sublime dress fit the high tight curve of her breasts; from there the silk and linen draped to mid-thigh with stunning effect. Given her long muscular runner's legs and the high heels, she wore the dress with devastating élan. Two years ago she could not have carried it off, he thought, admiring her. Now her young woman's self-consciousness about how she looked had faded to black, replaced with self-assurance. Not too many women he knew could wear that particular dress with Sylvie's cool confidence. The dress required everything about a woman's figure to be nearly flawless or risk seeming a caricature, a failed attempt to be something one was not. Without the physical and psychological attributes necessary to carry it off, the danger of ridicule lurked in dressing to match the airbrushed photos found in the glossy fashion magazines. Sylvie was ready make a statement.

They were met just inside the door to the casino by the floor manager and as he paid his respects to Sylvie and her dress, Will watched the crowd watching them make their entrance. For ten seconds the pure, undiluted sexuality of the tall blonde woman in a black dress pulled them from their machines and they blatantly stared. Will was reminded of water buffalo watching the sleek lioness moving at the edges of the herd. Once safely past them, they resumed their business and the wheels turned and the money jingled once more. They returned their attentions to the slim possibility of a pay-off, giving up the impossible fantasy of ever being with a woman like Sylvie.

"You're making quite an impression in that dress," Will observed as the manager walked them through the whirring, ringing din of the crowd pushing lighted rectangular bars on their gaming machines, or pulling down the long silver levers arming the right side of the slots.

"Thank you," she said simply and graciously, accepting the observation as a compliment. "This is the first time I've had an opportunity to wear this dress. Manfred bought it for my birthday," she informed him coyly. "You know, the birthday you have now twice forgotten."

Will grimaced. "If you like," he offered cavalierly, "I'll arrange to have your photo taken and you can send it to him. Include one of me, if you wish." He regretted the snide comment the instant it left his mouth and wished he would not be such an ass at times. Sylvie ignored the comments. In her book a little petty jealousy went a long way.

The floor manager introduced himself as David Red Cloud and seated them at an empty blackjack table reserved for unlimited play. The dealer was a young male that had suffered the unfortunate scarring of severe acne during his adolescent years. His long hair was pulled back into the ubiquitous pony tail worn by long-haired dealers in the casino, male or female. He greeted them as he broke the plastic surrounding the new decks of cards, shuffled them and placed them in the shoe. The floor manager removed the other two chairs from the outside comma of the table and set up a cordon of red velvet rope depending from brass stands that marked the table as private. Tonight they would play without the distraction of drunks, smokers, and inveterate talkers. As the dealer continued his preparations for play under the watchful eye of the floor manager, Sylvie leaned in close to Will and whispered in his ear. He could smell her perfume, the light delicate floral scent of the *Flowers of Rocaille* by Caron.

"I wore this dress hoping to seduce you tonight."

He pulled in another deep breath of her fragrance and lied like a Mafia Don testifying before a Senate subcommittee on racketeering. "You have to seduce my mind first," he said, playing hard to get. She laughed and smiled at the dealer, who missed his shuffle, dropped a card, and had to start over.

"That should be easy enough tonight," she observed. She ordered a scotch and ginger ale from the cocktail waitress, who said she absolutely loved that killer dress, but wouldn't dare wear it because her boyfriend would kill her right there on the floor if he saw her in it. Will was finally able to order a shot of Wiser's Very Fine, his favorite Canadian whisky, neat, no ice; eighteen-year-old if you have it. She said she would have to check at the bar since she did not recognize the brand. He was in luck when the drinks arrived, a good sign.

The dealer announced the table was ready for play. Will and Sylvie placed their first bets, each pushing forward a ten dollar chip. The young dealer pulled the first card from the shoe. As the cards came round, Will was dealt two tens and decided to double down, placing a 25 dollar chip in front of each card. The first card dealt him was the eight of diamonds. "Thank you," Will said, standing on the eighteen. The next card dealt to his second ten was the two of hearts. Will asked to be hit and received the five of diamonds. "I'll play these," Will indicated. Attention turned to Sylvie's cards.

"Rather extravagant tonight," Sylvie noted, looking carefully at her cards. "I'll play these," she told the young man dealing, who remembered too late to control his smile and maintain a professional demeanor of sangfroid.

He had dealt himself the five of spades showing. Covering his cards under the protection of his hands, he peeked at his hole card and surveyed the table.

Will leaned in to Sylvie's ear. "His hole card is a ten or a face card. He'll bet the fifteen and bust."

The dealer, named Jack on his employee's badge, turned over his hole card, the queen of hearts. To his fifteen, he drew the seven of clubs from the shoe and declared the bust. Will showed the eighteen and the seventeen, both winners. Sylvie paired a nine of diamonds with a jack of diamonds and accepted her winnings. She looked at Will, a question in her face. "I'll tell you later," he promised. "We're off to a good start."

They played for two hours, breaking once to let Sylvie use the bathroom. When Jack announced he was at the end of his shift and thanked them for playing with him, Will's pile of chips was now four rows deep. They declined to play on. Will tipped the waitress and the dealer handsomely as the floor manager David Red Cloud collected their chips and took them on a silver tray to the pay-off counter. He returned with seven hundred and seventy-five dollars for Sylvie and one thousand eight hundred and thirty dollars for Will. Red Cloud complimented him on his play and Will nodded.

"As a friend of the casino, may I have a word with you in private?" Will asked.

"By all means," the manager said, hiding his curiosity behind a professional smile. As he led them to his small office Sylvie wondered what Will was up to now. After they were seated, the floor manager steepled his fingers and gave the couple his complete attention.

Will said, "The young man who was our dealer acquitted himself quite admirably, given the distractions at his table. Unfortunately, he fell victim to my partner's considerable charms."

"I'm not certain what you mean, sir; although I might add, if you will permit me to say so, Detective Schumann is certainly the most alluring woman in the casino tonight."

"No doubt," agreed Will, "and therein lies the problem. "David Red Cloud waited for Will to explain. "You must promise me that the young man's job is safe if I tell you what I learned in observing him."

"Of course—unless he's guilty of some criminal wrong-doing; then I have to take action to protect the interests of the casino."

Will nodded. "He's guilty only of being a healthy young man, unconsciously reacting to very powerful stimuli. The young fellow was signaling Sylvie. He was telling her what his hole card was."

"He most certainly was not," protested Sylvie, coming to the young man's defense. She was genuinely puzzled by Will's statement, and not a little offended at the thought she was somehow colluding with the dealer to defraud the House. "Not once did he divulge what his hole card was."

"I agree that he did not orally tell you the information, but if you two will indulge me, let's look at the tape and I'll show you both what's happening."

Red Cloud made the call upstairs and they were watching the tape not five minutes later.

"Look carefully," Will said, "as he sneaks a peak at his hole card. If he has what he thinks is a winning hand, he immediately looks at me, then at Sylvie. If he thinks the hand is beatable, he invariably looks to Sylvie first, then to me."

Will paused the tape, rewound it, and then started it again. They watched Jack look at his hole card, glance briefly at Sylvie, then at Will. The House lost the hand. In four out of five instances where the House lost, he had looked first to Sylvie. When the House had the cards, he looked first to Will.

"Amazing," said Sylvie, watching the pattern emerge.

The manager wrote a quick note.

Will explained: "The dealer is unconsciously telling Sylvie the status of his hand because of his attraction to her. He wants her to win, which is only natural. He is displaying what's called a tell. A tell, as you know, is an unconscious nonverbal signal. Because of my training in semiotics, I'm able to interpret his nonverbal behaviors within the context of our play at the table; he's trying to help Sylvie win—which she did—so she will like him— which she does. At the same time, however, I used the information to help me with my play."

They waited a moment as the manager made a call to the chief. He arrived smiling. "What should we do?" he asked, once he was brought up to date.

"What I would do Henry, if you would allow me to presume, is show young Jack the tape and explain to him exactly what's happening. That's really all he needs."

Chief Henry Gray Wolf smiled serenely. It was an amicable decision and would prevent a lot of trouble. "I'll see to it myself. The funny thing is, Professor, we do give them a short course on tells during their dealer training. But at that age, they all think they're immune. Believe it or not, the women are even worse."

"Just between you and me, Chief, if you'll permit me the exaggeration. Even a blind man would have a difficult time dealing a straight hand to Sylvie in that dress." They all laughed at the self-evident and incontrovertible truth of the statement.

Will used the interlude to take out his winnings and placed them atop the lacquered table. "Because I took advantage, I'm obliged to return the money."

The chief pushed the wad of bills back. He would not hear of it. "Consider it an additional consulting fee for your analytical services. You have saved the House a considerable amount of money by discovering what you did and bringing it to our attention. No, sir. Please accept the money with our gratitude."

"In that case, I accept it gladly."

"You are welcome at the casino anytime," Chief Gray Wolf said. "But you, young lady, are restricted to the slots, the roulette wheel, or the craps table," he said with a wink of appreciation.

"I guess it's only fair," she acknowledged with a hint of resignation, and they said their good evenings.

As they walked down the hall to their room she said honestly, "I guess I have to accept the fact that I still don't fully understand I can have an effect on men."

Will took her arm. "Allow me to show you exactly what effect you do have, Miss." He swiped the card to unlock their door, flipped on the light in the foyer, and kissed the dress straps off over the smooth curve of her shoulders. The dress slid off the tips of her breasts and pooled above her bare feet. As she stepped out of the black pool of silk, he watched her. He shook his head as she reached for him, both arms open. "Who says you have to be lucky either in cards or lucky in love?"

"With you," she said, as he kissed her exposed throat, "luck evidently has absolutely nothing to do with either. And that's what scares me the most."

THEY SLEPT THROUGH the noise of the early risers, mostly families headed for the breakfast buffet. Like real gamblers they slept late. They turned their backs against the first shift of housekeeping carts and vacuum cleaners being pushed and pulled through adjacent rooms. The sun streaming through the seams of the curtains did not wake them. They woke to each other's smile and the irrepressible urgent need to use the bathroom. Sylvie beat him to the door so he ordered room service coffee and toast for her and a pot of tea with sweet rolls for himself. They showered together, enjoying the soapy clean slickness of each other's body, the sting of the hot water, and the fun of taking turns to wash each other's hair. The towels were white and thick and freshly laundered from the day before, and there were enough to use extravagantly. Sylvie was combing out her hair when

Will answered the knock at the door and received the breakfast tray from the room service cart. He signed the chit, tipped the waiter, and arranged the table for their breakfast. She was lavish with her use of butter on the wheat toast and cream in her coffee.

"You're going to get fat," he teased, "and that sexy black dress will have to go to charity."

She ladled in her fourth spoonful of sugar and stirred the mixture into a different color. "I thought you loved me for who I am on the inside."

"Certainly," he reassured her. "But your insides can get fat too."

She ignored him with a purpose, taking the coffee from the cup in little sips. "You didn't seem to have any complaints about my figure last night," she reminded him.

"I was needy," he replied, steeping his tea bag in the hot water of the silvered pot. He squeezed the bag between his fingers and dried them on the linen napkin spread across his lap. He poured himself a cup, sugared it, and added lemon for zest. He met her unrelenting gaze across the top of her coffee cup. "You're the best thing that's ever happened to me, *Hauptkommissar Sylvie Schumann.*"

"Thank you, Professor," she said giggling now. "It's nice to know the feeling is mutual."

He leaned over and kissed the cream from her lips. "If there is ever any doubt, just ask. It's easier for me that way." She nodded that she understood. After he finished his first cinnamon sweet roll, he jumped up, popped a tape in the VCR and swung the TV around. For the next two hours they watched an unceasing parade of characters walk up, sit and play blackjack at Randolph Baxter's table. They saw winners and losers, were amazed by how many played poorly and lost and did not seem to mind. In the second hour of viewing they were half-way through the Thursday tape.

They stretched out on the bed, Sylvie using Will's stomach for a pillow, when Will suddenly paused the tape, rewound it, and hit Play again. Two men, each with short haircuts, casually dressed in polo shirts and khaki pants, approached the table and sat, arranging their chips for play. The younger man appeared to be about thirty and seemed fit. He had the look of an ex-marine drill instructor, Will told Sylvie. His partner, and it was evident from the way the two interacted that they were a team, Will pointed out, was balding, about fifty-five and had lost his waistline inside a shirt too tight across the belly. They did not laugh or joke or make pleasantries with each other or the dealer. When an older couple took the two unoccupied seats at the table, they moved over to give them more room after a cursory acknowledgment of the couple's greetings. They played until the younger man's chips were gone—about thirty-five minutes—and left the table. They did not leave a tip.

"What do you think, Sylvie?" Will asked.

"I get goose bumps watching those two," she admitted.

Will nodded. "Trust those instincts."

"That's the same thing Roland once told me," she said, "and it was the best advice he ever gave me. Who do you think they are?"

"Not sure," he admitted. "But I'm more certain as to what they are. These two are professionals and that was their first contact with their victim. Because he doesn't know them, which is obvious from watching the tape, they feel comfortable in getting close to him so they can study him at their leisure."

"That's what they were doing," Sylvie said out loud as she realized Will was correct. "They were studying him like a pair of lions lying off in the distance while taking the measure of the weaker animals in the herd. Except with these two, they're face-to-face with their intended prey."

"Good way to put it," Will agreed. He rewound the tape once more. Viewing it again showed that the two were indeed sizing the man up coolly and objectively, studying him behind the blind of playing blackjack at the table.

Will and Sylvie ran through the Friday and Saturday tape of Baxter's shift, but the men did not appear again. Sunday was Randy's day off and the last time he was seen by anyone at the casino. "If we can establish that they checked out Sunday, we've made some progress. If you're ready, we'll pack and return the tapes to Chief Gray Wolf and have him make us a copy. We'll print off photos of the two gorillas and show them to the resort owners. This is important," he said.

She smiled in the face of his excitement; it had affected her too. "Not so fast, my dear *Professor Doktor*. I need to work off all that potential fat you're complaining about. If you don't mind..." she said taking him by the hand, and led him back to bed.

"Anything for the sake of your health," he mumbled into her kiss.

CHIEF GRAY WOLF was impressed by their discovery and promised to Fed-Ex a copy of the tape. He also promised to show photos, digitally enhanced from the videotape, to all clerks in the hotel and at all other places where the two men might have stayed. As he walked them out to their car he thanked them again for their good work, and after he held the door for Sylvie, shook hands with Will. He handed him a check, folded.

"A downpayment and a retainer for you and your team. When the case is resolved, I'll cut you another check."

Will placed the folded check in his leather coat without looking at the amount and thanked the chief for his help and hospitality.

"One last thing," Chief Gray Wolf said, holding them for another minute. "For Roland," he said, and handed Will a wrapped package.

Will studied it for a second or two and then beamed. "Moccasins."

"Leather from a deer I hunted and whose skin I tanned. Hand-cut and hand-sewn by my wife when she heard of Roland's wish. Tell him to wear them in good health."

"I will do so gladly," Will assured him and promised to stay in touch after their return to the cabin in the North Woods on Lake Kabetogama. In the Forester and on the highway heading north Sylvie delicately slipped the check from the inside pocket of his black leather sport coat and read the numbers. She let out a low whistle at the sum. "If this is the retainer, I can't wait to see what we get when the case is solved. Add this to the money we are getting from the sheriff's office and I might be able to quit my job with the *Kripo*.

Will took a quick look to satisfy his own curiosity. The check was made out to him for the sum of fifty thousand dollars. He looked to Sylvie and raised an eyebrow. "We?"

Chapter Twenty-one

Steak Dinner

The digitally enhanced photos taken from the casino's surveillance tapes arrived via the internet. Sylvie downloaded, printed, and handed the photos to Roland. He studied them closely and handed them back. "They have the look of professionals," he commented.

"Do you think this could have been a contract killing?" Will asked.

"It's a possibility we have to consider," Roland said.

Will shook his head and grimaced. "Great. Now we have to figure out why the Mob is involved with killing some poor guy nobody knows."

Roland shrugged. "Don't jump to conclusions. It might not be the Mob. It could be Armenians or Russians. And there are reasons other than Mob-related activities for hiring assassins."

Will agreed. "Here's what we do: I'll take Sylvie and run out to the Whispering Pines resort and see if they can make these two. I don't expect we'll get an ID on them but we can learn once and finally if these two were at the resort at the same time as Randolph Baxter, man of mystery."

Roland said, "Establish that much, give me a call at Popelka's and we will...I mean the three of us will sit and put the case together."

Will smiled at his uncle. "I'm glad I'm not working this one alone. In fact, I wish you could have seen Sylvie work her magic at the casino."

Roland grabbed his leather coat from the peg next to the door that led to the garage. "I know what you mean. She has become a very competent interrogator and that's a definite asset in this line of work."

Will dropped him off with a wave for Frau Popelka, and Sylvie moved up into the front passenger seat.

Don and Jean Berghammer, owners of the Whispering Pines resort, were getting ready to close things down for the winter. Jean was back for a weekend to help her husband with the myriad details involved in winterizing the camp. Don would stay until bear season closed. He had pulled an elk tag for Montana and looked forward to his hunting trip out west. Will and Sylvie had separated the two owners before showing the photos. Don Berghammer pointed with his tobacco stained index finger. "That was the pair. No doubt about it. They were with him in Seven," he said pointing a thumb over his shoulder to indicate Cabin Seven.

"Thanks, Don," Will said. "Go ahead and send Jean in."

She came through the saloon doors leading into the kitchen, wiping her hands on a dish towel. "Oh yes," she said with the surprise of remembering. "All three were in Cabin Seven. Do you think they killed him, Professor?"

"It's a possibility Jean, but mum's the word for the time being. All we have to go on presently is circumstance. The three were together—then Baxter, that's his name by the way, Randolph Baxter—turns up among the fishes. So let's keep it under our John Deere hats," he told her as Don came back in. Jean mimed pulling the zipper at her lips.

"Did you finger them?" Don asked his wife.

"There was no doubt about it," she assured him.

"Good girl," he said, and gave her a pat on the cheek. He turned to Will and Sylvie, who replaced the photos in her briefcase. "What's next for you two?" He patted his shirt pockets until he found his cigarettes for the day. He spanked one out of an open pack and lit it, waiting for Will to respond.

"Good question, Don. I suppose Seven has been cleaned and rented quite a few times since you saw these two men last."

Jean nodded. "It has been full almost every weekend this season."

"Good for you guys. No need to go through the cabin then. I do need to sit down with Sylvie and Roland and try to make sense of what we have learned so far. Once we get that figured out, we'll decide on the next step."

"Well, good luck to you guys," Don said with encouragement.

At the screen door, Will asked over his shoulder, "Any chance those guys paid with a credit card?"

"I already checked for you," Jean said, smiling. "And the car was a rental out of Duluth. I have the plate number, if that might help you," she said, hopefully.

Sylvie made a note but they both knew the plate number would come back as fake.

"When I get back from Montana and as soon as you get this case licked you, me, and Farley need to do some walleye fishing after the lake turns over."

"Thanks, Don. I look forward to getting in the boat with you soon." Will shook his hand.

"I think it's wonderful that you're trying to help that poor man," Jean said as they walked to the steps leading down from the lodge to the car park. "I'm sure it will mean a lot to his family."

"We'll stay on it until we get it figured out," Will promised.

Don held the door for Sylvie, careful to blow the smoke of his cigarette away from her. Don and Jean waved them up the hill as they drove back to Will's cabin.

Sylvie needed a little walk for herself and Will took the time to catch up on paperwork. When he came out of the den two hours later, she had just returned and was unlacing her hiking boots. "The leaves are starting to turn. It's just gorgeous in the woods. An artist could not paint so many wonderful rich colors." The cool of the afternoon had rubbed ruby into her cheeks, making the ice blue of her eyes even more apparent. He kissed her blonde hair and helped her pull the boots off her heels, then peeled down the wool hiking socks. He massaged her feet as she oohed. "Do you know that even your toes are pretty?"

She pushed a wrinkle into her nose. "Can you keep a secret?"

"Part of my job training," he promised.

"My toes are hairy."

Will checked each of her toes and the spaces between. "I see fungus but no sign of hair."

She slapped his shoulder, and then leaned forward to whisper in his ear. He could feel her warm breath in the shell of his ear.

"I shave them."

He made a point of clinically examining both feet again. "As I suspected. You are genetically part Hobbit. I just didn't want to say anything and risk embarrassing you. Your secret is safe with me."

With one bare foot against his chest she pushed him off the leather bolster and down to the floor. She straddled him, pinning his arms. "Don't you dare tell anyone, especially your uncle."

"Not a word," he lied, as she tickled him. "I promise!" He gasped as she reached the right spots.

"Liar," she said, as she stretched out atop his length, resting her body on his, rising and falling to the rhythm of his breathing. She felt absolutely at ease.

"Don't get too comfortable," he warned as she sighed her contentment into his ear. "We need to pick Roland up and put this case together."

"Okay," she agreed, at first disappointed in having to give up her comfort, then excited by the prospect of working with the two men. "Do I need to change?" she asked, sitting up and straddling his waist now.

He checked the nearly white blonde hair, eyes the color of Bavarian blue china with a touch of violet at the edges, and the perfect angles in her face. The nose was cute and well-shaped, if not a tad bit too long, but her lips were full and attractively formed, stealing attention from the length of her aquiline nose. She smiled fully, completely forgetting about her teeth, and patiently allowed the appraisal.

"Well, what do you think?"

"Keep those toes shaved and painted red and those pearly whites brushed and you'll be a perfect angel."

She stuck a big toe—nail painted crimson but hairless—into his ear.

"I mean do I need to change clothes?"

"I can't hear a word you're saying," he said, grabbing her foot by the ankle. "That's better. Just pull on a sweater for the evening chill—supposed to be cold tonight—put on some sneakers and we're out of here, if you ever let me up, that is."

She leaned forward and licked his lips with her tongue. "That's how Hobbits kiss."

"Yuck," he said, faking a grimace.

"Meet you in the garage in ten," she promised.

IN RESPONSE TO the horn, Roland came out of Lili Popelka's front door, shouldering into his black leather jacket. He opened the front door to the passenger's side of the vehicle and made Sylvie get in back. She gave him her best "you meanie" look but he ignored her, having seen it more than once. "Rank has its privileges," he reminded her.

"Chivalry should supersede rank," she grumped.

Will, grinning, looked over at his uncle as he strapped on the seat belt. "What the hell happened to your hair?"

Roland attended to the disarray in the mirror behind the sun visor. "You were supposed to call first."

"I know," Will said, laughing now as he backed down the driveway between the last of the flowers potted in the half-casks lining the pavement.

"Serves you right," Sylvie said, not yet finished with her pout from the backseat.

As they drove Will asked his uncle, "Do you want to know a little secret?"

Roland nodded, interested.

"Don't you dare," Sylvie threatened as she grabbed Will by the earlobe and started to twist.

"Okay, okay. Rest easy *Hauptkommissar Schumann*. Your secret is safe with me," he pleaded, hoping to get her to stop before she pulled his earlobe down to his shoulder.

Roland was disappointed. "Damn. I thought you were going to tell me she shaved her toes, or something freakish like that."

In the rear seat behind Will, Sylvie gasped, covered her mouth in surprise and blushed into her ears. "How did you know that?" she finally asked, her curiosity getting the better of her embarrassment.

Roland shrugged his shoulders under his leather coat. "I am after all an *Erster Kriminalhauptkommissar*," he said reminding her that he had achieved the highest non-administrative rank in the Bavarian state criminal police for good reason. Sylvie smiled at the back of her boss's graying curly hair, matted on one side.

In International Falls they stopped for brunch at a Chinese restaurant ubiquitously named the Golden Dragon. All three chose the buffet. When Sylvie came back with her plate piled high and sat, Will asked, "Are you feeding your tapeworm?"

She folded her napkin across her white thighs and khaki shorts. "I'm not talking to you or the *Erster*," she informed the table. Will poured her a cup of tea from the stainless steel pot in the center of the table and she thanked him as Roland sat and contemplated his Bird's Nest soup.

"It's better just to eat it and not think about it," Will suggested and Sylvie inadvertently laughed, her true good nature reasserting itself quickly and easily in spite of the ribbing she was taking. Roland finished his soup, pleasantly surprised at the delicate flavors, and when he returned from the buffet, they got down to cases.

"What do we have?" Roland asked Sylvie, getting the ball rolling.

She delicately patted the corners of her mouth with the red napkin taken from her lap. "We have a body recovered from the farthest reaches of the lake..."

"A serendipitous discovery," Will interjected.

"I was going to say that," Sylvie informed him politely, and Will returned to realigning his chopsticks in his right hand.

"The body was discovered and brought to the attention of the authorities," she continued.

"In other words, the discovery of the body was unintentional," Roland suggested.

"Correct," Will agreed, working his chopsticks experimentally. "The body was not meant to be discovered."

"Then why was the body denuded?" Sylvie asked.

"Perceptive question," Will acknowledged, genuinely impressed. This was exactly the reason for this kind of discussion. "In the event of discovery, however unlikely the possibility, stripping the body would make identification all the more difficult, to say nothing of the forensic analysis."

"And you conclude therefrom...?" Roland prompted.

"A professionally planned and executed murder."

"I agree," Roland said, looking to Sylvie.

"I agree," she said. "We have also established that a chemical agent was used to immobilize the victim— another indication of professional work." Both men nodded. "We have confirmed that during his shift at the

White Bear Casino, the two men on the videotape were in the presence of our floater, now identified as one Randolph Baxter. They have also been placed at Cabin Seven with Mr. Baxter at the Whispering Pines Resort. These are the facts of the case."

"Very good," said Roland. "The two of you have progressed to establishing two likely suspects for what plausibly is now a homicide and not a suicide. He paused for a moment, savoring his Broccoli Beef. "What don't we know?"

Sylvie took a delicate and cautious sip from her steaming green tea. There had been a time not too many years ago when she had been terrified by Roland's questioning. Now she understood that he had been teaching her to think through a case, examining each fact, checking every premise and questioning all assumptions. Now she enjoyed the sessions, regardless of the fact that more often than not, the intense scrutiny and objective analysis of information made her head hurt, in spite of a curious sense of elation that suffused her when they were finished.

Will took out his notebook. "We don't know who they are or where they are from. We don't know where they got the succinylcholine chloride. We have a name for the victim but we don't know if it is correct. I have the feeling we still don't know who he is."

"What do you mean?" Roland asked.

Sylvie interjected this time. "A person is more than just a name," she explained, frowning into her eyebrows. "A name is not necessarily an identity."

Roland tapped Will on the back of his hand. "Write that down: a name is not necessarily an identity."

Will grinned but Roland said, "However, even though we may tease our dear Sylvie, she is entirely correct. Why?" He directed the pressure of the question to his nephew.

"Names can be changed to hide or protect identities."

"Do you think this is the case here?" he asked.

"I do," Sylvie answered, emphasizing the pronoun.

"Explain."

"If you look carefully at his relationship with Jennifer White—Chief Gray Wolf's executive secretary—something is not quite right." At first, Sylvie had attributed Baxter's difficulty in sharing information about himself during his relationship with Jennifer White to the stereotype of the silent male. Now she was not so certain. What if it were something else? "What if he had somehow been forced to withhold aspects of himself or his identity? And does the U.S. Marshal have a role to play in any of this?"

"Beautifully reasoned and perceptive questions," Will said, making further notes before closing his notebook. "I think it is imperative that we establish Randolph Baxter's identity beyond merely naming him. In the act of discovering who he is we might very well discover what he was. A semiotic interpretation of what he was could lead us to hypothesizing a possible motive for his execution. He was killed for a reason and that reason no doubt is related to what he was. Without this information, I doubt that we can bring this case to resolution."

Roland and Sylvie agreed.

Will said, "I'll call the Marshal once we get some answers to our outstanding questions. In the meantime Roland should bring Sheriff Clayton up to speed. I'll contact some of my resources within the FBI and find out how to get succinylcholine chloride. Sylvie, use your computer skills and research every piece of public paper we can find on this guy: driver's license, voter registration, social security number—I'll help you with that—birth records, anything and everything we can get hold of to build an identity for this guy that transcends a mere name. We'll start first thing tomorrow."

The plan established, Sylvie excused herself for another trip to the buffet table. Will shook his head in disbelief. "Where does she put it all?"

Roland watched her with affection and appreciation. "She's finally in love."

"As long as she's not pregnant," Will said and took the occasion to reach at his feet for the wrapped package he had brought in with them. "Oh, by the way—and speaking of hairy toes—a present to you from Chief Gray Wolf."

Roland opened the package with delight. "Authentic moccasins," he declared, holding one up for everyone to see. He took his boots off under the table and slipped into the soft deer leather. "Like wearing gloves on your feet," he declared and reminded himself to thank the chief. Before they left, he took his new moccasins off and pulled his boots back on, not wanting to dirty the leather with a walk through the parking lot to the car.

SYLVIE WAS A wizard on the phone and a virtuoso on the computer. Under the auspices of Will's FBI credentials and with her formal International Criminal Police Organization (INTERPOL) affiliations, in a relatively short amount of time—three days counting the arrival of copied documents via Fed Ex—she obtained a substantial amount of information on Randolph Adam Baxter, deceased. She explained to Will and Roland that her internet search of public records established the following: his birth certificate showed that Baxter was born February 3, 1985 in Hudson, Iowa to Ruth and Adam Baxter, both parents now deceased. He had no brothers or sisters on record. He attended and graduated from Hudson High School. Four years later he graduated from Central College in Pella, Iowa with a degree in sociology.

Sylvie could not determine where he had worked after college—there was no record of military service either—until he showed up about a year ago at the White Bear casino. Will and Roland both made notes of the discrepancy, and Will asked Sylvie to order a copy of the birth certificate and the high school yearbook.

"His driver's license was valid and was issued a year ago in St. Paul, Minnesota. The DMV also reported that he owned a Mazda, on which he was still making payments. He had one MasterCard, obtained during his college years with a five thousand dollar credit limit. He rarely used the card and always paid the outstanding balance. His credit report came back with only two missed payments. He had not taken out any other loan except the car loan; there was no mortgage on record, no federal or state college loans. His credit score was average for his age. In the two years he had the card there was no indication that he had traveled outside of Iowa or Minnesota; there was no record of gas purchases, hotel rooms, or groceries. There was only one record of a lease, his current apartment, and it was entered into..."

Roland interrupted the briefing. "Let me guess: about a year ago."

"About a year ago," Sylvie affirmed and watched Will take note of the pattern. "His phone service, cable TV, auto insurance, visits to the dentist, all fit the pattern. All were initiated less than one year ago, consistent with someone having moved to a new location."

"Aha," Will said aloud, startling himself.

Sylvie looked up from her papers and waited. She continued her report when he said nothing further. "He had no criminal record, he was in good health, his medical files showed he had a mole removed from his back two months after he arrived in Hinckley; non-cancerous. His medical records did not extend back farther than this arrival in Minnesota. He had one subscription, already noted, in service for about six months. A call to the Social Security Master Death Index showed that his card and number had been issued when he was eighteen."

"At your request the Department of Justice persuaded the IRS to release his tax returns—casino dealers don't make a lot of money it seems—and as you have probably guessed, there were no returns prior to last year. That's all we have so far on Randolph Adam Baxter. And by the way, I chatted with Dr. Hansen in International Falls this morning. She confirmed that succinylcholine chloride is used primarily by anesthesiologists and veterinarians." She emphasized the latter word.

Will hmmmed for a minute. "That makes sense. They need to anesthetize their patients too."

"You've done a helluva job," Roland commended Sylvie. "Great information, given your limited time and resources."

Sylvie fairly beamed at the praise from her partner and her superior. He reserved his praise for truly noteworthy accomplishments. Roland took the view that it was silly to reward or compliment a person for doing their job. He preferred to acknowledge creative insight that resulted from long and deep thinking about a problem. He rewarded the perseverance and patience dedicated to a problem after others had long abandoned it as unworkable. He complimented one who took the courage to look beyond the ordinary, the mundane, and the routine, one willing to take a chance that might result in failure.

The longer he worked with Sylvie, the more he saw that she embodied those qualities: courage, commitment, and creativity. These were the essential values that coalesced into the characteristics of an outstanding investigator. In this instance, in Sylvie's case, and although he acknowledged and accepted his personal bias—in truth, he had developed a deep and sincere affection for Sylvie—a personal regard for her as a woman and as a friend that transcended their professional relationship. In this instance, her performance warranted the praise and he gave it unstintingly.

Sylvie was also one of those rare individuals on the force for whom praise, reward, or recognition—when justified and duly merited—served merely to reinforce her sense of duty and loyalty to the Job. She worked harder and with renewed energy. This self-same behavior had the collateral effect of slowly stripping away layer upon layer of cynicism Roland had laid on over the years to protect himself, the protective shellac that grew and hardened through time into the shield necessary to survive the dark side of the Job. Anyone else would have said Roland was just getting soft in his old age, but Will knew better and understood what was happening. Sylvie's youth, idealism, and enthusiasm acted as a counteragent to the years of accumulated bad experiences. Roland's job as her partner and superior was to temper her idealism with the realities of the street, moderate her enthusiasm so she would not burn out, and shape her youthful impetuosity into a more mature and rational deliberation. Without that, at least, Roland knew she could never become great; without that, she would never become anything more than merely competent. To that end, Roland acknowledged Will's contribution and he turned now to his nephew.

"Let's not overlook your 'aha' in response to something Sylvie said."

Will considered his uncle with unaffected admiration. "You caught it, you sly dog."

Sylvie looked up from her laptop screen where she was typing a summary of all they had just discussed. After she finished the file and printed out hard copies for the men, she knew they would study the document as if it were intended for submission to a peer-reviewed journal for publication. They would read for logic, rational argument, supporting evidence, facticity of claims, and validity of conclusions. Each inconsistency they found had to be addressed and resolved. She had come to realize that this method of case analysis, although tedious and time consuming, was often as important as the field work; perhaps more so with a case as difficult as this one.

First find, but then welcome the anomalies, Will told her, and then reconcile them. But never make the mistake of ignoring them. She knew Will's "aha" signaled his detection of exactly that sort of anomaly and she was excited to hear what he had discovered. He waited for her to save the file and she knew she was in for a bit of a discourse. Roland too arranged himself to be more comfortable in the leather recliner, hunkering down, anticipating the storm of words gathering on the horizon of Will's thinking.

Will took a deep breath, unconscious of the two smiles beaming his way. "I begin with the semiotic premise that there are essentially three kinds of identity. There is a socially constructed identity imposed on us by others. Our parents name us, our family passes along generational identity; we are judged, evaluated, rewarded, punished, and so on by the social institutions within which we interact." Sylvie and Roland nodded, each thinking of examples to corroborate Will's claim.

"We develop a personal sense of who and what we are and this sometimes is in contradiction of the ways others see us. In other words, some people are more self-defined than others."

Sylvie blushed and Roland grinned. Roland more readily fit the profile of a person given to self-determination. Sylvie, on the other hand, admitted that too often her sense of who and what she was depended on how others defined her, particularly her mother.

"A third form," Will continued, "results from the essential tension between the dynamics of these two forces. We often take the best aspects of a socially given identity and incorporate it with our sense of who and what we should like to be. A synthesis between the two identities—the social and the personal—arises, and identity thus becomes a process of identification, not something intrinsic or predetermined. That is, we are less fated to be who we are than most people believe. Great actors have this ability to reinvent themselves as they play different roles with such convincing skill that fans often identify the role or character with the actor." Will waited for either of the two to voice any contradiction or point out any flaw in his reasoning. None forthcoming, he continued.

"Identity then is inextricably bound with the history of the individual. Our sense of who and what we are changes and is modified over time. We aren't the same person at fifteen that we are at thirty, for example, although our name remains the same with the exception of some marriages, or the adding of titles and degrees, for example." He paused for a minute, taking the time to mentally connect his exposition to his forthcoming conclusion. "We are not getting a good sense of Randolph A. Baxter's historical identity. But we are getting a pretty clear sense of everything from one year forward. I consider this an anomaly worthy of consideration and further investigation."

Sylvie nodded to herself and made a note. Will had nailed it. She looked at Roland watching her, and then turned to Will. "You've always said that anomalies are important because of the questions they impose on our thinking. Can I try one?" She waited for his nod and then took the time to carefully formulate her question. "Why are we able to find facts of identity so easily one year forward, but run into so much difficulty when we try to discover the rest of the entirety of that man's life?" She looked directly at Will, awaiting his answer.

"I don't know the answer to that question Sylvie, but my hunch is that it has something to do with the phone call we heard on Baxter's answering machine back at his apartment. On that basis I'm starting to formulate a hypothesis which might lead us to a definitive answer. The important thing to my mind right now," Will looked quickly to Roland for confirmation, "is that we have established the question."

Roland laughed and wondered to himself how such simple things inevitably could be so important.

"And I predict that the answer will lead us closer to a solution for this case," Will concluded.

Sylvie was unclear as to how that might happen, but she asked instead, "How should I proceed?"

Will answered. "Let the question we've just established serve as our guide as we continue our search. And now that we have a firm jumping off point, I'm going fishing for walleye and you're both invited." Sylvie declined, eager to use the momentum generated in the discussion to push her database search forward. Roland said he would be glad to fish for a couple of hours.

"I might have something for you two by the time you get back," Sylvie said.

"And with a little luck, you'll have walleye for dinner," Will promised.

"I'll defrost a couple of steaks just in case," she said not allowing them the satisfaction of a face-saving rejoinder as she opened the laptop and lost herself among the nearly infinite strands of information floating like gossamer through the virtual space of the world wide web.

Chapter Twenty-two

Witness Security

Darkness pushed Will and Roland off the water and they were back in just under two hours, faces red from wind exposure, or their embarrassment from bringing home an empty net, Sylvie could not tell which. "Steaks all right with you guys?" she asked carefully.

"I would never refuse a properly grilled beefsteak," Roland admitted.

"Well then, why don't you two cook these beauties on the barbecue grill and I'll finish making an authentic German hot potato salad." She handed them the platter of seasoned porterhouse steaks and the opportunity to salvage their manly egos at having been skunked. A discussion of which wine to serve with dinner ensued and they soon forgot the absence of walleye for the table.

Directly in the middle of dinner, which Roland was enjoying with more than his usual gusto, the phone rang. Because it was such a treat—beefsteak prices were inordinately high in Europe given the fear of mad cow disease—Roland was loathe to interrupt his enjoyment of the particularly fine porterhouse covering his plate. He thought it might be Lili Popelka and he motioned to Will that he was not about to take any calls at the moment.

Sylvie teased him, "I never thought I'd see the day when beef was more important to you than sex."

Roland carved a succulent bite from the steak, examined its texture and degree of doneness on the tines of his fork, and chewed it with a look of heavenly bliss. "I can get plenty of sex," he said after he swallowed his bite and washed it down with the fine cabernet sauvignon from Paso Robles, California, Will served with the meal. "But a steak of this quality and size comes across my table only once every few years."

Sylvie smiled at the exaggeration, but Roland was not that far off in his assessment. Will had grilled the steaks to perfection: a vein of pink showed through the sandwich of gray as she cut herself another bite. From the wood chips Will had added to the gas grill flames she could taste maple-scented smoke in the meat. Will had gotten up to answer the phone and she heard him speaking German into the receiver and that diverted her attention from the steak. She wondered if it might be his mother. She had heard quite a bit about Hannelore, Roland's sister, and found herself wanting to speak with the woman.

Will could tell it was long distance. The voice on the other end politely asked in heavily accented English if he had reached the *Professor Doktor*'s residence and Will answered in German that he had. When Sylvie heard Will say "Manfred, it is indeed a pleasure to meet you," her heart suddenly raced in panic, as if she were about to fall out of the boat, and she knew without a doubt that Roland had noticed her sudden distress even before she was able to correct her smile.

"Keep quiet," she warned him, and he merely raised his eyebrows and took more of the excellent German potato salad Sylvie had made from the recipe of Will's mother.

She stood, walked over to the phone stand in the living room and waited to take the call, but Will—engaged in friendly repartee with Manfred—pushed her hand away as she reached for the receiver. Roland coughed into his hand as he saw her desperation and Will's apparent disregard of her growing embarrassment as the two men on the phone talked about her. After what seemed an eternity of pleasantries, he handed her the phone and stood watching and smiling as she greeted Freddi. She pushed Will back to his place at the table with a wonderfully forceful and angry stare. In a show of contrition he walked back into the open dining room, placed his napkin on his lap and resumed eating.

Roland fought off a laugh as he topped off Will's wine glass. "You really shouldn't be so mean to her. She's absolutely crazy in love with you and doesn't know what the hell to do about that ambulance chaser back home."

Will said drolly, "Please pass the potato salad," and helped himself to another substantial portion only slightly smaller than his first. He commented, "Just having a bit of fun at her expense. She's a big girl. She can take care of herself."

Roland nodded wisely at his nephew. "Just don't forget she is young and her inexperience with love makes her vulnerable. She's not jaded like the two of us. It's still heady intoxicating stuff for her and you've managed to turn her ordinary world completely upside down. So just you be careful," he warned gently.

Will suggested that his uncle perhaps overestimated Will's amatory effect on Sylvie but Roland was adamant.

"Trust me on this one; I know my partner, and I know you," he added and they agreed to leave it at that.

Sylvie leaned against the edge of the wet bar, her long legs crossed so that the beautiful shape of her quadriceps was delineated. She kept one arm barred across her breasts as she talked. Will got her attention, tapped his watch, and rubbed his index finger with his thumb, making the international sign for money being wasted. Sylvie looked exasperated, cupped the mouthpiece of the receiver with her palm and hissed at him in an indignant stage whisper, "Manfred's paying for this call, you idiot!"

Will feigned embarrassed surprise and Sylvie was forced to say into the phone, "No dear Freddi, you're not the idiot. I was speaking to someone else who is." She resumed the thread of their conversation in German.

"See, I told you she could take care of herself."

"That was a good one, though," Roland conceded.

Ten minutes later, after saying their rather clumsy goodbyes behind promises to speak again soon, Sylvie returned to the table and still somewhat distracted by the conversation, sighed deeply into her shoulders.

"It must be wonderful to be so much in love," Will said.

Roland cleared his throat in warning and Will looked quickly at him. When he looked back at Sylvie, from the catapult of her spoon she hit him squarely in the middle of the forehead with a dollop of potato salad launched across the table at her target. It stuck where it landed and did not move.

"That was an excellent shot," Roland judged as Sylvie stood in shocked surprise at her own unbridled audacity. The hand covering her mouth could not mute her gasping laughter.

Without missing a beat Will said, "I don't recall asking you to pass the potato salad."

"Sorry," she said quickly but unrepentantly, still amazed at what she had done, and ran her plate into the kitchen.

Roland reached over with his spoon, scooped up the dollop now slipping from Will's forehead and sampled it, "Too salty for my taste," he offered, and both Will and Sylvie laughed at the comedy.

After cheesecake topped with cherries, Will announced he would make a trip to Leech Lake the next day and they were both invited. Sylvie begged off without offering a reason, but Roland stepped in and said he would be glad to get away for a while. Will knew exactly what he meant. As much as Roland enjoyed the company of Frau Popelka, it was time for him to get away from her through absolutely no fault of hers. To the contrary, she was an amiable companion. Roland simply required his royal Bavarian quiet at times and the need had reasserted itself. He did ask about the reason for a trip to Leech Lake.

"A call to the alumni office at Central College in Pella, Iowa gives a last known address for one Randolph A. Baxter at Walker, Minnesota, right next to Leech Lake."

"Now that's interesting," Roland said, finishing the last bite of cheesecake off Sylvie's plate, with her permission. "It's worth investigating."

"Thought you might say so," Will said.

BEFORE THEY DROVE into the town of Walker, Will showed Roland parts of Leech Lake, a renowned musky and walleye fishery. Will told him he had once taken a forty inch musky, a relative of the northern pike, working a big jointed plug over the tops of a weed bed that dropped off into deeper water. In his opinion Leech was overrated for walleye and better for perch than advertised. The other difficulty of the big lake was its shallowness, unlike Kabetogama, Rainy, or Lake of the Woods. When the wind came up—as it often did—the lake swelled and rolled like an unstable washing machine and was just about as much fun to fish. Moreover, to his eye, the lake lacked the natural beauty of the Boundary Waters and Roland said that was certainly true, although from what he could see of Leech, it was not all that bad. Will allowed that he was probably spoiled by spending so much time at his cabin on Kabetogama. Just outside Walker they followed the signs directing them to the building that housed Social Services for the Ojibwe of the Leech Lake region.

The building was modern and relatively new; the asphalt paving the parking lot was still dark and the lines white and bright. At the front desk Will presented his credentials to the secretary and said he had an appointment to speak with Mr. Baxter. The young Native American woman at the desk could not have been much older than nineteen or twenty and she was flustered by the presence of the two men and their seeming importance. She twice pushed the wrong extension on her PBX console before she got the correct connection. She stopped her energetic gum chewing just long enough to announce Will and Roland, hung up and asked them to follow her. Roland thought the sneakers under her short skirt and nylons were an interesting statement, but when in Rome....

She showed them to Baxter's office, still too nervous to smile or stop her determined mastication. The office was as plain and nondescript as any other bureaucratic space in any number of countries: a metal desk and a chair on rollers, a computer on the desk, post-it notes on the computer screen. A tan sport coat hung from a stand in the corner, a wastebasket next to the desk held a brown lunch bag, and three stands of gray filing cabinets, one drawer in the first row by the door pulled open, held manila folders. A cork board on the wall behind the desk was filled with photos, mostly of Randolph A. Baxter holding some species of fish.

Baxter was darker than most Native Americans because he spent most of his free time on the water fishing, he said after Will complimented the photo of a nice musky big enough that Baxter strained to hold it with both hands under the gill plates. Will introduced Roland as his colleague assisting in the investigation of a missing person. Mr. Baxter looked puzzled, trying to search his memory for anyone he knew that might be missing. He acknowledged with a frown that he did have a cousin who frequently got liquored up on Friday night and occasionally disappeared for a weekend, but he usually stumbled out of the bush in time for work on Monday, Tuesday at the latest. Will assured him they were not there to find his cousin and the man visibly relaxed. After a few more minutes chatting about the fluctuating state of walleye fishing at Leech—and Baxter agreed with Will that the fishing had not been as good the last couple of years—Will segued into asking his questions.

Yes, Baxter had graduated Central College with a degree in sociology and had returned to Walker to work as a counselor in Social Services for the Anishinaabe. Will made a note in his book, then asked the man to state and spell his complete name with his place and date of birth.

"Randolph Adair Baxter, born March 1, 1965 in Bemidji."

"Interesting," Will said to Roland, who had also taken note of the discrepancy. "Did I hear you say your middle name is Adair?"

"Yes, sir. Adair. Named after my father's brother, Adair Baxter."

"If you don't mind," Roland asked, "would you please sign your name in its entirety?"

Baxter took out a sheet of stationery from a side drawer, pulled a pen from the wood stand that also held a small clock set below the engraved tribal insignia, and signed his name. He handed the paper to Will, who examined it and handed it to Roland. At first glance it was entirely possible to read Adair as Adam, given the man's cursive script.

"Thank you, Mr. Baxter. Since you've been so patient with us, we'll fill you in. We are indeed investigating a missing person at the request of the Anishinaabe Nation and the State of Minnesota. The name of the missing person is Randolph A. Baxter." They watched the man show his surprise. "However, his middle name is Adam, not Adair. And it seems he has appropriated some elements of your personal identity. There is also a physical resemblance. Your social security numbers are the same except for one digit."

Baxter pushed back from his desk. "Do you think I'm the victim of identity theft? To tell you the truth, I haven't had any problem with my credit card or car loan, or anything like that."

"No," Will assured him, "We don't think that's an issue in this case."

"Wait a minute," Randolph Adair Baxter said suddenly, and pulled open the bottom drawer of his desk. "What you gentlemen have told me finally explains this." He pulled out a copy of a magazine and handed it across the desk to Will. It was a publication of the Society of American Indian Engineers. Will studied the mailing label. It was addressed to Randolph A. Baxter, Walker, MN. "Everything is right except for one minor detail," Baxter said.

"What's that?" Roland asked.

"I'm not an engineer."

"Of course not," Roland agreed.

"But Randolph Adam Baxter might very well be," Will suggested, and asked if he could have the magazine for a day or two.

"Keep it," Baxter offered. "I just throw them out. You were lucky this came yesterday."

Will and Roland thanked him for his help and assured him that he had furthered their investigation. He walked them out to the Subaru and they shared hot spots for fishing on the lake before they parted.

SYLVIE WAITED AT the front door as Will and Roland returned the Subaru to the garage. Roland grunted and stretched, stiff from the inertia of travel and confined movement.

"I'm thirsty," he announced, taking his kiss on the cheek as Sylvie greeted both men. Will took his on the lips, but it was perfunctory and brief and he thought she could not be that impatient to start drinking pilsners. He knew it must be something else; she had learned something and was dying to tell them both. He could sense the tension in her. Outwardly she appeared calm and happy to see them, but she was an archer with bow at full draw in the instant before the arrow is loosed.

Roland looked after the beers so with Sylvie's help Will put together a platter of sliced cheeses—Havarti and Edam—smoked ham and turkey, gherkins, celery and carrots on the side, fresh rolls and butter and a good chunk of salami thrown in for good measure. Roland, already on the couch in the living room overlooking the lake, drained half the beer from his tall, thin pilsner glass that widened at the top. Sylvie brought the platter to the coffee table as he smacked his lips and took the foam from his mustache with the great drama and showmanship of deliberate satisfaction, justifying his need to slake his immense Bavarian thirst. He poured the rest of the bottle into the glass and loaded up a roll with cold cuts. Sylvie crunched a stick of celery stalk and Will pushed back into the big black recliner, beer in one hand, glass in the other.

Sylvie ate and drank and waited patiently while the men satisfied their hunger and thirst from their day on the road. Once both hunger and thirst were again under reasonable control, they briefed her with the results from their interview. From time to time she sat forward and typed notes into the laptop computer open on the coffee table in front of the couch. When they were finished she sat back and said, "Guess what I learned?"

Roland, who had also keyed in to Sylvie's need to share, ventured a guess. "Let's see, Will is actually married and has three children, all serving time in reform school."

Sylvie laughed at Will's comic expression of being found out. "Not quite," she said, too eager to share her information to elaborate on Roland's joke. "I have the phone records we were after." She smiled contentedly and waited for reactions. Nothing forthcoming, she said, "Well, aren't you going to ask me what was in them?"

Both men looked at each other, puzzled, and shook their heads. Sylvie was nonplussed. She had played this game before and knew she was being taken advantage of. "I'm reporting you both to *Direktor Hauptmann* for professional malfeasance," she said invoking the name of her and Roland's boss on the Bavarian state criminal police force.

"At least our malfeasance is professional," Roland noted.

"Indeed," Will contributed. "Nothing I hate more than amateur malfeasance." Both men shook their heads in agreement.

"Suit yourselves, you two comedians. If you don't want to know, I won't tell you!" She crossed her arms in defiance. The men called her bluff. "Okay," she said, giving in after just a few seconds wait. "The number we got off the caller id showed up monthly, as predicted, for just about a year and right up to the time of Baxter's disappearance. I also confirmed that the number is for one of the regional offices of the U.S. Marshals Service. And that, as you two gentlemen are so fond of saying, is highly significant." Pleased with herself and her contribution, she sat back again and took a self-congratulatory sip from her pilsner, golden in the glass, drinking down through the white crown of foam.

Roland looked to Will and on his behalf, offered her a job well done. "But what makes you think that information is significant?" he asked her.

Her smile of self-satisfaction dropped like a window slamming shut in the wind. "Well," she said as she snapped off a bite of carrot, "it has to be, doesn't it?" She looked to Will for help, who nodded vigorously.

"But what makes it significant?" Roland pressed. The time was good as any for a little instruction; his hunger and thirst from the road sated, he felt up to it.

Sylvie wrinkled her nose unconsciously as she considered the question. She knew she was not going to get any help from Will tonight as he was allying himself that evening with his uncle. She was on her own now. She raised her chin and cocked her head slightly to the side. "The chronosemiotics, as Will says. It's the timeliness: the monthly call indicates a pattern. A pattern generally emerges as the result of a causative factor."

Roland nodded slightly and even looked a bit impressed, but he was not yet finished with her. "Your speculations concerning the causative factor, please."

She took a deep breath and formulated the question out loud. "What caused him to make monthly calls to a regional U.S. Marshals Service office?" She took the time to think the possibilities through as the men refilled their glasses, then watched her think, an action that no longer troubled her. "He was required to make the calls." Both men immediately nodded and she smiled with the full force of happiness at having been found correct in her thinking.

"And why was he required to make monthly calls to the Marshals?" Roland asked, pushing her deeper into her analysis.

She shook her head. "That I do not know. There is nothing in his background to date that would indicate a need to report to the U.S. Marshals." Sylvie had learned early in her partnership with Roland to answer honestly when she did not know something, learning that such an admission almost always served as a necessary first step to discovering additional information.

"What do we know about the man?" Will asked, referring to Randolph Adam Baxter.

"Not much, actually. Everything we've learned in our investigation so far seems to indicate that his history, for all intents and purposes, starts about a year ago. He moved to Minnesota from somewhere, possibly Iowa since he is Meskwaki. He had a job and a relationship, but neither his co-workers nor his girlfriend know very much about the man. It's almost like he was hiding something, trying to maintain a sense of secrecy about his past."

"Hold that thought," Will told her.

Sylvie picked up the thread. "He was hiding who he was, at least the history of who he was."

"That's significant," Will said, with a little smile, "and will ultimately give you your answer." He let her consider the idea for a minute, and then asked, "What else do we know about him; that is, what are the indisputable facts of the case as it relates to his identity?"

"He's dead. Your analysis has established that he was probably murdered. We have tape from the surveillance cameras at the casino of the two men who might have killed him. And the second thing I need to tell you fits here. Dr. Hansen called to confirm that a second run of lab tests show conclusively the presence of succinic acid in the brain. Therefore, you were correct that succinylcholine chloride was used to paralyze the poor man, but keep him conscious, thus suggesting the professionalism of the killers. This tells us his murder was not random, impulsive, or a crime of opportunity. It was carefully planned."

Will and Roland watched her intently. She knew she was still on the right track.

"Now put it all together, Sylvie. Contextualize the pattern of monthly calls to a Marshal's office within the information you just reviewed for us."

"*Ach du Lieber*," she said in German, as the realization hit her. "It's a fake identity. Randolph Adam Baxter was created a year ago to resemble Randolph Adair Baxter in case somebody did a deep background check. Otherwise, his identity begins as of last year. It had to be a hit!" she exclaimed, referring to the murder. She pushed to the edge of the couch with both hands, now fully excited by the idea forming in her mind.

"The Federal Marshals..." Roland prompted.

"Ohmigod," she whispered as the idea crystallized around Roland's prompting. "Randolph A. Baxter, deceased, was killed while in the Witness Security Program. That would explain the creation of his identity last year and our inability to find any history of the man prior to that. He was calling to report in," she said behind the rapid intake of a breath.

"You have it dead on, Sylvie," Will said as Roland nodded his agreement. "I have no doubt I will be able to confirm through my FBI contacts that Baxter was enrolled in WITSEC, more properly the United States Federal Witness Protection Program. WITSEC is run by the Special Operations Group of the U.S. Marshals Service, itself an entity of the Department of Justice. And they don't enroll just anyone in Witness Security. It requires a request from a States Attorney to the U.S. Attorney and the final determination rests with none other than the Attorney General himself."

"So this had to be a pretty important guy?" Sylvie asked.

Will said, "Without a doubt. Witness Security costs the taxpayers a bundle of money and it's hard as hell to administer. Our next line of investigation then centers on the question, what made him so damned important to the Feds?"

Roland added, "And how is it that the program failed him? My information from Interpol in Lyon, France suggests this is a relatively rare failure."

"It is indeed. It suggests a force capable of penetrating the wall of secrecy surrounding someone taken into WITSEC. That takes resources and organization."

"We're getting closer," Roland suggested, agreeing with Will's reasoning.

"Thanks to Sylvie," Will said.

She smiled, accepting the compliment graciously, but admitted, "I merely confirmed the conclusion you two had already formulated. That's why you guys went to Walker today." She said it with admiration and respect for both.

Roland buttered and built another roll and stuffed it with meat and cheese, his appetite reawakened by all the thinking. "Don't minimize your contribution," he mumbled through a bite. "Without your organizational skills and talent for tracking down information through that damn computer, we would not have arrived at a verification of our conclusions." He took another bite that stretched the muscles of his jaw to their limit. Will and Sylvie looked on in amazement. After three minutes of careful and deliberate chewing, he swallowed. "In a sense, Sylvie, you not only provided many of the important pieces to the puzzle, you also arranged them in the proper orientation that allowed us to see the bigger picture. That orientation allowed us to see that Baxter had to have been placed in WITSEC, as Will calls it."

Will spoke. "Now, if you'll forgive me, and if Roland doesn't choke to death on his next bite from that sandwich, I have to excuse myself and make a series of confidential calls to rather highly placed sources," he said, exaggerating the cliché.

Roland mumbled something indecipherable and Sylvie took another sip from her beer, enjoying the crisp clean bitterness of the cold brew. She now felt justifiably satisfied with the contributions she had made.

Before he left to make his calls, Will came around to the back of the couch, kissed her on top of the head from behind and said, "We still have a lot of work to do on this case."

Sylvie laughed, not at Will, but at Roland's antics as he chewed a massive bolus of food into one side of his cheek, and with one finger, pointed insistently at the top of his head, demanding a kiss for himself.

Chapter Twenty-three

Locator Lake

To take advantage of the approaching Labor Day weekend, and as they waited for Will's federal contacts to respond with requested information, Will decided a break from detective work was in order. He knew federal offices would observe the holiday and did not expect a reply to his queries for at least four days. Sylvie looked forward to the four-day excursion Will had planned for them—a camping trip, but not without some trepidation. They planned to run up to the northwest shore of Kabetogama, hike the trail to Locator Lake, pick up a canoe left by the Forest Service on a reservation basis, and set up camp on War Club Lake, the second of four in a short chain of lakes. Will promised that this late in the season there should be no other hikers or campers to interfere with their enjoyment of the pleasant Indian summer that had washed most of the humidity out of the air and pushed the moderate daytime temperatures into the mid-fifties.

Will had called ahead to reserve the canoe and had just returned from the Forest Service Visitor's Center with the key to the padlock that kept the three canoes with paddles chained together. The ranger on duty assured him there were no other reservations, given the lateness of the season, and no one had called in with plans to camp or hike the area. That suited Will just fine;

he did not want the added worry of dealing with greenhorns and their tender feet when he had Sylvie along, already showing some nerves at being outdoors without the benefit of her comfortable place and familiar things.

Will wanted to travel light so they kept to the necessities: a three-season tent with a rain cover, needed in the North Woods no matter what the season; sleeping bags rated to 20 degrees below zero, but not down-filled because of the humidity and rain so often encountered; the luxury of a self-inflating air mattress; camp stove and cooking utensils; water purifier; flashlights and a battery powered lamp for the tent; and most importantly, toilet paper in a plastic bag. He also packed a survival kit against emergencies, which he added to the tent, mattress, sleeping bag, and cooking items stowed in his pack. Sylvie carried her sleeping bag, all the food and extra water, the lamp for the tent, all her personal items and extra clothing for both.

Will ran the Lund at speed toward La Bontys Point, slightly northwest of the jump-off point for the trailhead leading to Locator. Roland and Lili helped offload the gear onto the dock. They made a quick check and Roland asked if they had their collapsible fishing poles and small tackle box. Will patted his pack. He helped Sylvie shoulder into her backpack and she took the weight easily, adjusting the fit of the waist strap. Will kissed Lili's cheek and shook Roland's hand. "See you in three days," Roland promised, and returned Sylvie's wave. Will watched on the dock as Roland keyed the ignition of the big Lund and throttled the outboard to life. Roland reversed away from the dock, pointed the nose south and east and powered the big motor out of the hole, kicking up a rooster tail of water that spewed into the sky as the boat settled at speed into its long run back to the cabin. Will and Sylvie watched the boat—their last contact with the civilized world—disappear around the leeward side of an island and Will sighed.

"What's the matter?" Sylvie asked.

"My beautiful boat," he said wistfully.

Sylvie laughed. "Don't worry. Roland knows how to handle a boat and he's a wonderful driver."

"I know," Will acknowledged, "but this isn't the *Autobahn* and he doesn't know the lake. Not all the dangerous rocks are marked."

"Lili knows the lake. She'll take care of him."

"You're right," he said, smoothing a padded strap over his left shoulder. "If you need to use the bathroom, that's your last chance to do so in reasonable comfort," he said, indicating the outhouse set off to the side of the trail.

To indicate no, she shook her head with emphasis. "I'm fine. Besides, I hate the smell of those things."

He laughed at the apparent disgust in her face. "Breathe through your mouth when you're in there," he advised, but she was already moving out. "You sure you want to do this for the next three days?"

"No phone, no lights, no motor cars, not a single luxury," she sang. Gilligan and his shipmates had long ago washed up on the shores of German television. "We're castaways with only our wits and our survival skills to rely on." She paused for a minute. "I am really scared."

"Me, too" he said, feeding her anxieties. "I've never done this before."

She looked back over her shoulder quickly for reassurance and he could tell she was more excited than scared, but a glimmer of fear leaked through her grin, so he smiled to let her know he was joking.

She had once told him that since her father had died when she was five years old, she could count on the fingers of one hand the number of times she had felt truly safe. Maybe that is why she had joined the state police. And now, walking over the granite outcrop to the trail leading into the forest where she would have to camp and live for the next three days, she considered the man she was with. She felt an almost serene sense of security, a feeling that Manfred, for all the time they had been together, had never engendered in her. How strange, she thought, moving from the sunlight into the cool of the woods.

In the canopy of the deciduous trees, chlorophyll production had stopped in the leaves, allowing autumn colors to emerge. After two or three nights below zero degrees centigrade, the maples, hickory, oak, alders, and aspen would give their red, umber, gold, and silver leaves back to the earth. The conifers would stand largely unchanged, ever green but dropping needles and seed cones to the forest floor. As they passed deeper into the woods, they crossed a wooden bridge spanning a finger of water leaking from a marsh. In the distance Sylvie saw a large brown body move through the black water. As the creature turned it saw them watching. With an explosive slap the beaver pounded the marsh water with its spatulate tail and dived for cover.

"This is the second beaver I've seen since I've been here," she marveled. "I read in school that they slap their tails on the water as a warning sign, but I never dreamed that I would actually get to see and hear it in the wild. I'm amazed how loud it sounds."

Will pointed out the beaver's lodge set back in a small bay littered with willows that had been stripped of their leaves. "He's preparing for the coming of winter. He and his colony will spend the winter deep inside that lodge." It was time to move on—they still had ground to cover. Will wanted to find the canoe, load it, and paddle across the lake to set up camp before the sun set.

"I love the smell," she said, picking up her pace and taking the lead. "Everything is so fresh and clean. I love nature," she declared to the trees, the dark trail winding through them, and to the young eagle flying overhead.

More than anything else, Will was pleased she was happy, and the realization that her happiness was important to him came as a surprise. He usually let people look after their own happiness, but in Sylvie's case he decided to modify his philosophy a smidge. He was not so naïve to think he could really give her happiness, but he was still enough of a romantic to think he could at least contribute to it. After the first ninety minutes of hiking, he called her to stop. They found a pine tree large enough to sit under and use as a back rest. They dropped the heavy packs and pulled their wet shirts, moist from the perspiration of their exertions, away from their skin.

"Whew," said Sylvie, passing back the water bottle. "This is hard work."

"I thought you were in shape from all that running and physical training," he teased her.

"I meant being with you. This hike is a cakewalk. If you want, I'll carry your pack, too. From the way you're sweating, you look like you could use the help."

He liked her when she kidded him so. He appreciated the incongruity of her offer when she knew full well that he could carry his pack, hers, and her as well on his back, and still make it to the lake.

"The only thing I need right now, *Fräulein Schumann*," he corrected her, "is the full and sweet press of your lips on mine, and I mean now." Under the pine branches shielding their intimacy she kissed him long and hard, taking the taste of him as sustenance. After the breathless kiss she merely sat there looking into his eyes and face without speaking. He permitted the full and unabashed stare until he broke the line of his lips with a smile.

"You are the most beautiful man I have ever known," she whispered not to him but to the forest and kissed his cheek, which she knew he loved more than a kiss of the lips, he once told her. He believed that although it might be less passionate, he considered it to be more intimate. "What does that tell you, my handsome professor? What does this signify?" she asked, kissing his cheek again.

"It tells me that you care for me. You are giving me a kiss on the cheek, which you know I enjoy. A person who cares enough to give a kiss is a compassionate human being, my beautiful *Hauptkommissarin*."

She considered his explanation before kissing him fully and passionately on the lips, her mouth open, her tongue exploring his. "And this?"

"An offer of sex," he said, as he gathered his breath. "An invitation. You open yourself to me and use your passion to signal your readiness for more."

She defied him and shook her head. "It was about love, silly. And just so you know, I was faking it."

He stood and brushed the pine needles and humus from his knees and the seat of his pants. He gave her his hand and she rode the pull of his strength to her feet.

"And this?" he asked, gently cupping her breast and pressing against the nipple straining through the material of her sports bra and blue denim shirt. She laughed in the unaffected musical way he loved as she shook her head.

"That is only the wind," she explained, taking the weight of her pack.

He swung his heavy backpack lightly across a shoulder. "I am the north wind that touches you," he said in an instant of poetry he could not control. He felt foolish and young for saying it, but ultimately it was the right thing to do, and in his moment of vulnerability, she told him, "Yes, you are."

They held hands as they walked until the trail narrowed and forced them to walk one ahead of the other, Will taking the lead. He stopped occasionally to point out an interesting sight off the trail, such as a raccoon scuttling up a hickory tree. As the forenoon gave way to afternoon, they emerged from the forest and stood at the edge of a lake. He let her slip her hand into his, her long, elegant fingers warm from the exertion of the trek, giving her time to take in the panorama before her.

"It reminds me very much of the *Malerwinkel*," she observed, bringing to mind a memory of Germany where he had been born, an idyllic lake high in the Bavarian alps where artists posed their easels and painted the magnificent view of the serene lake shielded by granitic mountains.

"In a way, it does," he agreed. The moraine in which the water lay had been carved eons ago during the last Ice Age as the massive ice sheet retracted farther up into Canada. The sides of the lake were relatively steep, and the lake was longer east to west than it was wide north to south. Nearer to them the water looked almost the color of black tea; in the distance it seemed blue and green.

"The water is perfectly clear," he showed her, taking up a handful. "The bottom gives it this color so near to the bank. Farther out it will be forty feet deep in places. Let's get the canoe unlocked and loaded."

He pointed to the three aluminum canoes racked up on the shore upside down and chained together. An old wooden shed, its roof covered with moss, stood to the side, its oversized hinges rusted and its door padlocked. After he keyed the padlock securing the heavy chains that linked the three canoes together, he threw her the key tied to a plastic handle with the Forest Service logo printed on it, and had her open the door to the old shed. She found the paddles, seat cushions, and the life vests. In a show of strength that caught her off guard, he casually picked up the sixteen foot canoe, lifted it over his head and carried it down the steep slope to the lake edge, like a French voyageur portaging his canoe across land to the next waterway. He inverted the canoe again, hull down, and slid the fore-end into the water. After closing the padlocks on the shed and the chains on the two remaining canoes, Sylvie brought the packs down with the rest of the gear. He held the aft end of the canoe and she climbed in gingerly, rocking the canoe from side to side.

"Grab the sides for support," he told her, "and don't forget to lower your center of gravity." She bent her knees and leaned forward at the waist as she moved to the front of the boat.

"That's much better," she said, turning and sitting.

He handed her the packs for stowing. "Good job," he said, and passed back the broad wooden paddle. "Brace this across the sides while I push out and step in." He waited for her to get comfortable, and then pushed the canoe forcefully out into the water. At the last instant, when she thought he had waited too long and would be stranded ashore, he deftly stepped forward into the canoe, both hands holding the sides, his right leg trailing just above the water. Rippling the calm surface, the canoe glided silently into the lake away from the shore, and he brought his leg aboard and sat. Paddle in hand, he reminded her how to use her own as a rudder to bring the nose of the canoe around so he could continue paddling. With sure, powerful strokes he propelled them across the lake toward the far shore.

"This is wonderful," she said, shipping her paddle for a moment and thrilling to the quiet propulsion of the craft through the water. "This is what it must have been like three hundred years ago."

He looked around between strokes, taking it all in. "Not much has changed, thank goodness. The U.S. government did a wise thing back in 1967 when they declared this a national park and prohibited building. That's why the eagles and the beavers and the loons are back, to say nothing of the water quality. Sometimes people do get it right," he mused.

"I just can't believe how beautiful it all is," she commented, her own blonde, blue-eyed beauty contributing significantly to the scenery.

"Photo op," he said suddenly, digging his cell phone out of his backpack. There was no service, but the phone doubled as a camera, and Will had loaded an app that measured hiking distance, altitude, and direction. "Smile," he commanded, and she refused, taken suddenly shy in the midst of all the natural splendor surrounding her. He checked the orientation of the phone again to make certain he was not taking his own picture. "Say, 'I love pornography.'" This time she could not help herself and he almost missed his moment, taken by the radiance of her smile against the natural backdrop, but he recovered in time to hear the reassuring click that signaled he had made the shot.

"Your turn," she said, motioning for the phone, and he snapped one side of his camo Special Forces boony hat into place to give her his face in profile. He affected the look of an explorer surveying a vast, newly discovered terrain.

"You are such a ham," she said. "Now take off that stupid hat and your sunglasses too, so I can see those pretty, gray-blue peepers of yours."

"Steely gray," he corrected her, taking off the shades. "And these are not peepers; these are Mark VII Personal Optical Sensors; nor is this a stupid hat. Navy SEALS and Army Rangers wear them with pride; I have earned this hat."

She took the picture anyway, despite the idiot in the shot, and then stumbled aft to squeeze in next to him, nearly tipping the canoe in the process. "Sorry," she said, properly contrite while he steadied the rocking canoe. "I want a selfie of us together, as the Americans say," she explained, handing him the camera. She put her cheek to his and he extended his arm and asked, "Ready?" She nodded that she was. A second later he pushed the button tripping the shutter. She was entirely pleased with herself as she examined the photo.

"Back to your seat, please," he directed, steadying her with his hand on her behind. He was not above giving it a friendly squeeze in the process.

"Hey!" she cried out at the brazen familiarity and the surprise at having been taken advantage of in a compromised position.

"Think nothing of it," he said, assuring her. "Lewis took exactly the same liberties with Sacajawea and she never once complained."

She laughed at his idiocy and took the fishing rod he handed forward. While he readied his he told her, "Time to catch dinner."

She checked the drag as she had been taught and spun the blade on the white spinner bait. "What are we after, my great white Captain William?"

"Northern pike, my dear white-skinned Bavarian princess."

"Oh, boy," she said with genuine enthusiasm, and with a deft flip of her wrist sent the line reeling out toward the shore. She loved the challenge of a northern now and nothing, save a properly filleted walleye, tasted better.

Will grinned to himself. That's my girl, he thought, and cast his line into the distance. On her second cast she felt the attack of the northern before she saw him and even as she gasped in surprise, set the hook like a veteran. Will reeled in to avoid a tangle of lines and watched her fight the fish with enthusiasm and undisguised elation.

"That's a good one, Sylvie," he told her when he saw the fish near the canoe. Probably will go four pounds."

"What should I do?" she asked breathlessly when the fish had tired sufficiently to be handled.

"Hang on a sec," he said and dug his stringer out of the small tackle box. "Bring him back here a bit so I can reach his head."

She let out a meter or so of line and the tired fish lazily swam toward Will. He deftly grabbed him across the neck just behind the gill plates and once he had the writhing fish completely out of the water, unseated the hook from his jaw. "Perfect hook set," he said to Sylvie, watching with interest, then flipped the spinner bait back into the lake and out of the way so she could reel it in while he attended to the fish flopping at his feet. He put it on the stringer, which he tied to the other side of the canoe.

"Now what?" she asked.

"Get us another one. I'm hungry as a bear."

She did exactly that. They fished another hour or so and Sylvie caught four more fish after the second, one a fighting, dancing smallmouth which threw the spinner bait with a mighty shake of his head at the peak of his jump. Will caught three, all northern, but he spent most of his time controlling the canoe, keeping it parallel to the shore, trying to put Sylvie on as many fish as possible. He fished when he was able, quite content helping Sylvie enjoy her angling, which she assuredly did, genuinely excited each time she felt the heavy strike of a fish on the end of her line.

After her last catch and release, which she did by herself, proudly disdaining any help from Will or his pliers, he said, "Okay, bring your line in. Time to find a spot to set up camp."

She pouted as she pulled the spinner bait once more through the water.

"I know you're a fishing machine, sweetheart, but if we don't get our tent set up you'll be sleeping under the stars tonight," he explained. She shipped her rod and switched to her paddle. The two four-pound northern swam alongside the canoe, needing very little effort to keep up. Will took them further down the lake, all the while scanning the shoreline for a suitable location to put in.

"That might do," he said, pointing with the wide blade of his oak paddle, varnish peeling at the lip. She followed the line of sight, but it took her a minute to spot the feature he was interested in. Then she saw it: two slabs of monolithic granite lay in the water ahead of them, creating a natural U-shaped harbor. The granite emerged out of the side of a forested hill like two stone fingers extending from the top of a hand. In the hollow between the two knuckles of the fist, they would lay their ground cover and set up the tent. The slope rising up into the forest protected them from the north wind; the two granite massifs blocked the west and east winds. It was a good spot.

"Prepare to land," Will commanded as Sylvie turned the canoe in to the natural bay between the two rock outcroppings. She heard the nose of the aluminum canoe grind over the small stones of the short beach as it crunched to a halt in the sand. Will shipped his paddle after she was ashore, safe and dry, jumped out, lifted the nose and safely banked the canoe on shore.

Sylvie surveyed the landing and with an imperious look informed him, "This will do. See to my things, if you please, boy."

He bowed and complied, enthralled by the majesty of her beauty in the soft, late afternoon light.

Chapter Twenty-four

Camping

After clearing a suitable space of pine needles and rocky debris among the trees off the shore, they laid out the ground cloth, opened the tent and pushed in the flexible aluminum poles, staked the lines, and tied on the rain cover. The air mattress unrolled and self-inflated. Sylvie rolled out the sleeping bags and stored the packs and gear in the cupola at the front of the tent. Will cleaned and filleted the northern at the lake edge, a chore she would just as soon leave to him, although he had offered her the opportunity, gentleman that he was. Instead, she took on the task of collecting firewood and he had to laugh when she came back from her foray into the woods staggering under the weight of the load in her arms. She had piled the load too high and could barely manage a peek at her feet to assure her footing. He began to dig a fire pit and pointed to the side of his excavation. "Just drop it right there," he said.

Out of breath, with the top of her sleeve she dabbed at the sweat brightening her forehead. "There's more to be brought," she suggested.

"Knock yourself out," he told her. "We certainly wouldn't want you to get cold tonight." By the third load, they had enough wood stacked to build a fire large enough to land a cargo plane in a blizzard. He told her enough and hugged her for all her hard work, taking the scent of cedar, pine, and maple from her hair. He took his fire starting kit from the bellows pocket of his field pants, opened the plastic bag and handed her a match. "One is all we get," he said solemnly.

"You can't be serious."

"Serious as a heart attack. As you know, if we build our fire properly one spark should do it," he said. "However, we have played this game before and even a tenderfoot can start a fire with a match. Let's up the stakes. An authentic woodsman should be able to do it without the match."

Skeptical, she looked at the fire pit Will had excavated and lined with a ring of stones, and then at the insignificance of the single match. "You're crazier than I thought. You get that fire going without a match...," she said, thinking back to the one time she had tried to start a fire in the woods near the Hungarian border during an outing with her mother. She remembered how she had cried after using up the last of the matches in the box. They had slept cold that night, no fire to warm them. "You get that fire started without the benefit of a single match, and tonight you can have me any way you want me."

"This should be fun," he said, accepting the challenge. He saw the defiance in her blue eyes highlighted by the soft sunlight of the western sky. "Come here," he said. "I'll show you the secret. He reached into his pocket and pulled out a lighter.

"That's not fair," she yelled, slapping him on the shoulder. "All right," he agreed, "there's no need to get violent."

"First we need striking stones, then tinder." He took her by the hand and walked along the rocky shore of the lake.

"What are we looking for?" she asked.

"Two things: iron pyrite, also known as Fool's Gold." He stopped and pointed. "There. That shiny chunk will do."

She found what he indicated and brought it back. "It does look like gold. You think you can get this to spark?"

"Watch this," he said, as he pulled his small hatchet from his belt. He struck the pyrite against the steel head of the hatchet. Sparks flew.

"That is so cool," she said.

He grinned at her enthusiasm. "Pyrite is a Greek word for fire starter." He put the hatchet back into its cover at his belt. "But this would be too easy. And just so you know, it can't be stainless steel. It has to be a hardened carbon steel, like the hatchet.

She squinted and covered her eyes against the sun. "Now what?"

"That white quartz will do." He struck the white stone against the iron pyrite and sparks again flew. He danced away from the shower. She was more impressed with his footwork than the fireworks. On the way back to the firebed he stopped at a birch tree and scraped the papery bark with his pocketknife. "What I really want is this fungus called conch rot." He scraped with the edge of his knife until he had a soft ball in the palm of his hand.

"Now the work begins," he said, on his knees before the fire pit. He seated Sylvie as a windbreak and began the tedious process of striking the pyrite against the quartz. He had trouble getting the glowing orange sparks to hit the tinder ball. He realigned himself, narrowed his strokes, and fired a few sparks onto the tinder. It flamed for an instant before dying into smoke. Sylvie clapped, encouraging him. One stroke of the pyrite against the stone sent a shower falling into the dry tinder, and small fires erupted, flamed, and died. Sylvie looked disappointed for him. He set the stones aside quickly, cupped the tinder ball in his palms, and gently blew into the bundle. A tendril of smoke rose. He blew again and an orange flame crackled and licked at his chin. He carefully placed the nascent ball of fire atop the dried lichen and dead grasses in the center of the fire pit. He bellowed two more puffs into the tinder and it caught and crackled into flame. He turned and coughed the smoke out of his lungs, eyes watering.

"Next, we put in some wood shavings, but they must be absolutely dry or it will kill the fire and just smoke." He built a *tipi* of very dry twigs across the bolus of tinder. Around the *tipi* of thin twigs he carefully built a cage of larger sticks so that the top grid lay an inch or two above the point of the stick cone. He gathered together four or five sticks about the thickness of her wrist and laid these aside. He stepped back and examined his handiwork as the smoldering fire chewed into the wood and grew in size and strength.

She held up the single match, making it all the more significant. "I can't believe you did it. It's just as I have suspected all along..."

"What's that?" he asked, taking the bait.

"You are a caveman," she teased him.

"You're mine," he said simply, drawing her close for a sloppy kiss.

"Troglodyte," she accused him and pointed over his shoulder to the fire. A gust of wind had knocked down the carefully constructed geometry of his stick scaffold, drowning the flame in wood. He stood, hands on hips, thoroughly disgusted.

"Don't look so sad, pretty boy. You proved your point. She took the singular match he had given her and struck it against the friction of the sandpaper he kept in his fire kit. To shield it from the gentle breeze coming out of the north, she cupped the bending flame, protecting it within the cupola of her fingers and palm, and put it to the smoldering tinder, which caught the offer of the flame as it curled and sparked into light. Before the flame pinched her fingers, she dropped the match into the center and gently blew the sparking mass into tendrils of fire. Now the tinder pile glowed red each time she gently breathed air into the belly of the fire. The rebuilt stick structure smoked, hissed, and snapped into flame. She sat back on her heels and watched carefully. Will stood above her, admiring the steady progress of the flame.

"We did it," she said with a little girl's gleeful satisfaction.

"Indeed," he said. "You have a future as a pyromaniac." Just then superheated sap popped and the little stick tent shifted and collapsed across the center of the glowing tinder ball.

"Oh," she exclaimed, thinking the fire had again failed. He put his face to the embers and blew steadily. The fire caught, burning with some force now and the flames reached up and through the grid of sticks lying above the burning center. Another minute and these too ignited, so he fed in the larger sticks set to the side. When the fire announced itself in heat and light and sound, he added the larger pieces that would reduce to coals needed for cooking. The heat was such that they had to back away or risk being scorched and he said, "Madame, your fire is ready."

He looked up to see her unbuttoning her shirt. And much as he appreciated the view of her cleavage in her bra as she fully opened her shirt, he politely declined. "After dinner would be better."

She smiled and buttoned up. "Your wish is my command," she said, reminding him of her promise and her willingness to pay off in good sport.

"We have a long night ahead of us and we better eat because you're going to need your strength," he warned.

"Uh oh," she said rolling her eyes. "If you think you're man enough...."

He said nothing; merely pointed to the fire and grinned, then fed in another log. He arranged the stones he had collected off the shore and placed them so the fire would heat them. He set his griddle across the smoking stones and soon the butter he had cut into the pan sizzled, spat, and skidded across the iron bottom. Sylvie floured and seasoned the fillets, then dropped a packet of wild rice into the pot of boiling water set at the other end of the fire pit. He served her golden fillets of sautéed fresh northern pike, accentuated with the exotic flavors of wild rice on the side. She took her first bite of the steaming, snow white flesh under the golden crust, blew it from hot to warm on her fork, and then tasted. She closed her eyes it was so good.

"Absolutely delicious, Will."

"Ooops. Almost forgot," he said. He put his plate aside, scrambled up and headed down to the outcrop of stone in the water. He hurried back and presented her a bottle of chilled viognier from California's Central Coast region, a grape varietal new to her. Once uncorked and in their cups, she pronounced the wine acceptable, gleefully making a show of it, surprised at the unexpected luxury of wine in the wild. He touched his paper cup to hers. The luscious golden wine tasted of fresh apples, lemons, and honey. They toasted the dinner and the place and finally, each other. The wine proved a perfect complement to the fish and rice. They ate with gusto and stuffed themselves with fillets and drank down the entire bottle of wine, shared equally.

Will lay back groaning and Sylvie said, "Ohmigod, I can't believe how much I ate. I am such a pig."

Will propped himself on an elbow. "I've never seen a woman eat so much outside the circus."

"Shut up, you," she moaned, laughing at the truth in his hyperbole. "I have to pee. "Where's that toilet paper?"

"I'll do the dishes," he said, "while you go pee. Just remember: for a female boots point uphill, tush points downhill."

She considered the suggestion for a minute, then caught on. "Good idea," she said, shaking the roll of toilet paper for emphasis, and headed up into the trees.

When she returned she informed him for no particular reason, "That helped considerably." She watched him use sand from the short edge of beach between two granitic boulders to clean the pots and pans before rinsing them in the lake.

"Up for a walk before we lose the last of the day?" he asked. She nodded and he said, "When we get back we'll stoke up the fire again and I'll teach you all about s'mores."

They spent the better part of half an hour walking up the slope into the trees above the tent where they found a well-trodden deer trail. In a glade about half a mile from the campsite they stood holding hands, watching the last of the sun, the color of flame burning on a cedar bough, slip under the horizon. She gave him a quick kiss and he could taste a fleck of wine on her lips. She wanted to linger but he knew better. It would be dark soon and he had not thought to bring his small flashlight. They looked once more into the pink and orange sky, all that remained of the sun, and then walked the deer path back to the camp.

He added more fuel to the fire and showed her how to combine fire-toasted marshmallow with chocolate and graham crackers into a decadent sandwich. In the flicker of firelight he noticed the melted chocolate smeared on her mouth and kissed it clean for her. He tidied up the camp and she readied the tent for sleeping, setting up the battery-powered lantern for light. When she came out, she saw that for some reason he was building a miniature version of the campfire on the point of the granite slab that descended into the water. Darkness moved rapidly into the forest beyond them, settling in among the black green pines, turning the lake from blue to gray to ink. She looked up into the sky and saw the first twinkling smear of stars.

He was up to something and she waited patiently, watching him arrange a blanket next to the small fire. He put seat cushions from the canoe atop the blanket and she felt the cool breeze off the lake touch her cheek and fluff her hair. He called to her and she walked out along the narrow table of stone to where he waited by the fire. The heat of the burning logs reflecting off the granitic stone escarpment warmed her, and she could feel its heat radiate against her calves.

"Now you may undress," he told her.

She felt her breath catch in her throat when she realized what he had in mind. With the exception of her hiking socks, she complied and stood naked under the stars, feeling the sensual brush of the wind off the water on her breasts, and the heat of the fire on her behind. The disparate sensations both invigorated and excited her. She trembled as he unzipped his pants. Naked, he sat and she carefully straddled him, covering the cool length of his penis with her heat. She rocked against his thighs in time to the lap of the lake against their rocky outpost. He touched a finger to her lips. "Easy." He pointed to the fire. "I come when the fire dies, not before."

Her blue eyes widened at the challenge, but she nodded her assent, remembering her promise. She reveled in the heat their bodies generated against the cool of the night. She listened to the sounds of the lake and the forest behind them: the call of an owl ready to hunt; the cry of a loon trying to locate his mate. She thrilled to the sensation of his deliberate, cool kisses; the slow insinuation of his fingers across and into her body; the lascivious stretch of her legs around his hips. There were noises in the woods she did not recognize or understand, and she held him all the more tightly for it, basking in the security of his strong arms. She fought the need to finish, to move insistently and with urgency. Each time she neared her climax, he stopped her. She caught her breath and listened to the darkness all around them. As the lake gently lapped the shore she had an idea. She looked over to the fire now as a breath of wind caught it, ruffling the flames like the feathers of a bird on a high branch, and the embers that had burned to coal glowed as the fire relapsed when the wind dropped. She squeezed him with the slick muscles inside her, trying to pull him further up into her core. This time, he was forced to gasp against her throat.

"Where did you learn that?" he asked, after he got his breathing under control.

"Promise you won't tell anyone?"

He made a show of looking around, but she was serious in asking for his promise, so he gave it. "When I was a teenager I read books about the art of love-making, and before I ever had a boy I practiced because I wanted to be the best possible lover for my partner. At the time it was very important to me, but I had almost forgotten about it."

He kissed her neck and thanked her for remembering just in time. She looked once more at the fire, braced her heels against the rough granite and leaned back onto the heels of her hands. They both came as the fire rose into smoke.

THE RAUCOUS CALLING of crows in the trees above the tent woke him. He looked over at Sylvie curled deep in her bag, still sleeping like a baby, mouth slightly open, jaw relaxed, and a line of dried spittle running from her mouth to her chin. He grinned and reached over to run his fingers through the mess of her white-blonde hair. She looked for him and finding him, resettled herself in the warmth of the sleeping bag and said in German, "*Schlafe.*" Sleep.

He kissed her cheek, and amused by the innocence of her childlike insistence, told her to keep sleeping while he got up to relieve himself. He could not understand what she mumbled in return. After his pants, he pulled on his socks and boots but did not lace them, and stood outside the tent. He stretched away the stiffness of sleeping too closely to someone in cramped quarters and had a good look at the morning. A mist curled across the surface of the lake. In the east the first rays of the sun pinked the edges of the clouds, and then burst into orange flame below them. He stepped out on the flank of stone where their passion had killed the fire, and made his contribution to the waters in the lake. He remembered a quote he thought had once been attributed to Michelangelo speaking about his rival Leonardo's massive ego. "Every time he takes a leak into the river Arno, he thinks the water rises three feet downstream." He rather liked that idea as he finished and checked the height of the water at the shoreline. It might have come up a bit. His stomach grumbled, pulling him back from his nonsensical reverie. He had work to do.

He found a suitable length of larch with which to poke at the last cedar log lying on the cold fire near the tent. It smoked and smoldered as he pushed the ash away from the unburned wood. Last night's fire had taken a deep bite out of its center and had charred the ends. He dropped a bit of tinder and some smaller sticks on the white ash of the coals and blew. The tinder immediately caught and lit the sticks. In two minutes he had the fire going to his satisfaction, and as he waited for the wood to burn down to coals, he mixed pancake powder with water from his canteen. He did not have bacon or eggs, but he did have a soft jerky made from venison, from which he cut two helpings with his Buck knife. He settled the coals, warmed the iron skillet, and poured the batter in for the first cake. The smell of the pancakes and the jerky brought Sylvie out of the tent and into the morning, following her nose. She wore hiking socks, boots unlaced, her blue bikini bottoms, and her denim shirt unbuttoned over her bare chest. Her stomach was white, hard and flat, her legs long and sleek with runner's muscle. She pushed the sleep from her eyes and looked at him somewhat distressed.

"What's the matter?" he asked.

"Well," she said, "I have to go."

"Well," he echoed, "It's been nice camping with you."

This time she called him a *Dummkopf,* and said in measured and clipped tones, "I have to go to the bathroom but I don't know how." She was embarrassed by her confession.

"You don't know how?" he asked, incredulous. "And I thought it was the American school system that was failing." Despite the urgency of her physical needs, she had not lost her sense of humor and she laughed. She held up her hands, helpless. "I really don't know what to do."

"Just a sec," he said. He flipped the flapjack in the pan, noting its coppery brown color, and set the pan aside. "Come with me and I'll show you how to get started." He walked her into the forest and found a suitable tree, slender enough for her to hold, substantial enough to take her weight. He placed his feet shoulder width apart and showed her how to bend while holding the tree for support. They traded places. Using the toe of his boot, he scooped out a depression below the arc of her behind.

She shook her head. "I certainly can't do it while you watch," she said.

He pulled open the knot that loosely bound her shirt and kissed the tips of her breasts. "I don't expect you to. This tree was for demonstration purposes only." He flipped her the plastic bag containing a roll of toilet paper and sanitary wipes, which she caught easily in one hand. "Use this sparingly, and once you find a suitable tree, use the toe of your boot to hollow out a catch basin. When finished, drop your paper and wipies in too, and cover, like a pretty little kitty."

"I will," she promised, willing to sacrifice some degree of personal comfort for environmental correctness.

"And one more thing, Sylvie...," he called as she stepped gingerly into the tree line.

She turned to him and pulled her shirt closed across her breasts. "Yes?"

"Being that this is your first time, I would take the panties all the way off, just to be safe." She saw that he was being serious and she nodded.

When she returned she beamed with the self-satisfaction of accomplishment and finished dressing in the tent. She joined him out on the granite promontory, and accepted with delighted thanks, her plate of three steaming flapjacks.

"No more butter," he said, "but the maple syrup has butter flavoring."

She drizzled the amber liquid over the cakes and took a bite. "*Ausgezeichnet*," she said. She rolled her eyes after the second bite. "Simply outstanding."

They ate, one seated across from the other, and watched the mist rise off the lake like a thin cotton coverlet pulled back to expose the water's skin. This early in the morning the lake seemed more burgundy than blue or green. They watched a blue heron, hunched through the shoulders like an old man, stab at minnows in the shallows further down the lake shore. Breakfast done, she thanked him properly with a sticky sweet kiss. She wanted to save her venison jerky for later, but he ate his portion. She did the dishes and half an hour later they broke camp, loaded the canoe and paddled east under a rising sun.

Chapter Twenty-five

Pioneer Project

The Project Team Leader (PTL) was not having a good day. He had just this moment been informed that the North American Aerospace Defense Command (NORAD) in Colorado Springs had detected a ballistic missile launch from North Korea. U. S. Pacific Command based in Hawaii confirmed NORAD's data. The Hwasong-14 missile rose from Kusong, not far from North Korea's border with China, and landed in waters between the Korean Peninsula and Japan. Once he recovered from the initial shock of the intel, he thought the missile's almost 500 mile flight probably caused some severe anal puckering among the Japanese defense forces, to say nothing of the concern rampant among the South Korean Joint Chiefs of Staff and their American allies. The briefing served as further affirmation of the necessity for the PTL's project. And the news that day regarding the project's progress was only getting worse.

As usual, the team reported they were behind schedule and over-budget, although some project creep was expected. This, however, bordered on the realm of the criminal. He could not believe the numbers on the printout. There had to be a mistake. To get the contract you had to play the game: underbid and offer a timeline to completion no one could realistically beat. Once the military committed its financial and logistical resources, they were hooked. However, that did not mean the DoD budgeting office could not bring enormous pressure to bear. There were lucrative maintenance contracts to let and, of course, favorable consideration for future weapons projects. No, this was not like the old days of the eight hundred dollar toilet seat. It was now entirely possible that the Department of Defense could kill the project; he had seen it happen. The consequences of such a move for a subcontractor the size of his company could be catastrophic. He had been given the word: make the project work or the company goes down the shitter and we lose everything: personnel, the plant, the land, the equipment, stock options, retirement plans, everything goes. Failure this time was not an option.

He would have to push his people even harder and look for more corners to cut. If his company did not deliver on their end of the project, rumor had it they would be replaced, and word was out that a competitor for the original bid was being asked to ramp up again just in case. It was a very ugly rumor. The contract was the largest awarded to his company and without it he knew he would be looking for another job. He knew he had excellent and reliable people on the team who understood the realities of the project and knew how to play the game. He also knew that he was very good at what he did. He could deal with the cost-overruns and the delays.

He pushed the printout of the figures aside and examined the next document. He wondered if the day could get any worse. As he read, his day worsened. This news posed an entirely different set of problems that transcended the merely fiscal or budgetary, which could be managed. As he read more deeply into the horrible reality of the report, the problems escalated into the nebulous realm of the ethical and moral, dilemmas dreaded by engineers largely unprepared by their education and training to handle such philosophic issues. He looked at the signature for the chief software engineer: Dr. Nadipuram. That clinched it. Time for a face-to-face.

Daya Nadipuram, Ph. D., was without doubt his best and brightest software designer. Born in India, she was now a naturalized citizen of the U.S. but still wore her native sari to work. She preferred to work alone, not unusual among software types who spent most of their day poring over endless pages of code, line by line, until they destroyed their eyesight. LASIK, joked some of the engineers, was invented specifically for software geeks to restore their failing vision. A graduate of the top-ranked India Institute of Technology in Mumbai, she also held a Ph. D. from Caltech in computer engineering with an emphasis in software design.

As the PTL walked the short distance down the hall to her office, he remembered that Dr. Daya Nadipuram was seldom a fan of meetings, which spoke to her good sense, but the strength of the woman was that he could depend on her to do the job without having to hold her hand, as he was forced to do with many of the young hotshots out of software engineering programs at Renssalear, or MIT, or Minnesota. He glanced at his watch. She should be back from lunch and safely sequestered from the stares she engendered among the locals in town or the newbies on the site. The citizens of Cedar Rapids, Iowa, a town of almost 200,000 people, were still provincial enough that an Indian woman in a brightly colored sari above Nike running shoes caused them to turn and stare, but he was inured to the idiosyncrasies of his engineering staff.

"Hello, Daya," he said in greeting as he walked through the open door into her office.

She looked up from her terminal and smiled at the PTL. "Hello, boss. Thought you might be coming to pay me a visit. Care for a cup of tea?" He nodded and sat and waited for her to perform the ritual of pouring the tea. She knew how he preferred it, right down to the three cubes of sugar, no artificial sweetener. He would rather drink a Diet Coke, but he made an exception for her.

Besides, the ritual of drinking the Taj Mahal tea with her was calming, and it gave the two time to look each other over before getting down to business.

He looked into the expressive, big brown eyes accentuated by the arching black eyebrows and long lashes that did not seem real, but were. She was not at all an unattractive woman if you took the time to look carefully into her pleasant face, a luxury for which he rarely had time. As he sipped from the quail egg blue demitasse, he noticed her black hair shined with oil and that her skin was darker than his own. She smelled of incense and cinnabar. He considered why, now in her forties, she had never married. The obvious answer was that Cedar Rapids was not exactly a dating hotspot where an expatriate Indian woman might find a suitable mate of her caste, intelligence, and education. She stirred her cup of the lapchong-oolong with a small silver teaspoon, using the time to formulate her thoughts.

"The report I put on your desk this morning and the reason you are here, no doubt, is because I finished a computer run of the latest target acquisition software. When the results came out, I ran it again just to be certain." She motioned with a thumb to the stack of printouts on her desk. "I'm afraid I have bad news for you. Under every scenario within the model, the software failed. At its present stage of development," she said, avoiding his eyes by staring into the swirl of her teacup, "the Pioneer anti-ballistic missile system target acquisition software cannot and will not differentiate between a series of decoys and an in-coming missile." That was it. She was finished. She had nothing more to say. She took a sip from her cooling tea and ventured a look across the cup to see how her report had affected the PTL.

In a word, he was stunned and he did not care if she knew it. She had predicted as much. She was one of the few members of the team on whom he could depend for complete honesty. She did not mince words, she did not embellish or exaggerate, and she did not hedge or lie: she told the unvarnished raw truth. She provided the essential details and the facts and left others to draw therefrom whatever conclusions they might. She was a scientist and an engineer and a designer of software programs. She literally had written the book on target acquisition software for anti-ballistic missiles, an elaboration of her dissertation. If she said their company's current package would not work, then that is the way it was. The software did not work and no amount of testing or retesting could make it work. There was only one question to ask: "In its current configuration, can we use patches to make it work?"

She put her cup down. She had anticipated the question. She straightened the band below her breasts. "Given our current mission parameters, that is, the detection by multiple sensors first, of in-bound threats and, second, the ability to differentiate the ballistic threat from decoys designed to defeat the Pioneer, I would say, yes, eventually we can make it work."

He held his breath. He felt like a drowning swimmer with just enough oxygen left in his lungs to reach the surface before his chest exploded. "How long will it take, Daya?" What she had just said to him, he knew was designed to set up his question.

"Based on my computer modeling scenarios I predict it will take us, given current resources and budgets, a minimum of three years to solve all the problems."

Had she pulled out a .44 magnum and shot him between the eyes he could not have been more devastated. He felt the inexorable pull of the current, dragging him back down into the inescapable depths of hopelessness.

She saw the despair flooding his eyes. "I'm sorry, boss, with profound regret. I wanted this thing to succeed as much as anyone. I have five years of my life in this code. I remind you that from the time I left DARPA to come and work here, I have written memo after memo detailing my conclusion that the software cannot be ready within the time constraints by which we are bound. It's not merely a matter of hiring enough young people to write the code; it has to do with the incredible complexity and difficulty of the task. The requirements outstrip our capability at present. It's as simple as that."

There was nothing more to do. If it could not be done at present, it could not be done. His moral imperative at this point in his role as Project Team Leader was to inform the CEO of the company that the target acquisition software was not ready and could not be made ready in less than three years. It might cost him his job, but it was his duty and his responsibility alone to relay the information without hesitation or prejudice. It was his duty as an American citizen charged with contributing to the design and development of his country's new National Missile Defense Program. Anything less would be an abrogation of his duty and commitment to his company, his country, and his honor as a man. He turned back to Dr. Nadipuram. "I assume you have a full report prepared that details your findings and supports your conclusions."

She nodded and reached into the mysterious folds of her sari and pulled out a memory key. "Everything you need is here: simulations, analysis, report, everything." She handed it to him. He accepted the key.

"For the time being, this is for my eyes and my eyes only. I will set up a meeting and present it to CEO Davis first thing tomorrow morning. Are you prepared to testify to the accuracy and reliability of your findings?"

She nodded. She was not at all put off by the question. As both a scientist and scholar now working in the business world, she was fully aware of the need to support and defend her findings. Millions of dollars and people's careers were at stake. She rose from her chair in sympathy, now somewhat uncomfortable with what she had done. She understood the immense burden she had imposed on the Project Team Leader.

"Before I go, Daya...." She smiled and waited for the request. "Are there any other copies of these documents?" he asked, indicating the portable flash drive.

"You have the hard copy of my synopsis on your desk. Otherwise, all the original data and my analyses are on my hard drive, she said, pointing to her computer."

He thought for a moment. "Do you have a safe deposit box at your bank?"

She was a bit surprised at the question. It seemed rather personal. "I do. I have some of my mother's jewelry there, some insurance papers, and the like."

"Do this for me: burn another memory key, but tell no one it exists. Don't erase anything of your original files. Leave them intact. Take the copy with you and put it in your safe deposit box this afternoon. No. I take it back. Work late as usual. There will be less traffic, fewer eyes, and no one will be suspicious. Go to the bank first thing in the morning."

"How will I get it through security?"

He thought for a moment. "You know the female security guard, LaVinia Thomas, I think?"

"I do."

"She comes on at three and works until midnight. Hand her the key personally and let her examine it. Don't try to smuggle it through security. Tell her it contains some special Indian recipes you want to share with her. She's always talking about how much she loves to cook and try new foods. Download as many as you can off the internet and tell her to try four or five. Make sure you label the files on the key 'Indian Recipes.' Bury the computer modelling results and documentation in a folder with some strange Indian name. Have her upload the recipes on her computer at the guard station. She won't try to take them all if you indicate the ones you want her to have. Take the memory key and then go directly to your bank. Tell no one."

She agreed.

The PTL left her to find the recipes and download the information. He returned to his office and set up a meeting for the next day with the President and CEO Davis.

DR. DAYA NADIPURAM worked late into the evening as usual and, as usual, when she prepared to leave the building, the halls were quiet and the offices dark except for the rooms in which the cleaning crews worked. Instead of taking the elevator—to avoid meeting anyone— she walked the stairs down to the foyer where the security screenings took place and the guards had their station behind the grand curve of a marble counter top. As Dr. Nadipuram approached the security station, LaVinia Thomas looked up from her movie star magazine and smiled at the doctor, admiring the courage it took to wear such a beautiful flowing sari over Nike running shoes.

"Hello, LaVinia," Dr. Nadipuram said. "I have a little gift for you tonight." She held up the flash drive.

The majority of the engineers in the building treated Thomas as nothing more than a fixture, an inconvenience, and an interruption of their very important lives. Dr. Nadipuram, on the other hand, had always treated the large black woman with respect and often spent a few minutes with her, at least in the evening when Thomas worked the late shift, speaking with her personally and asking about her family. From these conversations Daya had learned that LaVinia loved to cook and loved nothing better than trying exotic foods. As Daya passed her briefcase over to be put through the detector, she handed Thomas the key and waited as she plugged it into the laptop on the polished granite counter.

"I have four or five recipes here from my mother that you really should try. If you like them, I'll give the rest of them to you as well. One is for curried shrimp and one for *appam*, a famous Indian pancake made with rice and coconut that goes great with stew. I hope you like them."

LaVinia Thomas beamed. She looked around quickly and adjusted her holster above her broad hips. Uploading the recipes would not take more than a minute or two and the building seemed empty at this hour. What harm could it do?

She grinned and waved Dr. Nadipuram around the marble counter where her computer sat on the shelf below the highly polished countertop. She knew she could trust the doctor. She swung the laptop around so both could see the screen. She let Daya take the mouse and call up the file registry for the flash drive. Out of curiosity, LaVinia moved in for a closer look. A number of folders appeared on the desktop. She watched Daya move among a number of folders labeled Breakfast, Lunch, Dinner, and Desserts. She clicked on three files to highlight them, thought for a second and said, "You'll want to try this one, too. That should be enough for now. Let me know if you have any questions about the recipes or the ingredients or how to make the meals. I'll be glad to help."

They watched together as the computer copied the files and informed them when it was finished. LaVinia was also greatly interested in having a look at the folder labeled Desserts, but she knew she must not be greedy. She would ask for it next time, to be polite. LaVinia removed the key and Dr. Nadipuram pulled a new key from her briefcase, inserted it into the drive, copied the files from the hard drive onto the key, removed it, handed it to LaVinia and made certain all record of the files had been erased in virtual memory and History. For safekeeping, she secreted the first key in one of the folds of her sari.

"Just to be safe," she told LaVinia, "we'll clear the Recycle bin as well and no one will be the wiser."

"This is so sweet of you, Dr. Nadipuram. I can't wait to try the shrimp curry."

"I thought you might appreciate the recipes. I'm glad to share them with you." She sighed. "And now I have to head home and do some more work tonight before I can get to bed. Tomorrow looks like an important day."

LaVinia Thomas walked her to the main doors and unlocked them for her. "Now don't you work too late, Miss Nadipuram. This damn company ain't gonna fail if you go to bed a bit early tonight."

"I think I'll take your advice, LaVinia. I have to be up early tomorrow as it is. Good night."

"Good night, Dr. Nadipuram." She watched the Chief Software Engineer walk gracefully into the night, the wind lifting the edges of her sari, her running shoes quiet on the concrete of the sidewalk as she walked to her car. Only when she saw that Nadipuram was safely in the car and the lights were on, did she close and lock the doors and return to her station. She could hardly contain the excitement of exploring the recipes she had been given.

The next evening, as she was standing at the stove stirring the curry into the shrimp, she realized in a brief moment of panic that she had forgotten to log in the memory key. She picked up her cell phone to call her supervisor, and then thought how silly. After all, who would care about a flash drive loaded with Indian recipes. She had seen it with her own eyes. The smell of the curry mixed with the golden yellow of the saffron took her from the phone back to the pan and she forgot the incident.

THE PROJECT TEAM Leader was at his desk even earlier than usual, and when his secretary arrived he asked her to hold all calls. From the time he arrived at work, he continued to struggle with his decision. He reaffirmed to himself that he had made the proper and correct choice. Now the difficulty lay in finding the right words with which to frame it. As the hour of the meeting approached, he looked at his hands. They were steady, but the mahogany in his skin glistened with perspiration. It did not matter; to others he appeared entirely calm on the outside despite the inner turmoil, but the sweaty palms betrayed him to himself. He had learned to live with it. He combed his brown fingers through his black hair, dark as anthracite, and moved his handkerchief from his back pocket to the front pocket of his khakis. He kept it there to soak up the moisture from the palm of his right hand in case he had to shake hands. He pulled a clip-on tie from his desk drawer, managed to squeeze the button at his neck closed, added the tie and shouldered into a dark blue sport coat. He put the memory key in the inside pocket of the coat and walked to the president's office.

Robertson—call me Bob—Davis was studying his monitor while the PTL waited for his executive secretary to show him in. He finalized a tee time, waited for the confirmation and logged off. He came around the enormous marble desk and greeted the Project Leader. "What can I do for you today?" Davis asked. He did not offer to shake hands. Instead, he indicated a glistening silver carafe of ice water inscribed with the company name and logo, but the PTL declined. Davis made the man wait while he poured himself a glass, added a slice of lemon with tongs and seated the man on the Italian leather couch.

The PTL studied his boss for a second or two, trying to get a read from his face. That face was tanned and almost dark as his own and seemed freshly shaved, no doubt professionally barbered with a stainless steel, straight-edge razor. His shoes, which seemed to match the soft leather of the couch, were immaculately shined. The smile seemed genuine; the boss seemed in a good mood. Perhaps the news climbing the grapevine had not yet reached the offices on the third floor. Like the PTL, Dr. Robertson Davis was a graduate of the Iowa State University at Ames, where he had finished a doctorate in physics. A Cyclone tried and true, whenever possible he hired graduates from his alma mater. That way they could commiserate with each other when the football team lost yet another game to their arch rival, the University of Iowa. He had season tickets for himself and a selection of passes, which he doled out to his employees from time to time as a reward for good work. Curiously enough, this season had opened with a victory over U of I, and part of his good humor was the result of the rather substantial bet he had won. Six more years like this one and he might break even. No, it was obvious from outward appearances that the president was unaware of the bad news.

The PTL summoned his courage once more and in his typical fashion, laid it on the line. "My software team tells me that the target acquisition program for the Pioneer is not mission ready or mission capable. I'm sorry to tell you this Bob, but we're not going to make it, given our current deadlines from the DoD."

He waited for the explosion but it did not come. Instead, Davis reached into the coat pocket of his Hugo Boss suit and withdrew what appeared to be a cigarette case. He pressed the spring-loaded clasp on the embossed silver lid and it sprung elegantly open into his palm. He removed a white capsule, popped it into his mouth, swallowed from the silver goblet, closed and replaced the case. Had he already heard the news after all? The PTL knew Daya Nadipuram would never leak information; her loyalty to the project and to the team was unquestioned. But someone else in the group might have talked.

Dr. Davis waited a moment for the anti-anxiety pill to settle and said simply, "That's not the news I expected. I have a meeting next week with the Director of the Missile Defense Agency. Each contractor on the Pioneer project is required to brief him on our operational readiness. You're telling me I will have to inform him that we're not good to go." His voice was flat and devoid of emotion, as if he were suddenly very tired. After three minutes of wholly uncomfortable silence CEO Davis said, "I depended on you. I hired you and gave you your first job out of Iowa State. You were my personal pick for PTL when we were awarded the contract for the Pioneer's target acquisition software. I put my full and complete trust in you." He shook his head dolefully from side to side. "Without that half-billion, we're not gonna make it." His voice rose a bit at the end of his sentence. He looked the PTL directly in the eye, defying him to say anything to the contrary.

The Project Team Leader shifted his position on the couch so he could face his boss more directly. This had nothing to do with betrayal. This had to do with feasibility and time. "I told you when we put forward the bid on the project that we could not meet the requirements set forth by the director of the NMDA in the time allowed. We might still be able to do it, Bob, but my lead scientist in software says it is going to take three more years, and she is not given to exaggeration."

"Goddammit," Davis screamed, becoming hysterical, the thin pane of his exterior calm shattered by the news. "We don't have three fucking years! We have until Monday of next week and then I have to stand up in front of all those military assholes and government contractors and every one of the Technology Planning Teams and admit that Tactical Missile Systems of Cedar Rapids, Iowa has failed to accomplish its Mission Essential Task. Goddammit. Goddammit. Give me the fucking report! He waited for the PTL to hand him the memory key. "Are there any other copies?"

"No sir," he lied. In that instant, he had made the ethical decision that as a citizen of the United States his country's security superseded his commitment to the financial viability of his company. There were greater and more important issues at stake here. The Israelis needed the missile defense system to quiet Iran's sabre rattling. And no one could predict what might come flying out of North Korea in the next year or so. "You now have the only copy. The original is on Dr. Nadipuram's hard drive. I have the synopsis of her analysis in a report on my desk."

Davis jumped to the intercom and instructed his secretary to personally run down—and he meant run, goddammit—to the PTL's office and bring back the synopsis. "That's good, that's good," Davis said, weighing his options. He recovered his smile and rebuilt his face around it. "For the time being, let's keep this between ourselves." He did not wait for acknowledgment. "Given the potential ramifications for the company, you understand. Lots of careers at stake here. If it gets out that we falsified or misrepresented our technological capabilities in the bid, there could be serious legal repercussions for all of us." He emphasized the last three words. He thought for a minute more as he wiped the perspiration from his forehead. For an instant, the PTL empathized with the man's predicament. He had built the company from scratch using principles developed from his dissertation. Suddenly his face brightened and he took a deep breath. "Does the program recognize the decoys?"

"Yes, that's the problem. The sensors slaved to the program detect everything, but can't discriminate between the warhead and the dummies. Essentially, if there are nine dummies and a warhead, it sends ten target verifications to the CPU guiding the missile, and this serves to overload the system."

"Aha, aha," Davis said. "So the software is fully capable of detecting an incoming ballistic missile."

"In a manner of speaking, but that's not the point..."

Davis shouted over him. "That's exactly the fucking point! Besides, we don't really know if the software will fail or not. It has only failed in modeling tests, right?"

The PTL shrugged his shoulders. "That's right, Bob, but come on. Who are we kidding here? In every computer test we've run the missile's threat recognition system can't differentiate between the real threat and decoys deployed along with it. It fails in every simulation we run."

Davis carefully shook his head. "I don't see it that way. This is not a failure at all. The software is working too well. All we need to do is refine it."

The PTL gave up. "Those refinements will take three years."

"Who knows that?"

"Dr. Nadipuram, who ran and reported the simulations to me knows. And because she reports directly to me given the sensitive nature of the findings, you know, because I report all findings from all my groups directly to you. That makes three of us who know."

"Why don't Daya's people know?"

"Each of the programmers works on a specific section of the code. As group leader, Daya compiled all the sections for the first time last week and ran the simulations. One section of code might work beautifully and logically individually, but when compiled, the system can still fail. It's a perfect affirmation of von Bertalannfy's theory that the whole is truly greater than the sum of the parts, as it is in this case."

Davis shot him a withering glare. "I don't need a fucking lecture on Systems Theory. Anyway, we can work that to our advantage." He took a minute and furiously scribbled a few notes. "Let's keep the system failure to ourselves, shall we? And I want you to fire Nadipuram. She's been nothing but a pain in the ass and an impediment to this project from the get-go."

The PTL sat up and squared his shoulders. "I can't do that, Bob."

Davis was momentarily taken aback by the man's blatant insubordination. "Why the hell not? You're her boss."

"She hasn't done anything wrong, Bob. If anything, she has been honest and forthright to a fault. Firing her would send a very bad message, one that could ripple through the company and destroy morale."

Davis steepled his fingers and thought for a moment, trying to ascertain the PTL's motivations. He concluded the PTL was merely standing up for his colleague in the face of adversity. He begrudgingly admired the PTL for that leadership characteristic. It explained his consistently high ratings from the colleagues he worked with. It was time to show some magnanimity. This was a positive ripple that could bounce right back to his office.

"All right. I sure as hell don't want to affect morale within the company until we have more information. The rats might want to jump the ship if they get the wrong impression." The PTL hid a sigh of relief, but Davis was not finished.

"Can you promise me your silence until after I report to the director at DoD?" On the face of it the request seemed reasonable enough, so he nodded. "I need to hear you say it," Davis said, ice in his voice.

The PTL looked him directly in the eye and said, "You don't ever have to doubt my loyalty, Bob." His loyalty to his country was resolute and unwavering and Davis completely missed the meaning of his statement, thinking it applied to the company.

"Good enough. That's all I can ask of any man. I always had you figured for a team player. Now let me take the ball from here on and we may yet get out of this cluster fuck with our sweaty shirts still on our backs. I'll let you know what I decide after my meeting in DC."

Mixed metaphors aside, the PTL was not in the least convinced.

Chapter Twenty-six

Attack

They took their time, not pressed by any sense of urgency or externally imposed schedule, motivated merely by whim and fancy and the long steady strokes of the paddle that propelled the canoe through the placid water. As they rowed the canoe, Will told Sylvie they were headed toward War Club Lake, the second in a chain of four small lakes in the forests above Lake Kabetogama. The last two lakes, Quill and Loiten, required portaging the canoe, so they decided to make their next camp at War Club.

Once out of Locator and halfway across War Club, Will asked Sylvie if she wanted to fish for her lunch and she nodded. He told her to head the canoe to a point of land that entered the lake ahead of them. At the end of the point grew a bed of reeds, natural baffles that calmed the water and provided a perfect hiding place for perch. Will positioned the canoe in about fifteen feet of water out past the edge of the reeds. On the end of Sylvie's line he tied a jig dressed with a small white twister tail.

"Cast in among the reeds, let the jig drop and swim the twister tail through. And don't worry if you bump the reeds. As you come out of them into the deeper water, let the jig drop some more, then reel up."

She waited while he tied his line and flipped it expertly underhand among the thin stiff grasses. She watched the speed of his retrieve. About five yards past the edge of the vegetation where the water deepened, she saw the line move sideways and he snapped the rod up to set the hook. He brought up a yellow-orange fish with black bars that marked it like a tiger. He told her it was in fact called a tiger perch.

"This is just about the size we want: ten inches or more, perfect for the pan." He put the perch on the stringer and warned her about the sharpness of the fan-shaped dorsal fin. They caught the perch in a school, and within an hour each had hooked twenty perch. They released most and kept enough on the stringer for a shore lunch and sandwiches later in the afternoon. It was fast and steady action and Sylvie thoroughly enjoyed herself. When he finally called her off, she was disappointed and wanted to keep fishing.

"That was nothing but fun," she said. After she stowed her rod she dipped her hands over the side to rinse them of the fish smell. She flicked the water off her fingers back at him. "I'm mad at you for making me stop."

"You can't catch every fish in the lake, girl. Give it a rest now and then. We'll have other opportunities. In fact, if you're good we'll fish for northern again after we set up camp and have dinner. Fishing for perch is fun, but it's a different kind of fishing than you're used to with me. It is great fun when they are schooled up and you can park and work the whole reed bed." He passed her the water bottle and a bar of chocolate to appease her.

"You up for a little hike after we land the canoe? I know a trail up ahead where we can stretch our legs before we put these perch in the pan where they belong."

"Sounds like a good idea to me. Now that I think about it, my ass is sore from all this sitting and I have to pee."

He paddled them to shore. "Thought you might."

He landed and she hopped out and held the nose as he scuttled forward, keeping his considerable center of gravity low and in the middle of the canoe. She did not run far back into the bush. As she did so, he properly beached the canoe, grunting as he pulled its heavy dead weight up over the rocks and into the grind of sand at the water's edge.

"That was important," she said as she came back down to the bank, a look of considerable relief on her face. "Should we take our coats for the hike?"

It was a good question. He looked up and gauged the wind and its direction. "I don't think we'll need them, but let's carry them just to be safe. Things can change up here in a heartbeat and, given the time of year, it would be prudent to err on the side of caution."

She mocked him. "It would be prudent to err on the side of caution. You sound just like a university professor."

"Old habits die hard," he acknowledged.

"Okay, fraidy cat, I'm ready," she said, showing off her command of English. She finished tying her coat through the sleeves around her waist.

"Take your water, too." He filled his pockets with a couple more candy bars and a plastic sack full of trail mix. As an afterthought, he added a baggie of the venison jerky. She sidled up and leaned against him as if he were an oak.

He took off her cap and kissed the top of her head. "I beg your pardon, *Fräulein.* Do you mistake me for a tree?"

"Not at all," she assured him. "Consider this simply a physical metaphor for our relationship out here in the wild."

"I see," he said. "A physical metaphor. Let's see if I can interpret the intended meaning of the metaphor. The sheer physicality of my masculine presence throws you off balance?"

"No."

"You have an inner ear problem?"

"No," she said, fighting back a smile.

"My skills as a woodsman and the scent of wood smoke in my shirt and hair have caused you to fall for me?"

She considered the possibility. "True, but not related to the metaphor."

This time he grinned. He shrugged his shoulders and held up his hands in a show of helplessness. "I give up."

She was disgusted with him. "That's the best you can do? And you call yourself a Ph. D.? Just where did you get that doctorate, out of the back of a magazine? It means I lean on you. I depend on you for support."

He stood there scratching his head, looking stupid, trying to comprehend it all, comically befuddled. He looked so silly she could no longer control her laughter.

"You are such a clown and I can't help you. All I can do is laugh at your silliness."

That's all he wanted to hear. "Let's get moving."

"Where away?" she asked. She remembered the phrase from a sailing book she had once read as a teenager.

"North," he informed her. "Always north, and you have the lead."

She took a step or two past him, stopped and turned back, looking sheepish. "And where exactly might that be?"

Being deliberately obtuse and taking advantage of her disorientation, he said matter-of-factly, "North is always north."

She considered this pearl of wisdom. When no further direction was forthcoming, she resorted to bribery. "I will kiss you if you show me the way north."

"As an officer of the federal government, I am immune to bribes," he informed her.

"Immune to bribes perhaps, but not to a Bavarian girl's alpine kisses." She kissed him passionately on the lips and he faltered, eyes closed, savoring the full effect of her kiss.

"This way," he indicated. He took her by the hand and headed north.

They hiked a snowmobile trail for forty-five minutes before they passed beneath an oak tree that sheltered a family of raccoons. The masked animals watched them shyly as they held tightly to their branches. The mother hissed down a warning. As a precaution the youngsters scrambled higher up into the tree. The mother suddenly leaped across to a branch on the next tree, tail up for balance, scrambled down and waddled away, hoping to draw the threat to her and away from her kit. Will and Sylvie moved on, leaving the three youngsters—watching them intently—in the top branches of the massive, ancient oak. Further up the trail they startled a blue heron into flight.

They found a log to sit on and had a quick snack for refreshment. After a ten minute break and a last sip each from the water bottle, they turned back. Will figured they would get back to the canoe just in time for a shore lunch. At the top of the ridge that sloped down to the tree line before the lake, they could see the water and the far shore. They walked the ten yards down, emerged from the trees and Will immediately stopped, holding Sylvie back with an arm.

"What's the matter?" she asked, seeing nothing amiss. Then it occurred to her. "The canoe is gone!" She looked up at him. "Did we come out at the wrong place?"

"That's what I'm checking," he said. He was past the moment of panic when he realized the canoe and all their gear was missing. They quietly walked down to the rocky shoreline. Both could clearly see the drag line where Will had pulled the fully laden canoe aground. "We're definitely in the right spot." He looked carefully up and down the length of the lake, checked the wind direction again and scanned the distance in hopes that the canoe had somehow floated off the landing and drifted with the wind. But he knew it could not have happened that way. The wind or the water or both could not have lifted the heavy weight of the canoe. Another force was at work. He slowly backed away from the scuff indicating where the canoe had been dragged and he dropped to one knee. He pointed to the imprint of Sylvie's Vasque hiking boots and then to the long deep imprint of his Danner hunting boot. Then, as expected, his eye picked out a third man track, intermediate in size, faint and barely discernible because it had been wiped with a cedar branch. He showed Sylvie the sign. It looked like the photograph of a boot print just beginning to develop in the chemical bath.

She looked at him carefully, trying to read his face as she comprehended the importance of what had happened to them. She could discern nothing from his eyes but his mouth was grim. "Any chance that this is some sort of North Woods practical joke? Could the ranger or Sheriff Clayton or someone else you know be having a joke on us?"

He had already considered that possibility and shook his head. "No. I don't think so. Someone stealing the canoe would be more likely, but not as a joke. It just isn't done up here. You don't play a joke that might cost someone a life."

As he rose from one knee to stand he heard the firrrp! of the first round, instinctively turning to the noise. The second caught him across the shoulder near the deltoid. The high velocity round tore through his jacket, shirt, and skin, lifted him off his feet and put him on his back. For ten seconds he lay stunned, eyes blinking, not hearing Sylvie's scream as the next round struck a stone near his head, sparked and ricocheted, producing a high pitched whaaang he could not yet hear. Then he felt someone pulling him further up the bank and he wanted to tell Sylvie he was not a canoe. Sylvie pulled and tugged him by the arms, and his head cleared all at once, aided by the pain in his shoulder that burned away the fog in his brain. Sylvie called his name as she grunted and pulled, trying to drag his dead weight up into the protection of two large boulders that lay just before the trees and out of the line of fire. She fell back on her behind, and he rolled over on his stomach and low-crawled on his elbows and insteps the last couple of feet to the tumble of granite, the boulders large enough to shield them both.

"How badly are you hit?" she asked. Unconsciously she was still trying to find her service weapon with one hand while she combed his hair with her fingers and brushed the sand from his face.

"I'm okay now," he said. He moved his left arm. It seemed uninjured. The pain was higher up between the deltoid and the side of his neck. He decided he would live, if the bleeding were not too profuse.

Sylvie inched up behind the stone cairn shielding them as she tried to establish the sniper's line of fire. She popped up, and just as quickly pulled her head back down. "He's in a tree on the other side of the lake where it narrows. He's shooting from about 500 meters. At least we know now what happened to the canoe."

Will frowned at her. The canoe was the least of his worries at the moment. He struggled up into a sitting position, resting his back against the granite shield. Sylvie slid down hard next to him, blowing the blonde bangs under her cap off her forehead. He took a minute to look her over. She was worried for him, but he detected no signs of panic or debilitating fear in her face. Her training had taken over. If anything, she seemed resolute, in control of herself and ready for a fight.

"Good girl," he said. "And I owe you one for pulling my heavy ass off the beach."

"I was just using you for protection."

A round chipped and powdered the stone above their heads and they flinched simultaneously, shielding their eyes from the spray of fragments as they hunkered down.

"We've gotta get outta here," he told her. "This guy is gonna come after us and try to finish what he started. He thinks he has the advantage."

This time she frowned at him. "Will, my poor shell-shocked darling, he does have the advantage!"

He shook his head. "He has a temporary advantage, which we will use against him, but we have one thing he does not."

She considered for a minute any possible advantage they might have and gave up. "What's that?" she asked.

"You," Will said. He was serious. "We're gonna crawl out of here lower than two timber rattlers, get back on that snowmobile trail and then we're gonna run like two Apache Indians running their horses to their knees. Can you do it?"

"I can run all day if I have to," she said without exaggeration.

He grinned. "If I'm chasing you.... Let's get the fuck out of here."

They crawled north behind and around the protection of the boulders on the slope and made it to the trees, two rounds snapping through the branches above. Then they were up and running, first in the sprint of fear and adrenaline, then in a steady ground-eating pace that took them two miles into the forest and away from the hail of bullets back by the lake. At the end of a third mile, he stopped Sylvie and they both stood in the middle of the trail, breathing hard and wiping the sweat from eyebrows and noses. They each took a good long pull from Sylvie's water bottle.

"Can you do a few more?" he asked.

"Miles or kilometers?"

"Miles."

"If we slow the pace a bit, I can do it. And more if you think we need to."

"Good. Let's say we run about an hour. He needs fifteen minutes to get down out of his tree, cross the lake to our side—maybe ten if he paddles hard—but I think he'll take his time. He knows we're not armed and he doesn't know what kind of shape you're in. He does know I'm hit, but not how badly. No, I don't think he'll run. He'll walk and track, say twenty minutes to the mile. It will take him two hours minimum to cover the same distance we cover in an hour. That will give us sixty minutes to prepare for him. You ready?"

"*Toujours prêt*," she said in French, quoting the motto of the Foreign Legion: Always Ready. "But hold on just a minute." She noticed that Will had tied his coat to his waist during the early part of the run from danger. His shirt was unbuttoned down the front to keep him cool. Even so, he had soaked through his Coolmax T-shirt. The dark green shirt, blackened by his perspiration, was soaked with blood down the left side of his back.

She lifted the flannel shirt carefully away from the shoulder as he knelt, giving her a better look. "Give me your handkerchief," she directed. He handed it up. She saw the ridge of muscle that rose two inches or so from the point of his shoulder up and into the muscles of his neck. Manfred's shoulder ran in a straight line from the neck to the long bony point where the arm dropped. She giggled. The round would have missed Manfred completely.

"What's so funny?" He waited patiently for her diagnosis.

"Oh nothing.... The bullet split your coat, your shirt, your undershirt and sliced you open like a knife across the top of your trapezius, I think it's called. It's not deep at all—you just got nicked, from what I can tell, but you'll have a nice wide scar there in the future."

She pressed the handkerchief in place and he flinched ever so slightly. As she studied the wound she realized how close she had come to losing him. Two centimeters closer to his neck and the bullet would have torn out his carotid artery. She swallowed and regained her composure. "Let's leave this in place because you'll probably bleed a bit more as we run."

He nodded. "Thanks, doc. It stings like Hell but that's probably due to the salt from sweating."

Before he started into his walk-run, he looked at the trail where they had stopped. Among the disturbance caused by the heavy soles of his boots, his blood spatters were evident. He was satisfied with what he saw. He gave Sylvie the lead and forced himself into a heavy-legged, slogging run. Sylvie, by contrast, was still light in her boots and refreshed enough to dance nimbly over the tree roots, downed limbs and jagged rocks that littered the rough trail. He sweated into his eyes and stumbled from time-to-time, kicking loose a stone with a curse or cracking through a branch, but through it all he kept his momentum moving forward. After another twenty minutes or so, he shot a quick glance at his watch. They had come far enough. It was time to make a stand.

Hands on hips, he bent at the waist, perspiration dripping from his forehead and spattering the leaves on the trail like drops of rain, his head steaming into the cool air of the late morning. The sweat he tasted on his lips ran clear and free of any salt, not a good sign. Further exertion would probably induce severe and debilitating cramps he could not afford. He would have to be left behind, sending Sylvie ahead for her own protection. He planned to use a similar scenario to his advantage, but so much depended on Sylvie at this point. His breathing once again under control, he looked up. She was waiting for him to recover, watching him, her cheeks flushed, face glistening with perspiration, her hands warm on his cheeks as she searched his eyes. Incongruously, she looked as if she had just stepped from the pages of an advertisement for Spring skiing in the Alps. "What are you thinking?" she asked.

"Do you ski?"

"What a silly question. Of course I ski. I was on the Olympic training team for Germany. Why did you want to know that?"

He grinned and shook his head. "There is still so much I want to learn about you."

"I promise to tell you everything about me once we get out of this *Scheisse*." She was being serious.

He recovered enough to share his plan. "He's got us outgunned, but we've got him outnumbered and outsmarted. We have to play to our strengths."

"And what exactly do you propose?"

"We set a trap. We set a trap using his expectations to lure him in and then we neutralize him." Will sat down on a rock and looked up the trail ahead of them, then back the way they had come.

"Time for a quick semiotic analysis, Sylvie, so we can set up the signs to deceive him."

She nodded her agreement, although still uncertain about where he was going with all this. She trusted him, of that she was certain. She had seen the results of his analyses, invariably correct in their conclusions.

"What does he know, Sylvie?"

"He knows there are two of us. He knows you are hit because he no doubt saw you go down. He knows he has a high-powered rifle with a sniper scope and a noise suppressor." She stopped there knowing that anything else would be conjecture.

"Good. What does he think based on what he knows? Treat each item of his knowledge as an interpretable sign," he said, helping her.

"An interpretable sign.... Okay. He saw you go down, but he does not know how badly you were hurt. He is likely to interpret your sprawl backward as taking a fairly serious hit. He saw me drag you to safety and help you run up into the trees. He probably saw the blood spatters from your wound on the trail before we started our run."

"Perfect," Will agreed. "We can use this to our advantage. We set up the signs so that it appears to support his conjecture. You're going to leave me for dead."

"No I'm not," she said, without any question or doubt in her voice.

"Sorry," he said, "Let me rephrase that. We're going to set the scene so that it appears you have left me for dead. Think about it. He would make the same decision in his own mind. If he's so badly wounded that he can't continue, he would send his partner on ahead. This serves two purposes: it contributes to the potential survivability of his partner and it slows the pursuer, thus increasing the chances of his partner getting away. We have to fulfill his expectations in order to close the trap."

"What do you need me to do? I mean how can I help close the trap? Wouldn't it make more sense to have me as the bait?"

"Good question, but I assure you that if he saw you the first thing he would do is think 'trap.' Remember, this guy is probably ex-military and probably rather old-fashioned when it comes to his perspective regarding women. He knows you weren't hit, so if he sees the 'damsel in distress' he won't believe it. He will believe that the male has used the female as bait in the trap. That's why I have to be the bait. Your leaving me is a plausible scenario because it fits his understanding of what is correct and what should be done. In his warrior ethos, he would send the weaker female ahead too, despite injury to himself."

Sylvie considered Will's analysis. Her face brightened as she stamped her feet and clasped her hands for warmth. The sweat was cooling rapidly under her soaked clothing. "There's one thing you haven't considered."

"What's that?"

"What if this guy is a feminist?"

Will stood up and hugged her gingerly, rubbing some heat into her back and shoulders. "Then let's hope for both our sakes that his enhanced testosterone overwhelms his social conditioning."

He sent her to look for a short length of hickory or oak from the trees bordering the trail and interspersed among the junipers, larch, and pine. She came back in five minutes with a piece about five feet long. While he was waiting, he pulled a lace out of his hunting boot. She handed him the pole and he sighted down its length. It was a good, fairly straight piece of wood, and despite a slight warp to the right, would do just fine. It was young and green enough to withstand a good amount of pressure before it broke.

"Too thin for a club," she observed.

"Right," he agreed. He used his Buck knife to cut a section out of the end of the pole about four inches deep. "But perfect for a short lance."

"Aha," she said in her high sweet soprano that made him look up from his work for just a second.

He pushed the handle of his knife into the center of the pole's end, but it did not yet fit. Out of the dense white wood he carved another shaving or two. This time the handle snugged in like a dowel. He wrapped the lace from his hunting boot around the end of the pole, further tightening the two fingers of wood against the handle of his big Buck knife. He tied off a couple of knots hard and tight against the lance and looked at his handiwork with satisfaction. He handed the weapon to her.

As she tested the balance and got a feel for its heft, he said, "Count on one thrust at the most, Sylvie. If you stick him in the gut or the heart, the knife will probably pull out of the lance. Don't let that surprise you. You will still have a nice length of hardwood in your hands. Swing it like a bat and try to hit the little baseball in his throat." Will pointed to his Adam's apple. "If you crush the cricoid cartilage, I assure you he will be finished, especially with four inches of steel piercing his thick skin."

Sylvie practiced a few thrusts up through the center of an imagined solar plexus, left foot forward as she lunged and pushed.

"No hesitation," *Hauptkommissar Schumann*, even if your only target is his back."

"Do I still aim for the heart then?"

"No. Too much chance of a rib deflecting the thrust. And we don't know what he has under his coat." He turned his head. "Go in right below the occipital ridge," he said. With his fingers he showed her where the back of the skull sat on the neck. "Don't go too high or the blade bounces off the skull. But even if you miss too low, you still might nick the spinal cord and that will suffice."

She shivered, more from the thought of what she had to do than from the chill of the wind drying the sweat on her body. It seemed to be getting colder by the minute and she could see her breath now as she exhaled.

Will looked at his watch and ran a calculation. "Time to get set."

"I'm ready," she said, "but it seems such a cruel thing to do."

He looked her over once more. He knew how hard it was to kill a human being, to say nothing of a trained professional. "If you fail, he will rape you before he kills you, Sylvie. No hesitation."

"No hesitation." She said it with conviction, and he knew she could do it. She had the training and she had something even more important that he was depending on: she was fighting for the life of her man.

Chapter Twenty-seven

No Hesitation

He showed her how the lay of the land could work to their advantage. The trail bended as it came out of the forest and into the small clearing where they stood. About thirty meters ahead by the up-thrust of boulders where he would prostrate himself, the trail rose on an incline and disappeared again into the woods. They would arrange things to make it appear he had given up, unable to negotiate the steep rise of the path into the trees. He would brace himself against the rocks as he waited for his pursuer. He intended to fall on his side, as if he had died or passed out and slid from the rock at his back. This would also present his bloody shoulder, now bleeding down the front as well, to the trail he said as he took off his coat. He folded it into a pillow to lay behind his head once against the rock. His coat ready, he looked at the trailside, grabbed a handful of freshly fallen leaves and crushed them in the palm of his hand. He used the tannins in the leaves as pigment to paint Sylvie's face in camouflage.

"I feel like an Ojibwe getting ready to go on the warpath," she said. She stood patiently and quietly while he painted her with ocher and red and brown. He stood back and looked at his handiwork.

"That hair is going to be a problem. You can see it fifty meters away, just as nature intended. He unzipped the green hood from his field parka, slid it over her head and carefully stuffed any stray tresses into the edges of the hood. He led her to a point where the trail emerged from the woods below them. "We'll put you down here so you're looking up the trail at me. You won't be able to see him coming until he passes you. We'll cover you head-to-toe with leaves." There were other mounds of leaves along the trail where the early autumn downfall had covered the rounded boulders along the trail.

"But shouldn't I be farther away from the trail? It seems like here I'm so close he'll almost step on me."

"That's what we want. The instant he sees the trail bend, he'll become cautious and try to look ahead as far as he can. He won't worry about what's at his feet."

"I see," she said. She sat down and stretched out on her back next to a line of small boulders. She tried to get comfortable, head pointing down the trail toward the stalker, toes pointing toward the rocks where Will would position himself. With her head propped up a bit she would be able to see Will, but not the approaching attacker. Will covered her with leaves taken from the forest, leaving the trail undisturbed. As he prepared to cover her head she said, "Lying in this position, even with my head at this angle I won't be able to see him coming."

"I don't want you to see him. He might be able to sense the eye contact. I want you to use your ears. In fact, soon as you hear him coming I want you to close your eyes until he walks by."

"I'm scared enough as it is, Will," she admitted. "If I have to keep my eyes closed I'll be mortified."

"Those baby blues of yours stand out like fog lights on a moonless night. Don't worry. You won't have to keep them closed for long. Now let's get this finished." He was firm with her because they were running out of time.

He carefully covered her head with leaves. Then in order to see exactly what their pursuer would see as he came up the trail and into the clearing, Will walked backward twenty feet or so in his original tracks, down the trail from the direction they had come, stopped and walked forward. As he came to the bend just before the clearing, he checked his line of sight ahead by looking up the trail to the rocks where he would be lying prostrate. Out of his peripheral vision he managed to catch the rise of leaves among the stones where Sylvie lay. It would be close, but if his attention remained diverted, the shooter would overlook her.

"Okay, sweet girl, this is it. I'm going to get in position. He should be here in ten minutes or so if we reckoned the time correctly. Keep absolutely still when you hear him and keep those peepers closed. He might stop like a good hunter and wait before he moves forward. He'll need a minute to survey the scene and make sense of what he sees. When his eyes lock onto me he'll want to know where you are, and his thinking should take him to the conclusion that you left me for dead and moved on. If he moves forward toward me, we'll know that we were right."

He knelt next to her and whispered once more, "No hesitation."

She answered him with her eyes. There was nothing more for him to do but get in place. He slid his back down against the face of the boulder and stretched out his legs. He pillowed his folded coat behind his head for support. He shivered involuntarily. The temperature continued to drop. He snuck one more quick peek at his watch, pulled a twig from beneath his behind, and looked the thirty meters down the trail to where Sylvie lay. All he saw was mounded forms covered in leaves, as if the rocks and boulders on both sides of the trail had been covered with the foliage of deciduous trees standing near the trail. The trail itself was nearly indiscernible. He could barely make her out. The camo job was good, but was it good enough to fool a trained professional? Time would tell. With nothing else left to do he let himself go limp. His body slid off the rock bracing him as if he had passed out or died and fallen partly into the trail.

Above her head and to her left Sylvie could hear the flutter of birds as they hopped and flitted from ground to branch to air. Far away she heard the hoot of an owl that reminded her of the fantastic night they had spent by the fire. It seemed an eternity ago. She closed her eyes for practice and forced herself to concentrate, forced herself to breath and slow her heart rate. She visualized what she must do, playing various scenarios through in her mind. She could do it. No hesitation. The stem of a leaf tickled her upper lip mercilessly, but she maintained her discipline and did not try to brush it away with her hands. Instead, she wrinkled her nose until the irritant moved just enough to be tolerable. She opened her eyes again. Her head was propped at just enough of an angle to give her an unobstructed view up the trail. With a shock, she saw Will's broad torso where he had fallen across the trail, his body facing her, and an instant of panic gripped her until she remembered this was part of their plan. She took a deep breath. That part certainly worked.

As she controlled her breathing, everything was remarkably quiet for a minute or two until she heard the caw of crows disturbed into flight and the angry chitter of a squirrel high up in a tree, disturbed and unhappy about something. She tightened the fingers of her right hand around the lance lying next to her. Her awareness of it made it manifest once more within the grip of her hand. Then she heard the unmistakable snap of a twig under a boot, a sound she had heard a hundred times today, and every sense in her body seemed a hundred times more acute. She could hear herself breathe through her mouth, so she closed it and used her nose. She felt her heart pummel her chest wall from the inside, as if trying to fight its way out. She ignored it and felt the stone against the back of her head and the lance along her right side. She listened and heard silence. The sparrows were gone and the scolding of the squirrel had subsided. She heard someone stop and breathe deeply.

She closed her eyes and hoped whoever it was could not hear the thunderous beating of her heart.

Out of one eye closest to the earth, open just a slit, Will managed to make out the figure at the bend of the trail. He was in full military camo. Even his boots and his rifle were camoed. Under his camo hunting cap his face was painted with lampblack and only his eyes were evident. As Will had predicted, the man stopped before emerging from the woods at the point where the trail straightened out of its bend. He had dropped to one knee and he was searching the treetops. Satisfied with what he saw or did not see, he stood and waited fully two minutes before he moved forward. His right boot was six inches from Sylvie's face as he scanned the trail ahead and saw Will's form. He immediately went into a crouch and brought his rifle to his shoulder. At this instant Will groaned and tried to crawl forward and gave up, both his hands above his head as he tried to pull himself off the trail. The man in the camo relaxed slightly and came off his gun, looking over the scope, but maintained his crouch. He looked at both sides of the trail where Will lay, motionless now. For good measure he scanned further up the trail where it climbed the slope up and into the trees. To be safe, he took a quick look back over his shoulder.

Most likely she had left him, unable to get him up the steep incline of the trail. From the looks of his bloody shoulder he should just about be dead. He came slowly up out of his shooting position, but kept his rifle trained on the dying man's chest. He heard the gurgle of a death rattle in the big man's throat and watched as the man twitched and died. Good, he would not have to waste another round. He moved carefully forward, sweeping the trail from side to side with his weapon.

As Sylvie heard the soft pad of the man's combat boots treading forward, she opened her eyes and waited a second or two as they adjusted to the light. She saw the back of a man covered in a camouflage hunting jacket walking deliberately away from her, step by cautious step. She flinched when she heard Will's death gasp. In that instant she was up and covered the five yards between herself and the man. She screamed, not a scream of fear, but an inadvertent battle cry as she lunged, thrusting the knife at the tip of the lance toward the back of the man's head. With a speed of reflex that amazed her even in the instant of its manifestation, he turned and brought his rifle up to parry her thrust. This action saved his life as Sylvie buried the blade to the hilt of the knife just below the man's collarbone. He gasped at the pain and stepped back as he had been trained to do, even as she pulled with all her might, trying to recover the knife blade. It remained lodged centimeters below the man's throat or he would be dead, spouting gouts of blood from the neck. She had the oak lance in her hands, raised it like a bat, and swung for the bulge centered in his throat. This time he blocked the blow easily as the pole cracked like a rifle shot across the steel barrel of his rifle.

To her horror, she saw that he was grinning now, utterly oblivious to the four inches of a razor sharp blade stuck into his body. She prepared to attack with her hands and feet, refusing to die so easily, as he calmly raised the rifle to his shoulder without bothering to sight through the scope. Before she could move she heard what she imagined could only have come from the throat of a mountain lion, and Will was on the man with a feral ferocity and speed that shocked her. He twisted the man's head between his hands with such force that she heard his spine crack like a shot from a Luger. She watched the man drop to both knees, still grinning, the surprise of his death darkening in his open eyes. He pitched forward onto his face and she did not have to look at him anymore. In the sudden stillness she heard only the labored rasp of Will's breathing. When their eyes met and they saw that each had survived the ordeal, she stepped off the trail and emptied her stomach.

She returned, once again composed, wiping her mouth sheepishly on the sleeve of her coat. "I usually only do that during autopsies," she tried to explain.

"You don't have to say anything," he assured her. "In fact, I think you were wonderful. You bought me just enough time to get the job done."

She looked down at the dead assassin and noticed his open eyes were dead blue. She watched Will going through his pockets and something suddenly occurred to her. "That was your plan all along, wasn't it? You didn't trust me to stop him, just to slow him up enough until you could finish him off. You had this thought through all the way, didn't you?" she gently asked.

"Not quite right, Sylvie." He rolled the man's dead weight up on a hip to get at his back pockets. "There was a very good chance you would stop him on your own, which put me in a position to back you up as needed. However, I also had to factor in the possibility that given his training and experience, he might be able to survive your initial attack. In that instance I was there to deliver the coup de main, and luckily, that's what happened."

She slowly shook her head from side to side. "The more I know you, the more I'm convinced luck has very little to do with it. I'm not mad at you, Will Sheridan. I'm just trying to understand you."

He accepted that. "I always try to have a contingency plan and that was it. We worked together as a team, Sylvie, and we succeeded in killing this bastard. I'm not sorry about that. This was a bad man with hostile intent and he would have left us both here for the coyotes and the bears."

He put his boot on the man's chest, gripped the handle of his Buck knife, and pulled it sharply from the dead man's body. A small amount of black-red blood pooled in the slit of the wound. He cleaned the blade on the sleeve of the man's camo parka, folded the blade, put it back in its leather holster on his hip and kissed her. "Yuuuck," he said. She laughed a little and cried a little on his shoulder as he held her. He winced quietly as she squeezed him too hard, but she did not care.

"I just can't believe you had it all planned. You used me as bait after all, just admit it."

He tried to hide the embarrassment of being found out behind a grin. "It's a good thing I'm a feminist. Now enough of this *Qvatch*," he said, using the German word for nonsense. "If you'll pardon the pun, we're not out of the woods yet." Despite the burning across the top of his shoulder, he held her protectively in the circle of his arms. He looked over her shoulder into the darkening sky. She could tell he was reading the signs again. She could also read in his face that he did not like what he saw. She shared his alarm. "What do you see Will, thunderstorms coming?"

He was forced to tell her no. "Snow is coming, and a lot of it."

"This early in the season?"

This time he nodded. "All this warm moist air boiling up from the lake that we had to run through is colliding with what they call the Alberta Clipper, a blast of cold air coming down out of northern Canada. When the two air masses smack into each other, and it looks to me as if that is happening as we speak, there will be heavy wet snow and lots of it, the kind of snow fall that knocks trees down."

She decided she did not much like the sound of that. She turned her attention instead to something she could deal with. "What do we do about this bastard?" She remembered the man's lewd grin as he saw her standing before him. A shiver traveled her spine like a spider crawling up her back.

Will picked up the rifle, a Weatherby .300 Magnum, and cleared the round from the chamber, ejecting it into his hand. He handed it to Sylvie. "This is a helluva weapon and this round would drop an elephant. The rifle has been specially modified, shoots a 220-grain Nosler round and has a noise suppressor. He handed Sylvie the rifle to hold. He pulled ten additional rounds from the two ammo pockets in the man's field coat and placed them in his own. The man carried no wallet, no identification, no papers, nothing that could link him with the rest of the world or in any way link him to his mission.

"Give me a hand here, will you?" Will asked and unzipped the man's coat. He also removed his hat from his matted black hair.

"I don't want to touch him," Sylvie said.

"You don't have to touch him. I want the coat because we might need it and I want to look at him." It was the younger of the two men at the casino in Hinckley. Neither Will nor Sylvie seemed surprised at the discovery.

"Why would he want to kill us?" she asked.

"Save that question for later," he said too brusquely. He instantly regretted it but saw to his relief that she had taken it merely as a command, and given the situation and their relationship, it was not at all unexpected or untoward. After stripping the man of his coat, Will grabbed him under the shoulders and Sylvie grabbed the heels of his boots. They lifted as one and his head slumped to the side as if he were asleep. They laid him out beside the trail in the same spot where Sylvie had lain in ambush. As they turned to leave she kicked him in the hip for good measure, rocking the corpse. "The bastard thought he was going to rape me."

"Jesus, Sylvie. That's not very professional," Will said, but he was grinning at her defiance.

After she purged her memory of the predatory look she had seen in the killer's eyes, she asked, "Where to boss?" and pointed a thumb up the trail like a hitchhiker.

"I'll feel better if we can get to the top of that ridge line and in among the trees before the big blow starts. He'll be okay here and we certainly know where to find him when we alert the authorities. Our next and most important need is shelter and a fire before everything gets covered with wet snow. And Sylvie, I meant what I said back there."

He took her hand in his. "You did one hell of an outstanding job and saved both our lives with your actions."

The sincere praise struck home. "I know you've studied martial arts and have a black belt in Tae Kwan Do, but where did you learn that move with the neck?" She was making conversation as they walked. She shuddered through her shoulders as she remembered the ghastly sound of the man's vertebrae snapping.

"The FBI sent me to a special martial arts course in Israel. It's called Krav Maga, and it's really a distillation of the very best self-defense techniques of all the martial arts. What the Israelis have done is get rid of all the useless stances, ineffective kicks and punches—you know, all the posturing and stuff that looks good in the movies but will get you killed on the street—and kept what actually works in real fighting situations."

"That's just like the Israelis," she commented.

"That's right. Those people don't fuck around when it comes to their self-preservation. Given their history, it's understandable that they would develop a philosophy of the fighting arts that says survive the initial attack, but then overcome the aggressor with efficient and overwhelming power."

"Will you teach me sometime?"

"No."

She couldn't tell if he were being serious or not.

Chapter Twenty-eight

The Cave

After ten minutes of hard walking they reached the top of the ridge and were within the forest again. Under the lowering clouds, the rising wind, and the dropping temperatures, Will and Sylvie pressed on through the forest. Will gave up the safety of the snowmobile trail, looking for something, she could tell, and there was urgency in the way he searched. Now and again he stopped and scanned the terrain. She was certain he was looking for something specific, but she did not interrupt to ask. She let him work the ground. Now deep in the trees, as the first soft flakes floated down like ash from a distant fire and melted in the heat of their faces, she was rewarded with a squeeze of her hand in his.

He pointed: "There. That should do us rather nicely if we have to hole up for a while."

She looked closely and carefully, but was unable to see the object at the end of his point. She shook her head. He pulled her by the hand. "Come on. I'll show you what I mean."

He took her down the slope of the ridge, sidestepping when it became too steep. The backside, as he called it, forced them to move around the larger moss and lichen covered stones left there by glacial retreats as if they had been jettisoned to lighten the load of the ice sheet shrinking its way back to the northern cold. Above a small ledge that stuck out of the hillside like an eyebrow, she saw the opening he was moving toward. It was about half her height and half again as wide. It was remarkable that he had spotted it at all from where they had been standing near the ridge top.

"Is it a cave of some kind?"

"Of a particular kind, if I'm as smart as I think I am."

She had no doubt about how smart he was. Once down into the bottom of the valley, they traversed on a diagonal ten yards up to the opening in the hillside. A massive log, broken in four pieces along its length, stretched across the top of the black hole like a fractured wooden mantel atop a fireplace. Scrub brush grew on either side of the opening; a stand of pines flared up and out a few feet below the adit of the cave, providing a natural windscreen for the opening. As they neared he held her back and put a finger to her lips. She stopped and waited while he dug for the small flashlight in his coat pocket. He turned the light on and adjusted the spread of the halogen beam through the lens. He followed the beam in head first, up to his shoulders. Then, to her dismay, he crawled the rest of the way in. The last she saw of him was the lugged soles of his boots. Had she not known better she would have sworn the hole had swallowed him, the preternatural mouth taking him in three successive bites. She heard the hollow echo of her name before he re-emerged, poking his head out and waving her to join him.

"It's an abandoned bear den."

She shook her head and sent a spray of wet snowflakes flying again. "I'm not going in there."

"Don't worry. If we don't make too much noise we won't wake her." For an instant she thought he was serious, but he laughed at the mix of trepidation and incredulity in her eyes. "It's just the two of us, really. The mama bear is gone to some other denning site."

"What if she decides to return?" That was a good question.

"We'll keep a fire lit and she'll smell us long before she tries to climb back in with us, so don't you worry. In fact, I need you to start collecting firewood. However, this time please keep it on the small side and hurry. We don't have much time before this storm lets loose."

She passed him the rifle and set about her task. He was out of the den and moving among the firs, stripping smaller dead branches from the living trees. He dropped the boughs into the small cave. When she returned with her haul he was rolling the second of two stones—about the size of a beach ball—in front of the opening.

"Our front door," he explained, taking the wood from her.

Reluctantly, she crawled into the black of the den. After she pulled her feet in she discovered she could easily sit up without bumping her head on the stony ceiling. As she turned to survey the den her head brushed an object hanging in front of her face and she gave a little shriek, which embarrassed her when Will shined his light up and she found it to be nothing more than a hairy root of some kind that had pushed through the roof.

"Sorry," she said, sheepishly.

He handed her the light so she could have a quick look around. She was sitting on a bed of pine and cedar boughs. So that is what he had been doing with the evergreens. The den was actually bigger than she thought. There was easily enough space to accommodate two people, although neither could stand.

"Sylvie!" He yelled loud enough to startle her. She thought the bear was coming. "I'm freezing my ass off out here. I need you to take these smaller stones and put them in a circle for our fire pit. They will also hold some of the heat. He passed the wet stones in quickly and she arranged them in a small circle in the dirt to the rear and the side of the cave opening. "Just right," he told her as she looked up for affirmation. She was shocked to see him wearing a coat of snow. He hunched protectively over their woodpile just outside the cave, trying to keep the wood dry, and he passed in handfuls at a time. She stacked the wood against the cave wall past their feet. He stood and slapped the snow from his clothes before he crawled in. He dripped melting snowflakes from his eyebrows.

"Will," she said as he turned and started to build the tinder pile for their fire.

"Yes, Sylvie.

"I think I should go pee."

He was too busy with the fire to be mad at her. "Good idea, but don't go farther than below the pines."

"I won't," she promised and crawled out. She climbed from her knees to her feet and disappeared into the gentle lazy veil of snowfall. During the five minutes she was gone the storm progressed into an unremitting vertical wall of white. She could see the stand of pines below her only as dark, indistinct forms in the background. She kicked a stone with the toe of her boot and cursed to herself as she stumbled. The larger boulders were now mounded with snowcaps. She squatted under the partial protection of the pine branch umbrellas, the trees already nicely flocked by the heavy snow. She got her pants down and fumbled with her panties, her fingers wet and numb with cold.

No time to mess around, she thought, and then she remembered with a twinge of false panic that there was no toilet paper. She improvised and reached out to scoop up a handful of the fresh snow to use as a wipe before what was left of the heat in her hand melted it. She gasped a little at the shock of the coldness, flicked the remaining snow and moisture from her hands, stood and quickly pulled up her pants. She turned to look at the rising steam where the stream of her urine had tunneled into the white snow. As she turned again to look up the hill, she was taken by a moment of visceral panic. She could see nothing but a shifting, virtual, white veil of snow blocking her vision of the den.

Still in the grip of her panic she wanted to run blindly up the hill in hopes that she would stumble upon the opening. Instead, she stood her ground and relied on her training to let the moment pass. She took deep breaths as she gathered her thoughts. She wondered what Roland, a seasoned mountaineer, would do in a similar situation. "Will!" she called up the hill and into the windblown snow. She tried to keep the panic from her voice. She waited. There was no answer. She called again, louder this time, cupping her hands next to her mouth. She heard his clear sharp tenor cut through the veil of snow. He knew exactly what had happened.

"Take four steps up the hill toward my voice, then stop and call again. When I answer, same drill. Start now!"

She took her four steps, making certain that they were up the slope. She stopped and called his name. He told her four more. Up she went. Again. Sometimes the wind took his voice and she was unsure of the direction. The blowing snow disoriented her. Then he called to her and told her to move to the right. She sidestepped until she felt the powerful bar of his arm and the strength of his grip as he pulled her toward the opening of the abandoned bear's den.

"There you are," he said, as if she had just walked up to his blanket on the beach. How could he do that? she wondered as she brushed off as much of the snow as she could reach. How could he keep his composure time and again, when she was scared to death? She scrambled in on her knees as he pulled her by the shoulders. She arranged herself on the mattress of pine and cedar while he rolled the two blocking stones in front of the opening to the outside. The fire was lit, burning, and drawing nicely, unaffected by the swirling winds outside. She could smell the wood smoke and feel the heat radiating off the stone walls of the cave. She pulled her hood back and shook out her hair. She noticed that he had placed the shooter's coat down as a ground covering atop their bed of pine needles and soft cedar boughs. He wiped her face dry with his bandana.

"Don't cry, little girl," he said. Unfortunately, this had exactly the opposite effect and the tears came uncontrollably. She let herself cry, let the tears run and flush away the last remnants of fear.

"That's the second time today you had to save me. I thought I was going to lose you again," she said. "You don't know how much you mean to me." She swallowed the last of the fear.

He took her face in both his warming hands, heated from the fire. "Sylvie, it will take a lot more than a paid assassin and a raging blizzard in the great white North Woods to keep us apart."

"You're a dummy," she said tenderly, sniffling. "We could both have been killed today, me twice." She hugged him.

"Well, if it's any consolation we might not last through the night. It's likely to get real nasty out there tonight."

Great, she thought, things could still get worse.

He saw the resignation in her face. "No. You have to look at the bright side. We still have each other."

He was trying so hard. "I don't want to die like Romeo and Juliet here in the bowels of our bear tomb," she pouted.

"But it is kind of romantic—wouldn't you say—if they were to find us frozen together for all eternity in love's last embrace?"

He was being silly now. "Is there anything to eat?" she asked, abruptly changing the subject to more practical concerns.

"I told you men were the romantic ones and women the pragmatists. Here I am caught in the rapture of romance and all you can think about is your stomach."

"You're obviously caught in the throes of hypothermia," she said, recovering her good mood.

He handed her the water bottle, a slice of the venison jerky, and the bag of trail mix. He decided it was best to keep the mood light, given the circumstances. "Here you are. I provide. I have given you shelter, the warmth of a fire, food and water. And Sylvie...."

"Yes, Will?" She answered through her clenched teeth, trying to tear loose a strip of venison, her mouth watering in anticipation of the salty spiced meat.

"If the food runs out and it looks like we'll starve to death, go ahead and eat me."

"Oh, shut up," she said, but could not suppress a little giggle. She chewed vigorously and passed back the water bottle. "We'll get through this if you can just learn to keep your wits about you."

He took a long pull from the bottle, savoring even the plastic flavor of the water. "That's my girl. Things could be worse. We do have shelter and the fire and enough food to keep the buzzards high in the sky for now. At the very least we can get through the night. For breakfast, I've still got some candy bars if we finish the trail mix tonight. We can melt snow over the fire in the plastic bottles if we run out of water."

"Won't the fire melt the plastic?"

"No. The heat will melt the snow before it affects the plastic if we keep it at the proper distance."

"Why can't we just melt it in our mouths?"

"A bite or two won't hurt," he cautioned, "but don't ever rely on that. The caloric expenditure required to warm the water inside your body is almost always greater than the benefit of the hydration, particularly if you have nothing to eat. Instead, it speeds the process of hypothermia and people die."

She laughed.

"What's so funny?" he asked, perturbed.

"You can't help being a professor, can you?"

He cuddled her in his arms, drawing her coat zipper up to her chin. "No more than I could stop wanting to be with you, no matter what the circumstances."

She fell asleep on his chest, lulled by the rhythm of his breathing. Only when she was deep in REM sleep did he gently move her aside, check the fire, and lie down again next to her, the fatigue and the fatigue alone finally taking her from him as he slept.

She woke once into the blackness—the dark paralyzing her—afraid to sit up until she remembered where she was. The fire had died down to soft embers that glowed momentarily when a tongue of wind lapped at the corners of the cave's mouth, touched the coals, then withdrew with a howl. She stoked the coals, added a few sticks to the sputtering flames and waited for the fire to take the wood. Only then did she curl back into the curve of his body, her back to his chest. A quick look over her shoulder and she was glad to see her big bear sleeping heavily but peacefully next to her. She put her head back down, ignored the cold, the mild pressure in her bladder, and the persistent hunger in her belly. She returned to sleep, taking the smell of the wood smoke in his hair into her dreams.

Chapter Twenty-nine

Moral Imperative

Lieutenant General Frank L. Simons had given his adult life to the service of his country from the time of his graduation at West Point to his current appointment as Director of the Missile Defense Agency, formerly the Ballistic Missile Defense Organization. Simons considered himself a missileer from the get-go and, unlike many of his peers who became line officers, did not wear the coveted Ranger patch. Almost every soldier who went through War College with him had qualified and won the right to wear the Ranger tab of the snake eaters. Such men had gone on to staff positions in artillery, infantry, and mounted cavalry. Early in his service Simons realized he was not a combat warrior in the sense these other men were. He considered himself and his career not one whit diminished by the fact that he did not wear paratrooper's wings. On the contrary, he considered himself and the men and women with whom he served superior to a Delta Force Ranger, a Green Beret, or even an Operator, as his Navy SEAL friends liked to call themselves.

From the time of his commission into the ranks as a second lieutenant, he had gone directly into the United States Army's Missile Command (MICOM). Service in this branch of the Army was reserved for the best and brightest of the highly trained and highly educated soldiers working as technicians, tacticians, and logisticians. Simons was a highly trained technocrat who knew that future wars would depend on career soldiers like him: men and women who could win wars with their brains, not their brawn; men and women capable of planning, designing, and executing a national missile defense system.

By force of habit Simons reached to push his glasses up on the bridge of his nose until he remembered he did not have to wear the damn things anymore. At fifty-eight, his presbyopia had advanced to the degree where he needed glasses for reading and driving, but they were nothing but a nuisance. Two months ago LASIK surgery corrected his vision. He could see better now than when he was at West Point, but he had yet to break the habit of pushing his glasses back up the slide of his nose as he read a document. He scratched the side of his head above his right ear where the hair was short and bristly, more and more gray showing through the black. It was going to be a long day of meetings according to the agenda brought to him by his executive officer, Major Marsden. He had set aside the entire day for the most important of the major contractors building the Pioneer anti-ballistic missile, a new ground-based interceptor (GBI) designed to replace the aging and outdated Minuteman III.

The Pioneer missile system was designed to serve as a key component of the Exoatmospheric Interceptor Program (EIP), a missile defense program created as a deterrent to the growing number of potentially hostile nations capable of fielding a ballistic missile with sufficient range to carry a nuclear warhead targeted for the United States or its allies. Given the advancement made in the intercontinental ballistic missile programs of Iran and North Korea, the Pioneer program could not be allowed to fail. A pet project of the president, word had come down from the secretary of defense in no uncertain terms that the project had been mandated to succeed. Now riding on the back of the current hysteria surrounding terrorism, the project had been infused with billions of taxpayer dollars. With worsening geopolitical situations in North Korea, Pakistan, and Iran, the message had come through clearly and unambiguously: failure was simply not an option.

After a series of embarrassing failures that had been spun into successes, in less than a year a dummy ballistic missile would be fired from Meck Island, one in the chain that constituted the Kwajalein Atoll, and a Pioneer missile would be launched to intercept and defeat the incoming threat. This time there would be no homing signal attached to the dummy warhead, which had accounted for the rare successes in the program to date, but the media had discovered this fudging with the test. This time the dummy warhead would be protected by a series of decoys. It would be, without doubt, the most severe test of the Pioneer to date. Radio, television, and the print media would all be there, more than a thousand critical eyes on the test, watching and awaiting the results. Future congressional funding was dependent on a successful test, a test that could withstand the scrutiny of the doves in the halls of Congress and all the naysayers more than willing to point to the Pioneer's deficiencies and spiraling costs. His personal advancement within the military depended on a workable missile defense program: this was his baby; he was the principal architect and designer. He reminded himself that the ultimate responsibility was his. The program could not be allowed to fail.

Lt. General Simons was well aware of the problem of trying to micro-manage a project the size and scope of the Pioneer missile program. He had done everything possible to put the best available persons into crucial leadership and management positions. One area he could not control, however, was the letting of contracts and subcontracts. He could only exert his power post hoc, that is, after the contracts were in place and the companies who were awarded them subsequently came under his purview. This was the weak link in his organizational schema and he knew it. Accordingly, he had taken great pains to accommodate the weak link. Every contractor's CEO, without exception and regardless of the size of the company, was required to report progress directly to him and the Pioneer Committee responsible for the Technology Master Plan. Simons preferred to keep the PC-TMP small as possible. Today he would sit with Dr. Jack Watson from Defense Advanced Research Projects Agency (DARPA) and Brigadier General Cliff Morningside to hear the first of five scheduled presentations. Watson had come over from JPL in Pasadena some years ago and had a reputation for being a creative problem solver. Cliff had been a year behind him at the Point and was a star halfback on the football team that had defeated Air Force and Navy in the same season, helping Army win the coveted Commander's Cup. Morningside was a good man and represented the Joint Theater Air and Missile Defense Organization (JTAMDO).

In about half an hour the three would convene the Pioneer Committee under top secret closed hearings and receive the first presentation of the day, a progress report on the target acquisition software (TAS) for the Pioneer. Dr. Robertson Davis, CEO of Tactical Missile Systems in Cedar Rapids, Iowa, would give the presentation. Simons thought for a minute. He remembered he had a cousin somewhere in Iowa, or was it Idaho? No, it was Davenport Iowa, on the Mississippi, he remembered. Why anyone in his or her right mind would want to live there was beyond him, especially if you knew anything about the North Central winters in January. Perhaps it was the pheasant hunting; he knew one of his young adjutants was mad for upland game bird hunting but if memory served, he preferred South Dakota to Iowa due to the paucity of public lands in Iowa.

Just ahead of his assistant's gentle tap at the door, his Apple watch beeped, reminding him of the meeting. The LTG was also reminded that he had a press conference scheduled later that afternoon following the last of the five presentations. At the press conference he intended to announce publicly the first full-scale theater test of the Pioneer anti-ballistic missile system, a test that would demonstrate to the citizens of the United States, her allies, and all potential enemies of state, that the future defense of the country's air space and borders was now being secured.

THE PROJECT TEAM Leader at Tactical Missile Systems could not believe his eyes when he read the headlines in the *Des Moines Register* the day after the briefing attended by his boss. "New and Improved Pioneer Set for Test: All Systems Go." He read further: "Lt. General Frank L. Simons, Director of the Missile Defense Agency announced today from the Department of Defense that the nation's latest anti-ballistic missile, code-named the Pioneer, will be ready for its first real-time test in less than a year. According to Simons, a dummy warhead aboard a 'hostile' incoming ballistic missile will be launched from the Kwajalein Islands and intercepted by the Pioneer, the latest generation and new vanguard of this nation's missile defense program."

"Simons said the United States is in the process of developing and deploying a national missile defense system pursuant to the National Missile Defense Act of 1999. The Pioneer anti-ballistic missile is slated to become the backbone of our deployed strategic missile forces. The latest version of the Pioneer, known as a ground based interceptor (GBI), contains sensors to track a target missile, a communications system, a battle-management system, and a prototype radar, Simons explained, making the Pioneer one of the most complex and technologically advanced missiles every fielded. Simons announced further that all systems were now operational, ready to be integrated, and ready for testing."

In a feature sidebar, the PTL read more about Simons.

"Lieutenant General Simons, speaking from the Department of Defense offices at the Pentagon, is Director of the Missile Defense Agency, formerly known as the Ballistic Missile Defense Organization. The Director is charged with running the nation's national missile defense program (NMD), which includes five major components: 1. The Pioneer—a ground based interceptor (GBI); 2. An X-band Radar (XBR); 3. Upgraded Early Warning Radar; 4. Battle Management: Command, Control, & Communications (BM/C3), and; 5. Space Sensor Technology."

At this point the Project Team Leader stopped reading and put the paper aside. He was not interested in the side-bars explaining the components of the NMD program, the highly censored description of the missile itself, or the full color graphics illustrating how the interceptor was designed to work, hypothetically. That word had not appeared. The reporter had written the story as if everything were fait accompli. He shook his head. Somebody was in for a big surprise. It was obvious to him now that Davis had lied to the director. The PTL was certain of one thing: the missile would fail its field test. Even with a year left before the firing, there was insufficient time to correct the problems in the software. He knew Davis was trying to buy time, hoping that the additional month would be enough time to write the patches. The PTL knew this was merely posturing to postpone the inevitable. The failure of Tactical Missile Systems to deliver on their promises could very well defeat the Pioneer.

ONE WEEK AFTER his boss's testimony before Lt. General Simons and the PC-TMP, the Project Team Leader had slept in longer than usual on the Saturday of his up-coming flight to Washington, DC. He attributed the extra hour or so of sleep to his higher than usual levels of stress. Normally, on the weekends he was up and out and fishing for bass on Coralville Lake. As he waited for the taxi to arrive and take him to the airport he sat on the couch thinking about what he had to do, considering the possible directions his moral imperative would steer his life. The curtains were drawn and the house was muted and quiet, perfect for thinking. Ever the engineer, he had studied the problem from every possible angle and point of view.

The easy way out would have been to kill the report. He could have put the blame entirely on Daya and her group of software engineers and saved his own ass. There was only one problem with that solution: Dr. Nadipuram, from the time she was hired, had steadfastly maintained to anyone willing to listen that the Software Group could not complete its task given the timeline imposed by CEO Davis. The PTL, once he was certain and had the hard facts in data on his desk, had stood behind her initial report and had made supporting arguments on her behalf. At the time, Davis had brushed off the damning report and promised his team—and this was strictly confidential—that the full package would not be needed for the interceptor tests.

He had been wrong. To protect his company, it now occurred to the PTL, Dr. Robertson Davis had been lying through his teeth to the director of the Pioneer committee. The cold hard facts were that the Pioneer anti-ballistic missile would not be able to distinguish between an in-coming ballistic threat and its accompanying decoys. The upcoming test was to be observed by the Department of Defense, DARPA, JTAMBO, senators serving on various national defense committees, generals of the Army and Air Force, and the usual gaggle of broadcast journalists and news media reporters. Doomed to failure, they would send the results of the embarrassing test around the world. The consequences of such negative publicity could result in delaying the program for years, and in the worst-case scenario, Congress could vote to limit appropriations or shut it down completely as they had done recently with two other high profile and very expensive weapons programs.

The PTL shook his head as he thought about the political ramifications and, even more importantly, the future of his company and his role in it. It had taken years for the Missile Defense Agency to overcome the growing criticism mounted by scientists and lawmakers alike, arguing that the program was ill-conceived, too expensive, and not feasible given the technology currently available. A failed test would add fuel to the firestorm of criticism. There was much more at stake here than one or two executives' jobs or the viability of a small contractor for missile defense guidance systems in Cedar Rapids, Iowa.

DURING THE DRIVE to the Eastern Iowa Airport south of Cedar Rapids, the PTL took the time to reflect and reconsider the actions he had taken in defense of his country. He remembered the smell of the plastic payphone at the all-night convenience store along I-380—perhaps the last working payphone in all of Iowa—where he had dropped a dime as they used to say in the movies. After half an hour of getting bounced around throughout the Pentagon he managed to reach the offices of the Director of the MDA. After giving his credentials and expressing the urgency of his need to speak with Simons directly, he was patched through to the lieutenant general's cell phone.

Simons listened skeptically while the man on the other end identified himself and stated the nature of his business. Before the call ended, his staff had reserved a flight for the man to Dulles from Iowa—not Idaho. Simons wanted a face-to-face meeting with the PTL. He wanted to look the man in the eyes and get a sense of who the man was and what he was dealing with. He wanted to learn the man's motivations and intentions. That could not be done over the phone. The lieutenant general decided for security purposes and given the highly confidential and sensitive nature of the interview, to see the man alone. Simons was prepared to sit and listen to the Project Team Leader from Tactical Missile Systems, Inc., located in Cedar Rapids, Iowa and hear him tell his story. If everything checked out and after a thorough vetting of the PTL, Simons planned to bring the man back for a full debriefing. For security purposes and not to raise red flags by having the PTL take more time off to fly back to DC, during the call they agreed to meet at a location to be determined, but somewhere in the vicinity of the contiguous cities of Cedar Falls and Waterloo, where there was a small regional airport.

AS HE WAITED for his flight to DC via Chicago to be called he thought more about Daya. She had come to his office, resignation letter in hand, prepared to give a standard two weeks notice. He had refused the letter, and told her that he had saved her job if she would accept a reassignment. She seemed none too sure about that plan, so he explained what he had in mind. He told her he needed time to work some things through, time to see how things were going to shake out and, despite what might happen with Davis and the company, he would do everything he could to protect her. Once he had a grip on the situation, he told her, he would call her back into his office and terminate her position under the auspices of a layoff. She agreed to the plan.

On the day of the termination he assured Daya that when she filed for unemployment, she would receive the full amount of the benefits coming to her, such as her 401k. He helped her pack, under the guise of safeguarding company intellectual property and top secret information, and suggested to her that she should take this time to visit her family in India. A few days later he drove her to the airport and as she wished him well and goodbye he thought her eyes had misted just before she turned and walked away.

THE PERSONAL MEETING with Lieutenant General Simons, an impressive and likeable man, had gone well, to his mind at least. "Don't worry, son," the LTG assured him. "This is not the first time we have had to deal with a situation like yours." But his face had blanched when the PTL told him the truth of what he knew, a truth that directly contradicted what CEO Davis had told the LTG in the meeting of the Pioneer Committee. Before the conclusion of the interview, a second meeting had been agreed to, one that for security purposes would convene in Iowa. The LTG then called in his XO, Major Harold Marsden, and introduced him to the PTL. "Major Marsden will see to it that you get back home to Iowa and he personally will call you to schedule our next meeting. Just so you know, I want a technical representative from the DoD to sit in with us and help ask the right questions." The PTL assured him that he expected nothing less.

He came away from the meeting impressed with the LTG. Now more than before, he was convinced he had made the correct decision for himself, for his company, and for his country. Marsden took him to dinner in a staff vehicle, a monstrous black Chevy SUV with driver, and personally walked him through Dulles, bought his ticket and left him with TSA at the expedited pre-check security lane.

His plane received clearance to land at Cedar Rapids airport in the middle of a thunderstorm slickening and painting the runways black as a lake under the light of a half-moon. Safely down, the aircraft turned and headed for the gate, running over towers of light reflecting off the wet mirror of the runway. The PTL blew out his cheeks in relief, grabbed his bag from the overhead bin and went to call a taxi for a ride home. At about the same time the PTL flew home from his meeting with Simons, CEO Davis, during a layover in Chicago, dropped a dime of his own to an old colleague he had once helped win a rather lucrative government contract.

THE CALL FROM Major Marsden came less than a week later. It took the PTL about forty-five minutes to drive to Waterloo, a John Deere town, and he was surprised when he saw the exit for the town. It had not changed much over the years; still dirty, drab and gray with the look of a Midwestern industrial town that had suffered the ravages of the farm crisis in the eighties and the massive layoffs at the various factories around town after the housing crisis and recession in 2009. He could remember a time when anyone who wanted a job paying more than minimum wage would kill to work for Deeres, as the locals called it. He had even thought about it upon graduation, but had taken the job at Tactical Missile Systems instead. Looking back in hindsight now, that had not been his brightest career move. At the time, he had been certain that he did not want to spend the rest of his working life designing cams for the drive shaft of a big green tractor.

As a young man he had hunted near Dunkerton and out by Dike when a flush of pheasants could number in the hundreds. Those days were gone, he though wistfully, as he drove west on University, looking for the hotel. Too many farmers riding John Deere combines and tractors now farmed fencerow to fencerow, growing corn not for feed or seed, but for another ill-conceived government program: ethanol. As the farmers jumped aboard he had watched the gradual erosion of hunting habitat. Lush fields of native prairie grasses and flowers once reserved for set-aside programs were now raped by the plow. Tree-lined ravines were bulldozed flat and filled in. Sloughs capable of holding large coverts of ringnecks were destroyed, either burned down, mowed over, plowed under and planted with corn or beans to get a few extra bushels of yield per acre. Ironically, the price of corn and soybeans dropped as the yields—supported by the more aggressive use of chemical fertilizers and herbicides, combined with bioengineered, fast-growing varieties—

increased. And then the government had nearly killed the set-aside program, funneling the money into ethanol subsidies, forcing the farmers to put even more land back into production.

He shook his head in disgust as he pulled into the parking lot of the mom and pop hotel. Even an engineer could figure out why the kids were leaving the family farm and the state in droves, and why South Dakota, with its progressive plans for habitat management, had overtaken Iowa as the pheasant hunter's destination of choice. It was a sad state of affairs and his reminiscences had not improved his mood as he walked to the reception desk and asked for the clerk to call room number 15 and say the code name he had been given. He was directed to the far end of the hotel farthest from the street and on ground level. There were only two or three other cars in the parking lot.

A young man, very fit with a very short haircut, greeted him, but did not smile. He seemed uncomfortable in his ill-fitting suit. Before he entered the door, the PTL was asked to show his company id, which he did. The young man studied it carefully, looked into his face twice, thanked him, and then knocked and opened the door. The guard followed him inside and informed him that he was to be searched first by hand and then by wand. He extended his arms and was patted down. It was a thorough search. He could not help but smile at the men waiting in the room. His keys triggered the detection wand, but the young guard seemed unfazed. His search finished, the guard nodded to one of the men in the room.

Lt. General Frank Simons in a conservative gray suit and red tie greeted him with a handshake and apologies for the security screening. He asked if the PTL wanted anything to drink. He said a Diet Coke would be fine and the young man returned from outside with the can and a bucket of ice. He popped the can and poured the foaming liquid into an unwrapped plastic cup. An unsmiling, middle-aged woman sat ready at a table, her transcription machine atop her heavy, panty-hosed thighs. She had taken her pumps off. There were two other men in the room with Simons. The first, Major Marsden, the LTG's executive officer and adjutant, he had already met. The second was introduced to him as a leading civilian expert in target acquisition systems, working for the Defense Department. He was a handsome man, probably in his late fifties and had an understated aura of competency.

The PTL knew such men and liked them, having worked with them from time-to-time on various projects for the military. They were usually retired officers in some technical branch of the services now working for DoD as civil servants with a government service rank of GS-12 or higher. They were part of a cadre of true and dedicated professionals who had given their lives and careers to working for their government and their country. The PTL considered them true patriots, regardless of political affiliation. The man was there to vett him, to determine if what he had to offer was legitimate, verifiable information. The technical representative from the Department of Defense had a strong and steady hand and clear blue eyes shining with intelligence. The PTL liked him immediately. After handshakes all around and everyone was seated, Simons started the proceedings.

"I want to go on record and tell you how much I appreciate what you are doing for your country. I consider it nothing less than an act of heroism. I also want to assure you that we will do everything we can to protect you, and when this is all over and done with and you need a job, I will personally see to it that you get one."

The PTL appreciated what the lieutenant general was telling him, more so now as he saw the stenographer record what had been said. He knew that the government's treatment of whistleblowers left a lot to be desired. Simons's formal pronouncement on the record made him feel a lot better. Guided by the questions from the technical expert, the PTL blew long and hard on the whistle of truth and told them everything he knew.

When he could not think of another thing to say, he stopped and looked at his Casio watch. To his amazement almost two hours had passed, the Diet Coke can stood empty and all the ice in the plastic cup had melted. The technical representative to the DoD had asked sharp and incisive questions concerning the company's work. There were instances where the PTL was forced to reveal proprietary secrets, and the man waited patiently while he worked through the years of conditioning and training that forbade the PTL from discussing or revealing top secret information.

The lieutenant general listened quietly and attentively, only occasionally asking a question of clarification. For the most part the men conducting the interview sat back in their chairs and let the PTL tell his story and answer the expert questions posed by the tech rep. Simons did not like what he was hearing, but he appreciated the PTL's decision to come forward and tell the truth, regardless of its potential impact on the mission's success. Of one thing he was certain: his country depended on and needed men like the PTL, despite the consequences of their actions. He knew the man's life would invariably change, possibly for the worse in the short term. He had seen it before: men and women of higher moral purpose and a value system that did not permit them to defraud or to lie or to cheat, particularly when it affected the security and welfare of their country. How ironic, thought the LTG, that such men and women were becoming increasingly hard to find.

To his mind these were the true patriots. Regrettably, all too often they were left with little to show for their courage other than disrupted lives, the hate and scorn of their co-workers, and more often than not, termination from their jobs. He looked at the man sitting quietly across from him and waited as the technical representative finished his notes from the interview. The

PTL, to his mind, was exactly the kind of man his country depended on, the kind of man the lieutenant general was sworn to serve and protect against all enemies foreign and domestic, the kind of man Simons wanted to serve with. Unfortunately, such men and women were becoming a rare breed. The LTG smiled at him and looked at the stenographer. She finished typing the last symbol or two into the machine, picked it up off her lap and went into the adjoining room.

"This is my promise to you. I intend to bring the full force and retribution of the U.S. Department of Justice to bear against Dr. Davis. Under sworn oath that bastard had the balls to look me directly in the face and lie his ass off in front of every one of the committee members, so help him God. He is screwing with me, screwing with my program, and I will see to it that he is charged with high crimes and prosecuted to the full extent allowed by law. Personally, I consider what he has done to be treasonous, and when the time is right, I will take his head for that reason." He said it without anger or emotion. He paused for a moment while his adjutant made a note, and then continued. "I want to enroll you in the government's Witness Security Program. I think it's in your best interest at the moment, given the way things could shake out. I'll contact your state's attorney general and have him initiate enrollment proceedings." He nodded again to Major Marsden, who made the note. "On my recommendation, he will contact the U.S. Attorney's office, where the final judgment for admission is made, but I can assure you that you will be enrolled. In fact, I can promise you a pre-admittance briefing the day after tomorrow."

The PTL thanked the LTG, but asked for some time to think about it. Simons assured him they could wait until Monday. He was given a number for the U.S. Marshals, which he could call night or day, if and whenever he thought the move was necessary. He was reminded that in the Witness Security Program or not, he would be the chief witness for the prosecution against Dr. Davis. The PTL accepted the responsibility and asked Lieutenant General Simons if he knew what might happen to the company or his co-workers. It was a good question and the LTG scratched his cheek, stubble emerging at the jaw line. He made a mental note to shave again on the plane back to the Pentagon.

"Because you came forward as a representative of TMS, we won't hold the company liable. We'll bring the case against Doctor Davis personally, since there seems to be no sign of collusion. In fact, from what you've told us you and your colleagues have done your level best to do the right thing. Most likely, and this is what I've seen happen in similar instances, we'll move in a senior vice-president of our choosing to manage the company in the interim. I'll see to it that the contract is maintained, an issue I know troubles you quite a bit. Don't worry about it; I'll take care of it," he promised the PTL. "And you make certain that you take care of yourself."

They shook hands again all around and as the PTL walked out into the parking lot he felt as if a concrete block had been lifted from his shoulders, his conscience clear.

Chapter Thirty

Go No Go

When she next awakened there was enough light in the den to make out the stony ceiling of the cave and the roots that pointed down at her like the gnarled fingers of a witch in her book of German fairy tales. On her back, as she quickly turned to find him, her head turned inside her hood and the lights went out. She struggled to pull the hood away from her eyes so she could see again. She heard him chuckling. She sat up and gave him a thorough once over. "You look like Hell," she told him in her objective opinion. His thick, wavy hair was matted down in spots and stood out in others. His beard grizzled his jawline. "You're the only man I've ever known whose beard is black, brown, blond, and red." She let her fingers travel over his face, reading the Braille of his stubble. The feel and the blend of colors fascinated her.

"When I was a baby my hair was light blond, the same color of my mother's hair. It fell out and came in black. My grandfather had red hair mostly, and my father's hair is jet black."

"Both my parents had blonde hair." He was not surprised. She rolled over on him. It utterly amazed her that she could stretch her entire length, almost six feet, atop him and not touch the ground with any part of her body. It was like lying on a living platform that rose and fell. She was nose to nose with him and playful. "You also smell like a bear." She wrinkled her nose for appropriate emphasis.

He remained stoic, refusing to rise to the bait. Finally he said, "Get off me."

She refused immediately, recalcitrant to the last, smiling her defiance into his face. She rode the gentle swell of his breathing. To her eye he looked even more rugged and handsome despite the circumstances and the mess of hair, which she tried to tame with her fingers. And the smell was not offensive; if anything he smelled of pine boughs, cedar needles, wood smoke, and man. She adored his smell.

"You talked a bit in your sleep last night," he told her.

She was interested. "What did I say?"

He teased her. "I don't know. It was all in German."

"You speak German."

"You said, '*Ich hab' dich Lieb,*' and I think you were saying it to me."

She blushed immediately, the red flush touching even the tips of her ears and swell of her throat. "I was evidently dreaming of Manfred and telling him that I loved him. I was dreaming of the man I love."

"I'm sure you were," he said with a knowing smile.

She pushed herself off him and crawled up to the opening of the bear den for a quick look outside. "Oh, my," was all she said. The wind spit snow into her face and swirled over the dampened fire, staying just long enough to agitate and inflame before it disappeared and let the fire hide once more down in and among the coals. "It's still snowing."

"You have a cute ass for a she-bear," he commented. "And thanks for the weather report."

She wiggled it for him. "I'm a hungry she-bear, and thirsty too, and I do have to go to the bathroom."

"I've got two candy bars for you, plenty of water, and you're going to get your bum wet and cold. So don't go too far away out of a sense of modesty."

"I won't have to if you promise not to look."

"I wouldn't dare intrude on a girl's need for morning privacy."

She kissed him before venturing out. "I'm not a girl, silly; I'm a she-bear."

She came back in short time, flocked with snow, demanding the water bottle and the candy bars. They ate together, sharing the water bottle. "Drink as much as you can," he said. "We need to force water to avoid dehydration."

She nodded and gulped. "Well, what do you think, big bear?"

He looked doubtful. "I've never had sex with a bear before." He stopped to think for a moment. "Actually, that's not quite right. I once knew a girl from…"

She cut him short. "I don't want to hear about it, Romeo. I meant what are our chances for getting out of here alive?"

"Mine are actually pretty good, but yours…." He stopped when he saw the look on her face. Although he was grumpy from lack of sleep and food, he did not want to be mean. He was merely trying to delay telling her the inevitable truth. "We've been pretty lucky this far. If our luck holds we can still get out of this with our skins on. Water won't be a problem and we can live without food for about a week."

She shook her head adamantly. "I can't." She saw that she had restored him to good humor. She knew he was grumpy because he did not like having to tell her the bad news. She fully understood what he was trying to do. He was being protective. In their present situation it was not such a bad thing. She frowned into her eyebrows. She was always having to protect Manfred, the poor dear—he just couldn't help himself. She felt a gentle tapping on her forehead.

"Earth to Sylvie."

"Sorry. You were saying…."

"It's the weather. They can't search or come for us in this storm. They can't get in the air and they can't get across Kabetogama. Even if they could they have no idea where we are, only a general idea that we started at Locator. So we can't depend on a rescue party pulling us out of this. For one thing, we're not overdue yet in the strict sense of the word. Roland assumes we still have our tent and all our gear and provisions, hunkered down waiting out the storm. We've done it before in the Alps. To be honest, Sylvie, I can't risk taking you out in the storm. We wouldn't last an hour. The wind chill is probably around zero degrees Fahrenheit. We can survive the snow and the travel, but not the wind. So there's nothing left for us to do but ride it out, lay low, and conserve our energy and our strength. In other words we have to hibernate like two fat happy black bears in the woods."

She saw the logic of his decision. She tried to make a contribution. "What about firewood?"

He had hoped she would not notice. "Not good. Through the light of day I'm only going to feed in enough to keep the embers going or we won't have enough to get through the cold of the night."

She did not seem all that worried about their dwindling pile of firewood. "We'll just cuddle for warmth."

Through the day, on the hour, he made her do five stomach crunches and five push-ups with him; and yes, she could do girly push-ups from her knees. After lunch he gave her a full body massage to keep the circulation going and she reciprocated. If anything, the storm raged and howled against their combined efforts to survive it. Sylvie was forced to say, "I don't know how all the little creatures of the forest can survive this." He did not have the heart to tell her that some of them would not make it: they usually froze to death in such adverse, unseasonable conditions.

THEY GOT THROUGH the long hours of the day by telling stories of their youth; Will tapped into his vast reserve of experiences as an athlete, some of them hilarious. She particularly enjoyed the one from his freshman year as a discus thrower at a major track meet in Eugene, Oregon, during a typically cold and blustery Pacific Northwest day. His name was announced as the next thrower. Already nervous, a freshman in competition against two world class throwers and one current Olympian, he hurried to get out of his warm-up uniform. In his haste to remove his warm-up pants and strip down to his running shorts, he accidentally hooked his thumbs into the pants, his shorts, and his jock strap, and mooned 20,000 track and field fans that very cold and windy spring afternoon. She thought that was absolutely hilarious, especially after he told her that the fans rewarded him with an enthusiastic round of applause.

Tired of talking, they dozed from time to time, but never together, one always keeping a drowsy eye on the sleepy fire, burning just enough to stay lit. In spite of the grumbling of her stomach—loud enough to be heard through all her clothes—she said not one word in complaint, knowing that he was as hungry as she, perhaps more so given his size and greater caloric need. When darkness finally pushed the light out of the cave, he stoked the fire and told her to sleep, the better to conserve her energy for the cold temperatures the night would push past the fire.

Despite his good intentions to the contrary, he too dozed off when he could no longer keep his eyes open. He woke with a start, his heart racing in his chest when he realized he had fallen asleep on watch. Next to him Sylvie shivered in her sleep and he could hear the chatter of her teeth as her body fought to raise its core temperature. He took stock of their diminishing pile of firewood. It would last the night, but he doubted whether it would get them through the next day. Screw it, he thought. Better to have a bit of warmth now rather than die by degrees as the temperature dropped throughout the night. As he fed in another short stick of cedar the fire bloomed in the rich oxygen of the cold night air and momentarily brushed the cave walls with soft orange light. He felt the radiant heat reflect over them as he added one more stick. He gently placed himself atop Sylvie, blanketing her with his body, supporting most of his weight on his elbows and knees. She stopped shivering and smiled in her sleep. At that instant he swore to himself that even if he had to crawl back the entire way on his bleeding hands and knees, he would get her out of this mess.

A few hours later, she woke. "God, I'm stiff," she announced, stretching from finger to toenail. "It's all those stupid push-ups and sit-ups up you made me do. I feel like I'm back at the Academy." She looked over at him. He was already fast asleep.

She took a double watch so he could sleep four hours uninterruptedly, a deep restful bear sleep he so desperately needed. When he did awaken he gently reproached her for letting him sleep through his watch. She told him in German to shut up and to stoke the fire just a bit so she could sleep one more time before the diffuse morning light washed out the last of the darkness lingering in the cave. She fell instantly asleep. She thought she heard someone calling to her in her dream. She had just stepped from her morning shower and, as usual, her small bathroom was cold, the window open so the mirror would not fog. Someone had taken all the towels and the little water heater above the tub had run out of hot water again before she could rinse the white suds of the shampoo from her hair. She thought she heard her mother call from the kitchen. She was nervous and cold, her hair wet, her arms crossed at her breasts.

"Sylvie," Will hissed under his breath, finally getting her attention and her eyes to open. He had a finger to his lips. It was light outside. He was at the opening of their den, on his belly, his legs splayed into the cave like a marksman in the prone shooting position. "Hand me the rifle," he whispered. As quietly as she could above the bed of pine and cedar branches and Gore-Tex, she passed him the rifle, barrel first. He moved over a scootch and motioned her forward. Her mouth opened in surprise.

Reflecting off the broad white expanse below them, the sun was so bright she had to blink streaming stars from her eyes. She squinted into the glare and tried to see what he saw. She could not believe how much it had snowed. There were no more edges in the world; the snow had smoothed out and rounded almost everything in the landscape into soft undulating contours. Granite boulders looked as soft and fluffy as her grandmother's goose down pillows. The limbs of the firs drooped under the weight of their snow load. Everywhere she looked there was brilliant white silence. Suddenly a cap of snow shifted and slid from a cedar branch, which snapped upward, now relieved from the pressure, the noise disturbing the serenity of the snow-dampened panorama. Then she saw it.

In the distance past the pines that served as their windbreak and another two hundred meters or so below them, a stag lifted his head and stood watching, the spike of his ears turning to the sound. He went back to nuzzling the patch of ground he had scratched clear with his front hooves. Will sighted through the Leupold scope and to his chagrin, noticed that his breath had fogged the lens. Sylvie saw it at the same time and reached into his back pocket and pulled out his bandana. He wiped the moisture from the lens. He gritted his teeth and sighted through the scope, centering the cross hairs on the deer some 600 yards away in the valley below. It was nearly an impossible shot at that distance, one that he would never attempt during hunting season out of respect for the animal, but now he had no choice. He had to make it. He unscrewed the sound suppressor to increase his chances for making the shot.

"Cover your ears," he warned. She cupped her hands to her ears and pressed. He sighted through the reticle again, calculated the drop of the bullet given the distance to the target and the elevation, and pushed the safety off. Half way through a slow, conscious exhale he squeezed the trigger. The rifle thundered back into his shoulder and nearly deafened him. He quickly cleared the round, slammed home the next, and slapped the bolt down. The deer had jumped and he knew the shot had struck because he had seen the snow fly where the bullet had puffed the pelt. Whether it was a killing shot, he could not tell because the deer was now gone. He reset the safety and tapped Sylvie, hands clamped tightly over her ears, eyes scrunched shut. "Come on, Pocahontas, we've got some tracking to do."

They crawled out of the den into the glaring white brightness of the day and plowed their way through the thigh-high accumulation of snow. They skidded down the slope to the flat where Will had seen the buck. There were blood spatters where he had jumped. They followed the disturbance he left in the snow and found him on his flank, not twenty yards farther into the woods. "That Weatherby Magnum is a helluva rifle," Will said. He touched the nose of the rifle to the moist nose of the animal. It did not move.

"He's beautiful," she said, sadly. "It's a shame we had to kill him. How are we going to get him up the hill and back into the den?" she asked, her stomach talking now.

He laughed at her sudden need. "Do you plan to eat the whole animal?" he asked. She shoved her hands more deeply into her coat pockets and stamped her feet to keep them warm. The cold bit at the contours of her cheeks, reddening them. She could not help it if she was starving. He opened his Buck knife and handed her the rifle for safe keeping. "We'll take the tenderloins and I also want the hamstrings."

"What in the world do you want those for?"

"Look back at the way we came down."

"Oh. Looks like two snowplows forced their way through."

"Right. We'll be dead from fatigue in fifteen minutes of pushing through that heavy wet stuff. While I butcher the deer, your job is to find four saplings about a meter and a half in length, and about as round as the rifle barrel. Don't worry if they have small branches or needles or even leaves attached, but they should be live and supple. Take the Buck knife. I'll use my pocket knife for the deer once I get a cut started through the fur."

She looked at the knife. Dubious, she said, "It'll take forever to cut through those trees, even ones that small."

"Bend them first and break them with your boots. Off you go."

She pirouetted on the ball of her boot and set off to find suitable candidates for harvest, although she still could not imagine what he wanted the saplings for and he was not telling. It took her the better part of an hour, bending the four saplings she found, twisting, pulling, stomping on the bend, and finally cutting through the green woody strands of fiber exposed by all her effort. In spite of the cold she felt herself starting to sweat, so she took a break. After less than five minutes she was again cool enough to work. As best she could she trimmed the young trees into poles, put all four over her shoulder and in one of the paths plowed with their shins and boots, tromped back up the slope to the opening of the den. She skirted the bloody tinge of the carcass bleeding up into its snow sarcophagus and regretted again the death of the animal. The smell of roasting venison wafted down the slope and almost brought her to her knees with hunger. She handed in the poles. Will examined them with a critical eye.

"You've earned your lunch."

All she could do was sit there staring at the fire, saliva running from her mouth like a slobbering dog chasing a coon, Will said. "I can't wait any longer," she told him. She watched a thick strip of venison roasting on a spit and darkening atop the last of their precious firewood. "Just slice me off a piece of that one and I'll eat it raw."

He pushed her back on her behind. "Just wait five more minutes, my fine young cannibal. In fact, you can help me while the meat cooks." He handed her one of the sapling poles he had stripped. "We're going to make snowshoes. Pre-shape the poles by bending them around your knee, careful not to snap it, and try to get it into the shape of an ankh." She knew what an Egyptian ankh was and as he carefully cut lengths from the long hamstring tendons of the deer's legs, she formed the pliable green poles into a curvilinear shape. "Good job," he told her. He stretched the tendons out to dry on a small rack of twigs above the meat roasting on the fire. Once their work was finished, he asked for his knife back. He cut a chunk from the roast dripping juice at the end of the three spits holding it above the flames. It was rare and still moist with seeping blood but hot to his touch. He handed it to her on the point of his knife blade. "There. Tell me what you think about that." The roast venison, much more rare than she preferred, was the first real food she had given her stomach in almost a day and a half. The taste of the deer meat was so profoundly delicious she literally could not speak.

"Okay. Don't say anything," he told her, and grinned as he cut a portion for himself.

As she chewed she remembered a story Roland once had told her. "Roland said there was a time when he and your father poached a stag back in Bavaria at the request of a local restaurant owner. I guess the hunter who was supposed to supply meat for the inn had been injured or some such thing, and they took it upon themselves to remedy the venison shortage."

"My dad told me the same story. After they brought in the deer, the rest of their stay at the resort was free."

"Must run in the family," she noted.

He laughed. "The venison is certainly fresh, but I can't say much about the accommodations."

They gorged themselves on the venison, hot and smoking. When she could not manage one more morsel of meat, Sylvie sat back against the stone wall of the cave and produced an inadvertent and unexpected—even to her—burp of surprising proportion and volume. She tried to hide her indiscretion behind her hand and a look of mortified, child-like innocence. But Will was having none of it.

"Sylvie," he admonished her by merely saying her name.

"I'm a little pig," she admitted.

"Yes, you are," he agreed. He reached over and cleaned a trail of brown juice from the corner of her mouth and the curve of her chin. "We need to build the snowshoes now."

"What can I do?" She had never built snowshoes before.

"Your job is to finish stripping the needles from the pine boughs we've been lying on while I tie the saplings into frames. What we don't use we can feed into the fire to keep us warm before we set off."

She was unsure about the reason for tearing up her bed. "Are we moving?"

He laughed. "Yes. We're moving and we have a helluva journey ahead of us. We have to make it back to War Club Lake through three feet of snow as we try to follow a trail that has disappeared." He thought for a minute. "Although that might work to our advantage, on second thought, if we can hike a straight line to the lake. We'll stay with the trail as long as we can, hiking from point to point."

"What do you mean by that?" she asked as she stripped needles.

"We pick a landmark in the distance—one we know is still on the trail and we hike to it. From there we establish our next landmark, and so on."

"I see what you mean." She watched as he deftly bent and shaped the saplings into frames that very closely resembled the oversize racket heads she used when she played tennis with Manfred. Tennis was his only active sport. "Did you know I can beat Manfred at tennis?" She made conversation as they worked.

"No, I didn't know that. How does he feel about that?"

The question surprised her. She had taken for granted the fact that she could outplay him on the tennis court, or in any athletic endeavor, for that matter. "He has always been a gracious loser, ever the gentleman."

Will decided it was in his best interest to let that one pass. "Hand me three or four of those sticks you stripped, will you please?"

She handed over what she had done so far and watched him for a moment as he sized them, laid them across the frame, and tied them into place with lengths of the deer tendon, now dried into pliable strips. She watched with admiration as the snowshoe took shape. "Is there anything you can't do?"

He smiled at the indirect compliment. "Get back to work."

She put a handful of cedar needles to her nose and breathed deeply. "I love the smell of fresh cedar. You know, Freddi would never have approved of you shooting that deer."

Will set the first shoe aside, satisfied with his craftwork, and began the second. "Why not?

"He's very active in the Green Party and he's against all forms of hunting and killing animals."

Will cinched a knot tight. "How noble of him. He would have let you starve to death in service to an ideal?"

Sylvie laughed out loud at the absurdity. "You are my protector."

Will looked worried. "I haven't got you home safe and sound yet. Maybe you should hold on to Freddi a while longer."

Sylvie considered the proposition. "Maybe you're right. We still have a long way to go, don't we?"

He nodded. "I've been thinking about that, Sylvie."

She thought he was talking about their relationship, but he was not.

"The decision to go must be as much yours as it is mine. We're faced with the very real possibility that we might not make it. Here at least we have shelter and food." He was serious.

She scooted next to him so that they sat shoulder to shoulder, watching the last of the fire smoke into the meat. "Tell me what you think could go wrong." She could tell he needed to talk it through with her.

He picked up the second completed snowshoe and started the third. "We don't know if these will work, or how long they will hold up."

It was a good point. "We'll take five minutes and test them with a stomp around the outside of the cave. We can take extra strips of those tendons as ties, and if something breaks, we'll repair as we go," she suggested.

He gave her a quick kiss on the cheek, sensible girl. "We'll be racing the sun. We have to get to War Club before dark."

"We can do that easily. We're both in excellent shape."

"Have you ever walked in snowshoes?"

"No," she admitted, "but I've skied cross-country since I was five years old."

That was welcome news. It would help matters. "Okay. Say we make it in good time. We're assuming we will find his canoe there," he said, referring to the dead man they had left alongside the trail.

It seemed an eon ago, she thought. "It will be there," she assured him. "He certainly didn't swim across the lake to our side."

Will was not so easily convinced. "We have to get across the lake and paddle all the way back to the northwest end where we initially picked up our canoe. Then we have another cross-country hike ahead of us to La Bontys point on Kabetogama. That assumes Maggie and Roland are able to get there now that the storm has broken and are still waiting for us if we miss the pick-up time. We can't afford to spend a night out in the cold and snow without protection of some kind. We don't know if the tent is still in our canoe after two days of blizzard. Goddammit!" He threw down the last of the snowshoes, willing to show her his frustration. "It's just too risky." He sat glowering and as she watched the fire glimmer, she let him simmer in silence for a while.

"Okay. Let's consider the other option. Say we don't go. What happens if we wait here? We've got food and enough water to survive."

He considered the possibility, scratching at the bristles of his beard with fingers blackened by the smoke and soot of the fire. She could hear the rasp. He took a quick look outside and up into the sky. "A high pressure system is over us now by the looks of those cirrus clouds. That gives us two, maybe three days, of stable weather, if we're lucky. Roland shows up as scheduled, no us, returns home and calls out Rescue. They can't start till tomorrow because it will be dark by then. They don't know where to search, as we discussed previously, and now there's all this snow to contend with. Given the logistics, the organizational hassles, and the problems with weather and terrain, I think we're looking at a minimum of three more days in the den, Sylvie. And that's if they can spot a signal fire from the air with a pontoon boat. They can't get a helicopter in here because the forest is too dense. They have to take us out on foot or on dogsled."

"What about snowmobiles?"

"That would solve most of our problems, but the big lake isn't frozen over yet and they..."

She put a finger to his lips. "I've made up my mind. I would much rather put my trust in you instead of the others. I want to go. We'll take our chances and trust our intelligence, our skills, and our physical conditioning to get us back."

"I don't much like leaving things to chance, but you nailed it. I would rather depend on us than on other factors. I agree. We go."

They shook hands on it.

Chapter Thirty-one

Trek

Once they agreed on their plan they made ready to leave. Still early in the morning, they had enough time to break camp before starting the hike back to War Club. Will cut strips of venison to take along and Sylvie stoked the fire with the pine and cedar bedding they had slept on. She melted snow into both their water bottles and they forced water until they could drink no more.

"I can hear my stomach slosh as I move around," Sylvie said, unable to take one more sip of water.

"Good enough," Will told her.

It was time to try out the snowshoes. He tied the first pair, somewhat smaller in size than his, to her boots. She happily tromped around the outside circumference of the cave. Before too long she had the hang of walking on the snowshoes. There was a definite trick to lifting, stepping forward, and then lifting the next shoe forward, but soon enough she was showing off by tromping short distances while he strapped his on. "They work perfectly, my big handsome smelly mountain man. I have to admit you are a genius."

He was up on his and moving about and he had to admit they did the job. He was forced to agree that he was, indeed, a genius. Then Sylvie had a stroke of inspiration that made him doubt his own brilliance. In the midst of her jubilation she said, "Let's cut some poles for trekking."

He felt like an idiot. He should have thought of it himself. It would make the work of travelling across the snow infinitely easier. "Excellent idea," he told her.

It did not take them long to find suitable lengths of young pine and strip the branches down to poles. With the addition of the poles for stability and pushing through the snow, they were able to negotiate the top of the snowfield with some degree of dexterity. The overnight temperatures had crusted the snow with a thin cap of ice, which helped. They crunched through the ice with each step they took, the snowshoes preventing them from sinking deeper into the white cushion of snow pillowing their feet.

They stood at the mouth of the bear den and Will doused the last of the smoldering fire with snow. He stuffed his coat pockets with extra lashes and small branches in case they broke one or two in their snowshoes. Sylvie had the extra meat in the plastic bag that previously contained the gorp, and each had a full bottle of water. Will picked out a landmark along an alley of trees and it was time to get moving.

Sylvie stopped for a minute and looked back. "I'll miss our little bear cave. If we were going to stay in it much longer, I could have really fixed it up. I already had some curtains picked out for the entrance."

He laughed. "Come on, Sacajawea. We have miles to go before we sleep."

"Who is this Sacajawea and should I be jealous?"

"She is the young Native American who helped Lewis and Clark during part of their trek from St. Louis all the way to Oregon. They even hit parts of the North Central States. You should not be jealous but you should be vigilant all the same."

He set the pace, not normally his habit or style. He preferred overwatch to lead and let Sylvie take the lead when they walked or ran together. He enjoyed the luxury of watching her and seeing that everything was going well. Today, however, it was more important that he follow his line and make it to the landmark he had chosen, so Sylvie brought up the rear. He had another reason for leading, but kept it to himself. He knew that despite her excellent physical condition, he was the stronger of the two and at some point that would come into play.

At each landmark—a unique tree, or large granite outcrop, or even a rise in the geography—they stopped and together picked out the next point in the line of their march. It was slow and laborious going at times, but Will liked the progress they were making. The snowshoes were holding up beneath their boots and the poles proved an invaluable asset in propelling them forward while, at the same time, helping to maintain balance when going down slopes. After the first hour, about a third of the way by his reckoning, he gave Sylvie a longer break, letting her sit to rest. He cut a portion of the tenderloin big enough for both to share. Steam rose from her head as she sat chewing, her blonde hair darkened by the moisture of her sweat. "You look like a little locomotive," he said.

She wiped sweat dripping from an eyebrow and tore off another chunk of the venison with her incisors. "I do feel like I've been pulling a train up the side of an Alp."

"Ready?" he asked, giving her a hand up at the same time. He knew stopping too long could be deadly. They were both sweating hard and hypothermia was a risk if they waited too long to recover. In the second hour they found the bend of the trail where they had been attacked. Their assailant was still there under a grave of pure white snow, his head, torso, and feet three distinct oversized mounds. Under the shroud of snow he was a caricature in death; he had become a real snowman.

Farther down the trail the wind had piled the snow into drifts, making further progress impossible, and they were forced to give it up. They tried to maintain a southerly direction as best they could, picking out landmarks and moving toward them with the hope that at some point they would reacquire the snowmobile trail marked by signposts, just to be certain of their direction. As they side-slipped a rather nasty incline down the side of a small hill, Sylvie caught the toe of her snowshoe, pitched forward and slid headfirst the rest of the way down the slope. He was at her side almost immediately, having watched the drama of her fall and subsequent slide unfold. She sat in a heap, sputtered and spit snow from her mouth. He helped wipe her face with his bandana. "I know," she said as he helped her to her feet and found her trekking poles. "Now I look like a little toboggan."

Well into the second hour he further slowed the pace. If anything, the snow was deeper off the trail and the ice crust had melted under the radiant heat of the sun. Sylvie lagged farther and farther behind and he had to wait for her to catch up when they reached their landmarks. She said nothing but he could gauge the depth of fatigue in her face. The fall had taken its toll and had cost her valuable energy. They had to keep going. Stopping was not an option. A conspiracy of factors beyond her control brought her down again. Lack of sleep and adequate food, the cold, the exertion, the psychological stress of not knowing whether she would live or die, each element alone was not enough to stop her, but all the elements working in synergy finally forced her to her knees. She was frustrated and angry. At one time or another in her life she had experienced all these factors—sometimes one or two working together—but never so many all at once and with such overpowering force.

She had been struggling to keep up even though she knew Will had slowed considerably to help her along, and she knew she was lagging too far behind. She could not keep her mind from wandering and once Will had to call her back in line as she meandered away, following some imaginary path in the warmth and security of her imagination. She was proud of herself and her training and the focused discipline of her mind that kept her moving despite the numbing fatigue. Only her conscious, concerted effort allowed her to lift one leaden snowshoed boot after the other, using the poles to help steady her shaking arms, moving forward, always forward, eyes locked just ahead of the next step, and never once, ever, complaining. Then all at once, in spite of the best efforts of her iron will, her outstanding conditioning, and her youthful indomitable pride, suddenly she fell sideways to the snow. Her eyes were open in terror. No matter how hard she struggled she could not get up. She did have the strength to cry out in shame or even to cry. She could only lie there, rasping the cold air into her burning lungs. She lay half on her back in the cushion of snow, feet twisted in the snowshoes, the lower half of her prostrated body twisted on her side. Defeated, she closed her eyes.

He was on her in a second. She was shocked by the intensity in his voice when he called her name. Startled, she wondered what she had done wrong. He knelt next to her on one knee, his upper body blocking the sun, placing her face in shadow. Her sunglasses had dropped in the snow when she had fallen. He studied her for a minute or two, trying to read the signs, or in this case, the symptoms. She moved her head back and forth to let him know that he should not bother. She was finished. She had let everyone down. She wanted to cry. She knew she was dying of exposure. "Save yourself," she managed. "Go on without me." Her voice was coarse and she was frightened by the way it sounded. It was her mother's voice after a night of drinking and cigarettes.

He grabbed the front of her coat and pulled her up into a sitting position. How could he still be so strong after having suffered so much? He had broken the trail for her the entire way, plowing through the snow ahead of her so that her going would be that much easier. She knew what he was doing. He never liked to lead. She watched him clean her glasses and wondered how he had gotten them off her face without her knowing. While she waited, she sang a little song she had learned in her third year of school. She stopped when her voice cracked, and she was embarrassed again. He put the glasses on her face. Much better. In the open spaces between the pines and the conifers the sun reflecting off the snow was blinding. He made her drink from the water bottle.

"Let's get you up and on your feet," he said.

She rode the pull of his powerful arm up to a rubbery weak-kneed stand. He led her to a downed tree, swept clear a place for her to sit and lowered her to the fallen larch. It felt good to sit. She was feeling better. "You bonked," he said. She looked around for her poles. She did not know the word. He explained. "You depleted all the glycogen in your muscles. It happens to long distance runners and cross-country skiers when they use up all their energy reserves. Without much fuel left to burn, the body does a near total shutdown. We call it hitting the wall, or bonking."

"You mean I'm not going to die?" She sounded curiously disappointed.

"Not anytime soon."

"I thought I was doing to die of hypothermia."

"That's still a real possibility. We have to get you up and moving again soon as possible."

She turned her head away from him. The good news had enlivened her somewhat, but now she was visibly distraught knowing that she most likely would live.

"What's the matter, Sylvie?" he gently asked.

She looked into his eyes, desperation and shame in hers. "I think I peed my pants."

"Big pee or little pee?" he asked.

She wondered to herself what difference did it make? She was angry with herself now. She was a grown woman, and the fact is she had peed her pants like a little girl, and she felt compelled to tell him. Men could be so stupid at times. "Just a little leak," she confessed, "as I fell, I think. I couldn't help it. I tried but it was too late. I could feel the warmth of the moisture in my panties." She sighed deeply, helplessly resigned to the inevitability of being judged. She felt small.

He cut her a strip of the venison. "It's nothing to worry about. The most important thing now is for you to eat this."

"I can't," she said, waving it away.

He insisted and she relented, taking a bite, forcing herself to chew slowly and deliberately with barely enough energy to work her jaws. She had to work the dark meat with her mouth open.

"I'm ashamed," she said, after a swallow or two. She asked for another drink to help with the mastication. "I peed my pants like a four-year-old girl."

"So what?" he said. "I got so drunk once I threw up in my girlfriend's lap."

She winced at the thought picture. She wondered if he was telling the truth. "That's disgusting. Weren't you embarrassed?"

"Not really."

"Why not?"

"The smell triggered the same effect in her. She got even, so to speak. I thought it was all rather romantic: two lovers puking on each other."

Sylvie scrunched her face into a mask of disgust. "That's just gross. Don't you dare get drunk and think about throwing up in my lap." She was gradually forgetting about her own difficulty. She tore another bite from the tenderloin strip and chewed with better effort. After a swallow, she repeated. She washed it all down with more water. "I feel better now," she offered, and continued to eat. He sat next to her on the fallen log. She looked into his haggard face; he seemed gaunt and tired and near the end of his seemingly inexhaustible strength, but his eyes were still bright and fierce. "You look like you just staggered out of Dachau," she said.

He laughed a little, more out of relief at her signal to him that she was recovering than at the morbid humor.

She waited for him to say something and when he offered no rejoinder she asked, "Well, how do I look?"

He turned to face her and made a show of examining her carefully. He finger-combed her matted blonde hair behind her ears. Her face was gray and dirty with smoke and fatigue, her lips thinned and chapped by the elements, her baby blue eyes swimming in the cold. "Good enough to throw up on. Despite what you've just been through, I have to say surprisingly good," he lied.

The lie was exactly what she needed to hear. Her chin came up and she tore one more mouth-filling chunk off the hunk of venison and said defiantly, "Don't you dare." He smiled and ate what remained of the smoked deer meat.

"Do we have much further to go?" she asked, strong enough now to worry about the answer.

He lied again, knowing what she needed now more than anything else, more than food or water, was hope. She needed to believe that she was going to succeed in spite of it all, and he knew that if she convinced herself that the end of their journey was near, she could push herself the rest of the way despite her fatigue. He knew the human body could be pushed far beyond the limits of endurance imagined by most people so he told her, "We're almost there, Sylvie. And since we have time left, we'll slow the pace down a bit too."

She motioned for her poles. "I can make it."

"I know you can, sweetheart. I never doubted you."

When Will stopped after what seemed an interminable slog through the pristine and undisturbed snow that appeared to stretch forever ahead of them, she bumped into his heels. She walked with her head down, too tired to keep her chin up, even the muscles of her neck exhausted. She leaned up against him, breathing great gouts of steam into the air. He turned around and watched her, amused. "Now you're a little dragon."

She did not share his amusement. This was their third stop since he had told her there was not much farther to go. Granted, the stops had been more frequent and the rests somewhat longer, but here they were again, stopping and resting. She regained control of her breathing and had enough energy left to say, "My ass is dragging, that's for sure," showing off an idiom she had learned from Roland. She no longer had the courage to ask how much farther.

He grabbed her by both arms just below the shoulders and step by tamping step, turned her to face down the slope from the ridge where they stood. Now her mouth opened in surprise. "The lake." Where the water touched the shoreline there was a meniscus of ice covered with snow. It was as if someone had outlined the inside edges of the lake with white, making the water look almost black in comparison.

"The lake," he said, confirming her observation. "We made it. And there's still plenty of open water if we find a canoe."

She was on the verge of tears and could feel her blue eyes brimming. Her vision swam for a second or two, she was so happy. As they took in the glorious sight of the lake below them, she took stock. Her thighs burned and trembled with fatigue; she could barely lift her arms and had just enough strength left in her hands to keep her poles from dropping into the snow. She felt as if she had been beaten across the back with a plank. She was so utterly and completely exhausted that she wanted to do nothing else but sit down in the snow and cry quietly.

Instead, she sniffed and asked for his handkerchief again and blew her nose into it, buying time to compose herself. She tried to hand it back, but he told her to keep it in such a way that she could only laugh. About two hundred meters up the lake from where they had exited the woods, they spotted the gleam of the sun off the aluminum hull of their assailant's canoe. They hiked to it, removed their snowshoes, and Will dumped the accumulated snow out of the belly of the canoe.

He loaded Sylvie into the canoe, handed her the rifle, then the paddle, snowshoes, and poles. He waited for her to get set before he pushed off. Will guided them immediately across to the far bank of the silent lake where they found their canoe still loaded with all their gear.

To save time they decided to leave it with the exception of a paddle for Sylvie. She had revived enough to help paddle every other stroke or so. They slid along the lake's quiet length, the only sound the dip and splash of water as they propelled the canoe forward until they reached the narrows that joined War Club Lake with Locator Lake. Sylvie greeted their push through the opening into the larger lake with a "Yahoo" and a smile back at Will. About ten minutes later she noticed that for some reason he had shipped his paddle across his lap and the gunwales of the canoe, and smiled forward at her.

"Okay. I give up. What do I look like now?"

He ignored the question. He smacked the open palm of his broad hand against his forehead, already reddened by windburn and exposure to the sun. "I just remembered something."

She slumped forward, resting on her paddle, too tired to guess, but she gave him the courtesy of looking back once more. "Don't tell me you forgot something back at the bear cave."

He grinned. "There is a feeder tributary that runs from Kabetogama into Locator!"

"What's a feeder tributary and why should I care at the moment?" Out of the sun and in the shadows of the trees lining the bank, she was numb from the cold blanketing her fatigue. At the moment she had neither the will nor the interest to translate the words into German.

He did it for her and explained, "There's a creek Sylvie, not too far distant from where we originally picked up our canoe. In some years it's deep enough for a boat on the Kabetogama end—I know because I've fished it for smallmouth and northern, but it narrows and shallows up the farther we get into it. Unfortunately, I have no idea what it's like from the Locator end running back to Kab."

"But we're in a canoe."

He grinned like a maniac. "That's exactly the point, my very tired but still very beautiful voyageur." The whites of her startling blue eyes were shot through with blood, her nose sunburned a dangerous red, her luscious full mouth chapped at the lips and cracked at the corners. "We can probably get a canoe through it, even if we run into a thin skein of ice."

"You mean we won't have to walk anymore?" She could hardly believe what he was saying. The thought of another trek through knee deep snow, even with the advantage of the snowshoes, filled her with dread. She was prepared to stay behind in a makeshift snow cave and wait to be rescued, if it came to that. She would willingly sacrifice herself for his safety. What she heard him say next almost made her cry with relief.

"I can't promise, but there's a very good chance we can make it all the way through in a canoe. That means no more walking through the ice and snow."

He found the mouth of the little stream connecting the two lakes and she marveled. She had not seen it in the distance. The shoreline looked the same to her, unbroken in its unchanging similarity. All of a sudden, she felt him rudder the canoe to the left and they were in the creek, moving through the reeds at either side of the opening. The deeper they moved in, the more narrow it became and her paddle, if she was not careful, brought up black gouts of swirling mud from the bottom. In other places the nose of the canoe crushed through a skim of ice trying to knit both snow covered banks together. Once, as they passed under the branch of a pine stretching over the creek, Will was inundated with a dump of snow as the branch let its load fall. His sputtering misfortune gave her a good laugh.

When she turned forward again she noticed the waterway broaden by degrees and minutes later she saw the great expanse of the blue water lake stretching to the horizon. Out of the mouth of the creek and in the small protected bay naturally constructed from the lay of granite at the opening, they shipped their paddles for just a moment to get their bearings. To the right they saw La Bontys Point and tied to the dock, Will's big red Lund, waiting for them. Will pulled back the sleeve to his coat, exposed his wrist and checked his watch. He said to Sylvie, "I hope Roland and Lili aren't mad. We're over an hour late."

She reached back and kissed him anyway. Despite all they had been through, he had managed to get them back safe and sound, just a little over an hour late.

Roland was startled when they slid silently up alongside the Lund. Bundled up in a new white snowsuit, he looked like an Eskimo. "You guys are late," he said after he examined them both thoroughly. "And you look like you've been through Hell. We were starting to worry."

Lili helped steady the canoe as Sylvie stepped out and up onto the dock. They hugged, relief evident in Lili's face. Roland shook Will's hand and accepted a hug, mildly surprise at the show of affection. After Will went to Lili and Sylvie to Roland, who kissed both her cold windblown cheeks in greeting, Will looked at Sylvie and in one voice they said, "Man, do we have a story to tell you guys."

Chapter Thirty-two

Best Shot

When the PTL returned to work the Monday after his debriefing, his secretary gave him a warning look and informed him that CEO Davis was waiting for him in his office on the third floor. The intense interview before Lieutenant General Simons had worn him out flat and he had not slept well. Despite his fatigue, the PTL could sense the tension pervading the third floor of Tactical Missile Systems. He expected the worst, and after he was called into the CEO's office, he was summarily fired. He told Davis calmly that he could not be fired without cause.

Davis yelled, "This is my goddammed company and I can do whatever I goddamn please! I don't need anyone telling me what I can or cannot do, especially when it comes to protecting my company. You were, and I emphasize were, the team leader on this project and you failed to deliver. I put my trust in you and you failed. Now I'm going to hire someone who can get the job done instead of telling me what I don't want to hear. You have until noon to clear out your desk and turn in your keys, cards, and codes. There will be a man from Security with you to make sure you don't do anything not in the best interests of this company. Now get the hell out of my sight and out of my office!"

There was nothing left to say. The PTL did as he was told. By coincidence, the security guard that morning was LaVinia Thomas, covering an early shift for a partner, and he could tell in her face and demeanor that she was sympathetic to his plight. She apologized for having to do her duty. She went so far as to help him carry a box out to his truck and load it into the cab behind the seat. After the last trip, he signed the appropriate release forms, noticed that his secretary was crying silently, and assured her that things would be okay. He picked up his nameplate and was escorted down the hall past Dr. Nadipuram's office, where he stopped for a minute. Thomas pulled at the broad brown leather belt below her waist as she tried to hitch up her shiny polyester trousers, looked up and down the hall, and nodded as she waited for the PTL. He did not recognize the new man at her desk.

He remembered the concern in Daya's soft brown eyes, the emotional mist making them seem even larger as they said their goodbyes at the airport. She had decided it was indeed in her best interest to leave the country for three weeks under the guise of visiting a sick relative in India. She had asked him to please stay in touch, which he promised to do. To his surprise, she had hugged him briefly. He wondered if she was happy, visiting her friends and family in India, away from all the turmoil that had swept through the company like a Midwestern tornado roaring through town in the spring.

At his truck again, LaVinia Thomas, entirely uncomfortable in her brown security uniform and creaking leather belt, awkwardly offered to shake his hand, and he did so gladly. Without a look back he drove from the parking lot through the gated campus and out of the research park onto the interstate. He drove the ten minutes to his house, unloaded the boxes from his office, and made a call to a number just outside Tama, Iowa.

THE OLD FARMSTEAD on the Settlement was not easy to reach unless you knew where you were going. If you lived there you knew, and if you were coming to visit, you were a friend and also knew. The difficulty in finding the place was compounded by the unsigned, unimproved gravel road reached as you turned off the last of the blacktop. The house, perched with some dignity on the rise overlooking the 160 acres, was badly in need of painting, but after his grandmother had died, had been in this state for at least ten years. The outbuildings had not worn much better through the years of standing up to the harsh Iowa winters and blistering summers. The barn was in the best shape of all, because Grandfather sometimes cared for his livestock more than his own creature comforts. The red color was still bright, befitting the Red Earth People, but that is not why he had painted it red. With its prominent location on the rise past the farmhouse, the brick-colored building could be seen from any outlying perimeter edging the farm. It served as a homing beacon, a fixed landmark used for orientation, and the PTL could remember many happy hours on the fender of the big green John Deere tractor as he helped plant corn. The same tractor was parked in the aluminum shed that also served as a garage for the farm.

He drove past the chicken coop and startled a few hens into scattered, flapping hops. On his right he saw the low-lying farrowing building for the hogs, now long unused. He missed the fresh pork on the table, but certainly not the smell of pig manure leaking from the sty when the wind shifted. Smoke in the chimney bent to the wind and Ranger, the prettiest blond Labrador retriever a man could ever want to pet, ran up to the truck, his bark changing from warning to recognition. The PTL parked by the front door and renewed his acquaintance with Ranger, who was delighted to welcome back a long lost member of the pack.

Grandfather waited behind the screen door in his faded red, long underwear, and gray and white wool hunting socks. He liked to tell people that this longjohns were originally white and over the years had picked up their color by prolonged contact with his skin. As he opened the screen door for his son he complained, "Why do you have to hunt so goddammed early in the morning? We can get just as many birds in the afternoon. It just doesn't seem sporting to kill a creature so soon after its breakfast and while it still has the expectation of a good day ahead."

He motioned to the chair at the oaken dining table, older even than his grandfather, its top scarred by decades of casual use. "How are you, Grandfather?" he asked. He settled into the mismatched, uncomfortable cheap aluminum chair, the Naugahyde backrest cracked down the middle and split down the sides.

"I'm eighty-seven and I miss the warmth of my bed and I haven't had my breakfast yet," he said, struggling into his Carhartt coveralls. He pulled out a chair for himself and pulled on his hunting boots. The PTL noticed that although worn—the toes pointed up at an angle from the floor and there was not a touch of color left in the leather—the boots had been treated with waterproofing beeswax that made them shine in the light. As his grandfather leaned forward to lace the boots, his long white hair fell forward into his eyes, obscuring his view behind the veil of white.

"Do you want me to braid it for you?" the PTL offered.

"No thanks, boy. I'll just pull it back and tie it off before we go. Do you want a cigar?" He went to the refrigerator and loaded the front side pocket of his hunting coat with smokes. He filled the front pockets of his Carhartts with enough venison jerky for two. The PTL shook his head as he watched the old man go through his pre-hunt rituals. It never ceased to amaze him that his grandfather could shoot and smoke at the same time.

"Suit yourself." He pulled his hair back, tied it into a ponytail, and put on his blaze orange baseball cap. "I don't know how anyone can shoot without a cigar for balance." He went into the living room and returned with his shotgun still in its protective case. "Did you bring shells? You know I only shoot fours and I haven't had time to get into Tama and buy some more."

"I brought you four boxes for today, Grandfather."

"Smart aleck, overeducated, overpaid, worthless in the field grandson," he said, proud of the man who came to see him at least once a week, more often during hunting seasons. He called to the Lab sitting patiently on the porch, sweeping the ground with the broom of his tail. "Come on, Ranger, let's get us some birds." He opened the door to the PTL's truck and Ranger jumped in, taking his place between them.

"You could put him in back where there's plenty of room, like a normal dog," the PTL complained. He pushed the dog over so he could get at the ignition. Ranger did not mind the push in the least, being a good-natured dog to begin, having learned the patience necessary to live in peace and harmony with an eighty-seven-year-old man. As the truck backed out Ranger immediately pressed tightly against his old master, ready and eager for a ride across the farm.

Grandfather scratched Ranger behind the ears. "Nope. Ranger is not a normal dog. He rides up front with me so he can scout the territory. A good hunting dog knows what to look for if you just give him half a chance. He can't see beans riding in back."

At this point Ranger took leave to fart and ignored the PTL's obvious discomfort at the noxious smell. His Grandfather, rather than lowering a window, puffed a cigar into smoke. He looked over at the PTL. "I'd appreciate it if you wouldn't fart in the cab. It really bothers the dog, you know."

All the PTL could do was roll his eyes and then roll down a window. "How's that?" Then he started to laugh.

"He has a very sensitive nose. Really," his grandfather said to the dog, rubbing the retriever's luxuriously soft ears as he commiserated with him, "some people have no manners at all."

The PTL put the truck into full-time four-wheel drive and headed along the periphery of a cornfield harvested two weeks ago. The corn had come out earlier than in years past as it had been an unseasonably warm autumn. Pheasant hunting, because of the unusually warm weather, had not been good, at least not as good as in years past. The dusting of snow on the ground would certainly help matters.

They talked as they drove the rutted farm road. The PTL observed that too much land had been taken out of the conservation reserve program and put back into production. Of course bean and corn prices had dropped precipitously, right along with the quality of the pheasant hunting. All the razor sharp minds with their razor cut hairstyles back in Washington could not seem to figure out that relationship, he said to his grandfather. The old man puffed on his cigar while he considered the issue and Ranger showed his tongue to both men. "And how come all your cigar smoke doesn't affect that dog's sensitive nose?" the PTL wanted to know.

His grandfather ignored the logic of the question. Instead, he spoke to the previous issue. "It's not about hunting or conservation, boy. It's all about making money." He motioned with his cigar, indicating where they should park.

The PTL drove the truck through an open gate leading into a set-aside field still enrolled in the CRP, heavy with native prairie switchgrass pushing through the white snow salting the ground. Glad to have the snow to improve hunting, the PTL was also glad it was less than two inches deep. The going would not be so tough for his grandfather and he would be able to stay in the field and hunt longer. The snow would also serve to gather the birds, grouping them into coverts for protection against the elements. He parked and they got out of the truck quietly, leaning into the doors to close them. Ranger quickly ran to the back of the truck and relieved himself. Grandfather took the opportunity to do the same, pouring his morning coffee in spurts into the snow.

The PTL drew his Benelli from the soft gun case stored behind the seats, loaded in three shells, and checked the safety. He uncased his grandfather's gun, a semi-automatic Remington 1187, his one concession to old age. For most of his hunting life the old man had carried a 12 gauge Remington 870 pump shotgun, but he could no longer shuck the gun fast enough to drop multiple birds on the rise. He handed the gun, smelling of Rem oil and cleaning fluid, to his grandfather, relieved and ready to hunt. "It's loaded with the safely on," he told him, but the old man checked it anyway. "What's the matter? Don't you trust me?"

The white haired man bit off the soggy end of his cigar and spit it into the snow. "Of course I trust you, boy. But this isn't a matter of trust. It's a matter of safety in the field. Now do you want to talk or do you want to hunt? Today, if it flies, it dies," his grandfather warned the field, and his grandson chuckled. He started every hunt with those words. He thought it brought them luck. He instructed his grandson as they walked down the slope of the hill toward a ditch filled with high grass, Ranger following his nose. "If you see a rabbit run, I'd be glad to have a couple for my table, and if you spook a turkey, shoot that too. Or a deer, I'll take a deer for certain; these fours we're shooting will drop a buck if we get close enough so don't hesitate to take the shot."

"Okay, Grandfather. Don't worry. Anything that moves we shoot; to Hell with conservation or hunting laws."

Grandfather stopped short and puffed the end of his stogie into a lash of flame as he considered the lay of the land. "My land, my life, my laws. Besides, who's going to throw an old Injun like me in jail? And pardon me for reminding you of what you already know, but it was the likes of me that used to run this entire Settlement long before you were even a gleam in your father's bloodshot eye."

The PTL nodded an attestment to that factual truth and resettled his green John Deere hunting cap. He knew and did not need to be reminded. He was justly proud of his forebears. His father had been chief after his grandfather, and for a time there had been talk about him one day taking on the leadership of the People. He had had other ideas. About ten yards ahead Ranger locked into a point, rigid from black wet nose to blond tail tip, directing the men to a thick clump of foxtail. They moved up slowly and waited for the bird to flush, but nothing happened. Grandfather rolled his cigar between his teeth from one edge of his mouth to the other. "I'm starting to freeze my skinny Injun ass off waiting for that bird to wake up and take his morning shit. I told you it was no good hunting this early in the damn morning when all civilized creatures should be resting warm in their beds."

"I'll go in," the PTL told him, grinning. "You stand your ground and take the shot, so heads up." He walked into the clump of grass ahead of the dog's unwavering point and kicked up a hen, shitting and flying all at the same time. The suddenness of the bird busting up out of the cover startled the PTL and he rocked back yelling "Hen!" afraid that his grandfather would shoot anyway. Instead, he saw the old man's eyes crinkle with glee under the orange baseball cap that had Chief embroidered in red letters across the front. As the PTL regained his footing a second bird jumped up—a rooster this time—following the direction of the hen's flight. The big bird cackled his displeasure as he rose, rocketing from his hiding place in the grass, and the PTL watched in horror as his grandfather swung his shotgun in an arc following the bird's flight, never raising the gun above the level of his hip. The old man fired and a tongue of flame licked after the shot. The rooster, long barred tail streaming behind him, tumbled in mid-flight, somersaulting back down into the thin skein of snow. He hit the ground, bounced in the trampoline of the grasses, then fluttered and died just before Ranger scooped him up and returned him to the shooter, the yellow Lab's tail dancing high with pride.

"How do you do that?" the PTL asked, incredulous. He should know better by now; he had seen the old man do it time and time again, although it violated every principle of good shooting taught him by his father.

"I'm not out here to have my picture taken; I'm out here to put birds in the bag," he explained as he loaded the dead rooster into the back of his grandson's game pouch.

"Nice shot anyway, Grandfather, despite the unorthodox technique."

The old man studied his grandson, of whom he was inordinately proud. He was strong and independent and had made his own way in the world. When the time was right, he would come back to lead the Meskwaki. For the time being, he knew his grandson had other concerns and needed the benefit of his counsel. "Talk while we hunt this ditch; the birds are holding tight and Ranger will let us know when he gets a nose full."

The PTL explained everything that had happened in the weeks past and the decisions he was struggling with. The old man threw away the stub of his cheroot and ground it into the stomp of his hunting boot. He pulled off his right glove, pawed through his coat pocket for a replacement. The first time he drew out another shotgun shell. "Can't smoke that." He replaced it and found the cigar. He peeled the wrapper, put it in his coat pocket, licked the cigar with his tongue, and lit the end. He pulled the glove back on, flexing his fingers against the cold. "Why do white men always have to fuck up everything?"

They walked in silence behind Ranger, keeping their line and their distance. The dog worked the edge of the creek bank. As they approached the bend of an elbow populated with a stand of cane, Ranger got birdy. "Stay alert," his grandfather warned him just ahead of the flush.

He pushed the safety off, mounted the gun to his shoulder and watched the flush. Hen, hen, hen, and then a rooster showed its ringed neck. He started his swing well behind the bird, and as his barrel moved past the white ring at the pheasant's neck, he fired and dropped the bird cleanly. He looked for other roosters in the commotion and saw his grandfather locate a cock among the rising spread of birds. The old man shifted his cigar again and tracked the fleeing bird. He fired once and missed, slightly behind the fast moving rooster, kept swinging and fired again, this time hitting the bird, causing him to drop a leg. His third shot an instant later dropped the bird. His grandfather whooped a war cry and shouted, "I love these goddamned semi-automatics! Why did I ever wait so long to get one?" Ranger helped them collect the birds. He kept one for his bag and slipped the smaller of the two birds into his grandfather's vest.

"What would you do, Grandfather, were you in my situation?"

"I would consult my spirit guide and ask for a sign." When his grandson did not reply he said, "When you get a flush like that out of the cane, birds flying in every goddamn direction, you have to stay calm and pick out one rooster and swing on that bird and that bird alone. It's not like shooting partridge where you can sometimes just shoot right into the covey rise and drop a couple or three. We did it exactly right and we have two birds to show for it," he said with obvious satisfaction. "I've seen hunters in similar situations swing on a bird, give it up to pick up another one, find yet another cock and wind up watching everything fly into the next county, all the time wondering why they didn't pull the trigger. You can stand and watch the birds fly, Grandson, or you can take your best shot and live with the consequences. Now, no more talking. One more bird and I'm outta here," he said, teasing the younger man.

Before the sun reached ten o'clock in the gray sky, they both had their limits. He drove Grandfather and Ranger back to the farmhouse and helped clean the birds. He left them all for his grandfather's freezer. His grandfather asked one question only while they ate together. "Will I see you again before I die?"

"I don't think so, Grandfather."

"My spirit guide disagrees. A white princess will bring you back to me."

He knew better than to talk against his grandfather's vision. "We shot well today."

The old man nodded. "Our last hunt together was a good one."

"Yes, it was."

After lunch, he helped his grandfather wash the dishes and asked him if he needed anything before he returned to Cedar Rapids. Not wanting to prolong the inevitable, he left before the dishes dried. They said their goodbyes like warriors and the men they were. Ranger wagged his tail just enough to be polite, sensing the fatality of one last parting. Out of habit, the PTL drove the white graveled road slowly to keep the dust down until he remembered the snow.

AFTER DAYA NADIPURAM had dropped the bomb on his desk, the explosion reaching all the way up to the CEO's office, after his subsequent meetings with Lieutenant General Simons of the Missile Defense Agency, and the day after seeking his grandfather's counsel, the PTL knew he had another decision to make, one that most likely would take him far from his home. He took comfort in doing what he always did when he was still working and needed time to decompress and think things through.

The PTL went fishing on Coralville Lake, a reservoir complex of water and campgrounds about 5 miles north of Iowa City. Under a cloudy sky with almost no wind, he caught the lake in the midst of the fall turnover, a time when the lake inverted itself and the cool water below the thermocline rose up and dissipated the waters warmed by the summer months. The cool water brought the fish up off the deep and energized them as they began their feeding to fatten up for the approaching winter. The bite was on and he caught more than twenty largemouth bass, one pulling the needle on his handheld scale up to five pounds. He released all the fish. It had been a good day on the lake.

Before he began the 25 mile return trip north on I-380 to Cedar Rapids, as he pulled his boat onto the trailer behind his pickup truck he heard the strange but familiar kuh-kuhk of a ringneck rooster pheasant. He turned and in the early evening light, saw the male bird glorious in his late fall plumage, head and tail held high and proud before he casually strutted into deep switchgrass bordering a fence. The PTL took the sighting as a sign and felt immediately better for what he was planning to do. That night he slept deeply and without interruption, his dreams filled with visions of pheasant hunting with his grandfather. The next day, he got up early and drove to a the convenience store just off the freeway outside of Cedar Rapids, where he had found the payphone that still worked. He called a number he had memorized, and within the flush and flurry of the chaos that had become his life, fired his best shot.

Chapter Thirty-three

Recovery

Will woke into an enormous sense of relief, one similar to finding your keys in the last pocket of your coat. Through the glaucous eye of sleep, he looked over to the digital clock radio on the nightstand next to his bed. It was exactly the same brand and model in the bedroom of Randolph Baxter's apartment and read ten something. The uncommon coincidence pulled him further into wakefulness. He winced as he rolled onto his side again and pushed his face into the warmth of the pillow. He felt the pull of the tape across the bandage where it pressed into the wound atop his shoulder. He gave the pain a minute to subside and thought about the events of the last few days.

Dr. Alan Merkin had a family practice in Ray and served as the on-call physician for the Resort Owner's Association. A long-time friend of Will's, he came to the cabin immediately after the call to his pager. He took Sylvie first, hair still wet from her shower, and treated her for a mild case of frostbite on the tips of her fingers and, in spite of her nearly complete physical exhaustion, pronounced her in good health. He prescribed sleep and lots of it and saw to it that Roland and Lili put her to bed. Will had followed Sylvie into the shower off the master bedroom and waited patiently while she thoroughly cleaned his wound with antiseptic. He was too tired even to wince when the alcohol bit into the exposed flesh. As he waited for Merkin to finish with Sylvie, he took some beef broth Roland had prepared and sipped it, observing the doctor examine Sylvie. After the doctor turned to Will and gave him an affirmative nod, Will kissed Sylvie into her bed and watched with a sense of relief and satisfaction as she fell asleep before he could pull the covers over her shoulders.

He felt himself fading fast from the combined effects of the warming shower on the outside of his skin and Roland's warming broth inside. He tolerated Merkin's inspection so he could finally get to bed. Dr. Merkin recleaned the wound, which stung him into deeper irritability but he made an effort to maintain his good humor out of respect for his friend. "I could put in a stitch or three, but you'll have a larger scar if I close it with these butterfly Band-Aids alone and then cover it with gauze."

Will knew the doctor was offering him a choice. He did not want to bother with the hassle of finding someone to take the stitches out later. He usually did it himself if he could reach the knots. "I'll live with the scar, Doc," he said. He preferred another seam in his hide rather than the tattoos many guys sported as signs of manhood. His future scar had been fairly won and would show nicely in comparison to the collection of cicatrices Roland had picked up over the years. "Just tape it and slap the gauze on. I can barely keep my eyes open."

"Thought you might say that." Dr. Merkin smiled and reached into his large black medical bag. The travelling bag was a shiny leather antique handed down from his father, also a physician, and Merkin continued to carry it because patients expected to see it at his side. It was a symbol that signified healing and comfort, Will told him one day as they were fishing together, so he dragged it around from patient to patient. He kept the majority of his emergency medical supplies in his Jeep Wagoneer, and reloaded as necessary.

Finished with the patch of Will's wound, he stepped back to examine his handiwork and liked what he saw. After all these years of practicing, and all the advances in medical science and technology, he still derived a basic satisfaction from the laying on of hands so vital to the art of healing. The powerful man sitting bare chested and in his skivvies on the edge of the bed was diminished by fatigue and exposure; he saw it most in the paleness of the skin drawn too tightly over the bones of the face and in the hollows below the bloodshot eyes. He had no doubt that Will's remarkable fitness had brought him through the ordeal unscathed except for the scratch left by the bullet where it had creased a furrow into the skin overlaying Will's trapezius.

Will managed to lift his chin one more time to look up at Merkin as he snapped the medical bag shut. "You'll live, but you need to sleep and take it easy for the next couple of days. You're also dehydrated and I would put an IV into any other man."

Will nodded. "What about Sylvie?"

The doctor helped him swing his legs onto the bed as Will groaned under the effort, more from fatigue than pain. "This is merely my medical opinion but she is quite possibly the most beautiful patient I've had the pleasure to see during my thirty-five years of practice. And I say this as a scientist and a physician who has seen the human body in all its myriad imperfections and permutations: she's a stunner, that one, and except for the mild frostbite, the exhaustion, and the dehydration, she'll be fine with a couple of days of sleep, food and rest, so leave her alone. I'll check back on you both in three days. I want to take another look at your cut to make certain there is no infection. I'll leave a tube of antibiotic cream with your uncle. Now get some sleep."

Lili and Roland stood in the doorway to his bedroom, waiting for the doctor to finish. Lili helped him get under the covers as Roland helped Dr. Merkin shoulder into his fleece-lined sheepskin coat. "You did a good job bringing her back safely. She will be fine when you wake, Professor," Merkin said before he turned to go.

Will stretched into the warming comfort of the feather bed. "Send me the bill, Alan."

Dr. Merkin shook his head. "Take me walleye fishing instead."

"You got it, Doc," Will mumbled. As Lili turned off the light to his room he fell instantly asleep.

HE LOOKED OVER at the clock again. He had misread it. He had slept until just after one. He heard the knock on the oak door to his bedroom. It was Roland checking on him. Will called him in. Roland butted the door open and backed in, carrying a tray of soft-boiled eggs, rolls, butter, assorted lunchmeats, and a fresh pot of steeping tea. Will sat up in bed, his stomach growling to the smell of the fresh bread. "Hello, nurse," Will said. "How's Sylvie?"

"Still sleeping like a baby," Roland told him waiting to set the tray across his lap after he sat up.

"Mouth open and drooling?" Will patted down the feather bed, scooted up into sitting position and propped a pillow behind his back.

"That's the way she always sleeps, ever since we started working together," Roland informed him. "And one of those rolls is for me."

Will cut one in half, slathered it with butter, lined it with lunchmeat and handed it to Roland, sitting next to the bed. "And how would you know that?"

"Too many late night sessions working cases back at my apartment. She takes the bed in the spare room where you usually sleep when you visit. I have to wash the pillow cases when she goes home."

Will mumbled a chuckle through a bite of the freshly baked rolls brought by Lili from the restaurant.

"How are you feeling?" Roland asked Will.

"A little stiff and sore, hungry and thirsty, but otherwise surprisingly good," he reported. He tore off another bite of roll and butter and chewed with pleasure. Roland reached over and prepared two cups for tea; in one sugar and milk in the English fashion for Will. Will's father had preferred it the same way. In his, Roland took only a little sugar and a splash of lemon. Stirring his tea Will asked, "How do I look?"

Roland grinned at the question. "For the sake of your continuing recovery and particularly in consideration of your mental health, I advise you to avoid all mirrors for the time being; and think about shaving very soon."

Will raised his eyebrows as he sipped the tea. "That bad?" He scratched his beard with the other hand and could only imagine what his dark, wavy hair looked like tousled by so much sleep.

As the color returned to Will's cheeks and the clarity to his eye, Roland allowed that all things considered, he did not look all that bad and Will had to agree that he did not feel all that bad, now that he had slept out and was taking nourishment again. The men talked quietly and ate together, Will sharing with his uncle the account of the shot that had nearly taken off his head. He told Roland how they had first escaped the assassin and then trapped him. They discussed the luck of finding a bear's den, empty, and how bravely Sylvie had conducted herself throughout the ordeal. Will could see the pride in his uncle's eyes, for himself and for Sylvie, the partner on whom he had often depended for his life. For a minute Will thought he might have spotted the beginnings of a tear welling up as his uncle stood, removed the breakfast tray and set it on the chest of drawers near the bed. It might have been the steam from the tea. At that instant, wearing nothing more than a thigh length T-shirt, Sylvie came bounding into the room and jumped onto Will below the protective cushion of the feather bed, kissed him quickly on the lips and demanded, "Feed me!"

Roland laughed and gathered up the breakfast tray. "You two get reacquainted and I'll go get breakfast for Sylvie." Will asked for more tea and another roll.

Sylvie snuggled in tight and before the naked length of her body under the T-shirt worked its uncontrollable magic, he slid out from under the feather bed and ran to the bathroom. "Hey! Come back here!" she commanded, to no avail. He closed the door but was not long in returning and they were in each other's arms and fast asleep again when Roland returned with her breakfast. He left the tray, heavily loaded with extras such as reading materials, chocolate, unsalted cashews, cheeses, and kiwi fruit. Before he closed the door he declared the day to be a *Ruhetag*—a day of quiet and relaxation—and he left them to spend the rest of the afternoon in bed together. He left a note telling them he would be at Lili Popelka's for the evening if they needed him. He doubted very much that they would. The ringers on the phones were switched off, the answering machines on. No one was expected to visit, and he left them to continue their rehabilitation, the warm, comfortable cabin left entirely to themselves.

ROLAND RETURNED MID-MORNING of the next day, rested and recovered from the anxiety and travail of getting them home safe and sound, and he was happy to see them, happy that they looked so good, and happy for their sense of togetherness. They reported that they were fit and ready for duty.

They spent the rest of the day building the case, as they called it. Sylvie entered all the information they had acquired since their last session together. Roland sat next to her on the oversized leather couch, sharing his notes on the case. Will was in his easy chair, stretched full length, half-listening to Roland's commentary as he thought through the attack at War Club Lake. The attempt on their lives was not random; therefore, it was intentional. An intentional act was always the product of some motivation. What motivation? They were getting too close to solving the problem of Randolph Baxter's true identity. Signification? Baxter's identity would bring them closer to discovering who the killers were. Signification? Identification of the party who hired the killer would most likely follow. Were the killers hired or did they act on their own? Will's experience suggested these were trained professionals for hire with possible connections to the underworld. Signification? The services of such men did not come cheaply. A contract had to be let, the assassins located and engaged, and expenses paid, all suggesting an individual of means and contacts. This implied someone with money and status. He cleared his throat and took a sip of his iced tea from the oversized glass.

In a light, powder-blue sweater over khaki slacks and without bra or makeup, Sylvie was beautiful in the soft late afternoon light that filtered through the skylights and cast her in a muted radiant glow. There was no doubt she loved working with Roland. She seemed content and as happy as he had ever seen her, working the keyboard, linking files, and asking questions. Will sighed into the heaviness of his chest. Some small part of him envied their partnership, their coalition of professionalism and trust and most importantly, their years of friendship. Sylvie caught him staring and when he did not look away, she gave him a warm and caring smile that he could not help but return, and then resumed his thinking.

It had to be someone with the wherewithal and more significantly, the need to hire two professional hit men. This implied a relationship with the victim and the agent of his death. One did not casually assume such risks and expenses to kill strangers. No doubt about it; the two were somehow linked. A jealous lover? It didn't seem to fit the details of the context. A drug deal gone awry? More plausible; this would explain the link with Witness Security. It was possible that Baxter was in the program because he was providing the feds with evidence in return for protection. Will made a mental note to further consider this possibility when the phone rang. He answered as Roland and Sylvie waited expectantly.

Special agent Angelika Valesa was calling from the FBI's Special Investigations Unit at Quantico, Virginia. He recognized the voice immediately.

"Hi Angie. It's good to hear your voice again." He could imagine her smiling, pushing the freckles on her cheeks up under her big blue eyes. Valesa, given her Polish heritage and red hair, had a complexion to match and he used to tease her about the bottles of sunscreen she kept on her desk, at hand, and in her purse. Less than ten minutes of exposure to the sun caused the freckles under her eyes and atop her nose to flame red as her hair. Agent Valesa was his primary contact when the Bureau first hired him to consult on cold cases. She was a competent agent and a hard worker. He genuinely liked her and knew the feeling was mutual.

"Before we begin I want you to know that I'm calling you from an untraceable burner cell phone so I can tell you how mad I am at you because you only call when you want something from me," she pouted into the phone.

He laughed, and seeking to sooth her with his charm, said in an affected Scottish brogue, "Now, now Moneypenny, you know I only have eyes for you."

She laughed at his bad James Bond impression but he assured her that they would be working together again soon enough, if the Bureau could afford his fees. Placated to just the right degree she turned to business just in time for Will's taste as he noticed the interested and quizzical looks exchanged between Sylvie and Roland. He cupped the receiver and whispered so they could hear.

"FBI, with information."

Roland nodded emphatically, but Sylvie pursed her lips together even as Will said, "Go ahead Agent Valesa, I've got my notebook handy."

"I got a call from the U.S. Marshal's office in Minneapolis wanting to check on you and verify your credentials. I assured them you were everything you represented yourself to be."

"That was very generous of you, Angie."

Sylvie looked up again from her keyboard at the laptop.

"You owe me and I intend to collect next time you come east for a visit." She did not wait for an affirmation. "The officer with whom I spoke—a rather highly placed individual I might add—was one very unhappy government servant. These guys aren't used to having someone penetrate their security, Will, and then knock off one of their enrollees. To make matters worse, you come knocking on the door asking all sorts of embarrassing questions and now they think they have been compromised a second time."

"Not at all," he explained. "We just figured it out."

Special Agent Valesa laughed at the understatement. "I know that," she agreed. "I have absolutely no doubt that you just figured it out in that handsome oversized head of yours. Who else could do that with so little information?" she asked rhetorically. "But the chief marshal doesn't know that and he thinks someone breached his security, and he is one really pissed off Stetson wearing cowboy. I settled him down and filled him in and, although he's not prepared to send over the case folder on Randolph A. Baxter —I think he's still doing a CYA—and until he gets his ass properly laminated for protection, he's not going to play ball."

Will nodded into the phone, felt silly and said, "I see. That explains his reticence to talk with me about the case. Did you inform him, however, that I have sufficient grounds to conclude that Baxter's disappearance was not a suicide but more likely a murder, and an assassination to boot? And I would think that the murder of a person enrolled in the WITSEC program makes this a federal case."

She giggled. "I told him essentially the same, but not with quite that intensity. By the way, the assistant director agrees and asks if you would be so kind as to keep us informed of your progress in the investigation."

He knew he was being flattered but chose to ignore it for the time being. "Thank the AD for his confidence in me and please assure him that I'll forward progress reports in a timely fashion." He let Valesa continue.

"The CM was being hardheaded as a Minnesota bull moose and said until an official determination is made stating Baxter's death as a murder and not a suicide, he would not release details of the case."

"That son-of-a-bitch."

"I know," she commiserated, "but I sweet talked him a little bit."

"I have no doubt about that, Angie. You are one sweet talking girl. To that I will attest." He heard her giggle again. "What did you get out of him?"

She paused, using her position to dramatic advantage. "What's it worth to you, Professor?"

He laughed loudly into the phone, disrupting Sylvie and Roland again, and he ignored their indignant glances. "Let me put it to you this way, Agent Valesa. I will personally see to it that you are rewarded for your special initiative in this case, and that's a promise."

"Well then...," she said, envisioning the possibilities, "I have no choice but to tell you what I know. The chief marshal said if you were—and I quote—so goddammed smart, then you shouldn't have any problem figuring out the rest of the case. His words, Will, not mine. I already know how goddammed smart you are, among other things." She did not elaborate. Will waited. "He did say, however, that you were on the right track in identifying Mr. Baxter..."

"That's good to know," Will interrupted.

"...Except for one thing."

"What's that?" he asked, pen ready.

"Your man is not Ojibwe.

"No kidding?"

"Nope. But you were close."

"How close?"

"Real close. He is Meskwaki."

"Damn. You sure about that?"

"That's what the marshal said. Meskwaki. Does that help?" she asked hopefully.

"Damn right it does. It is highly significant and corroborates what one of our sources told us." He smiled to himself when he heard her smother another giggle, this one at his expense, no doubt.

"One more thing, Will. I doubt if Baxter is his real last name, but I couldn't get that out of the Chief Marshall no matter how hard I tried. I had to stop before I pissed him off further."

"You did the right thing by backing off," he assured her. "I owe you one, Angie. And I expect to be in touch soon. Thanks again."

"Glad to help, Will, and please let me know when you get to town."

"I'll do that. Bye bye." He heard her say goodbye, replaced the receiver and turned to his audience waiting so patiently and expectantly.

"Road trip," was all he said.

"Road trip?" Sylvie questioned. "Where to this time?"

"Yep. Iowa. Cedar Rapids, Iowa, I think."

"Planes, trains, or automobiles?" Roland asked.

"It's twelve hours by car, or thereabouts. I say we fly. We can get a hop from International Falls to Minneapolis and from there to Cedar Rapids."

Sylvie already had the flight schedules up on her laptop screen. "I can book the trip right now if you want."

"Get two seats. One for Roland and one for myself."

Her face flooded with disappointment, but ever the good soldier she nodded and started to book the flight. "Two tickets, one for you and one for Roland. I guess that means I'm not going," she said, pouting through her lower lip.

Will played dumb. "Who said you weren't going?" He looked over at Roland who disavowed any knowledge.

She looked across the top of her screen at him, perplexed. "I just heard you say two seats, one for Roland

and one for you." She looked at Roland for confirmation and he nodded vigorously.

"Yes. That's exactly what I said. But that doesn't mean you're not going. I thought I would take you on my lap, with your permission of course."

Much as she appreciated the thought she immediately booked a third seat. "Will that be Visa or MasterCard, sir?"

He lifted a hip, pulled out his wallet and threw her his American Express Corporate card. "This is now a federal case. They lost Baxter and we found him. Let the government pay for my expenses."

THE NEXT DAY, at Dr. Merkin's insistence, they stopped at his office in Ray. The M.D. accepted a kiss on the cheek from Sylvie, which put him in a surprisingly good mood despite himself and the troublesome day he was having. He made Will remove his polo shirt and ignored the grumbling about messing up his hair. He gently pulled the tape and gauze patch from his shoulder and studied the raised pink line. "No infection and healing nicely. Certain to scar but I can inject it later to reduce the size."

"Not on your life," Will said.

He waited as Merkin swabbed the wound again with antiseptic before applying a fresh bandage. Merkin sat back as Will deliberately shouldered into his black polo, careful not to muss his hair. Once he had the shirt suitably settled across the broad expanse of his shoulders, Sylvie came over and mussed his hair in spite of his careful attention to dressing himself.

Merkin smiled at the horseplay, waited for it to end and said, "Finish the antibiotic regimen and keep your tetanus shots up to date. When are we going fishing?"

"I'll call you when we close this case and I want you to know that you've got a guaranteed seat in my boat for the walleye opener in the spring. And Alan..."

"Yes, Will."

"Change the line on your reels. I know how cheap you are but those lines need to be replaced at least once every two seasons, not every five years. We wouldn't want to see a grown medico cry when the line breaks under the weight of an eight pound screamer, now would we?"

The doctor showed them to the door. "Old Farley Nilsson tells me the same thing. It just drives him nuts when he sees that sun-damaged, frayed and knotted monofilament. But I promise. I'll have fresh line on for the opener."

Will made a mental note to rig an extra rod with new line for his friend.

ABOVE A TOWERING line of thunderheads, the British DeHavilland two-engine, propeller driven aircraft bounced them from International Falls to Minneapolis-St. Paul. To grateful thanks, Will had given out two extra sets of the foam earplugs he used for hunting and flying. Ears suitably protected, the three managed to survive the turbulence and the drone of the big propellers chewing up the air. From Minneapolis, a 737 jetted them down to Cedar Rapids, and Will used the time to brief Roland in the aisle seat on his left and Sylvie on the right in the window seat. This seating arrangement, although extremely uncomfortable for Will, gave Roland access to the female flight attendants and Sylvie access to the geography under the wing. He opened his case notebook and waited until he had their attention.

"An irony, to begin," he told them. "According to Roland's research, the Meskwaki of Iowa were traditional enemies of the Ojibwe to the north. Officially designated the Sac and Fox by the U.S. government, who got it wrong once again, the Meskwaki, as they prefer to be known, are the only active American Indian tribe in Iowa. They own their land, purchased from the State of Iowa in 1857. They are considered a tenacious and self-determined people who resisted Anglo-American acculturation. The French named them the Fox in the

1600s, but they call themselves Meskwaki, the Red Earth People, or People of the Red Earth. That will make sense when you see Iowa soil."

Roland asked, "Where does the Sac part of the name come from? I couldn't find the linguistic origins of the name."

"I'm getting to that," Will told him. "In 1730, the so-called Fox formed an alliance with the Sauk, or Sac, to fend off the Europeans, no insult intended," he said with false deference to Roland and Sylvie. "In 1804 a band of Sauk ceded land to the American government. This band separated from the tribe and became recognized by the Americans as the Sac and Fox of the Missouri. The remaining group was called the Sac and the Fox of the Mississippi, which forms the eastern border of the state of Iowa. By the way, the Missouri forms the western border and that's why Iowa is roughly translated from the Indian word as the beautiful land between two rivers."

"I like that," Sylvie added. "It seems very poetic."

Will resumed his briefing. "Between 1832 and 1842 the U.S. forced this group to cede their lands and move to a reservation in east-central Kansas. After ten years a group of Meskwaki separated from the Sac and Fox, returned to Iowa, bought land in Tama County, Iowa where they live to this day and fiercely maintain their culture and beliefs. And whatever you do," Will cautioned the two, "don't call it a reservation. It is a settlement and enjoys certain sovereign rights including tribal police and laws and a casino called, simply enough, the Meskwaki Casino."

"While we are there I want to see the Mississippi," Roland told him.

"Me too," Sylvie said happily.

"Tourists," Will sneered as they prepared to land in Cedar Rapids, Iowa, the Cedar River gleaming gunmetal gray in the intermittent sunlight below the wing.

Chapter Thirty-four

Tracking

The investigative team landed at the Cedar Rapids airport, collected their travel bags, and walked over to the car rental agency where they had arranged to rent a vehicle. At the counter Will signed the papers and collected the keys to a Lincoln Navigator. He declined the collision insurance.

"Please let me drive it," Sylvie begged when she saw the enormous size of the vehicle. As a matter of safety he quickly and firmly denied her request. She crossed her arms and mounted a beautiful and nearly perfect double lip pout of such intensity that it stopped both men in their tracks.

"What are you doing?" Will asked.

Roland knew his partner's moods well enough by now to stay out of imminent danger.

"I don't understand why you two will not let me drive. I am perfectly capable of driving this tank. I am a highly qualified and competent driver. I have passed all the pursuit courses required of Bavarian state police officers and still you two will not let me drive." The attractive pout transformed first into indignation, then defiance as she looked first to Will, then to Roland, both hands on hips for emphasis.

"Don't include me in this," Roland warned, his tone of voice gently but firmly reminding her that he was still her superior officer. To underscore his authority, he took the front passenger seat. As he buckled in and looked around he said, "Rommel didn't have Panzers this big."

Sylvie grew more upset standing next to the vehicle and would not move, chin up, arms crossed under her breasts. Will stepped around her and opened the door behind Roland's seat.

"I am not going to have this conversation with you standing here in the airport parking lot. Get in." He used his command voice and although his tone was quiet and measured, it carried an underlying intensity that signaled he would tolerate no further insubordination. She stepped up and slid onto the capacious leather seat behind Roland.

She said in passing, "I hate you."

He waited until she cleared her long legs and settled in before he chunked the door closed. He heaved himself into the driver's seat, strapped the seatbelt across his chest, keyed the ignition, and looked over at Roland.

"In all my years at the university I never experienced such gross insubordination as this."

Roland shrugged helplessly. "It's the quality of the training candidates receive coming out of the police universities these days. Now you know the hell that is my professional life."

Before he could put the SUV into Drive, Sylvie punched the back of his seat with a finely executed left jab. "I have a need to drive! It is a biological imperative and you two are conspiring to stifle my natural urges. That is neither a good thing nor a healthy thing," she warned. The two men looked at each other. This changed everything.

"Listen, Sylvie," Will said. "When we get to the hotel in Tama-Toledo you can drive around in the parking lot to get the feel of the vehicle."

"Oh good," she said with glee, clapping her hands for emphasis. "I get to drive," she announced.

"That was much too easy," Roland said in amazement.

"I just want to drive," Sylvie said ruefully and settled back, contented. "And when we get back to Germany, I want to drive our newest Leopard tank," she said to Roland, referring to the German army's enormous battle tank.

Will winked at Roland. The silence was blissful, but twenty miles down the road Sylvie interrupted the hog report on the radio and they missed the futures price for corn and beans.

She said suddenly, "I don't hate you anymore," and returned to her sightseeing.

"Thank you Sylvie, that means a lot to me," Will acknowledged, looking back at her through the rear-view mirror. He looked over at Roland in silence and the two men exchanged raised eyebrows.

They checked in at the hotel and left a few flyers with the desk clerk. He promised to show them around and gave the men their card keys. Roland had his own room adjoining Will's suite where they set up the computers, faxes, and printers and hooked up their gear to the Wi-Fi internet cable access provided by the hotel.

"Which bed do you want?" Sylvie asked Will as they left Roland to unpack in the next room. Before Will could answer she made her selection: the queen bed closer to the bathroom.

"Thanks for asking," Will said as he threw a T-shirt on the bed next to the curtained window. She jumped him, knocked him on the bed, and rolled him over to straddle his chest and pin his arms under her knees. "Don't make me have to kick your ass," she warned. She was showing off her command of American idioms.

"Get off me, you European psycho. I'm taking you to the hospital to have you checked for mad cow disease."

She laughed and dismounted after a quick kiss on the lips. "This has nothing to do with eating beef. It has everything to do with you frustrating my female instincts. I need to drive large fast armored vehicles with lights flashing and sirens howling."

"You'll just have to contain your vehicular exuberance for the time being. Remember where we are. We have to respect the traditions of these people or we're going to leave here with zilch, nada, nix. *Verstehst du?*"

She nodded that she understood, being a stranger in a strange land and all that, but biological urges were not to be trifled with and clearly superseded anthropological customs. She assured him again that the biological clock on her need to drive was ticking.

"You're a silly goose sometimes," he told her. In deference to her biological imperative, as she called it, Roland let her sit in the front seat as they drove to the casino.

THE CASINO WAS larger than Will remembered and there were more people in the red carpeted rooms, coincidentally the same color as their SUV. The manager greeted them and told them the casino had recently undergone an expansion. Once the manager understood their reason for being there, he promised to show the flyer around and post them by the cashiers' windows. Unfortunately, he did not recognize the man in the photo. In fact, he questioned if the man in the sunglasses was indeed a red man. He did seem awfully pale in the picture. Will's face turned red as the manager's as Will assured him it was because the man had an indoor job, like the manager's. With a warning look of disapproval, Roland pulled him by the arm away from the man.

The next stop took them to the Visitor's Center. The director greeted them with courtesy and made a show of looking closely at the picture before assuring them that he would show it to other Meskwaki whom he knew, then kindly showed them out. At the administration building, the head of the Tribal Council greeted them warmly and asked if they were enjoying their visit, which they were, and although he did not recognize the man in the photo, he guaranteed them he would post it where others could see it as they came and went. He promised to pass along the word that they were in town trying to identify a tribal member and would invite everyone to cooperate fully. To show his sincerity, he checked the flyer again for the phone number and address. He walked them out to the Navigator personally, exuding warmth and expressing his gratitude for the hard work they were doing. Inside the massive vehicle once again, Roland shivered through his leather jacket, frustrated.

Back in Tama they pulled into a local watering hole, bothered the bartender with a flyer, and slid into a booth toward the back. From their high-backed booth in the corner they could see the comings and goings of the regulars and they sipped their beers as they waited for their pork loin sandwiches. Even Sylvie looked a bit glum.

"Jeez," she said, having adopted one of Will's favorite expressions. "I feel like I'm back in Potsdam before they raised the Iron Curtain and dropped the Berlin wall. Everyone is afraid to talk."

"I warned you," Will told her. "We just waded through a river of obsequious bullshit." For privacy, they switched to Bavarian dialect as the early dinner crowd filled the place. "These people do not take lightly to outsiders coming in and mucking about in their affairs. They are a fiercely independent nation and they distrust whites and, for the most part, with good reason."

"I understand," Sylvie said. She sipped from her American beer, not liking it much. "But all we're trying to do is solve the murder of one of their own. By the way, Will, this beer tastes like dishwater."

To Roland's amusement, Will nearly spit into his glass. "For your information, *Hauptkommissar*, you happen to be drinking one of America's finest commercial brews."

The waitress, a middle-aged red woman still attractive but grown a bit heavy through the butt and thighs of her denim jeans, arrived with a tray set under three plates and baskets of French fries. She had her eye set for Roland. "Here you are." She dealt a plate and a basket next to each paper setting. "We don't often get foreigners in here, no offense."

"None taken," Will said, switching back to English. He accepted the offer of the red squeeze bottle of ketchup from her apron, then the yellow for the mustard. She leaned in to Roland's ear, conspiring to whisper a secret.

"Just between the two of us, the local folks get a little unsettled when they hear someone speaking French."

"Of course," Roland said immediately. He apologized for the social gaffe on behalf of his colleagues. She seemed genuinely flattered by his good manners.

"Where you all from, if you don't mind me asking?"

"Not at all," Roland assured her gallantly. We're from Alsace, on the border between France and Germany."

"Oh, I see," she said pleasantly, although she had never heard of Alsace or had any idea where it might lie on the map. "Can I get you anything else?"

"We're fine for the moment," Will said, "but if you wouldn't mind, please take a look at this missing person flyer."

Without looking at it for more than a second, she did a quick survey of the bar before she took the flyer from Will and, to his surprise, folded it and put it in the pocket of her scalloped serving apron. She looked at Sylvie and smiled ruefully. "They sure have pretty girls in Alsace. I'm glad I don't live there."

Sylvie thanked her for the compliment and asked her why she wouldn't want to live there.

"Hell, if all the girls are pretty as you I'd never be able to keep a man. It's hard enough as it is for a single girl living in this town."

"Oh, I would think you wouldn't have any problem at all," Roland told her, and she positively beamed. She turned to the sound of the serving bell dinging on the counter of the cook's window and saw the waiting plates ready for pick up. She left without excusing herself. At the end of the meal she returned and asked if everything was all right and if they wanted a piece of pie. She could recommend the apple but warned them to stay away from the lemon meringue. When they politely declined, citing the generous portions of the breaded pork loin that had covered their plates, she thanked them, wished them well during their stay in the U.S. and slipped Roland a tightly folded piece of paper. Will paid the dinner but let Roland leave the tip.

BACK AT THE hotel Roland showed Will the little note. "I might be able to help," was written under a telephone number and a time to call. It was signed "Mary." Five minutes after the time given on the piece of paper Roland called the number. She did not think it would be a good idea for them to come visit her, but... She asked, "Where are you staying? No problem." She would come to see them at the hotel. She needed fifteen minutes at the most.

Half an hour later they heard an older model Dodge pick-up truck in need of a new muffler rumble into the parking lot. After she switched it off the engine dieseled and shuddered, then backfired through the muffler before dying. No one seemed to mind. It was almost three in the morning.

Roland met her in the parking lot and brought her back to his room. She wore blue jeans and cowboy boots and a freshly ironed western shirt with snap buttons. Her black hair was combed out and fell to her shoulders. Her lips were red, slick and wet. Hanging from a shoulder strap, she carried a black bag shiny as her lipstick. He seated her at the round table in Will's room and asked if she cared for a drink and she said yes, she needed one. Roland poured a round for everyone and after the first drink of Crown Royal, which she drank down all at once, waited for him to fill her glass again. She took the flyer from her purse.

"I think I know him," was all she said. "But you have to promise me that you'll never mention that I came to see you."

"We guarantee your anonymity," Roland told her.

She liked the sound of that; it seemed official. She politely asked whether she could ask one more question before she started her explanation. Roland nodded and topped up her glass, tumbling the ice with the whisky.

"Why are the French so interested in this guy?" she asked, genuinely puzzled.

"That is a fair question, dear Mary, and if I tell you it must stay our little secret, *non*?" Will and Sylvie cringed as Roland overacted his role. He nodded toward Sylvie. "*Mademoiselle Schumann* and I are experts at locating missing persons and we have been hired," he pointed to Will with his plastic cup, "to help zee incompetent *Americans*." Sylvie coughed politely behind her hand, hiding a giggle. Will scowled, a clear admission of his inferiority.

It all made perfectly good sense to Mary. She understood bureaucratic screw-ups and the need to bring in hired experts. The explanation and the alcohol relaxed her. She took the flyer from her purse, put on reading glasses and studied the picture in earnest. She removed her glasses, folded them and replaced them in their red velvet carrying case, and shook her head. "I don't know.... When you first showed it to me I thought I was certain; now I'm not so sure anymore."

"Trust that first instinct," Sylvie told her. "It's normal to have doubts. But sometimes we react to things on a different level below the surface. It's not always about what's logical and rational. Sometimes we react to things unconsciously and emotionally first."

"That is so true," Mary agreed, drawing out the word so. "Take my last boyfriend: I just knew there was something about him that wasn't right. But nooo, I didn't trust my instincts and now that bastard is serving time in Joliet. I don't think I'll ever get back the two hundred dollars I loaned him. That was my rent money," she sighed and resigned herself to another sip of the excellent whisky. "Live and learn, I guess." They all drank to that.

Roland redirected her attention back to the flyer with a question. "Who do you think he is?"

She shook her head doubtfully. "That's just it. I don't remember his name but I'm almost certain that I recognize him. He always wore a baseball cap. I know that. I think he was a senior ahead of me in high school. Yes, that's it. He was two years ahead of me. I remember his first name now: Randy. I know that he was quiet and smart, that much I remember." She said it with finality, finished her drink and smiled at Roland.

"This will help tremendously. You have established for us that he is Meskwaki and attended the tribal school. That's excellent and much more than zee Americans have been able to discover." He looked very smug and twisted the end of his mustache as a Frenchman might do. He graciously pointed the neck of the whisky bottle at her cup but she waved him off with a blush. "Is there anything else you remember about him, his friends, the sports he played in school, where he lived, anything that might come to mind?"

She wanted to remember but it was a long time ago. "Well, not that long ago," she giggled, not wanting to reveal her age. She shook her head very slowly from side to side. Then she tapped her wet red lips with her index finger, the nail long and shiny with red shellac. "I vaguely remember something about him winning a scholarship for his good grades. Yes, that's it. It wasn't a sports scholarship; it was for his academics and not athletics. Everyone was talking about it at the time." She frowned. "It was still pretty unusual back then—an Indian getting an academic scholarship to go to college. Isn't that sad?" she asked rhetorically. "The reason I would remember that is because I think he had a scholarship to Iowa State. I remember thinking to myself how lucky he was and what a bright future he had ahead of him. He had a chance to actually do something with his life." She looked ruefully at the empty cup and ice cubes swimming in their own water, sorry now that she had declined

Roland's offer of a refill. Her eyes glistened and Sylvie was quick to hand her a tissue, which she accepted with thanks. She checked herself quickly in her compact mirror to make sure her mascara had not run and, satisfied with the results, she stood.

Will told her that she had been very helpful and said that on behalf of the American government and the expert French team he was empowered to compensate her for her time. She waved at him and said she was just trying to help but her eyes widened and she quickly accepted the four crisp, new, hundred dollar bills. She quickly folded the bills and secreted them in her purse.

"Really. I didn't do this for money."

"We know that, Mary. We're paid consultants," Sylvie explained. "Likewise, we have consulted you and it's only fair that you be compensated." Mary looked again to Roland, who nodded.

"Consider it our little contribution toward the rent."

She laughed at that one. Roland picked up the whisky bottle and two fresh plastic cups from the dresser. "Care to finish this with me next door?"

She blushed momentarily and, without hesitation said, "We won't need it."

Will showed them to the door and warned Mary about Frenchmen. He told his uncle to come and get them when he was ready to start the next day. They would need to make a trip to Ames, home of the Iowa State University Cyclones.

SYLVIE'S SHRIEK OF delight was a fair approximation of a war cry when, after brunch, Will threw her the keys to the monstrous Lincoln. They waited patiently for her to finish her happy dance in the parking lot.

"I'll sit in the back, if you don't mind," Roland said, declining the offer of the passenger seat. Sylvie slowly steered the untracked tank into traffic, smiling the entire time.

"Did you learn anything new?" Will asked his uncle.

"A gentleman never tells. However, Mary White Feather, in every regard, was an enthusiastic delight.

"I don't mean sexually; I mean about the case."

His uncle shook his head and briefed them as Sylvie commanded the giant SUV onto the interstate, mostly ignoring Will's imprecations that this was not the *Autobahn* and the speed limit was 65 miles per hour. They spent the rest of the trip in silence, concentrating on Sylvie's driving.

In Ames, at the Iowa State University Alumni Center, given their legitimate and official need, they received a computer-generated list by year of all students who had graduated from the College of Engineering. Unfortunately, due to the restrictions of the Family Educational Rights and Privacy Act (FERPA) of 1974, they were able to get information only about the name of the student, date of graduation, home address, telephone number and any directory information if so permitted by the student. They were given a couch and a table in the large waiting room ringed with aerial photos of the university depicting its change and growth over the years from an agriculture college to a major research university with roots in agriculture as the state of Iowa's land grant institution. As they riffled through the printout the task seemed daunting. Even with three persons working, it might take three days to get through all the names.

Will did his best to help his team get started. "The problem is that we don't have a legitimate last name, according to information given us by the chief marshal, and this is compounded by the fact that not all students release their hometowns to the directory."

"We have a field that indicates gender, but not race or minority group," Sylvie noted, thus reducing the scope of their burden.

"This might help too," Will added. "I know that the Witness Security Program often lets enrollees keep their first names for obvious reasons. Last names and middle initials are often chosen at random from the phone book, so we can't use logic or analysis to reason through those. I also know that many tribal members have what we would consider a white man's last name so we can't depend on it being a typical American Indian name, but then again, it might be."

Roland looked at Will. "You just said it could be any kind of last name. You're not helping."

Will pursed his lips and said "Sorry. I'm frustrated."

Sylvie patted him on the back. She understood frustration.

They divided the list into thirds and began their search, following the tip of an index finger down the long list of last names, looking for males with the first name of Randy or any variation thereof. Five minutes into the search Roland looked up, his finger holding his place, and announced "Got one."

Will leaned in from his left, Sylvie from his right, and they bumped heads over the print out and said "Sorry" simultaneously while Roland laughed at the natural comedy. Will rubbed the bruise on his temple and grumbled.

"Jeez, Sylvie, you've got a hard head." He read the name. Randolph C. Darian. Home address: Newton, Iowa. "Probably not," Will said. "But let's mark it just to keep track in case we can eliminate it.

Sylvie found the next Randolph in the graduating year she was looking through. The last name was Simpson, the middle initial J and the hometown Decorah, Iowa.

Will shook his head but had her underline the name for future reference. "Good trout fishing up around Decorah," he said as a matter of fact. The next two possibilities were eliminated because of out-of-state addresses, one in Illinois and one in Minnesota. Will finished his list and set it aside, waiting for Roland and Sylvie.

"Okay," Will said with some exasperation, "we have exhausted all the possible last names with the first name of Randolph. For the sake of trying to get lucky, let's now search using the first name of Randall, which is fairly close to Randolph."

"Worth a try," Roland said and Sylvie nodded.

The first three Randalls on the list were noted but did not fit the timeline they needed, two being too old and having graduated too long ago. One was currently enrolled in the Engineering major. Sylvie looked up from her list. "Hmmm," she said, inviting Roland to look over. "Randall Bruce Wahkahchai, home address withheld by request."

Will felt the hair on his forearms rise as he heard the name. "I have a good feeling about this one, a very good feeling. Let's put it on the top of our list for that graduating year. The chronology is right."

Sylvie looked over at Will. There was skepticism in her voice. "You have a good feeling about it? The master analyst, the paragon of cold hard objective fact and rigorous emotionless scientific investigation, is going on a feeling?"

Will lectured her. "A competent investigator does not overlook the intangible. When reason and analysis is not possible it is perfectly acceptable to rely on the investigator's instincts guided as they are by years of experience and hard work. Right, Roland?"

"Whatever you say Will." He winked at Sylvie to let her know he was humoring his nephew, but all in fun.

"Come on, you two. If we hurry we might catch the dean of the College of Engineering still in his office."

RATHER THAN TRY to find another parking spot, they decided it would be quicker to walk across campus to the Engineering building, guided by their campus map and directions from a friendly student who stared unabashedly at Sylvie. They studied the list of names and offices on the glass case inside the door of the building and found the office number for Dean Gregson. His secretary, in response to Will's FBI credentials, showed them to an inner office, the door already open.

Dean Gregson, a small man in a small suit, nearing retirement age, switched his computer off, came around his desk and greeted them with handshakes. They made small talk as they sat, Gregson asking about a colleague at Iowa Polytechnic State University, where Will had been a professor. They commiserated about the status of professors' salaries in the state of Iowa and the horrible budget situation, as usual. They wondered if the brain drain would stop anytime soon and decided it probably would not, given the winters in Iowa and the higher salaries in other states. Will explained the reason for their visit in his official capacity as a special agent for the Federal Bureau of Investigation and showed him the name of Randall Bruce Wahkahchai. The dean's face immediately lifted in recognition.

"It's been a few years now; in fact, back then I was the Head of the Electrical Engineering department and I had Randy in two of my classes. Department heads in those days still taught a class or two as part of their duties. One of the best students I ever had. He's a Meskwaki, you know." He was not quite sure why that particular piece of information caused all three of his guests to smile simultaneously.

Will handed him the picture. Dean Gregson studied it and frowned.

"Something has happened to him. It's not quite the way I remember him but the shape of the head, the hair and the features seem about right given the passage of time. If you don't mind my asking, why is he so white in this picture? He looks like Michael Jackson."

Will explained the reason for their visit and confirmed the dean's suspicions.

"Excuse me just a moment." He picked up the phone and asked his secretary to bring in the yearbook for that year's graduating class. An older student on work-study brought the big volume into the room and handed it to Dean Gregson. He thanked her, checked the index and opened the collection of pictures to the page for graduating seniors in the College of Engineering. He found the picture of Randall Bruce Wahkahchai and compared it to the photo on the flyer. He pulled at the beard feathering his jaw.

"By the way, if I remember correctly, the meaning of *Wahkahchai* in Meskwaki is Crouching Eagle. Even as a young man he carried his name with a certain nobility. That's not a very good likeness but I still think that's your man," he said, and turned the book around for them to compare.

All three nodded simultaneously. They had their man. There was no doubt they were looking at a younger, darker version of the man on the flyer. Under his name was a list of his hobbies and affiliations, including campus clubs and membership in various societies. The one in particular that caught their eye was the Society of American Indian Engineers. "I'm convinced now that we have found and identified our man," Will announced formally and the dean smiled, happy to have helped.

"You've been extremely helpful," Will told him.

"I just thought of something. Sally!" he shouted through the opened door, not bothering with phones. Sally, his executive secretary, or chief administrative assistant to the dean, as she was more properly known, stuck her head in. "Please bring me the list of all the Iowa companies who employ our engineers, if you would be so kind."

She saluted her boss playfully and two minutes later had the spiral bound folder on his desk. "I don't know what I would do without that woman," he said with genuine admiration and she smiled over her shoulder at him as she walked back to her desk to answer a ringing phone. "We try to keep an updated list of all the companies hiring our graduates. It helps us with fund raising, placing our students in internships, and getting them jobs. The dean rocked back in his high-backed leather chair, crossed his wingtip shoed feet across an open file drawer, and leafed quickly through the pages in the binder, allowing that it might take him a minute or two.

"No hurry at all," Will assured the dean, although Sylvie was showing signs of hunger. On the way in she had studied the vending machines with a predatory interest while she waited for Will to get them orientated in the vast building.

"Here it is," Dean Gregson said. "He was hired by a group called Tactical Missile Systems or TMS, Incorporated. They are primarily a government contractor. In fact, if memory serves, they recently landed a pretty hefty contract for the Pioneer anti-ballistic missile defense project for the feds. The Pioneer is a legacy project designed to replace the Minuteman III in our new missile defense program. They're located in Cedar Rapids, by the way."

Will thanked Dean Gregson for his invaluable information and as he walked them out, Sally made for them a copy of the page with the address of the corporation's headquarters, phone numbers, contact persons, officers, and a description of their mission as a company. At the front of the massive stone and glass building they stood for a minute and looked at each other in disbelief. They could hardly believe how quickly the case was coming together.

"Don't mean to be a pest," Sylvie said with apology, "but all this footwork is making me hungry. And when I get hungry, I get a little—how do the Americans say?—bitchy."

Roland and Will looked at each other as if this were a surprise of startling proportion. "I could eat," Roland added.

As a reward, Will took them to a grill-your-own steakhouse he knew in Des Moines. The expense account treated them to filet mignon wrapped in bacon for Will and Roland, and Sylvie, to their astonishment, selected and grilled a twenty-two ounce Porterhouse steak and ate every last bite, including a baked potato the size of a coconut.

After dinner, stretched out in the comfort of the back seat, she slept most of the way on the return to the hotel, Will and Roland talking quietly about the case as they drove back to Tama-Toledo.

Chapter Thirty-five

Nadipuram

Sylvie was late to breakfast and groggy at the table of the restaurant across the street from the hotel. She complained of a lingering stomach ache. Her complaint alone was enough to merit the men's attention, but what she reported next interrupted their meal. She had not slept well through the night—not unexpected, sleeping in a strange bed in a strange place—despite Will's presence in the bed next to hers. More than the minor gastronomic distress, a recurring dream had disturbed her sleep, and while the symbolic elements of the dreamwork seemed familiar, her sense of anxiety in the dream had increased. She knew only that she was searching to find her way in the dream and that she was trying to help a faceless man. And yes, there was water and a canoe. She seemed somewhat embarrassed as she again shared the elements of her dream with Will and Roland. With prodding from Will, she remembered more elements of the dream. She was still dressed in a white, fringed buckskin dress, but this time she saw herself paddling the birchbark canoe with a purpose, as if she knew where she must go. A man without eyes sat in the front, a new element she had remembered.

The men shrugged at her discomfort so she ignored them and resigned herself to black tea and two slices of unbuttered toast, although she had studied with considerable interest the picture of the hearty breakfast skillet on the plastic menu before deciding it might not be the wisest choice, given the delicate condition of her stomach. She was unable to resist, however, the grape jelly in the cute little packets that came with the order of toast. The pretty picture of the purple grapes on the cover sold her.

The men patiently waited for her to finish, and her mood improved as her stomach settled. They had two stops ahead of them on the Meskwaki Settlement, they informed her, and an appointment with the CEO of TMS, Inc. in Cedar Rapids later that afternoon.

After breakfast, with uncharacteristic docility, Sylvie accepted the offer of the back seat. On the short ride to the Settlement Will offered his semiotic interpretation of the dream. His reading of the recurrent symbols suggested that she was at a point in her life where she had to make an important decision about the direction her life was taking. The dream also symbolized her confusion regarding her relationships. The water symbolized life and life changes. The feeling of uneasiness she experienced had the hallmarks of a classical Freudian anxiety dream.

She thought about it and said he was probably right, but there was something else about the dream: a feeling of resolute purpose that cut through her anxiety, and she insisted this too should be considered significant. She sensed the emergence of a newfound strength emanating from deep within her psyche acting as a motivating force, driving and pushing her to help the poor man in the dream. She asked Will who he thought the guy in the canoe might be. At the manifest level of the dream it had to be Randall Wahkahchai and Sylvie and Roland agreed. Will did not offer his interpretation of the latent symbolism: he was certain the man symbolized Manfred and since no one asked, he kept it to himself.

They all agreed, however, that whatever the interpretation of the symbolic content, it was an interesting dream, particularly the newfound element she expressed as a sense of purpose. Roland, ever the pragmatist, thought it had more to do with the case than with relationships or personal growth. Will suggested it probably had more to do with a protein overdose from the night before than anything else, and Sylvie suggested he was probably an idiot more than anything else.

The first stop took them back to the offices of the tribal headquarters of the Meskwaki Nation where they were assured that one Randall Bruce Wahkahchai was indeed enrolled. Will asked if a residence address on the Settlement was listed. The clerk seemed reluctant.

"I'm not supposed to release that information."

Will showed his credentials and informed the clerk that they were investigating a federal matter and gently reminded the young man that all federal laws applied to the Settlement. The man excused himself, left the information counter and went back to his desk to make a phone call from his office. He spoke into the receiver but watched them during the course of his conversation. After a minute or two he nodded, hung up the receiver, pulled a sheet from his memo pad next to the phone and wrote down an address. He brought the piece of paper to Will, and on the large map of the Settlement on the wall, showed him how to get to the address. Will thanked him for his help and they set out to find the residence, but not before Sylvie commandeered the driving position in their land tank.

A YELLOW LABRADOR retriever barked a greeting as they drove up to an old farmhouse showing the need of a new coat of paint. Will introduced himself to the friendly animal and after accepting a good scratch behind the ears, the dog returned to the porch, wagging his tail. An old man, long white-silver hair untied, waited for them behind the screen door. Will introduced himself again, showed his credentials, then introduced Roland and Sylvie as consultants on the case they were investigating.

"You let the woman drive," the old man said as he opened the storm door for them to enter.

"She has a gun," Will said, and the old man's face crinkled into a smile of perfect white teeth.

"I doubt that she ever has to use it," he observed. He took her hand in his and looked up into the cobalt blue of her eyes. "This is Ranger, my loyal companion and hunting partner." The Lab pressed his great golden head against Sylvie's thigh, demanding to be petted.

"What a beautiful dog." She dropped to her knees and gave him a proper scratching. He dropped to his side and rolled over, exposing his underside.

"He's shameless," the old man said. "Come on in and have a seat. Sorry about the mess, but at my age orderliness is pretty low on my list of priorities. Successfully finding my teeth in the morning is more important."

Will and Roland sat on the musty couch. At the old man's suggestion, Roland folded up the dog's blanket and neatly placed it over the arm of the bolster before he sat. Sylvie sat in the middle, Ranger's head in her lap, his gorgeous brown eyes swimming with gratitude as she stroked the top of his head and pulled at the velvet of his ears. He wagged his tail to show his contentment.

"Just push him away if he gets to be too much of a pest. We don't get a lot of visitors out to the farm these days and he has to make hay while he can."

Sylvie commanded Ranger to sit, which he did immediately, and after a last pat on the head, stretched out on the floor, draped over both her feet, his tail thudding against the threadbare carpet. The old man, in worn blue jeans faded almost as white as his hair, and a new red flannel shirt that must have been a gift, sat in the leather easy chair. He was having trouble with the lever and could not get it to recline.

"Goddamn this chair," he said, cursing its reluctance and its aging mechanism. "Everything starts to break down as it gets older," he warned them. He gave up, settled back and said, "You've come about my grandson, haven't you?" Will nodded. The old man sighed. "I had a vision that he had drowned, but I couldn't see his face. I knew he might be dead, but it troubled me most that I could never see his face."

Will explained how an anonymous body had been found in mid-June at Lake Kabetogama on the Boundary Waters of Minnesota, and how the three had taken on the case, believing it to be a murder and not a suicide. The old man nodded and said Randall would never have committed suicide, so they were right to trust their instincts. He listened quietly as Roland picked up the thread of the narrative. Roland explained how they had tried to rebuild the man's identity piece by piece and give a name to a man no one seemed to know. The hardest part had been breaking through the artificial barrier of secrecy imposed by Randall's time in the Witness Security Program, and the reluctance of the U.S. Marshals office to share information regarding the case. Will explained to him the role played by the Ojibwe and Chief Gray Wolf.

"I owe a debt of honor to my brothers in the North," Chief Wahpellah said aloud so that he would not forget the obligation. After thinking for a minute the chief said, "I have no doubt Randy asked to be placed with the Ojibwe, knowing our connections with Chief Gray Wolf's casino."

When Will and Roland finished telling their story, the old man, his eyes clouded with the milk of time and grief took a cigar from his shirt pocket, stripped off the cellophane wrapper and drew fire from a long match into the rolled tobacco. He smoked and thought as Sylvie coughed politely into her fist.

"I am Randy's grandfather and I am still the tribal chieftain of the Meskwaki. My son, Randy's father, died in action in Afghanistan. Randy would most likely have taken my place after I died, and I will be ready to die soon." He did not say this to win their sympathy. He simply stated the matter as a fact. "I am an old man and this will be my last hunting season."

Will asked what he hunted and Chief Wahpellah told him pheasants now, but later he would hunt for deer, and if the snows were not too heavy, pheasants again. Will smiled and told him of the many years he had hunted pheasants not too far from the Settlement. The chief nodded. "I know of you and your two hunting partners. Steve and Tom, I believe were their names. We knew of your expertise in the field. The three white men who could hunt almost as well as Meskwaki." Chief Wahpellah waved holes in a cloud of cigar smoke that made the dog sneeze. After his vision cleared, he noted the effect of his surprising compliment. The big white man blushed into the throat of his blue polo shirt. Wahpellah smiled and said, "When you are finished with your work, you three will hunt with me."

"It will be an honor," Will said, on behalf of Roland and Sylvie."

The old man drew more smoke from the cigar and let it settle in his lungs before giving it back to his nostrils. "I have to ask you a serious question."

"By all means."

"Are you certain he was killed by white men only?"

Will explained the presence of the two men on the video tape at the White Bear casino and the subsequent attack on him and Sylvie at War Club lake.

"You are a very brave young woman. I know now why he lets you drive." He tapped an inch of ashes from the cigar into the saucer of his palm. "I have seen you before."

Sylvie shook her head and politely said she certainly would have remembered him; but no, they had not met. The old man smiled. "In my vision," Chief Wahpellah explained, "I saw a white maiden in white ceremonial robes, her eyes blue as the spring sky and she had come a very long way across the great waters to help me find my grandson. This was my vision: my grandson was blind and could not find his way home by himself. The white princess led him back to me."

In spite of himself Will felt a chill crawl his spine and looked over at Roland in amazement. Sylvie sat with her mouth open, the full import of her dreams now evident. The three detectives turned and looked at each other, simultaneously remembering that Chief Gray Wolf of the Ojibwe had had essentially the same vision.

Roland said, "It is good then that we have found each other and your grandson will come home to where he belongs."

Will agreed. "But we are not quite finished with the case. We must still discover why Randall was killed so we can bring those responsible to justice."

Chief Wahpellah nodded. "Such men cannot be allowed to walk free." He then told them the story his grandson had shared with him the year before on their last pheasant hunt together.

Will assured Chief Wahpellah they would return to Tama after their visit to Cedar Rapids and TMS.

"It will be a good hunt," the chief promised as he walked them to the SUV. As he shook hands with Roland he said, "Tell Mary, my grandniece, that she was right to trust her instincts about you."

As they drove off the Settlement and headed for Cedar Rapids, Sylvie said, "That has to be the most remarkable interview I have ever experienced. I still have goose pimples on my arms." She paused. "And I can't wait to go hunting with Chief Wahpellah."

From behind the wheel Will thought for a long time about why he had suddenly decided to let Sylvie drive after they obtained the address to the farmhouse. Perhaps it was nothing more than a sign.

EDWARD M. BERNARDO, in a gray pinstriped suit above a white shirt and red power tie, tried to be helpful as possible. The new CEO of TMS, truth be told, had only been in the position for the last six months after the company had been placed in receivership by the federal government. He opened his hands to them, hoping that they would understand. Dr. Davis, former CEO and founder of the company had unexpectedly retired, a surprise to everyone in the company, you understand, although he retained his seat as president of the Board of Directors. Yes, Bernardo knew of the resignation of the Project Team Leader of the Pioneer program, a man named Randall Wahkahchai. No, he did not know Mr. Wahkahchai personally, only by reputation in his former role as Chief Financial Officer. Occasionally he had seen the PTL professionally during meetings when he was required to brief the top executives. Please understand that although TMS was a relatively small company of less than five hundred employees, he did not rub shoulders, so to speak, with the engineers.

Yes, he had known Dr. Davis personally but they did not socialize. His sudden retirement in the middle of the Pioneer project was a shock indeed, you understand, and there had been rumors that it was something personal between Dr. Davis and Mr. Wahkahchai. The two men were often at odds as to the direction the project should take.

The last he heard, Dr. Davis was in the Bahamas, aboard his yacht, and he did not, unfortunately, know the whereabouts of the PTL. The conditions of his appointment required that he report directly to Lt. General Frank Simons, Director of the Missile Defense Agency. It was a distinct honor to serve his country and work toward such an important goal. Here was his address at the Pentagon and the phone number to his office at Redstone Arsenal in Huntsville, Alabama. He wished them good luck with their investigation into the disappearance of Mr. Wahkahchai. He was always glad to help and took pride in his open door policy and willingness to work with government agencies. As they stood to leave and shake hands, Bernardo recalled that Randy Wahkahchai had the reputation of being a good company man. The company could use more employees like him, you understand.

They understood.

Will, Sylvie, and Roland took the elevator down to the first floor and walked up to the reception desk where they had to return their visitor's passes and sign out with Security. LaVinia Thomas accepted the return of the temporary passes and gave them the clipboard to sign. They were the only visitors for the day. She studied all three signatures and then looked at Will who was just about to thank her for her kindness.

"Doctor, can I ask you a question?"

"Of course," Will said and smiled.

Ms. Thomas looked around at the routine traffic of employees moving within the building. Everything seemed ordinary; nothing seemed out of place. Nevertheless, she leaned forward and whispered her question. "Is this by any chance about Randy Wahkahchai?" She asked the question cautiously, afraid that it was none of her business.

Will looked at Roland and then Sylvie as if deciding whether to include Ms. Thomas within the circle of their confidentiality. They nodded discreetly. "Just between us, as professionals?" he suggested. Immediately she nodded her emphatic agreement. "Yes," Will told her quietly. "We're here on his behalf." Her sigh of relief was audible.

"Don't believe the half of what they tell you upstairs."

"We never do," Roland assured her, smiling.

Ms. Thomas was immediately taken by his accent and squared the Sam Brown belt over her ample hips. Sylvie stepped back a bit as Roland moved closer. "Did they tell you he resigned?" she asked, skeptical.

"That's amazing," Roland said. "That's exactly what they told us. LaVinia Thomas beamed the white smile of most of her teeth at them.

"Well, don't you believe them for a minute," she said rolling her eyes in emphasis. She leaned forward across the counter so that her bountiful breasts pressed against the marble countertop, her leather belt creaking. "Telling you this might cost me my job but I trust you guys. Davis fired that poor man and covered it up to make it look like a resignation. That's all I know." She finished with an emphatic "Umhmm!" She slipped back on the heels of her black orthotic shoes, shored up to take the burden of her weight, and took her proper place on the stool behind the counter. She was satisfied now that she had said what needed to be said. Mr. Wahkahchai deserved as much. She breathed heavily for a moment or two as she recovered from the exertion.

Roland looked first at Will, then at Sylvie. "That's a very important piece of information," he lied. "As friends of Mr. Wahkahchai, we thank you for it. We also want to assure you that as fellow law enforcement professionals, we consider what you have told us privileged information."

Ms. Thomas, her breathing once again under control, although she was sweating a bit now said, "I'd do anything to help that man. He was a fine man and treated everyone with respect. I hope it helps you guys." She was sincere in her concern.

Will promised her that it would. On the spur of the moment, just as they turned to leave he asked, "Did Mr. Wahkahchai have anyone at work, besides yourself, in whom he might confide from time to time?"

Her eyes widened and she nodded. She thought of leaning forward again to whisper the name, thought better of it given the effort, and wrote the name on a memo pad instead. "I'm not supposed to do this." She tore the page off the pad and handed it to Will. "I wrote her home number there too. I know she won't mind."

They thanked her again for her invaluable assistance and she waved them out the glass doors as she answered a ringing phone on the bank next to her terminal.

Once outside and walking through the parking lot to Visitor's Parking, Sylvie wanted to know the name on the piece of paper.

"No name," Will joked. "It's LaVinia Thomas's home number and a message to Roland that he should call tonight but not before seven."

Roland grinned, knowing better, but Sylvie grabbed the slip of paper and read the name: Dr. Daya Nadipuram.

"Let's make a call on the cell and see if she's home," Will said. Their run of good luck continued when she answered. After a considerable amount of persuasion and explanation she reluctantly agreed to see them. She emphasized more than once that she was no longer employed by TMS. Will told her that was exactly the reason why they should talk. Her directions to her house were given with a scientist's attention to detail. They pulled into the driveway of a house in an established neighborhood where the lots were nearly a half-acre each. The driveway was concrete and fronted a three-car garage. The house was two stories clad with aluminum siding, and there were lace curtains even on the basement windows. Will surmised that the basement had been finished as a result.

Dr. Daya Nadipuram answered the soft chime of the bell after the first ring and showed them in. Before they sat, Will made the introductions after which Dr. Nadipuram invited them to share tea. She promised them an authentic Kashmiri chai, a blend of black and green teas, which she had brought back from India not two weeks before. They accepted and she went into the kitchen just as a kettle whistled for her attention. Roland and Sylvie sat together at either end of a long couch and Will settled into a comfortable padded chair at the foot of a glass coffee table. The chair's twin sat at the opposite end, which Will surmised was reserved for Dr. Nadipuram, given the eclectic mixture of gardening and engineering magazines racked in a wicker basket at the side of the chair.

She returned with a scrolled silver tray supporting tea service for four. She had included finger sandwiches and small cakes. The tea was excellent. An original blend from the Himalayas, she informed them, served with a spot of cream and honey for sweetness. In the tea they could taste cinnamon and cloves and a touch of ginger. The ceremony of presenting and drinking the tea allowed them to study Dr. Nadipuram.

She seemed to be a quiet, albeit confident woman and her furnishings in the living room reflected her sense of self. Understated elegance, Will thought to himself. Roland was certainly paying attention. Sylvie and Daya smiled sweetly at each other, genuine and unaffected by the presence of the men, as the two women took the time to study each other. There was nothing gaudy or cheap on the shelves; in a corner of the room a *sitar* rested its gourd belly on the rug, its long thick neck touching the wall. Will asked if she played. She smiled politely across her cup and said, "Regrettably, no." The instrument had belonged to her father, an accomplished musician and student of *raga*, but she had never learned, content to sit at her father's knee while he contemplated and played the intricate musical forms that combined passion with elegance.

Her father had died recently and the *sitar* had been left to her, built from her father's hand. She crossed her legs, almost long as Sylvie's, elegant and modern in tan slacks below a V-necked cashmere sweater. Will thought it must certainly be an authentic Kashmiri garment—it had the fine hand and drape of an exquisite item, the lightest possible brown that beautifully accentuated the black sheen of her long straight hair and her luminous brown eyes. Her face had grown thinner since her lay-off at TMS and the roundness of her face had transformed into an attractive angularity. Intelligence radiating from her eyes suffused her face.

Dr. Nadipuram was particularly impressed with Sylvie's rank and accomplishments and despite the distance of continents and cultures between them, the two were simpatico after ten minutes of conversation. Will saw both women visibly relax through the shoulders. It was easy to understand the similarity between the two. Both were intelligent and beautiful and had persevered and prospered in typically male dominated fields. Both managed to retain their essential grace and femininity as an expression of their identity as women. It also became evident, as Daya poured them a second cup that, in spite of her struggle against an Indian culture that placed by far a greater intrinsic value on males, she neither hated nor feared men. In fact, she had chosen to study at a largely male university and had taken her graduate degrees in a field dominated by men. She had chosen her path and followed it with enthusiasm and confidence.

As Will watched her, he concluded that he was in the presence of a singular, exceptional woman who liked and got along well with her colleagues at work, most of whom happened to be men. After Sylvie explained her professional relationship with Roland and shared how he had carefully helped her manage her career, Daya looked at him with a newfound respect and said, "Sylvie is very lucky to have someone who cares so much about her in so difficult a job."

Thumb on his jaw, Roland stroked his mustache with the inside of his index finger and matched her charm. "I simply told her to watch and study carefully everything I do, then do exactly the opposite."

Daya laughed with the enthusiasm of a young girl. Will noticed that Roland was inordinately pleased he had made her laugh. Something about the woman seemed to captivate him. Roland did not give in easily to most women, but Daya had managed to catch his full attention. Will regretted that he would have to change the subject even as the two were getting more comfortable with each other. Although she seemed friendly and open to them now after getting to know each other, Will was still uncertain as to where her loyalties lay. He decided to proceed carefully so as not to alienate her or disrupt the still fragile seine of friendship they had managed to weave in their short time together.

He looked quickly at Roland, ever the consummate professional despite the fact that he had allowed Daya Nadipuram temporarily to enchant him. Roland returned Will's glance to let him know he had his full support to proceed. Sylvie too had taken notice of the woman's uncanny understated confidence and observed her with respectful admiration. Will had no doubt that in the days ahead he would be seeing something of Daya in Sylvie.

Chapter Thirty-six

The Return of Wahkahchai

The time had come to test for loyalties. "You mentioned that you are no longer employed at TMS. Would you share with us your reasons for leaving?" Will asked.

Dr. Nadipuram uncrossed her legs, sat back and rested her hands atop the arms of the chair. She seemed untroubled by the question, although she did take a deep breath. Her answer was certain, precise, but intense. "Although Dr. Davis had instructed Randy Wahkahchai to fire me, he did not do so immediately. After consulting with me, Randy removed me from my position as chief engineer of the software division on the Pioneer project. I was reassigned to our testing division; the engineers call it the 'shake and bake' division because various electronic components are subjected to various stressors such as atmospheric, heat, cold, pressure, and weight, and so on until failure. In terms of the company hierarchy, it's equivalent to demotion from general to lieutenant, to use a military analogy. It's basically a division for young engineers fresh from college managed by senior men burned out or incompetent to the point where shaking and baking things can't get them into further trouble. It's necessary work and it helps the young engineer understand the details of what we're working on, but certainly is no place for a senior engineer with a doctorate. Shortly before Randy disappeared, he formally let me go under the guise of a lay-off"

"Most likely the result Davis hoped for," Roland commented.

"Also the result I hoped for," she said mysteriously.

Will made a mental note to revisit the point but another question pressed.

"Why did Mr. Wahkahchai not fire you upon instructions from Dr. Davis?" Sylvie asked, before Will had a chance to pose the same question.

"That's a very good question," Daya allowed. "There were two reasons, I think. Keeping me on but sequestered away allowed Randall some needed time to prepare himself for his interview with Lieutenant General Frank Simons, head of the ballistic missile defense program for this country. He told me this in strictest confidence. He said it was his duty and his moral obligation as an American citizen who truly loved his country."

Roland nodded. He understood patriotism.

"I think that once Randy made his decision and got his case together, he gave me my walking papers so that I could collect the full amount of unemployment coming to me. It also allowed me to save my pension and find a new job, which I start next month, by the way. I also got to spend some time with my family back in India."

Will nodded as he took notes. "I'm beginning to make sense of Wahkahchai's actions. He was a very smart man and it is evident that he cared very much for you. It is clear to me now that he sent you to India for protection."

Nadipuram closed her eyes briefly in acknowledgement; she had not considered this aspect of Randy's asking her to go to India. Now she understood why he had been so adamant. "I respected him," was all she added.

"How would you characterize your working relationship with Dr. Davis?" Will continued.

The question startled her. She had expected that such a question would be about Randall Wahkahchai. She started by hedging a bit. "I respected him for founding the company and creating so many opportunities for so many bright, dedicated people." She paused and frowned. "To use an analogy, he struck me as a father unsure of himself and thus was never completely comfortable with his children. This made him an intolerant disciplinarian. His management style—which I have always believed is a reflection of one's parenting skills—bordered on the authoritarian. I know that comes across as an exaggeration, but that's what I saw. I certainly appreciated the opportunity he gave me, but I didn't enjoy working for him, not that that is important. He is one of those creative, narrow-minded and stubborn men who cannot be told no when it affects the realization of their vision. Please don't misunderstand me; he could be pleasant and charming when it suited him, but when it came to making and keeping TMS a successful enterprise, you could say he was an amoral and driven man. That's what I mean," she explained.

The next question also surprised her.

"Would you say he was driven and amoral to the point where he would do almost anything to ensure the success of his company, even to the point of doing something illegal if he thought it would ultimately benefit the company?"

She moved slightly forward in the chair and took the time to adjust a small ruby earring in her right ear. She thought before answering, considering the implications of the question. "As many successful and accomplished entrepreneurs, Dr. Davis, in addition to his excellent education and creative genius is, in my opinion—and I think the word describes him perfectly, a narcissistic egomaniac. He takes everything regarding TMS personally. If you insult the company, you insult him."

"His sense of self and personal identity is wrapped up in the public image of the company," Roland suggested.

Will smiled to himself.

Daya folded her hands in her lap and said, "You have it exactly right." She paused to take a deep and cleansing breath. Will was certain now that Daya Nadipuram's composure was in some way related to her practice of yoga. She had a selection of books on her shelves relating to the different styles and practices of the art.

She elaborated. "When Randy Wahkahchai, who, as you know, was our designated Project Team Leader, told Dr. Davis, as he was ethically and morally obligated to do, that the software program would not work and could not work for the time being, I am certain that Davis took it as a personal affront, a breach of trust, if you will. And this in spite of our personal warnings directly, and in memos and official reports keeping him apprised of the situation."

"Would you say he was in denial?" Will asked.

"That is not my area of expertise." She paused. "That said, his denial was pathological."

All three detectives grinned at her.

"And Will finds that highly significant," Sylvie said to Daya, as a co-conspirator.

Will was forced into laughter at the observation. It was evident that Sylvie had already come to an opinion regarding Nadipuram's loyalties.

Daya looked first at Sylvie, then at Will. "I like the fact that he can laugh at himself. I don't think I ever saw Davis laugh at himself once. I found that very strange indeed."

"With these two," Will said drolly, indicating Roland and Sylvie, "I get plenty of opportunity to humble myself. They have an unerring knack for letting the air out of my tires, so to speak."

Daya summed up. "They help keep you centered."

As Will considered the state of his psychological equilibrium, Roland asked, "Was there animosity between Dr. Davis and Mr. Wahkahchai?"

She shook her head sedately. "No. It was entirely professional. Wahkahchai was seen as an impediment to the success of the project and was therefore removed."

Will let Roland continue his line of questioning. "So you suspect that he did not resign but was fired instead?"

"Wahkahchai would never resign. He was a man of honor. He did what he had to do." She stopped there.

Will pushed her. "And what was that, Dr. Nadipuram?"

"He told the truth. He took the evidence that the software program could not differentiate decoys from the true ballistic missile threat directly to Dr. Davis. I know this for a fact," she added, anticipating the next question. "He came to me personally in his capacity as PTL, and friend, I think. He wanted to prepare me for any repercussions." She turned away for a moment as her eyes misted. "He took it all upon himself when he could very easily have used me as the scapegoat. All other phases of the project at TMS under Randall's control were integrating nicely with the software: sensors, tracking radar, battle management systems, everything was working except the damned threat recognition software. I told Davis when he hired me that it would be the most difficult aspect of the contract. To his credit, he immediately acknowledged that, but he also recognized that the logic and structure I had created would work in time. Unfortunately, TMS had neither the resources nor the programmers to finish the code on time. We're talking about millions and millions of lines of complex code. We needed parallel processing and the supercomputers at DARPA to run the simulations. And we didn't always get it. There just wasn't enough time." She sighed heavily.

Now that he had a sufficient understanding of the situation at TMS, Will decided it was time to include Daya Nadipuram as a friend of the investigation. He told her the story of Randall Bruce Wahkahchai's death.

After Will concluded his narrative, she excused herself suddenly and hurried to the bathroom. She returned five minutes later and it was obvious she had been crying.

Daya Nadipuram took a minute to carefully study the faces of the three detectives as she pressed a tissue to the corners of her eyes. She had picked up Will's frustration at the fact that Davis, upon leaving the company, had no doubt purged all records of the Project Team Leader's report. When Dr. Nadipuram confirmed those suspicions, Will slumped back in his chair. Roland and Sylvie shared the trouble in his face. They too understood the consequences for the case. She excused herself again and went into her bedroom. She returned with a flash drive memory key in her hand and presented it to Will.

"You'll need this," she said and reseated herself. "I have the original locked in a safe deposit box at my bank." The act of making a contribution to the case contributed to the reassertion of her composure. "I don't mean to sound all mystical and Far Eastern but I truly believe that it is Karma that has led you three to find me. Wahkahchai was afraid something might happen and he asked me to make this copy of the report, just in case. I give it over to you for safekeeping and in hopes that everyone will learn the true story of the man Randall Wahkahchai was."

Will accepted the memory key with gratitude and excused himself. He hurried out to the rented SUV and returned with his lap top. He inserted the key, copied and saved all the files to his hard drive and created three additional keys, one for Sylvie, one for Roland, and one for himself. The others talked as they waited for Will to finish the copying. He returned the original to Dr. Nadipuram. She studied the black plastic key—it seemed so light, insubstantial, and small in her hand—as she considered the ramifications of the information it contained, and then formulated a question for Will. "Do you think Davis is implicated in Wahkahchai's disappearance?" She corrected herself. "I should say murder." Although she had asked the question of Will, all three nodded.

Will explained. "I don't think he pulled the trigger, but I think he hired the hit men."

Roland's next question to Daya bordered on the brilliant. "Do you know if Davis had any ties to organized crime? Or were there any rumors to that effect?"

Daya nodded. "From the time I hired on there were persistent rumors that some of the start-up money had come from the Mafia in Chicago. I thought it was nothing more than silly talk trying to romanticize the history of the company. But now that I think of it, no one really knew where the money came from. Davis certainly didn't have the wherewithal to start a company so soon after his doctoral work. We just thought it was from a venture capitalist in San Francisco that saw the value of Davis's original work."

The next question made the case. Sylvie asked, "Did Davis by any chance have a girlfriend? We know he was married and divorced but it seems he never remarried."

Again Daya nodded. "In fact, the rumor is that he took her along on his yacht to the Bahamas. To be honest, I never liked her. She seemed cheap and brash to me, right down to her platinum hair and oversized artificial breasts. She worked as a veterinarian's assistant, if I remember correctly," she added as an afterthought. "Although I can't imagine why that would be relevant. They met when Davis brought his dog to the vet's office to have a paw stitched up."

Will startled everyone in the room by sitting bolt upright in the chair, an action which caused his foot to accidentally strike the underside of the coffee table and rattle all the cups, saucers, and spoons. He ignored it, jumped out of his chair, ran over and kissed Sylvie fully on the lips. "Sylvie! You're a genius," he said unabashedly.

"I told you so," she said to Roland, who grinned, although it was clear she was still uncertain as to the immediate and current signification of her brilliance. She gave up. "I'm really a genius?"

"Unquestionably." Will looked to Roland, who had already worked out the link.

Dr. Nadipuram was as confused as Sylvie but smiled good-naturedly.

"Succinylcholine chloride," Roland explained. "Will had hypothesized that a chemical agent was used to immobilize Randall Wahkahchai before he was killed in order to make his death appear to be a suicide. The drug, until fairly recently, was considered virtually undetectable. When Will asked for a full drug assay of the brain tissue, the report showed traces of succinic acid."

"No doubt the byproduct of the body breaking down the chemical," Dr. Nadipuram observed, remembering her chemistry.

"Exactly," Will said. "And there are basically two kinds of professionals who have access or cause to use the drug. Anesthesiologists, which had been my first guess, and veterinarians."

"And Davis's girlfriend just happened to work for a vet. Now isn't that an interesting coincidence?" Daya said.

Will grinned. "I would go so far as to say it is highly significant."

Sylvie and Roland groaned simultaneously, which did not affect Will in the least and he again asked to be excused while he made a quick call on his cell phone in the kitchen. He returned with news. "I can get the last flight out of Cedar Rapids into Chicago and on to Washington, D.C. from there. I need to speak with Lieutenant General Simons at the Pentagon and with his consent see about swearing out a warrant on Davis. We have an extradition treaty with the Bahamas and the sooner we serve the warrant, the better." He paused and then shrugged. "It's probably better if I go alone. That means I'll have to leave you two in a hotel for the next two days or so. I'm sorry about that, but I promise to make it up to you both when I return."

Roland and Sylvie assured him they understood and would not mind waiting at the hotel. At this point Daya interjected. "I won't hear of any such thing. Roland and Sylvie are welcome to stay with me until you return. This house has four bedrooms and I would appreciate the company." It was agreed.

Roland looked at his watch. "I don't know about you two, but I'm ready for dinner. I say we drop Will off at the airport, and then we'll let Dr. Nadipuram choose a restaurant for us—our treat—for helping us put the case together."

She asked everyone to call her Daya and said Roland's idea was wonderful.

WILL, FLASHING CREDENTIALS, made the flight because they held the plane for him. In Washington, he was met at Dulles airport by Lieutenant General Simons's executive officer, waiting with a car. Will briefed Simons and handed him a copy of the reports on the software problems for the target discrimination system on the Pioneer antiballistic missile. Simons tapped the key with his finger.

"This is what Randall Wahkahchai promised he could produce and the reason I wanted him in the Witness Security Program. He had given us half the document— for his protection, he said. I'm not very happy with the U.S. Marshals office right now, but no agency is infallible. Despite their outstanding record, they do lose a man from time to time, but keep that under your hat, Doctor."

Will understood that the lieutenant general was not excusing their actions, he was merely explaining them. Will could also see that the news he had brought Simons deeply disturbed him. There was no doubt now that the rebuilding of the nation's missile defense program would be significantly delayed. Nevertheless, despite these setbacks, Simons was determined to move forward.

Lieutenant General Simons thanked Will again and put his driver and car at his disposal. As he saw Will personally to the waiting vehicle, at the door he said, "Please remember me to your father. He's one of the best we ever had when we were working together in Missile Command. I appreciate that he took time out from his golf game to fly to the Midwest on such short notice to sit and debrief Mr. Wahkahchai. His technical expertise continues to be invaluable to the Department of Defense." Will promised he would pass along the lieutenant general's good wishes upon his return home.

AT FBI HEADQUARTERS in Quantico, with the full support and backing of Lieutenant General Simons, Will made a full report to the assistant director and waited just long enough for a judge to swear the warrant for Davis's arrest and extradition.

As he waited for the plane back to Chicago the next day, he was greeted by a special agent who informed him that Bahamian Port Authorities were holding Dr. Davis and his girlfriend for questioning. Two men from the Bureau had already been dispatched to bring them back to the U.S. for charges and trial. The day after he returned to Cedar Rapids, a team of agents came to debrief and depose Dr. Nadipuram. In the meantime, Will had called International Falls and made arrangements for the release of Randall Bruce Wahkahchai's body for its return to the Meskwaki settlement.

Will was informed by the debriefing team that they would need two to three days to conduct their interviews. As much as she wanted to attend the funeral of Randall Wahkahchai, Daya Nadipuram knew she could serve him best by staying with the agents as they prepared their case against Davis. Will, Sylvie, and Roland met the plane carrying the remains of Randall Bruce Wahkahchai and returned him home to the Meskwaki Settlement. He was given a proper burial according to the ceremonial customs of the Red Earth People. He was once again on his home lands and was laid to rest next to his mother, father, and grandmother, who preceded him in death. The day after the funeral, Chief Wahpellah made good on his promise to take the three pheasant hunting.

SYLVIE DID HERSELF proud, dropping the first rooster that flew within range of her gun. She stayed close to Wahpellah's side, who regaled her with hunting stories and expert shooting, however unorthodox. By early afternoon they had shot their limit of three birds each. They had dinner with the chief at the farmhouse. Will and Sylvie helped with the preparation of the birds, while Roland and Wahpellah talked over good Canadian whisky. After the outstanding dinner, they said their goodbyes. Chief Wahpellah handed Will a letter for the Chief Henry Gray Wolf of the Ojibwe Nation and once again thanked the three for the return of his grandson. Wahpellah personally handed Sylvie into the driver's seat and they said their goodbyes, Ranger barking and wagging his tail.

The next day, with Daya's home cleared of the debriefing staff, Will promised Daya, Sylvie, and Roland a trip to the Mississippi. Roland's girlfriend, Lili Popelka, had sent word that she could not wait any longer for them to return as a daughter in Florida was ready to give birth. Farley Nilsson had agreed to take over the restaurant until she returned after the winter season. She promised to Skype and hoped Roland would too. He saw no reason not to as he genuinely enjoyed his relationship with Lili, and Sylvie promised to explain what Skype was.

As they prepared for the daytrip, Roland asked Daya if she knew how to catch a walleye, and she replied that she did not, but was certainly willing to have him teach her. Roland looked quickly at Will who immediately invited Daya to travel and stay with them at the cabin in Minnesota in gratitude and in exchange for the hospitality she so graciously had shown them. With a serene smile intended for Roland, she accepted immediately.

Chapter Thirty-seven

Missile Test

After his meeting with Professor Sheridan, and satisfied now that CEO Davis of TMS would soon be apprehended, Lieutenant General Simons took the time to remember with fondness and great sadness the extraordinary individual he had come to know as Randall Bruce Wahkahchai. Almost a year ago, one week after receiving Project Team Leader Randall Wahkahchai's testimony and learning the truth of the Pioneer missile's radar and detection system flaws, Lieutenant General Frank L. Simons felt as if he had been knocked down by the blast of a booster rocket exploding on the pad during a failed test-fire. The rest of the information on the memory key Dr. Sheridan had given him confirmed his worst fears. He no longer had the luxury of hoping for the best. The deadline for the full scale test of the Pioneer antiballistic missile system was fast approaching and the test was doomed to fail. The software program needed at least another year, more likely two, before it could be made to work properly. Those were the cold hard facts he had to deal with.

BACK FROM HIS meetings at the Pentagon, the LTG was once more in his office at the Redstone Arsenal Army base ten miles southeast of Huntsville, Alabama. Unfortunately, despite being home again, his day was progressing from bad to falling in the shit-hole worse, and the digital clock on his desk still did not show 0700 hours. Now this.

The Government Accountability Office had released its latest report and analysis of his intercontinental ballistic missile interceptor program, with specific reference to the new Pioneer project, now becoming ever more crucial to the nation's missile defense systems. The hard copy report in his hands did not make for pleasant reading. After the introduction, the GAO report offered an overview of the program's history and he read that too, checking for factual accuracy and errors. At least the research was good, to his eye and to his knowledge.

The Missile Defense Agency (MDA) currently headed by Lieutenant General Frank L. Simons at the nearly forty thousand acre facility at Redstone, had its origins in the Strategic Defense Initiative. Proposed by President Ronald Reagan in 1983, SDI was intended to combine ground-based interceptors and orbital platforms of lasers and missiles in space, which earned it the tongue in cheek nickname "Star Wars." SDI fell under the aegis of the Defense Department and in 1984 became the Strategic Defense Initiative Organization. Shortly thereafter a paper written by the eggheads at the American Physical Society concluded that the Star Wars program was not feasible given the technology existing then. Coupled with the ending of the Cold War and the subsequent reduction of nuclear arsenals world-wide, political support for SDI waned and withered, finally and formally dying in 1993. Under President Bill Clinton, SDIO was renamed the Ballistic Missile Defense Organization and in 2002 the name was shortened to the Missile Defense Agency. Simons chuckled at that one: a rare case of a bureaucratic department adopting a shorter name.

After the terrorist attack on the U.S. homeland September 11, 2001, President George W. Bush, with characteristic incompetence rushed deployment of the ground-based missile system, which became operational in 2004, in a manner of speaking, Simons editorialized, never a great fan of the Bush administration. He knew the GAO to be a non-political and non-partisan investigative arm of Congress, but what he read next galled him as a citizen, an engineer, and as a war fighter.

The MDA had cost U.S. taxpayers more than forty billion dollars to date. Part of that problem, according to his highly trained military mind, was that the Bush administration, already struggling to prosecute two ill-advised wars off budget in Afghanistan and Iraq, had exempted the Missile Defense Agency from standard procurement and testing regulations. A West Point graduate with a Master's degree in Engineering from MIT, Simons regarded this move as a strategic and fundamental error that continued to undermine the program's progress and reliability on his watch. And therein lay the crux of the matter that occupied and tormented his thinking today.

He did not need the GAO report to remind him that the program's success was a dismal failure by any standard or criterion. Less than nine out of seventeen attempts to intercept incoming ICBMs had been successful, and even that statistic was stretching the truth. In order to trumpet some semblance of success to the public, the interceptors launched by his predecessors had been given every chance to succeed, and still failed. The missileers of the Pioneer program knew the time of launch, the trajectory, the speed, and a host of other factors crucial to intercepting an incoming ICBM, including conducting the exercises during daytime and in optimal weather conditions. Significantly lowering the speed of incoming missiles had resulted in a few hits. The one attempt at a nighttime intercept had been a dismal failure, Simons recalled.

Overcoming the more intractable problems of guidance, tracking, and interception required extraordinary data and telemetry integration by software running on the tactical computer aboard the Pioneer

ABM. At the time, Simons thought hiring Tactical Missile Systems in Iowa would give him a workable solution as MDA waited the three years necessary to prepare for the upcoming test shot, using that time to reengineer other systems and boosters for the missile. The last attempt three years ago had been a failure. His agency could not afford another loss. The CEO at Tactical Missile Systems had promised him a workable solution to all the software problems well within the three years Simons had given the company to write the code. Davis had lied through his teeth, forcing the LTG to rewrite his timelines and test fire schedules. Now this.

As he read the GAO's conclusion, he reached for his roll of antacids. In the clear, unambiguous terms of the document, the GAO concluded: "The record suggests that an operationally useful defense capability does not yet exist." In disgust at the unvarnished truth memorialized in the document, he fed the pages of the report into the shredder, hoping that the machine specialized to handle top secret documents would digest the pages better than he was digesting his breakfast eaten at the Officer's Club earlier that morning.

He stared at the scale model of the Pioneer missile on his desk. Designed as an exoatmospheric rocket of three boosters more than 60 feet tall, it was capable of carrying a 150 pound kinetic kill vehicle. Granted, the rocket presented profound engineering challenges. In all fairness to his team many had been solved, he was proud to admit to himself; many, but not all, in of one of the most complex engineering and scientific challenges he had ever faced. The problem lay in the system's overall complexity; specifically, in the guidance and sensor technology designed to fly the missile, separate the kill stage and locate and fly it independently to target an incoming ICBM, lock on target, differentiate the aggressor from any and all decoys and deliver the kinetic kill vehicle on an intercept course that would result in destroying the hostile incoming missile. Simons shook his head. And all this at speeds of 4 miles per second.

He loosened his tie, put his feet up and closed his eyes. After almost an hour of uninterrupted hard thinking in the chair, he had a solution. It was time to quit feeling sorry for himself, solve the problem, get out of his chair and get it done. The thunderstorm that had rolled over the Arsenal on its way up to Huntsville—after lighting the blue-gray skies and rumbling through the building like a rocket booster at full burn on a test pad— had cleared the air of heat and oppressive humidity. As the last rumble faded into the distance he began to solve the problem. I command this operation, he reminded himself, watching the storm move on. Responsibility for the success or failure of this project is mine, and in that thought he knew he had the beginnings of a solution. Based on his interviews with Randall Wahkahchai, he knew—despite the lies that bastard of a CEO had told him—the TMS software will fail, given the current parameters of the test. He also knew there was insufficient time for Tactical Missile Systems in Iowa to correct their software problems.

He knew and understood all too well that it was inconceivable for him at this point in time, given current geopolitical events, to publicly postpone another test more than a week or so. He was fast losing the cushion of time the spooks had given his program. The fucking North Koreans had just put up a Hwasong-15, an ICBM capable of reaching the U.S. mainland. And intelligence briefings from the CIA suggested North Korea had sufficiently miniaturized an atomic weapon, making it small enough to ride atop the booster. Whether or not the package could survive entry and re-entry flight phases was another issue entirely, but the North Koreans were forcing the timeline. In his mind he further isolated the problem facing the upcoming test. The software as written by the programmers at TMS could not adequately differentiate between decoys popped out by the incoming missile and the missile itself.

According to systems reports from his engineers, he was secure in his knowledge that everything else was a go. The inescapable logical conclusion, therefore, he reasoned, is to change the parameters of the test. As he looked out his window into the brightening day, he cinched up his tie and thought to himself, thank you Jesus. Using the weather was an acceptable excuse that could help buy him just enough time to effect the changes he had in mind.

He picked up the phone and spoke with his executive officer, the bright young mover and shaker recently rotated back from the Afghan theater. "Harold," he said to the major, "get me on the next AMC flight to McChord. Make sure my golf clubs get on board, then call my wife and let her know this is an emergency TDY for at least two weeks. She will understand."

Major Marsden asked, "Usual staff and retinue this time?"

"No. Just the two of us for security purposes."

"Very well, sir. So noted. I'll get right on it."

"And Harold, put in a call to Colonel Raymond Lederer at the Army Garrison-Kwajalein Atoll. Kiss his ass a little and make it a formal personal request. Ask him to come alone. I know he plays so book us a round at Fort Lewis, but not too early. I hate striking a wet golf ball. And let me know if Air Mobility Command gets bitchy. I know this is a busy time for them shuttling personnel and materiel to Iraq, Afghanistan, and Frankfurt. Tell them this request is a Priority One, directed from the office of the secretary of defense. We'll email them the paperwork on our secure server ASAP."

"Understood, sir. Priority One."

"Thanks Harry."

"You're welcome, sir."

An hour later the lieutenant general's phone rang. It was his XO.

"Got a sit rep for you, sir."

"Proceed when ready," the LTG said to the major.

"Air Mobility Command was indeed in a bitchy mood but we straightened them out with some honey and some sugar and sweet talk, sir."

The LTG chuckled. "What did it really take?"

"One case of Chivas Regal."

"Bunch of damn alcoholics," Simons said. "Make sure it's charged to my personal account."

"Of course. Personal account," Marsden repeated back. He continued. "The scotch bought us two confirmed seats on a diverted C-5A Galaxy flight outbound from McGuire Air Force Base scheduled to arrive at Joint Base Lewis-McChord in the State of Washington. The flight will divert to Redstone under the guise of taking on additional fuel and then proceed to McChord. A staff car will be waiting to take us to the Fort Lewis Eagles Pride golf course just north of Lacey. Colonel Lederer, who we managed to track down at a conference in Honolulu, which saves him about fifteen hours flight time from Kwajalein, sends his regards and is pleased to meet you at the golf course for a round of 18 holes after we shower, dress, and eat lunch in the dining room at the clubhouse."

"Outstanding," the LTG said. "It's really a shame you don't play, Harold."

"Perhaps someday soon, sir. Right now driving the golf cart is more than enough challenge for me."

THE FLIGHT FROM Alabama took nearly five hours even in the relatively comfortable seats in the top section of the mammoth machine, a section that looked very much like a commercial aircraft. It was located above the cavernous loading area below their behinds. Once the largest plane in the world, the C-5A Galaxy landed the LTG and his XO south of Tacoma, Washington at McChord Air Force Base. The Pacific Northwest gave them an unusually clear and bright day and snow-clad Mt. Rainier, one of his favorite landmarks, shimmered in the distance. The waiting staff car, once luggage was acquired and loaded into the black SUV, drove them south on I-5 to the exit for the Fort Lewis golf course. Traffic, as usual, even during mid-day reminded him of a NASCAR race, cars and trucks traveling bumper to bumper in the three southbound lanes.

After parking, Major Marsden and Lieutenant General Simons stopped in the pro shop, confirmed their reservation, and were informed by the PGA pro on duty that most of the foursomes of women playing on Ladies Day should be just about making the turn to start the back nine. The LTG bought one sleeve of balls instead of two. They were likely to find plenty of lost balls abandoned by the female foursomes already out on the course. They had time to find their assigned lockers, shower, change into civilian golf clothes and shoes, and eat a bite of lunch while they waited for Colonel Lederer— ten minutes out—to arrive and join them.

After a short wait, Colonel Lederer, looking tanned, fit, and athletic, emerged from the locker room dressed and ready for golf. The three men shook hands all around, ordered lunch, and as they waited for the order to arrive, used the time to catch up on families, budgets, and politics. Finished with lunch, they headed for the driving range and each hit a bucket of red-banded range balls as part of their warm-up. Ten minutes before their scheduled tee-time Major Marsden ferried the commanders to the first tee. An announcement over the outdoor PA let them know they were the next twosome up. The LTG had insisted that they should not be paired with two other golfers to make a foursome, standard operating procedure on a busy day for the course, showing itself green and beautiful under the fine weather of the Pacific Northwest, an inviting day that brought more and more cars into the parking lot, now nearly full.

As the ranking member of the twosome, the LTG had honors and hit first. His drive started nicely but as it gained elevation, like a Chaparral missile locking on to its target, turned right toward the high linked chain fence flanking the boundary of the golf course. The fence was designed to give protection to drivers on the southbound lanes of Interstate 5, and in not so rare instances, northbound traffic as well. The slice gathered altitude and just before it cleared the fence to force a second drive lying in three, the ball caromed off the limb of a towering mountain ash, looped 30 feet into the air, settled on the right side of the fairway and rolled forward another 20 yards. The LTG handed his oversize Taylor-made driver to Major Marsden and said, "That's why I love this course. If you know how to play the trees, you can shoot a low round." The two men laughed in disbelief.

Colonel Lederer's drive split the fairway almost 300 yards up the course.

"Good drive," the LTG said, complimenting the shot. The two men walked together ahead of the golf cart carrying their clubs.

Four holes in and two new found balls each in the pocket of their golf slacks, the two men sat on the bench flanking the tee for the par four fifth hole. Marsden waited in the golf cart parked off to the side. As they waited for the foursome ahead of them to find their balls and hit their second shots, the LTG tapped his driver on the grass ahead of his knees. "Did you read the GAO report I sent you?"

"Yes, sir." He looked over at the LTG and resettled his Fort Lewis golf course cap. "Must be a real problem for you guys back in Redstone," he said ahead of a smile.

The LTG thumped his club on the green grass ahead of him and thought, that's why I like Lederer so much. He's a no-bullshit kind of guy and not afraid of a superior. "Don't be a smart ass, Ray, and quit letting me win. I know you're a two-handicap golfer. There is no way you should be losing to me, a seven-handicapper. From this point forward, balls to the wall, my friend."

"Roger that, sir. And while we're waiting, anything else I can do for you?"

"Funny you should ask. And what I'm about to tell you is top secret. I have a gut feeling that before we fire the Pioneer at your incoming hostile missile, the test burn of the rockets in the first stage booster will not go well at all. For some time now our engineers have been pissing and moaning about problems with the initial booster. The good news is," and here the LTG smiled, "a booster failure during a test burn is no big deal to us, despite how it might look in the papers. I can have another booster ready to go in about two weeks. This buys us some much needed time. It comes down to this: MDA needs a win. For that matter, the entire command needs a win, bad. You guys in the Space and Missile Defense Command will share in the glory if the next launch and intercept is successful. So we have to proceed on the assumption that failure, or at least the perception of failure by the public and the media is not an option, as my dear friends in the Navy SEALs are fond of saying."

"Understood LTG, but I just shoot them at you guys, as ordered."

"Exactly. And that's why I have to change the parameters of the missile coming out of Meck Island. This cannot be a blind shot. For reasons that are classified even above your pay grade and security clearance, once we get the Pioneer mounted on a replacement booster, I need to shoot at your incoming missile with both eyes open. That means I need to know trajectories and speeds in advance."

Such requests were not unwarranted or unusual. Marsden's firing teams at USAG-KA had done just about everything they could to ensure successful intercepts in the past, just short of programming their missile to detonate as the kill vehicle approached.

"And Colonel Lederer, this time I need you to send me one that deploys only two decoys instead of the usual number."

"I can do that."

The lieutenant general smiled. "And can you time those decoys to trigger just before my defender's kill vehicle strikes your bird?"

"That's a tough ask, LTG." He stood up, smiled at Simons, and checked if the last golfer in the foursome ahead had cleared. He watched with chagrin as she seemed to be aiming directly at the men waiting to hit on the tee. Before any of the three men could holler a warning, she swung and missed her ball lying in their fairway, almost fell over, regathered herself, reloaded, and with another mighty swing managed to scalp the top of her ball. It frog-hopped twenty yards across the fairway to her right and into the adjoining rough. She gave them a happy wave as she pulled her two-wheeled cart off in the general direction of her shot. Once the ladies were safely clear and off his fairway, Marsden realized they were playing not the hole ahead of his group, but the sixth hole that paralleled five, so he teed up his ball and to give them another margin of safety, took another minute to walk back to the LTG.

"My team can do it, but not in time for the launch as scheduled."

"What's it going to take, Ray?"

Lederer thought for a minute. One case of Glenmorangie single malt, eighteen years old. I can't get it at our Class VI store at Kwajalein."

"Done." The LTG stood and looked down the fairway, considering what the colonel had said as he tried to make sense out of the female foursome's convoluted play and travel across three separate fairways. He took off his golf cap and scratched his head before resettling the cap. "How much time do you need?"

"Let's see. According to the schedule we are one week from the test burn of the booster. The incoming missile is slated to launch a week after that providing everything goes well. But your instincts tell you that the booster will fail. If so, and we all know that nothing is one hundred percent certain in the world of rocket science, then that gives us two weeks to make the adjustments we need to meet the parameters you are talking about. That's cutting it much too tight even for my shakers and movers at Kwajalein. If you can give me an additional seven days I'll send you a missile even the French navy could track and shoot down." He returned to his ball and hit his drive flush on the screws. He watched the ball rocket into the air like a jet taking off from an aircraft carrier. The ball touched down and rolled to a stop 350 yards up the fairway.

The LTG patted him on the shoulder and said, "Impressive drive. You know, I just can't shake the feeling that we're going to have a booster problem on the pad at Vandenberg during a test of the rockets. There's also some inclement weather on the way, according to the long-range forecast. Here's the new timeline. We fire the booster in one week as scheduled. It fails. Who could have predicted that? Bad weather moves in the following week. We delay the test of the replacement booster one week due to the weather. Everyone understands that. We reschedule our intercept test for the following week, giving you and your crew three weeks to launch a hostile missile reprogrammed with the new parameters I have asked for. We can do this for the sake of the program, our country's missile defense, and for the sake our allies." He signaled to his XO. "Make it so, Major Marsden."

The LTG addressed his ball, gripped his driver and let it rip, hitting one of his prettiest drives in a long time. He was not the least concerned that the ball settled almost 60 yards short of the colonel's drive. He knew he could make up the difference on the two-tiered green. Sure it was fun to drive for show, but his real strength and the real money was made—as the pros like to say—putting for dough. His next shot, a seven iron, landed about ten feet short of the pin placed on the upper level of the green.

As he walked to the green, Lieutenant General Simons knew he had done what was needed to assure the success of his program. And a successful missile defense program benefitted the United States and her allies. This was the end game. He took a minute to read the putt, gauging the green's slope and distance. The grain of the grass grew toward the ball and this required a putt with some speed behind the roll. Too much pace, however, and the ball would travel below the hole, over a ledge separating the top level of the green from the lower, and roll back into the fairway. The other option was to leave the putt short and walk away with a par.

He took a deep breath and exhaled like a sniper on the target and stroked the ball. He knew immediately he had hit the putt with too much force. Despite its speed, with the unerring accuracy of a missile homing in on an incoming bogie, the ball sped toward the hole, broke left, reacquired the target, and jumped the hole. Instead of skipping completely over the hole, the ball hit the back edge of the cup. The carom lifted the white golf ball a foot straight up into the air before it dropped down into the dark, rattled, and settled in the hole for a birdie three.

Chapter Thirty-eight

Return Home

Will was forced to revise their travel plans after he received a call from FBI headquarters in Quantico, Virginia. Special agent Angelika Valesa informed him that agents working out of the Madison, Wisconsin office had located the whereabouts of one Stefano "Little Bull" Benedetto, the second and older of the two men in the video Will and Sylvie had sent to Quantico. Known as a "made man," Benedetto had risen through the ranks of the Cosa Nostra in Sicily as an enforcer and consigliere. In the U.S. he had made his reputation as a reliable hit man and occasionally took outside jobs for hire. He was known as the planner of the duo, his partner responsible for the actual hits. The duo's work outside the mob had made them "persons of interest" in two federal investigations tasked to investigate mysterious disappearances of high-ranking executive officers in the business world. Using the model of totalitarian governments, some companies, domestic and foreign, had taken to eliminating key competition by assassination.

According to Valesa, because of Benedetto's links to Sicily, the Bureau was able to tap his cell phone through a FISA Court warrant. Cell phone records pinpointed his location to a cell tower in the vicinity of a fishing camp north of Madison. During the heyday of the Mafia's power and influence over the meatpacking industry in Chicago, mobsters sweating from too much federal heat often disappeared to safe locations to cool for a time in the wilds of northern Wisconsin and upper Michigan.

Will was invited to take part in the apprehension. After informing his team of the good news, Will confirmed a seat on the next flight to Madison. "I'll be back in a day or two at the most," he promised. "Then I have a surprise for all of you."

Roland drove Will to the Cedar Rapids airport. Before he dropped him at the curb below the sign for his carrier, he put his hand on Will's forearm and said in German, "While you were at the Pentagon Sylvie got a call from Manfred. He asked her to marry him."

The news hit Will like a baseball bat across the shoulders. "What did she say?"

"She said she needed some time to think about it because we are winding down this investigation. She told him she would give him her answer after we return to Bavaria. You need to give this some serious thought," Roland said as they shook hands.

"I'll call you soon as we get the cuffs on Benedetto," Will said. He walked through the automatic sliding doors and found the ticket counter. The flight to Madison was on time, short, and grim.

THE FBI FOUND Stefano Benedetto in a cabin at a camp famous for its muskie fishing. He was taken into custody without resistance as he exited his cabin, fishing rod in one hand, tackle box in the other, the screen door flapping shut behind him. Under his floppy fishing hat, in his waders and boots, it was an ignominious capture of the infamous "Little Bull," considered armed and dangerous, but only to muskies, one agent quipped. In federal prison it would take him a long time to live down photos of the arrest. Informed of charges against him that included kidnapping and transporting a person across state lines on top of murder one, Stefano "Little Bull" Benedetto took a minute and crunched the sentence numbers in his head. The total time convinced him it was in his best interests to assist the state with their prosecution of Dr. Robertson Davis, CEO of Tactical Missile Systems in Cedar Rapids, Iowa.

On the drive back to Madison, Wisconsin, Will asked Benedetto how he and his partner had managed to track down Randall Wahkahchai in WITSEC. Evidently, Davis had contacted the two hit men immediately after Wahkahchai had reported the problems with the software design. They put a tail on him the very next day. The fact that he went into the program under a different name had posed no problem at all. Benedetto and his partner had gone to the casino to finalize the hit on Wahkahchai after they got the chemical to immobilize him from Davis's girlfriend, who evidently worked as a veterinarian's assistant. With that information in hand, Will thanked his fellow agents for their excellent work and the courtesy of the invitation to assist with the arrest. Two days later, Will returned to Cedar Rapids and shared the story of Benedetto's capture. His team's work was officially done and the case was closed.

IT WAS TIME for Will to share his promised surprise. Instead of flying home, Will wanted to take them on a road trip up through Iowa, Wisconsin, and then into Minnesota to show Roland, Sylvie, and Daya some of the pretty country in the north central part of the U.S. Unfortunately, they missed the best part of the late autumn when the leaves turn and the forests of the north-central states become redolent with color. Oak, elm, hickory, ash, and some sugar maple turned their leaves to autumnal colors before gently dropping them to the earth. But there was still enough red, orange, brown, rust, and yellow to evoke appreciation from the back-seaters as Will drove north along the Mississippi through New Vienna, Luxemburg, and the river town of Gutenberg on the way to Prairie du Chien. He stopped at Pike's Peak State Park where the Wisconsin River pushes its waters into the Mississippi. Roland and Sylvie were astounded by how much the rolling limestone bluffs and hills through which the river flowed reminded them of the Rhein near Koblenz.

In Prairie du Chien they stopped at Stark's, a sporting goods store that sold not only every sort of outdoor equipment from hunting boots to boats, but also, curiously enough, booze, an irony that did not escape Roland. Stark's was famous in that part of Wisconsin for its liquor and wine. When Roland saw the price per bottle on the Crown Royal he nearly had a seizure.

"It's all about the difference in taxes," Will informed them. "That explains why so many Iowa residents buy their booze and boats at Stark's."

Daya, to Will's surprise lingered among the single malt Scotch whiskies, so he put a bottle of Macallan and Glenmorangie in Roland's cart. Sylvie walked up to the cart, arms full of late harvest Rieslings from Germany. As Will paid for all the purchases, including a fishing hat for Sylvie with a picture of a leaping northern pike on the cap, he lamented the fact that he was turning into an enabler for his traveling retinue of co-dependent alcoholics.

After their purchases, Will spent the day driving through middle Wisconsin before re-establishing the home trail back to the Boundary Waters. He showed his group the apple country, then the rolling hills and valleys of the dairy farms, and they spent the night in the Wisconsin Dells, a town famous as the self-styled waterpark capital of the world. They slept in, had a leisurely breakfast and discussed plans for the trip back to the cabin at Lake Kabetogama. As they lingered over breakfast Will noticed the headlines in the morning paper. A test-burn of the first stage booster rocket under the new Pioneer anti-ballistic missile had taken place the day before. In a high-backed, red booth at the table of the local waffle restaurant, he read the highlights to a very interested audience.

Halfway into its test burn, according to reports from the Missile Defense Agency, the booster rocket flamed out and shut down. Nevertheless, in typical government fashion, the test firing had been deemed a success. At the news conference Lieutenant General Simons, director of the MDA, declared that this was rocket science, after all, and such unforeseen circumstances were bound to occur this early in the project's development phase. That's why they tested. His scientists and engineers had discovered a minor glitch in an extraordinarily complex, multimillion dollar system, Simons explained to the press. The flaw had been fault-located in the booster system, which was completely unexpected but fairly easy to fix. They would analyze the data and make the necessary changes, he promised, correct the problem that caused the rocket's failsafe system to engage and shut down the burn. Correcting the problem would delay the full launch test of the Pioneer interceptor missile by no more than three weeks, he assured the news media, and then only because of inclement weather set to hit Vandenberg, California in the coming week. He assured them that his team would strictly adhere to the following timeline: a test of the replacement booster after the weather cleared, and a full-scale test of the Pioneer's capabilities to follow the week after.

Will pointed out how the carefully worded press release avoided any mention of the word failure. "What do you think?" Will asked Daya.

"It's possible that the booster failed."

"But isn't that extremely rare?" Will asked.

She nodded. "Booster technology, although it is rocket science as Simons says, is fairly basic physics and hasn't changed much in the last few years. The failure is suspicious. I think it is a significant coincidence that the booster failed, given what we know about our inability to have the onboard software program driving the sensor technology up and ready for deployment."

"Yes," Sylvie said with mock seriousness. "But do you find it to be highly significant?" The entire table laughed at Will's expense and Roland quickly explained the inside joke to Daya. She seemed rather interested in the idea of semiotics and the study of significant signs and symbols. She challenged Will, to the amusement and encouragement of her new friends.

"How would you explain what happened, Professor, using semiotic analysis to interpret the event, of course?"

Will took a sip from his iced tea. "Here are the significant events. A booster fails and should not. The software for detecting and discriminating decoys from the hostile threat should be ready but is not. Given the planning, expense, and need for a public success, the test burn was designed to fail, thereby buying the program additional time to assure that the upcoming interceptor launch and interdiction is successful. However, we four know, as does Simons and his team that the interception is doomed to fail. He has bought himself the additional time, therefore, to cobble together what most likely will be interpreted as some semblance of a success. That's my analysis," he said confidently.

Daya looked at Sylvie and Roland, surprise and respect evident in her face and she turned to Will. "I think you got it exactly right and I find that to be highly significant indeed."

After the laughter subsided Sylvie shook her head and asked, "Does this happen often with military programs?"

"All the time," Daya said without missing a beat.

ONE DAY BEFORE he drove Roland, Sylvie, and Daya to the airport in Minneapolis-St. Paul, Will shared with them the report that a dummy hostile missile had been launched from the Kwajalein islands, was detected, and the new Pioneer anti-ballistic missile launched from Vandenberg Air Force base to intercept it. The incoming missile had deployed its decoys, as expected, although Will noticed that only two had been used instead of the usual number designed to confound the interceptor's sensors. The Pioneer anti-ballistic missile, after locating, tracking, and intercepting the dummy hostile missile, instead of relying on kinetic energy alone to destroy its target, detonated its warhead. In the explosive fireball of energy and light, the Pioneer annihilated the incoming missile and its accompanying decoys. According to Lieutenant General Simons, the test had exceeded all expectations and was considered by the Missile Defense Agency and all observers to be nothing less than a complete success.

ANYONE BUT A hardened old coot like Farley Nilsson would have moved from the cabin years ago. It was hard to get to, had only the basic amenities, and when the lake froze over, he was forced to depend on his old Polaris snowmobile for transportation to the mainland. But Farley did not care. In fact, he stayed for those very same reasons. He liked living alone, he did not need much in the way of creature comforts, and when you got down to it the old cabin just past the mouth of where Deer Creek ran into Slatinsky's Bay was his home.

The morning air indoors was chilly enough to cool the tip of his brown nose, and he stoked the black potbellied wood stove, agitating the embers enough to burn the hickory fuel he added. He put a pot of coffee on the stove and drank in the heat radiating from the belly of the black iron. His coffee made and steaming in the cup, his pants and boots on, he had a look out the open kitchen window, taking in the sharp crisp air of the early morning. The loons were gone and in another week at most the lake would swell with ice. The season was already too late in coming, he noted to himself. The overheated summer and the yearlong drought had pushed the calendar off the wall. Except for the storm that had trapped Will and Sylvie at War Club Lake—a false augury of winter—fall, like a barnacle on a boat's hull, had stubbornly refused to let go.

Farley stepped out to sniff the cold air outside the cabin door. A storm was on the way down from northern Canada, no doubt about that. He needed one more trip to lay in provisions for the time when the lake would be iced over but not hard or deep enough to permit travel by snowmobile. Better do it today, he told himself. As he turned he looked out into the bay and did not like what he saw. A large red Lund had drifted up into the shallow water where the reeds grew. Damned tourists! Somebody let their boat get away from them. Now he would have to go and save their tender footed asses. Then he thought better of it; it was much too late in the season for tourists. Only hardened locals like him would venture out this early to fish in the cold.

He went into the kitchen to get his binoculars. He sharpened the view until the stranded craft came into focus. Damned if it wasn't the Professor's boat. He was worried now. He hurried back in, finished dressing and pulled the Johnson on the back of his boat into service. It spluttered, coughed, and belched smoke. Farley coughed back, belched coffee, choked the throttle, and pulled the cord again. This time the motor caught and fired. He let the motor warm until the idle dropped before he moved the throttle from neutral into forward and motored down the creek to where it dumped into the bay. He pulled up alongside Will's boat, cut the throttle back to neutral and drifted in. He stood and saw the big man's body stretched out on the bottom of the big red Lund. He yelled his name. Again. The big man moved, drew up a leg and tried to turn over. At least he wasn't dead, but the wet stink of alcohol coming from the boat was enough to knock an owl out of his tree. "Will! It's Farley!" he yelled. "You gotta get up! I can't lift you by myself!"

Will turned to the sound of the voice and groaned, the morning light blinding him. "Go away, Farley. Just let me lie here." He rolled over onto his stomach again, pulled up the tarp he was using as a blanket, and was out.

Farley reassessed. He took the length of rope he had brought along and tied the two boats stern to stern. As he throttled up, the nose of the larger boat pulled out of the mud and swung around. Farley kept the speed down so the water would not wash over the transom of the boat as its rear dug into the water. After a short run up the creek, he pulled up to his dock. Still about ten yards away he gunned her a little and sure enough a nice wave washed over the back of the Lund, soaking Will into consciousness. He spluttered like Farley's old Johnson during a cold morning start, got himself to his knees and hands and with Farley's help, staggered onto the dock. Even Farley, used to a man's smell after a seven-day deer hunt in the North Woods, was forced to turn away as Will grinned and tried to thank him. "You're the only one I can trust, Farley," he mumbled. Will shook his head in lament. "She left me high and dry, old buddy."

Still on the dock and thinking of the smell emanating from his friend, Farley skinned him out of his coat and overshirt and T-shirt, all stained with the sweat of alcohol, got him seated on a deck chair and started working on his boots. "Who left you, big man?"

"Sylvie. She went back to Germany to marry that pussy Manfred." He looked at Farley. "What kind of name is Manfred, anyway? You're only supposed to have a name like that if you're a field marshal." He grinned, but his eyes closed and his head lolled.

With effort punctuated by grunts and groans from them both, Farley got him up again and through the door and into the cabin. He guided him onto one of the four stout oak chairs he had built himself and skinned Will's socks off his feet. "Stand up and take off your pants," Farley instructed, his sense of decorum allowing him to go only so far, even in the name of friendship. As Will braced himself with a hold on the back of the oak chair at the table, he got his pants down to his knees.

"Farley, I love you man, but I'm not like that," Will grinned ludicrously, as he started to sway. Farley caught him, maneuvered the big, heavy man to his bed and got the pants off his ankles before he swung the big feet onto the bed. They stuck out beyond the end of the mattress exactly the length of one hunting boot. Farley covered Will from naked toes to naked chest under a thick quilt. "You're a good man, Farley Nilsson. Come here so I can kiss you."

Farley grimaced, but there was tenderness in his gruff voice. "You go to sleep big man, and when you wake, I'll be back from town with supplies. You can stay a couple of days until you get her out of your system and we'll talk and fish until the ice sets."

Will rolled his head back and forth on the pillow. "No more talk, Farley. Just fishing. And bring me back a bottle of whisky, if you will."

"One bottle," Farley promised. By the time Farley returned from washing out the sodden clothes and hanging them on the line behind the cabin to dry, Will had rasped into a deep sleep, mouth open. Farley looked at the man with affection and a little sympathy as he slowly shook his head back and forth. He had been in love that much once in his life a very long time ago. He knew that it would take a lot of fishing and hunting and, no doubt, Crown Royal in the months ahead before the wounded heart would heal and the scar would set.

ABOUT THE AUTHOR

William Russell Sheridan, trained as a research scholar, earned an interdisciplinary doctorate in semiotic theory from a Research I university in the Pacific Northwest. After developing and publishing his new method for solving crimes using semiotic analysis, he served as special consultant to the Bavarian State Police, Interpol, and the FBI. He lives in California, where he is currently a professor at university.

www.ingramcontent.com/pod-product-compliance
Lightning Source LLC
Chambersburg PA
CBHW071243250626
47163CB00002B/303